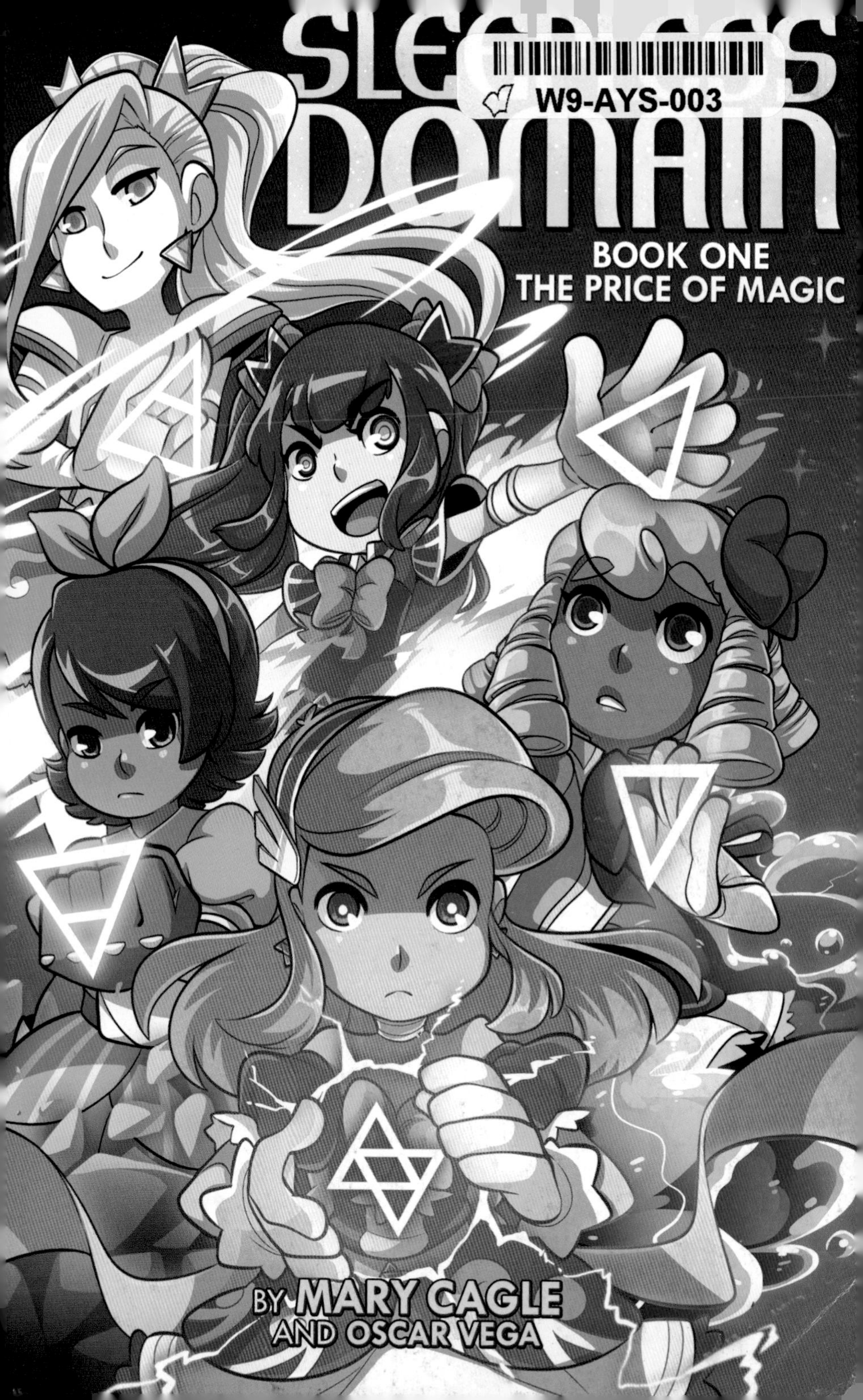
DOMAIN
BOOK ONE
THE PRICE OF MAGIC
BY MARY CAGLE
AND OSCAR VEGA

Sleepless Domain - Book One: The Price of Magic

Copyright © 2015-2019 by Mary Cagle.
Art and script by Mary Cagle.
Character designs and art for Chapter 1 & 2 by Oscar Vega.

Edited by Hiveworks Comics, LLC.
hiveworkscomics.com
sleeplessdomain.com

Seven Seas press and purchase enquiries can be sent to Marketing Manager
Lianne Sentar at press@gomanga.com. Information regarding the distribution
and purchase of digital editions is available from Digital Manager CK Russell
at digital@gomanga.com.

Seven Seas and the Seven Seas logo are trademarks of
Seven Seas Entertainment. All rights reserved.

Follow Seven Seas Entertainment online at
sevenseasentertainment.com.

Cover Design: Nicky Lim
Prepress Technician: Rhiannon Rasmussen-Silverstein
Production Assistant: Christa Miesner
Production Manager: Lissa Pattillo
Managing Editor: Julie Davis
Associate Publisher: Adam Arnold
Publisher: Jason DeAngelis

ISBN: 978-1-64827-650-7
Printed in China
First Printing: October 2021
10 9 8 7 6 5 4 3 2 1

CONTENTS

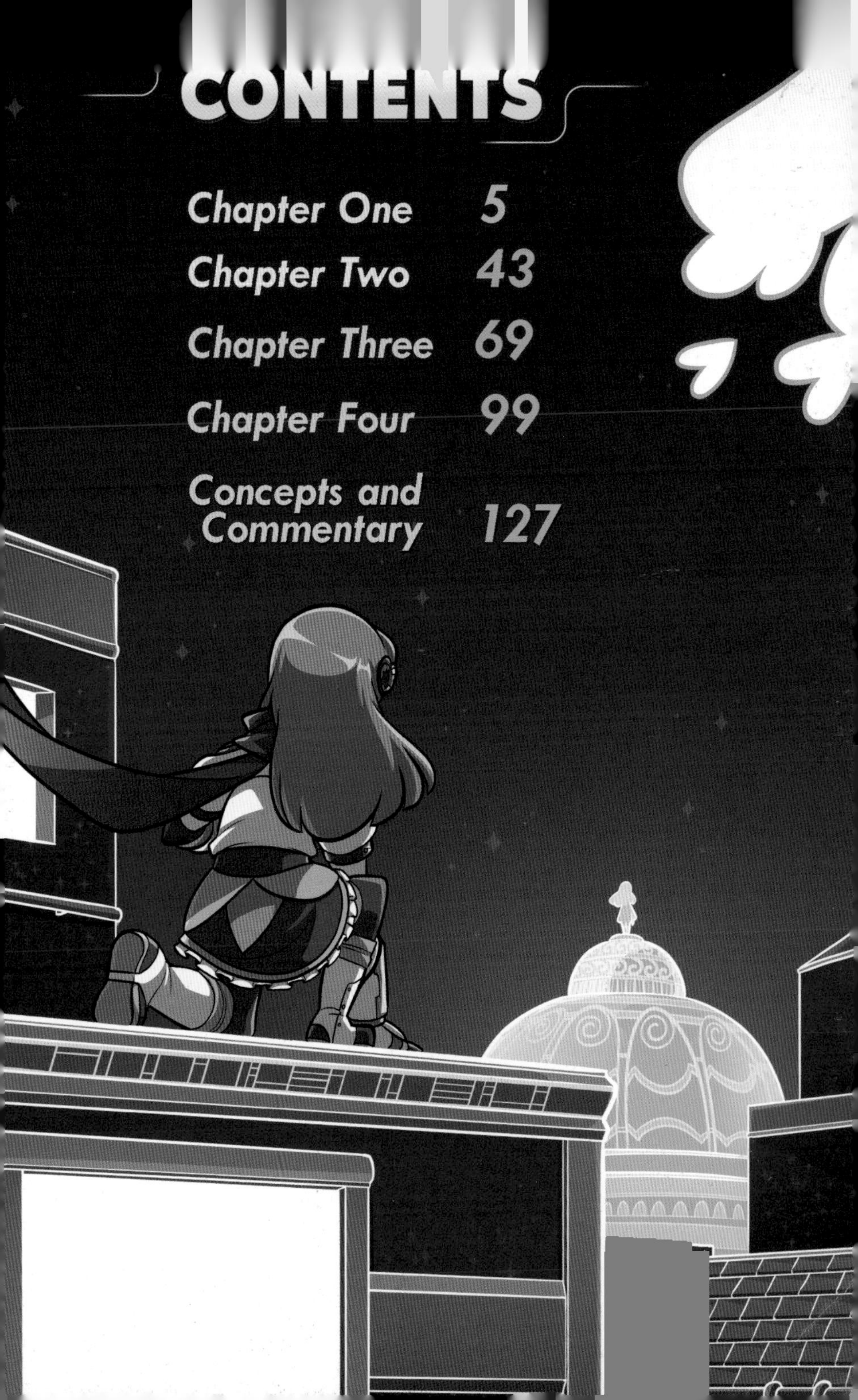

SLEEPLESS
DOMAIN

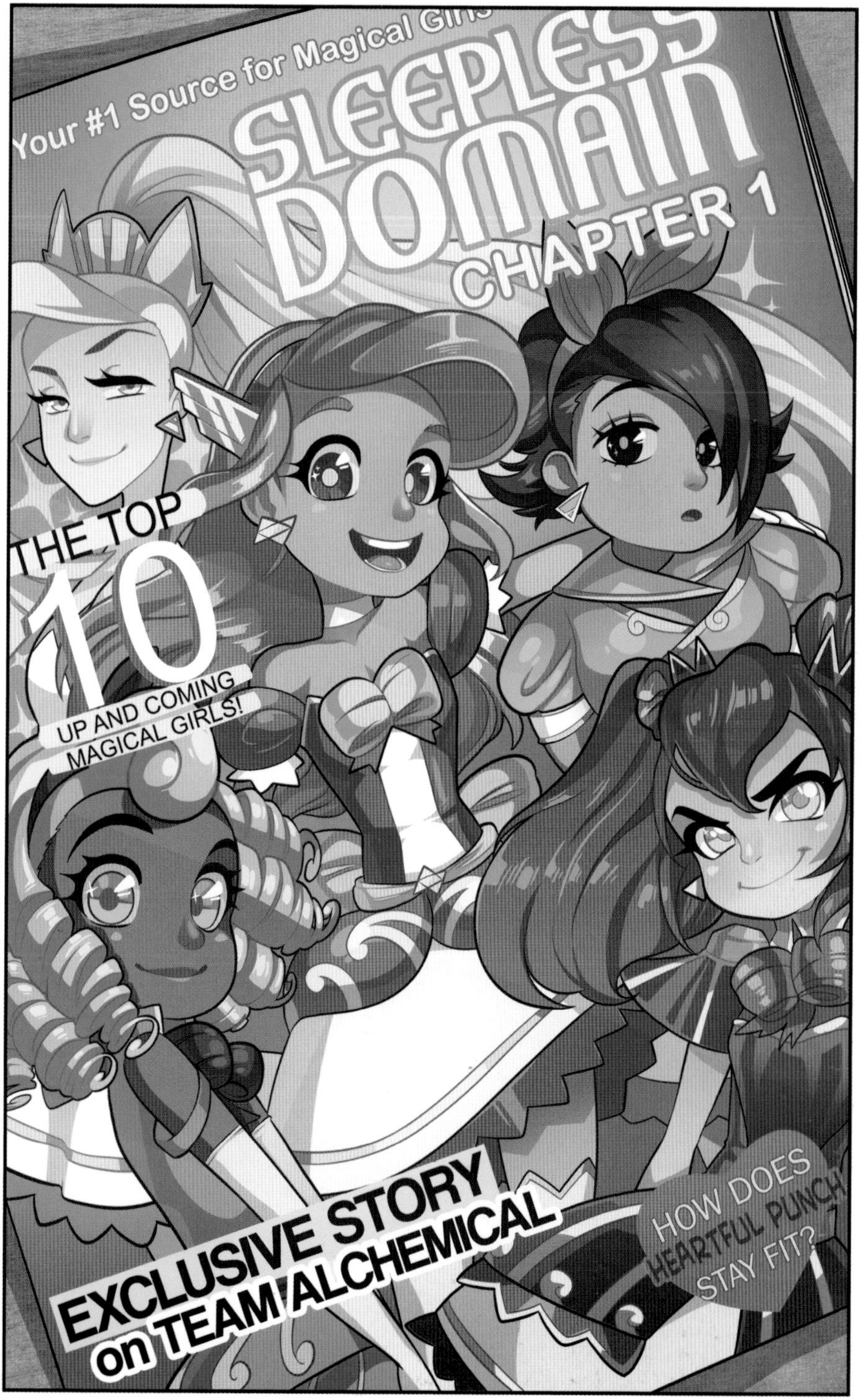
Your #1 Source for Magical Girls
SLEEPLESS DOMAIN
CHAPTER 1
THE TOP 10
UP AND COMING MAGICAL GIRLS!
EXCLUSIVE STORY on TEAM ALCHEMICAL
HOW DOES HEARTFUL PUNCH STAY FIT?

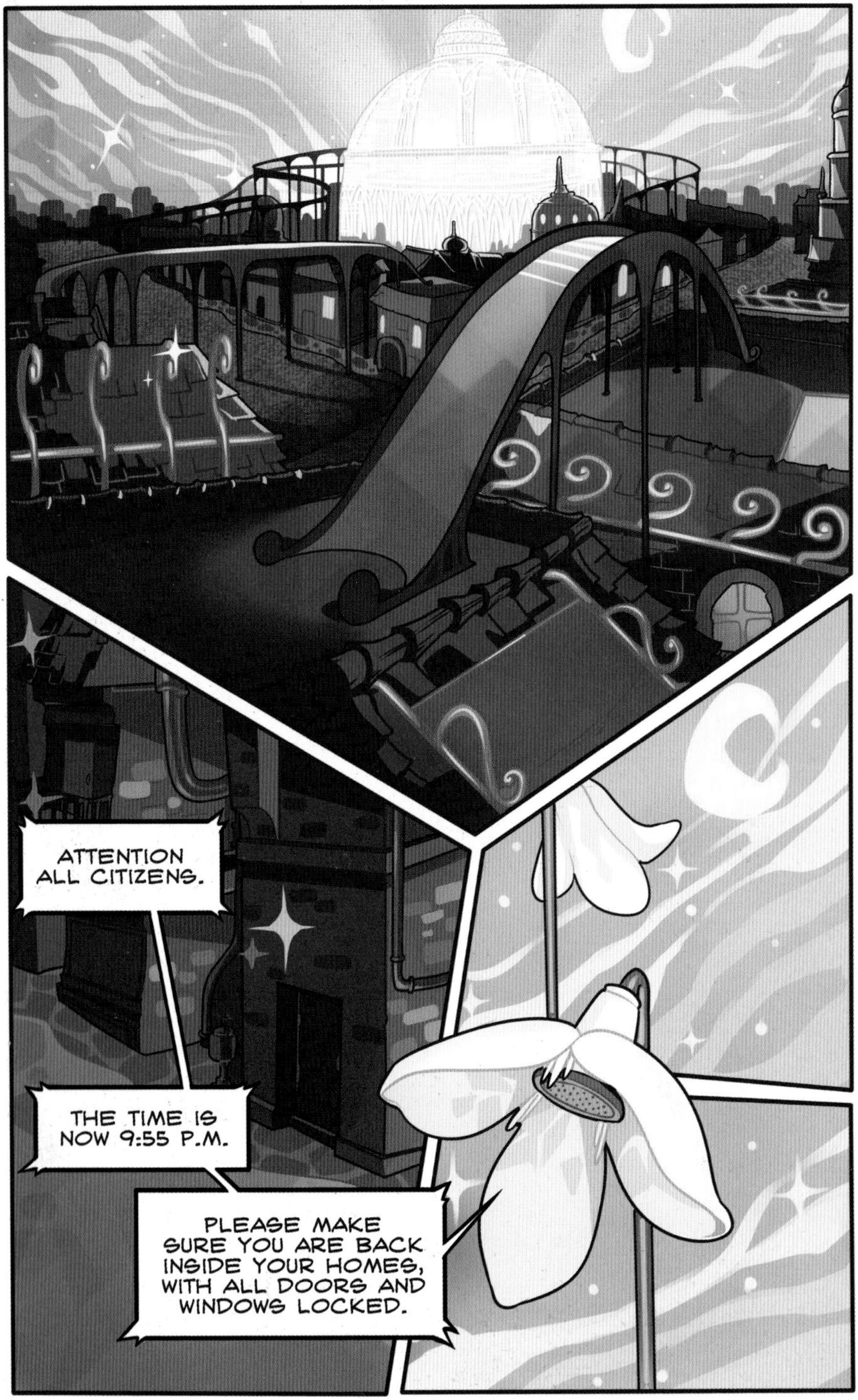
ATTENTION ALL CITIZENS.
THE TIME IS NOW 9:55 P.M.
PLEASE MAKE SURE YOU ARE BACK INSIDE YOUR HOMES, WITH ALL DOORS AND WINDOWS LOCKED.

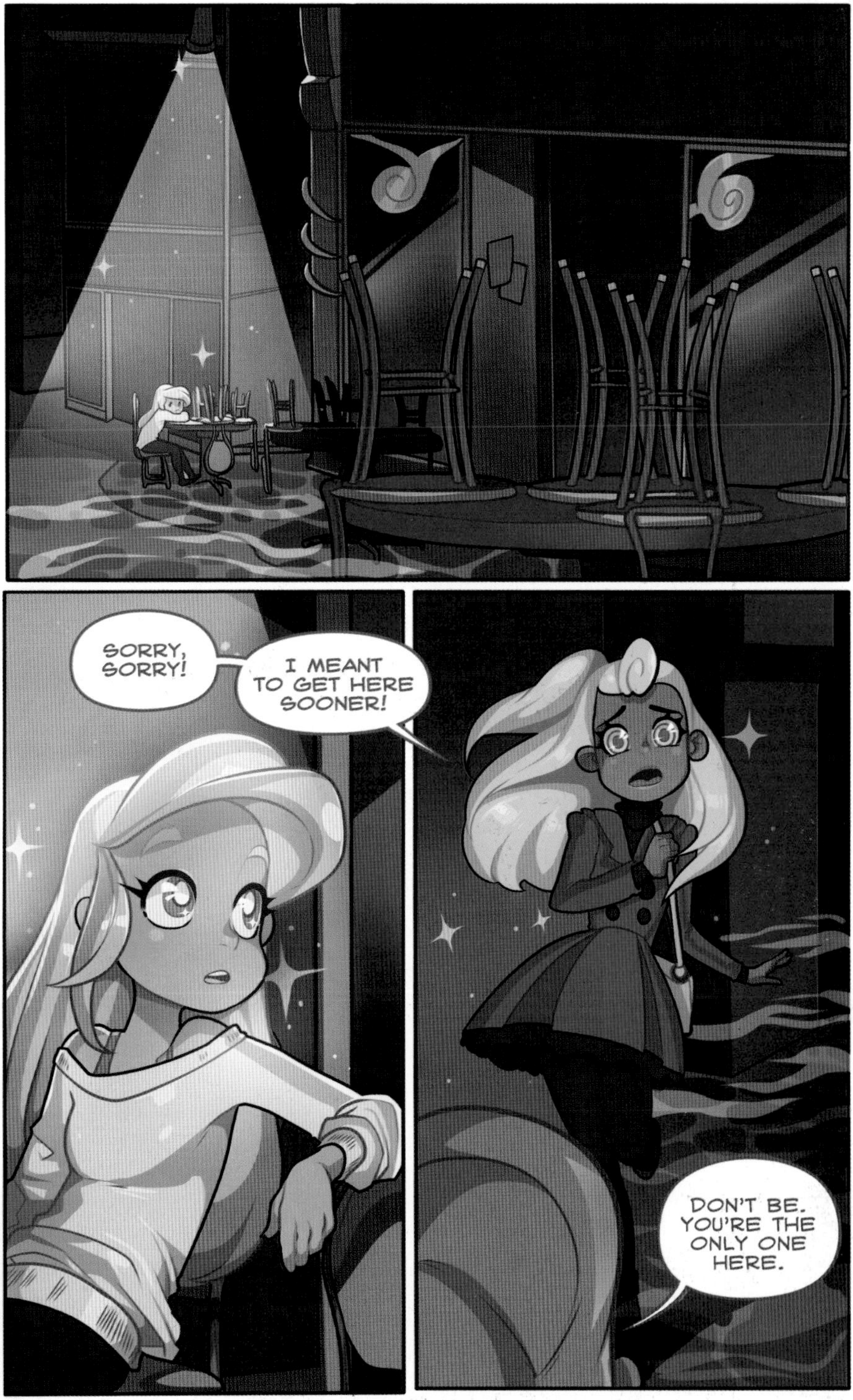
SORRY, SORRY!
I MEANT TO GET HERE SOONER!
DON'T BE. YOU'RE THE ONLY ONE HERE.

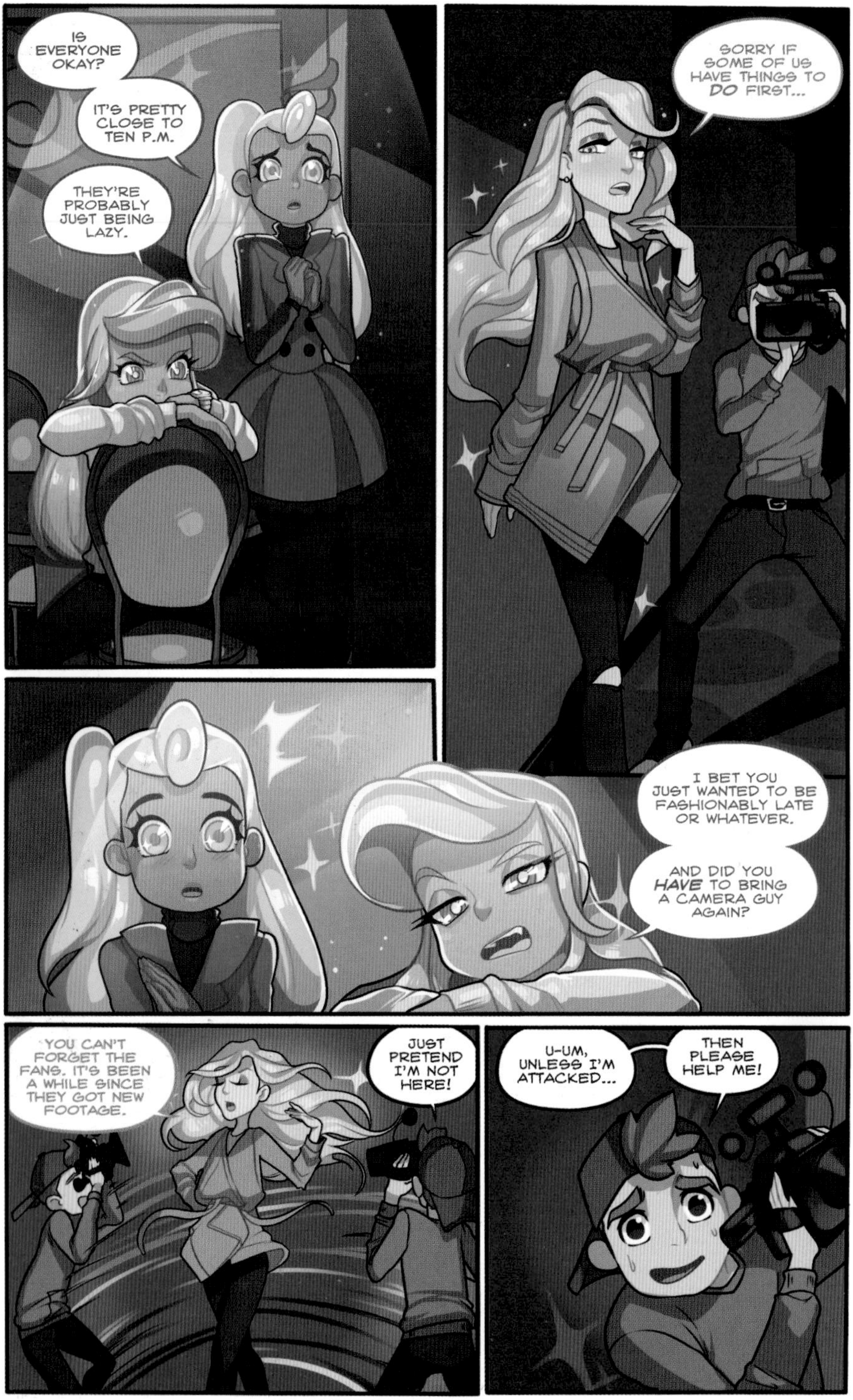

IS EVERYONE OKAY?
IT'S PRETTY CLOSE TO TEN P.M.
THEY'RE PROBABLY JUST BEING LAZY.
SORRY IF SOME OF US HAVE THINGS TO *DO* FIRST...
I BET YOU JUST WANTED TO BE FASHIONABLY LATE OR WHATEVER.
AND DID YOU ***HAVE*** TO BRING A CAMERA GUY AGAIN?
YOU CAN'T FORGET THE FANS. IT'S BEEN A WHILE SINCE THEY GOT NEW FOOTAGE.
JUST PRETEND I'M NOT HERE!
U-UM, UNLESS I'M ATTACKED...
THEN PLEASE HELP ME!

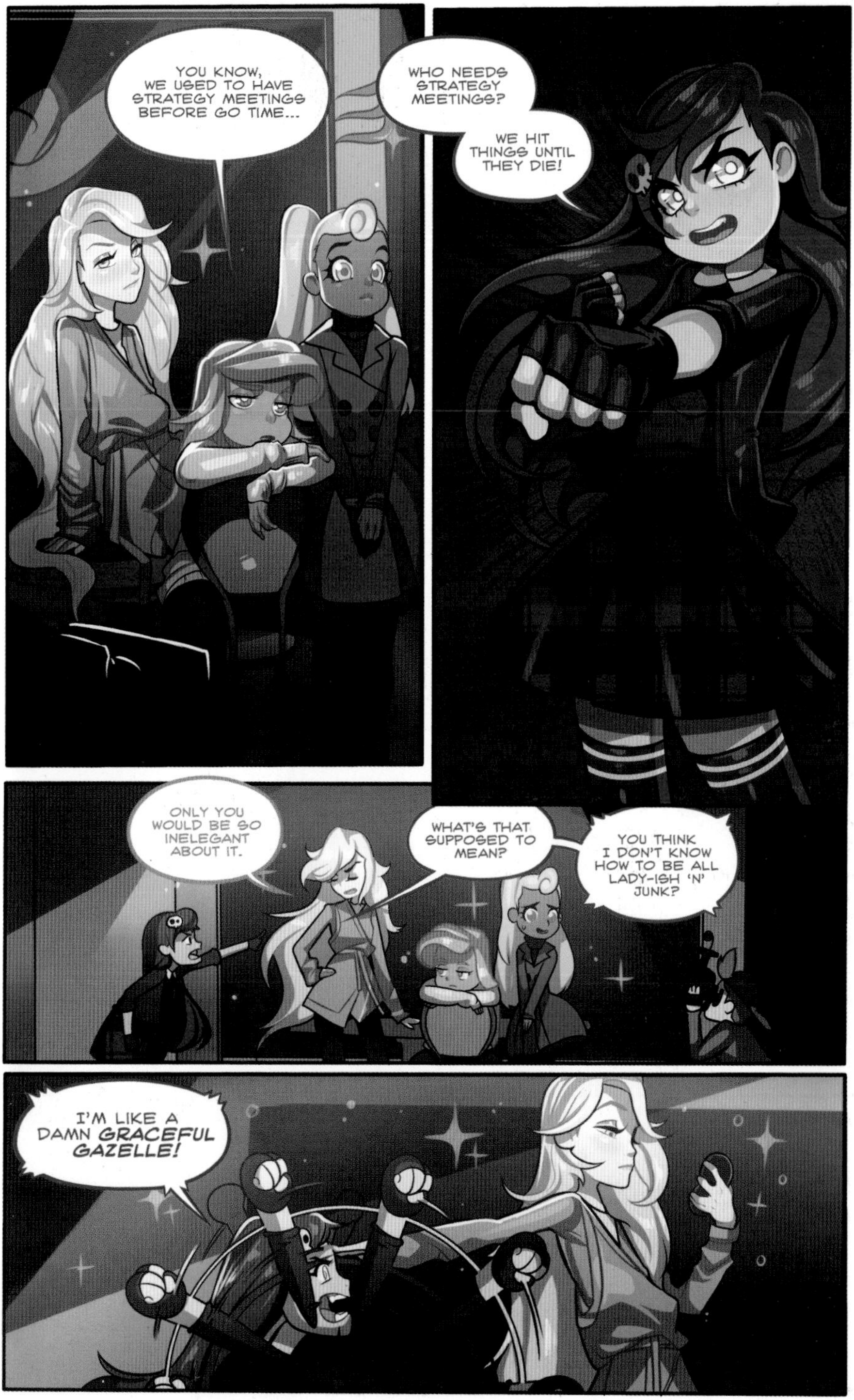

YOU KNOW, WE USED TO HAVE STRATEGY MEETINGS BEFORE GO TIME...
WHO NEEDS STRATEGY MEETINGS?
WE HIT THINGS UNTIL THEY DIE!
ONLY YOU WOULD BE SO INELEGANT ABOUT IT.
WHAT'S THAT SUPPOSED TO MEAN?
YOU THINK I DON'T KNOW HOW TO BE ALL LADY-ISH 'N' JUNK?
I'M LIKE A DAMN ***GRACEFUL GAZELLE!***

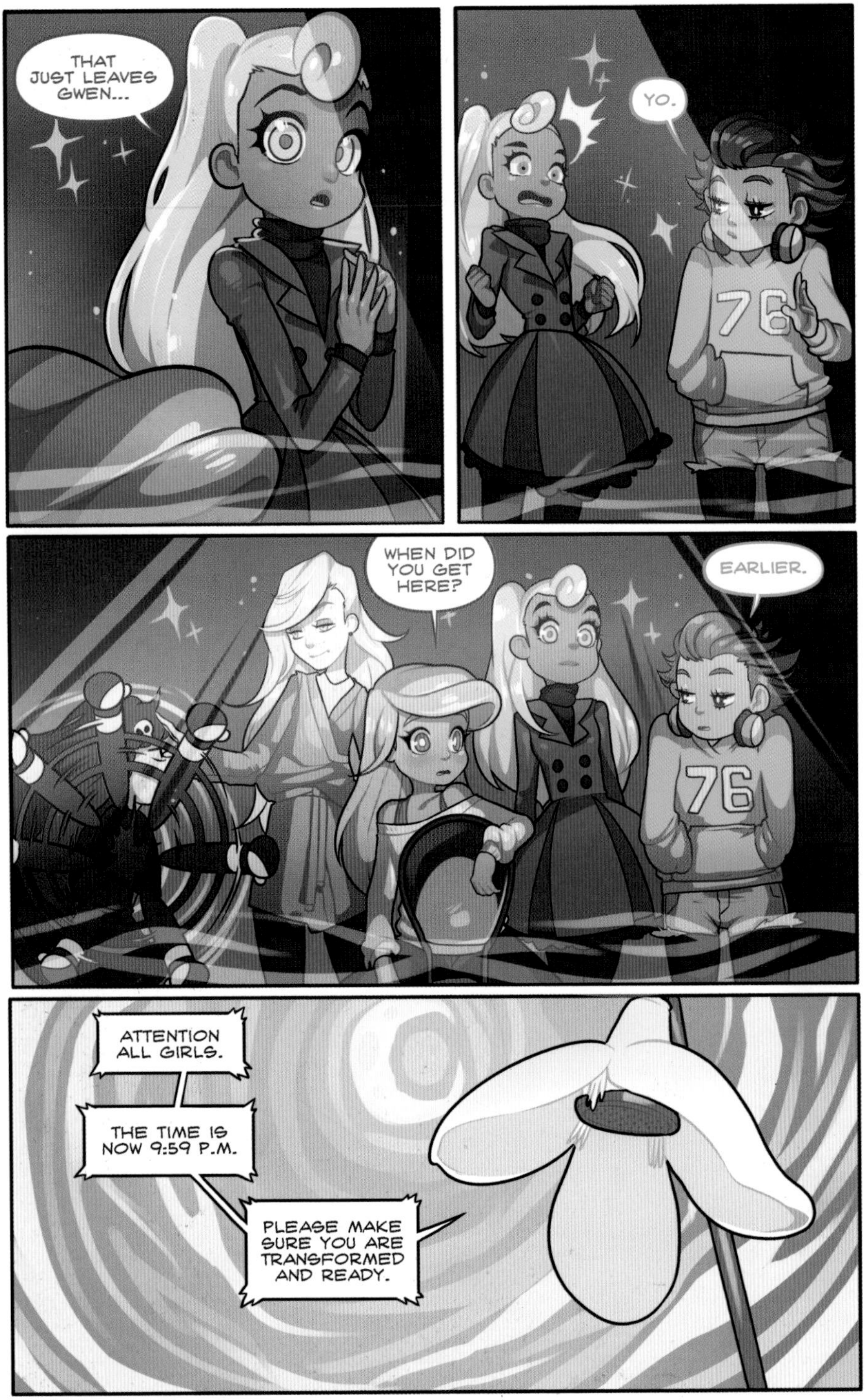

THAT JUST LEAVES GWEN...
YO.
WHEN DID YOU GET HERE?
EARLIER.
ATTENTION ALL GIRLS.
THE TIME IS NOW 9:59 P.M.
PLEASE MAKE SURE YOU ARE TRANSFORMED AND READY.

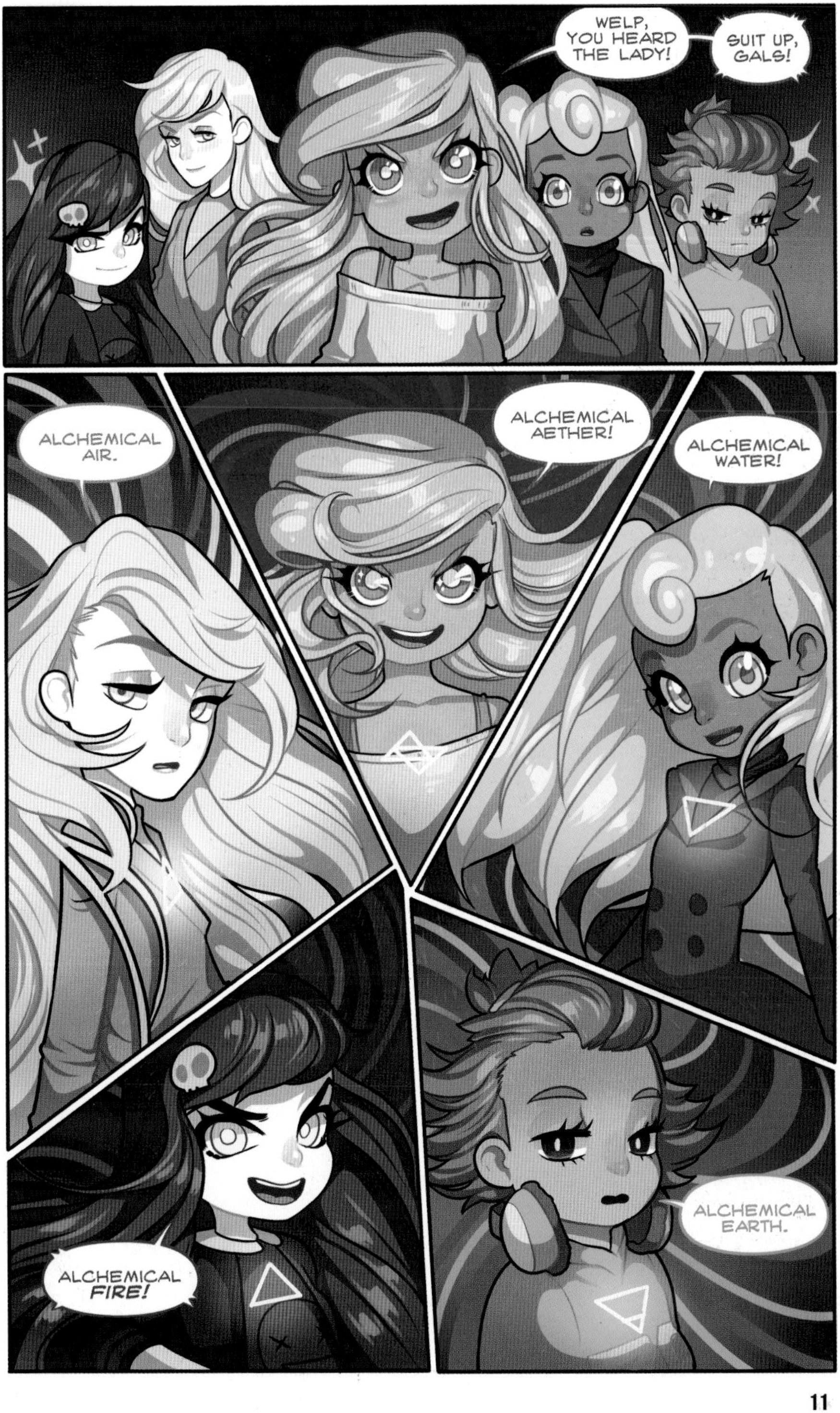
WELP, YOU HEARD THE LADY!
SUIT UP, GALS!
ALCHEMICAL AIR.
ALCHEMICAL AETHER!
ALCHEMICAL WATER!
ALCHEMICAL FIRE!
ALCHEMICAL EARTH.

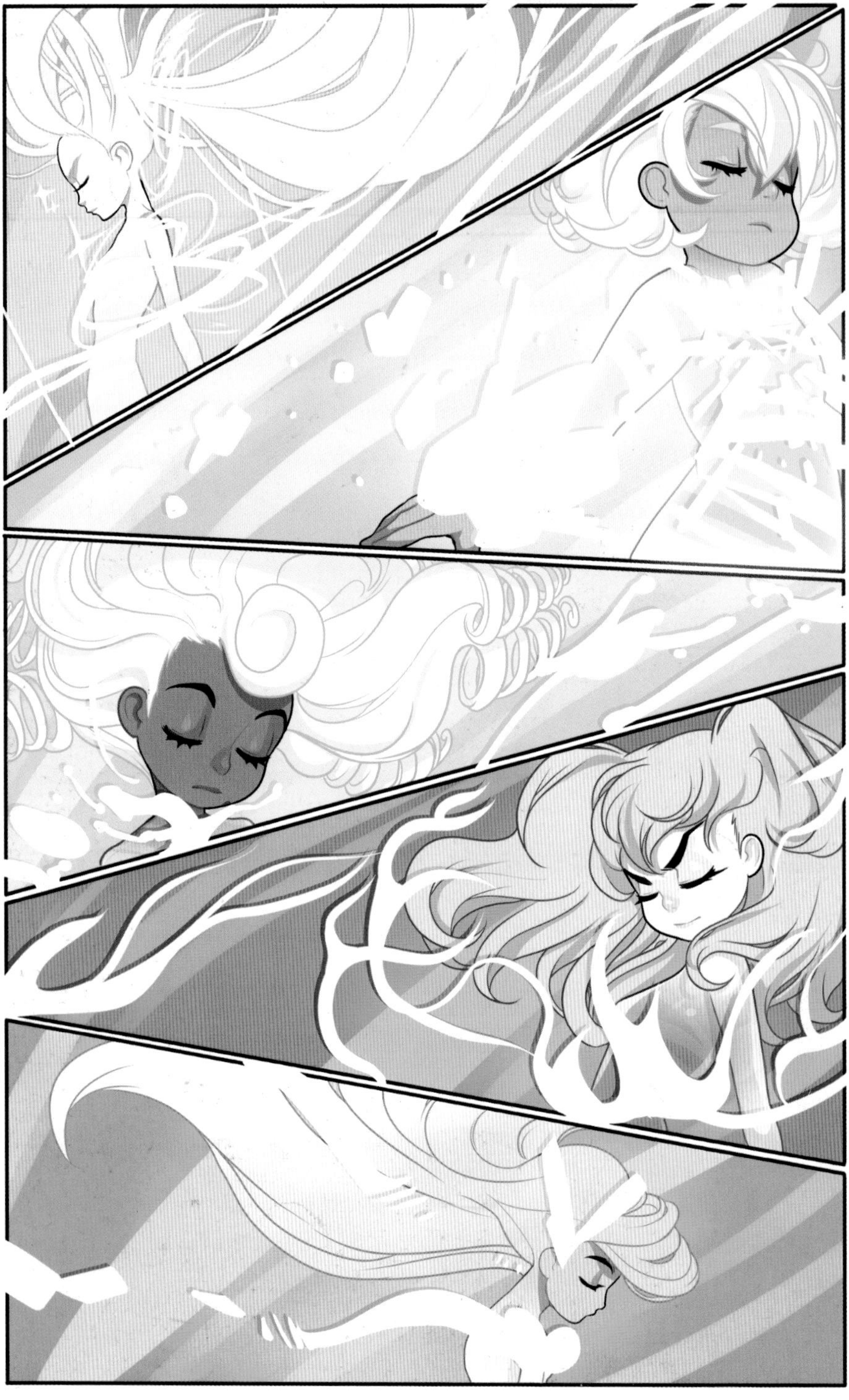

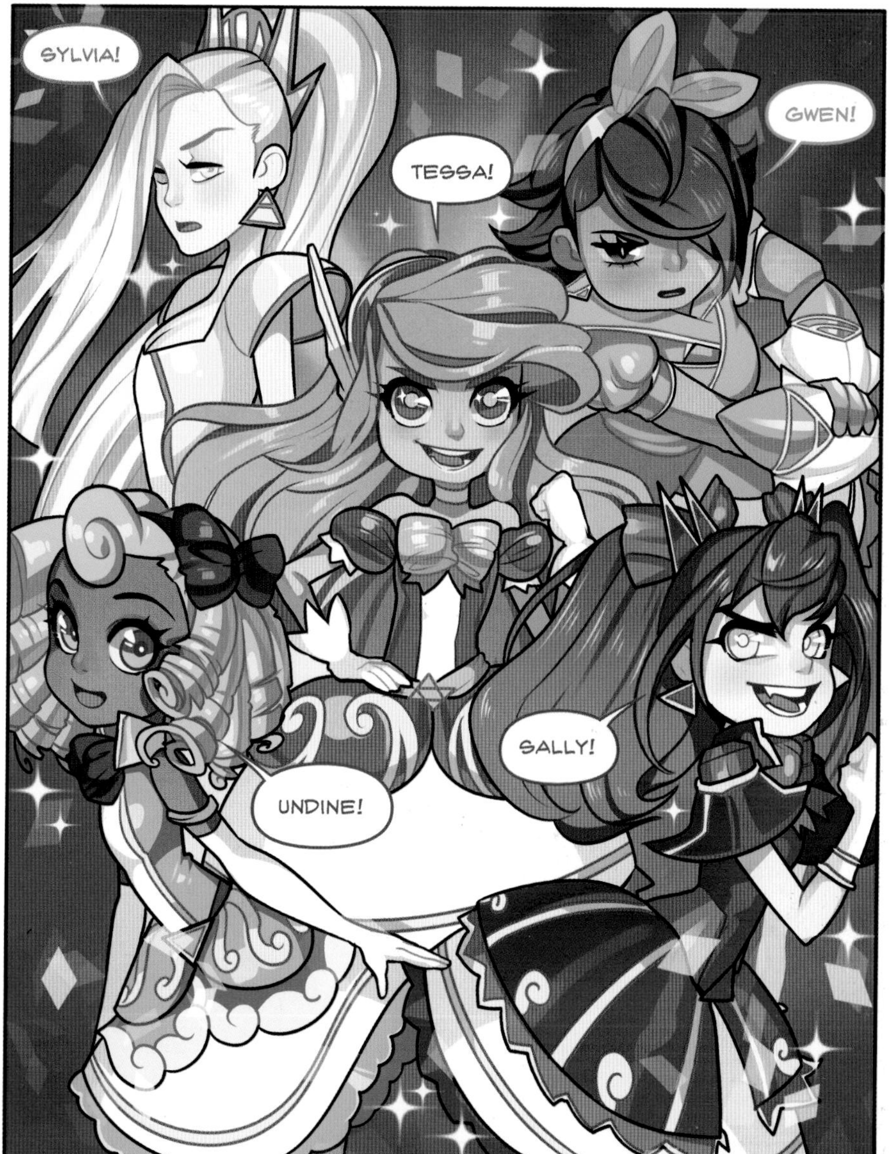
SYLVIA!
TESSA!
GWEN!
UNDINE!
SALLY!
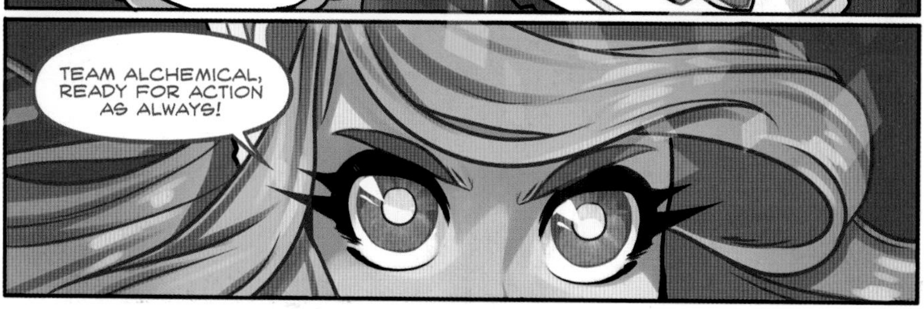
TEAM ALCHEMICAL, READY FOR ACTION AS ALWAYS!

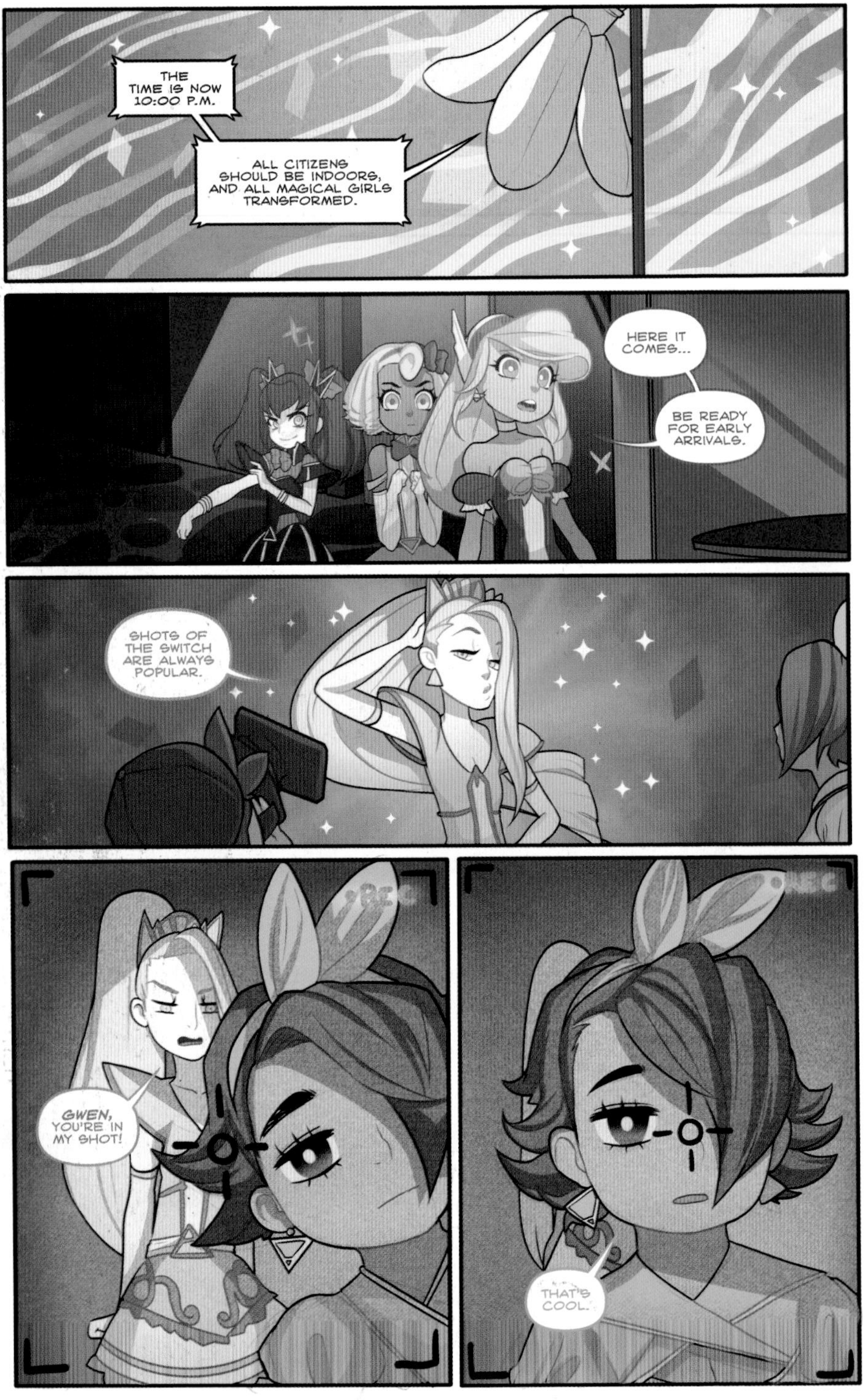
THE TIME IS NOW 10:00 P.M.
ALL CITIZENS SHOULD BE INDOORS, AND ALL MAGICAL GIRLS TRANSFORMED.
HERE IT COMES...
BE READY FOR EARLY ARRIVALS.
SHOTS OF THE SWITCH ARE ALWAYS POPULAR.
GWEN, YOU'RE IN MY SHOT!
THAT'S COOL.

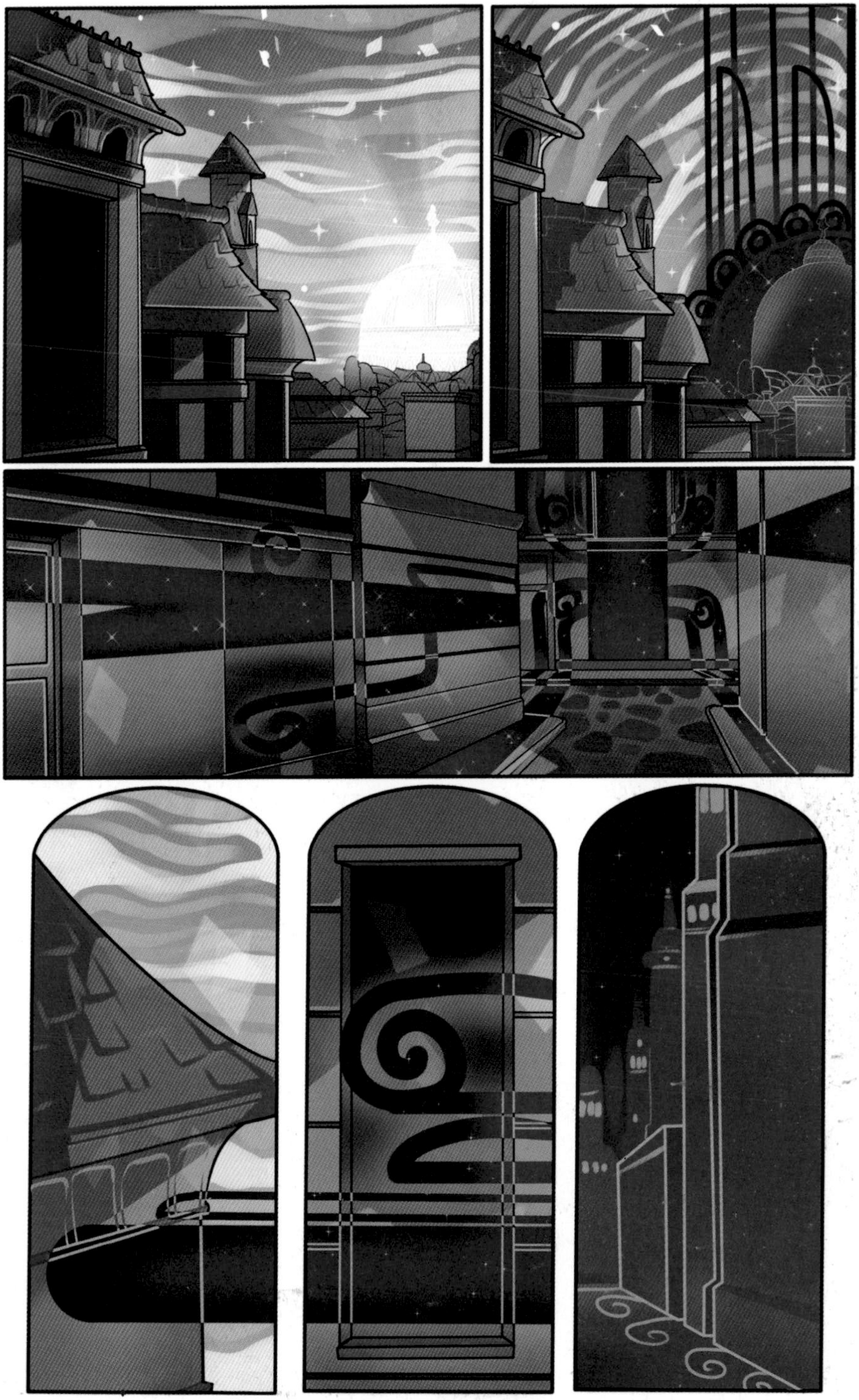

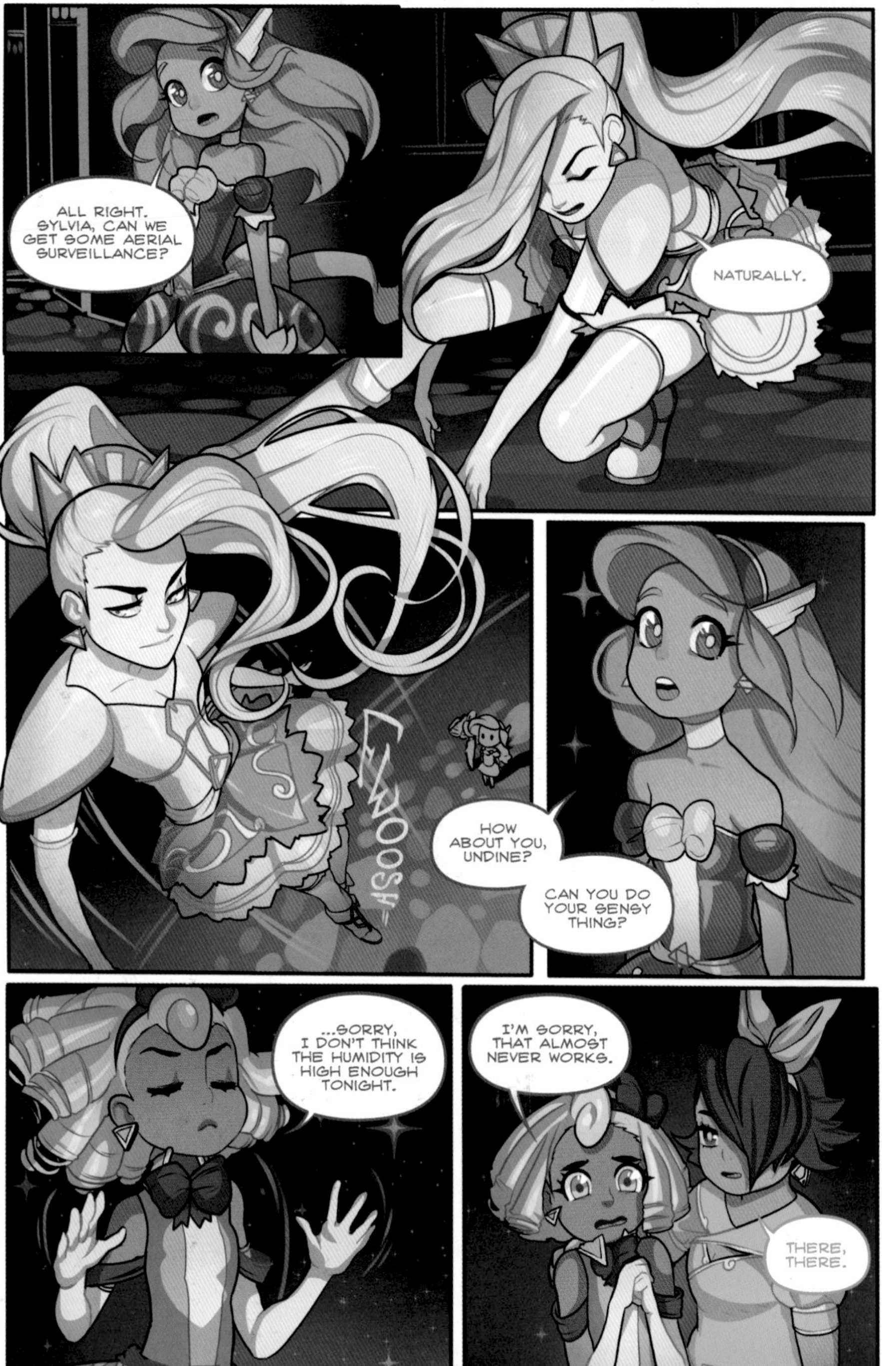
ALL RIGHT. SYLVIA, CAN WE GET SOME AERIAL SURVEILLANCE?
NATURALLY.
SWOOSH
HOW ABOUT YOU, UNDINE?
CAN YOU DO YOUR SENSY THING?
...SORRY, I DON'T THINK THE HUMIDITY IS HIGH ENOUGH TONIGHT.
I'M SORRY, THAT ALMOST NEVER WORKS.
THERE, THERE.

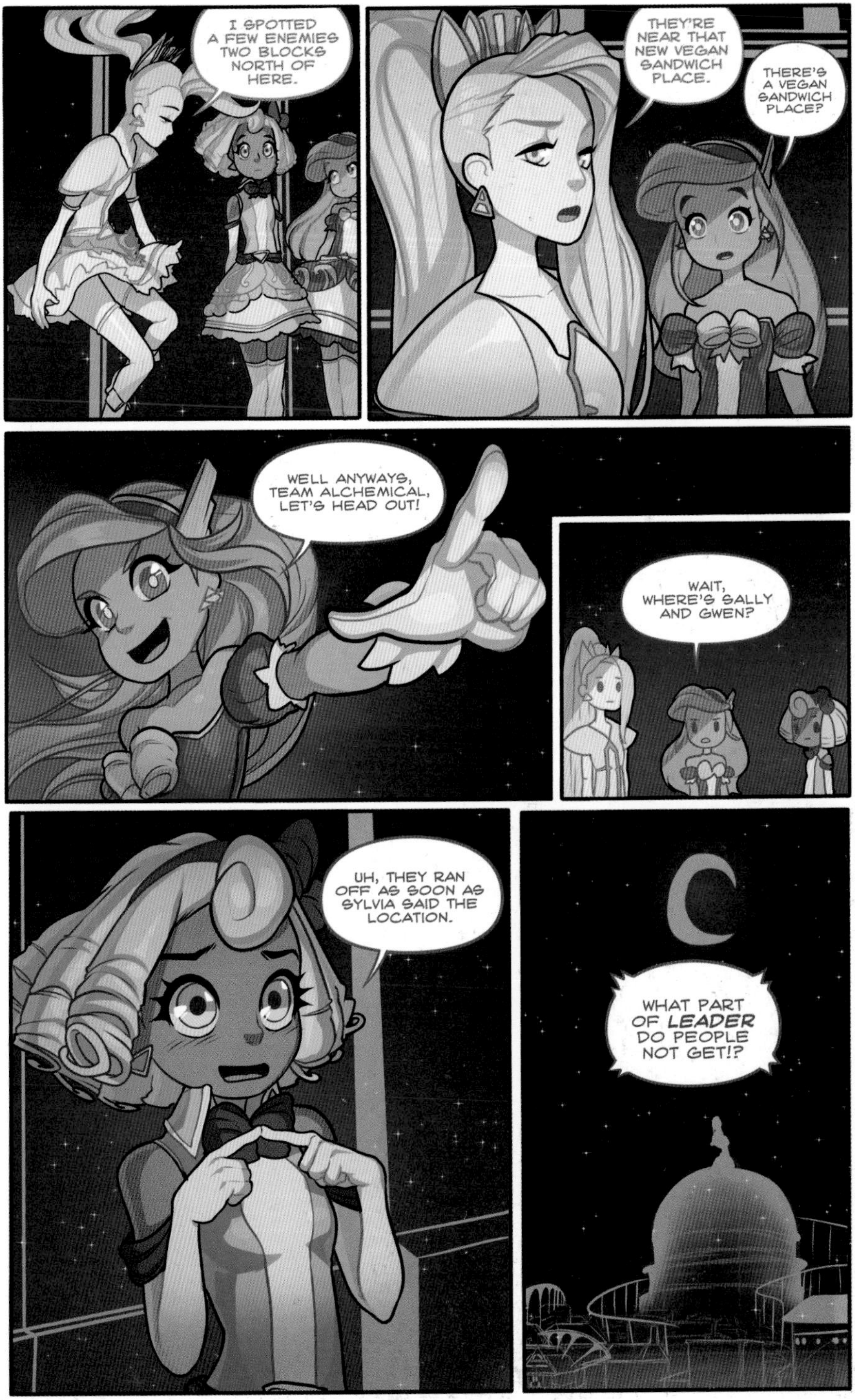
I SPOTTED A FEW ENEMIES TWO BLOCKS NORTH OF HERE.
THEY'RE NEAR THAT NEW VEGAN SANDWICH PLACE.
THERE'S A VEGAN SANDWICH PLACE?
WELL ANYWAYS, TEAM ALCHEMICAL, LET'S HEAD OUT!
WAIT, WHERE'S SALLY AND GWEN?
UH, THEY RAN OFF AS SOON AS SYLVIA SAID THE LOCATION.
WHAT PART OF **LEADER** DO PEOPLE NOT GET!?

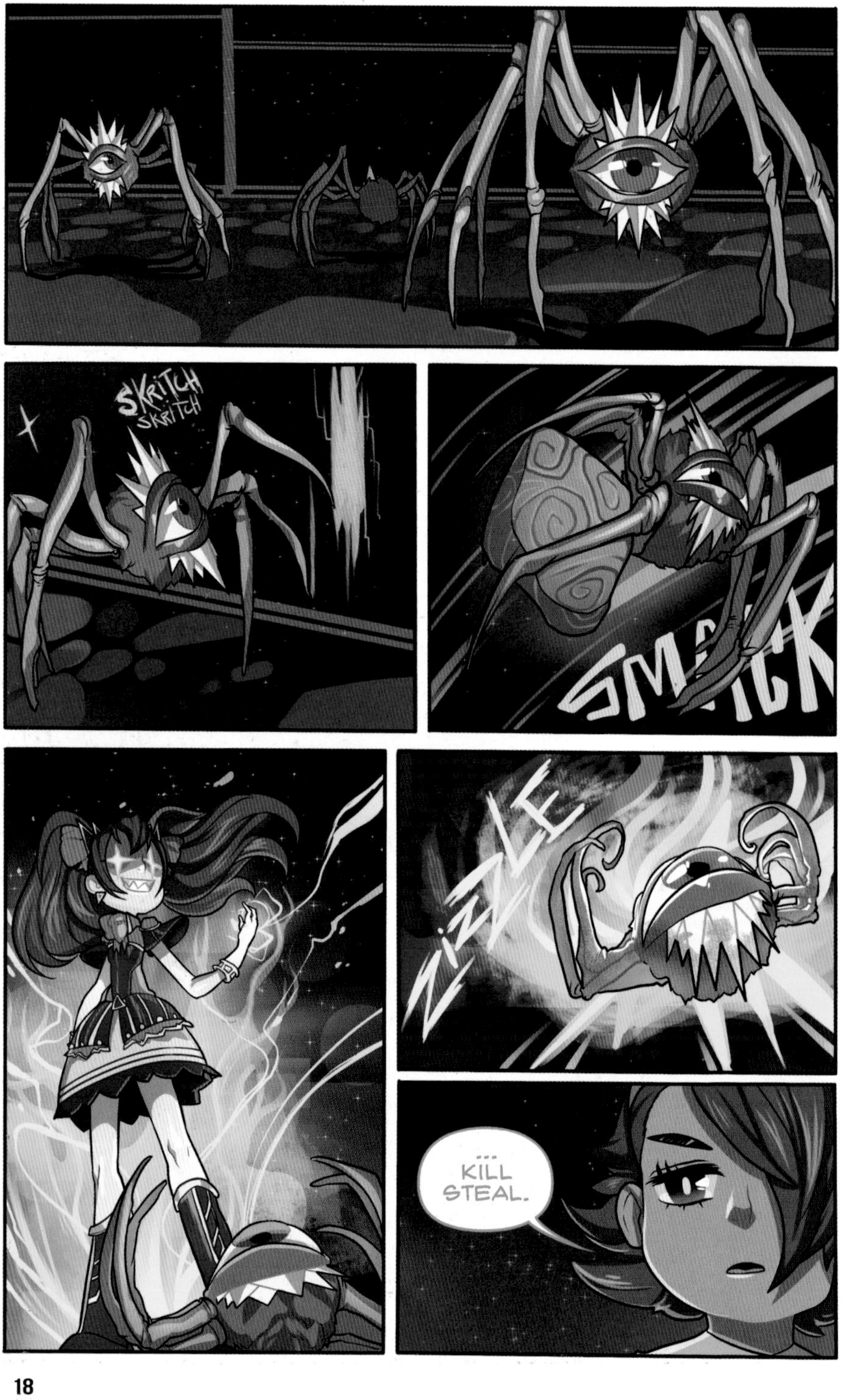
SKRITCH
SKRITCH
SMACK
ZIZZLE
... KILL STEAL.

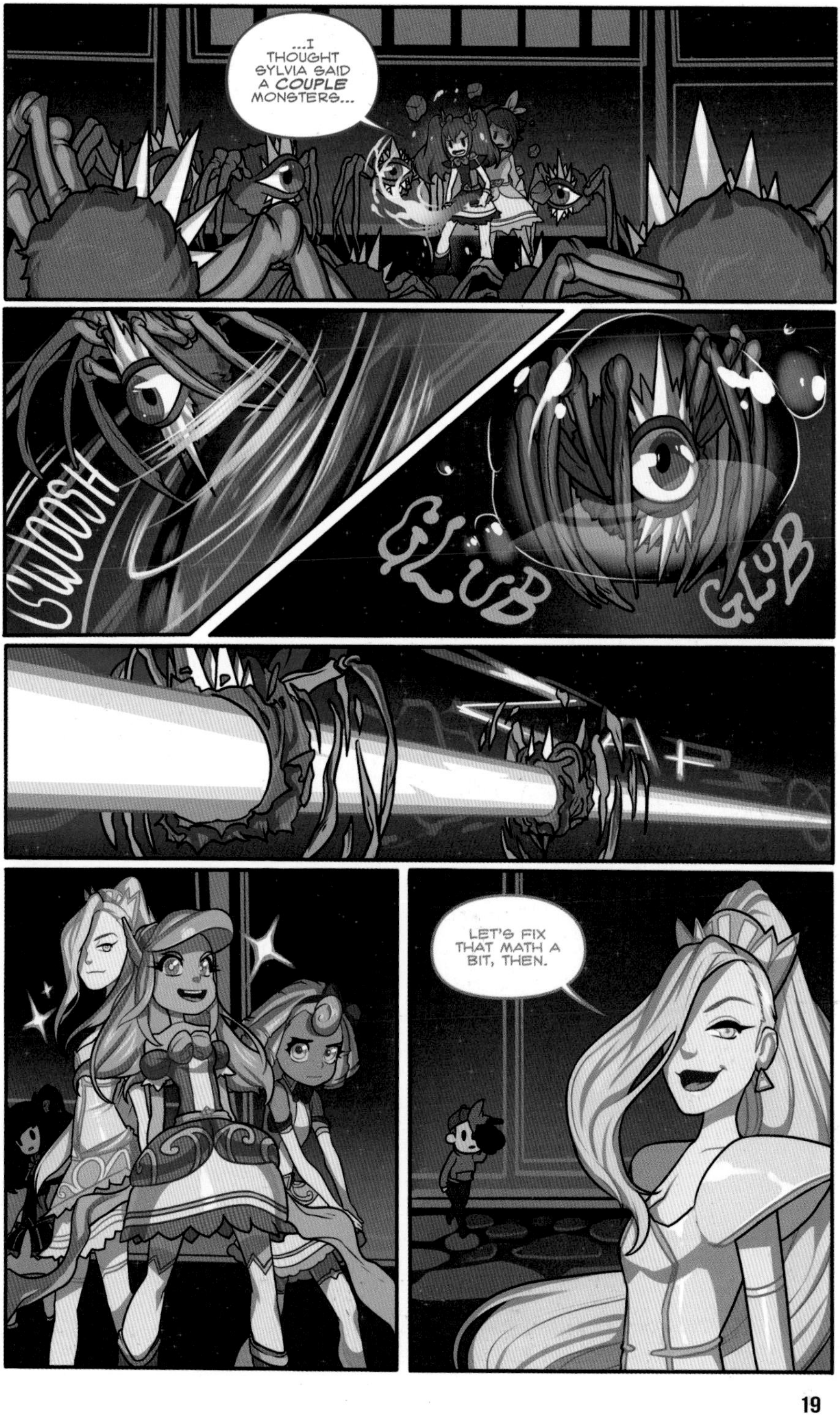
...I THOUGHT SYLVIA SAID A *COUPLE* MONSTERS...
SWOOSH
GLUB
GLUB
LET'S FIX THAT MATH A BIT, THEN.

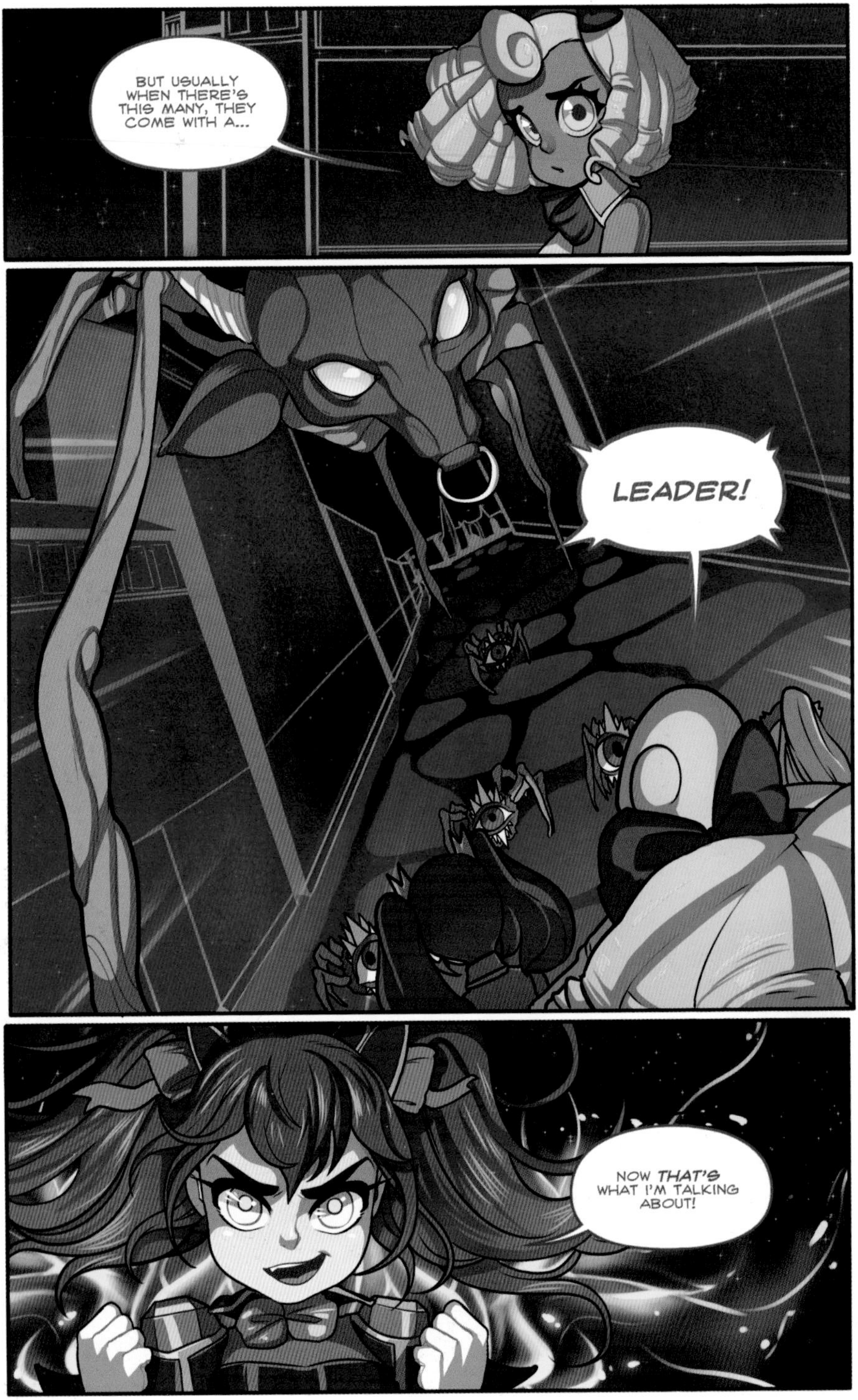
BUT USUALLY WHEN THERE'S THIS MANY, THEY COME WITH A...
LEADER!
NOW *THAT'S* WHAT I'M TALKING ABOUT!

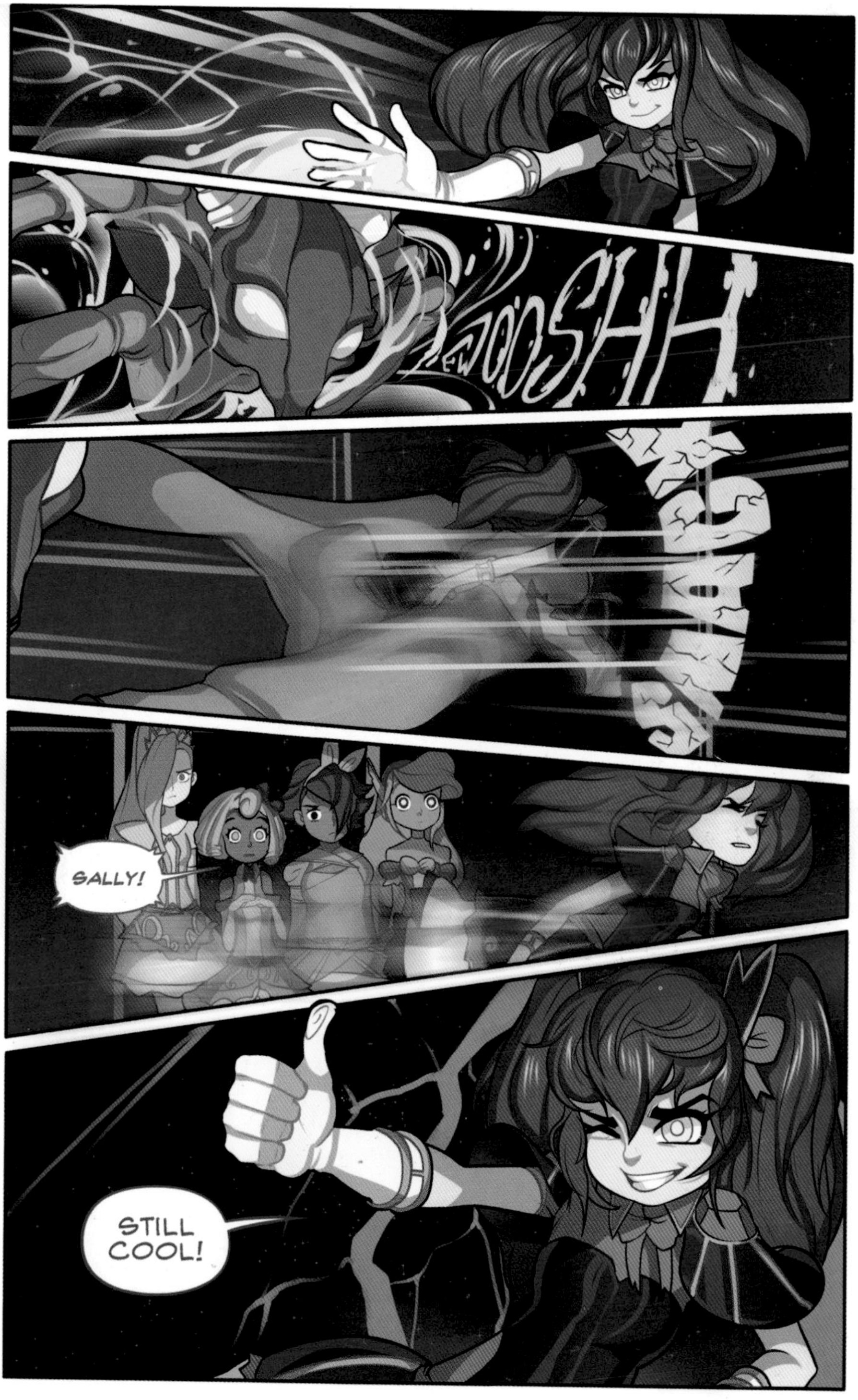
SALLY!
STILL COOL!

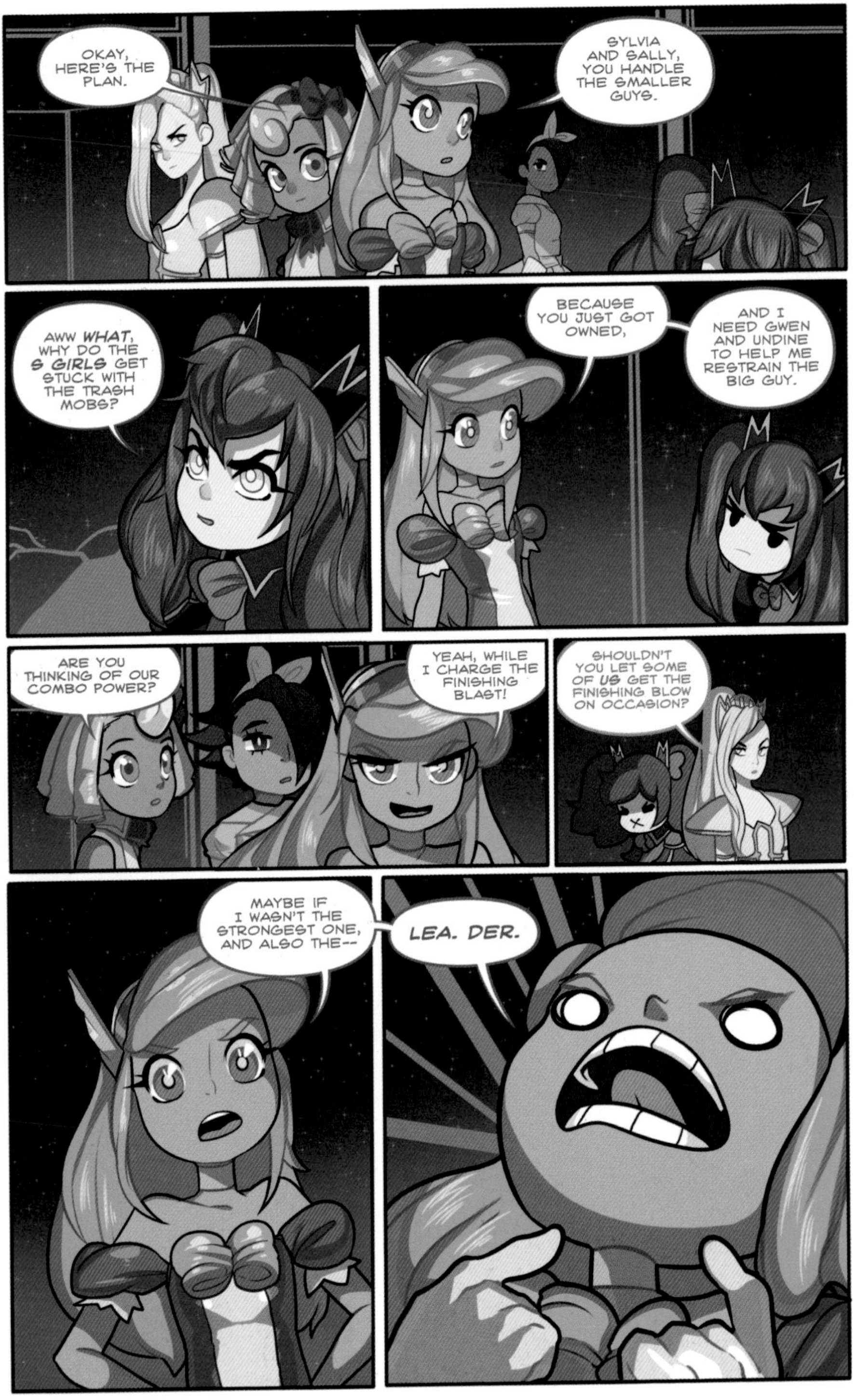

OKAY, HERE'S THE PLAN.
SYLVIA AND SALLY, YOU HANDLE THE SMALLER GUYS.
AWW *WHAT*, WHY DO THE *S GIRLS* GET STUCK WITH THE TRASH MOBS?
BECAUSE YOU JUST GOT OWNED,
AND I NEED GWEN AND UNDINE TO HELP ME RESTRAIN THE BIG GUY.
ARE YOU THINKING OF OUR COMBO POWER?
YEAH, WHILE I CHARGE THE FINISHING BLAST!
SHOULDN'T YOU LET SOME OF *US* GET THE FINISHING BLOW ON OCCASION?
MAYBE IF I WASN'T THE STRONGEST ONE, AND ALSO THE--
LEA. DER.

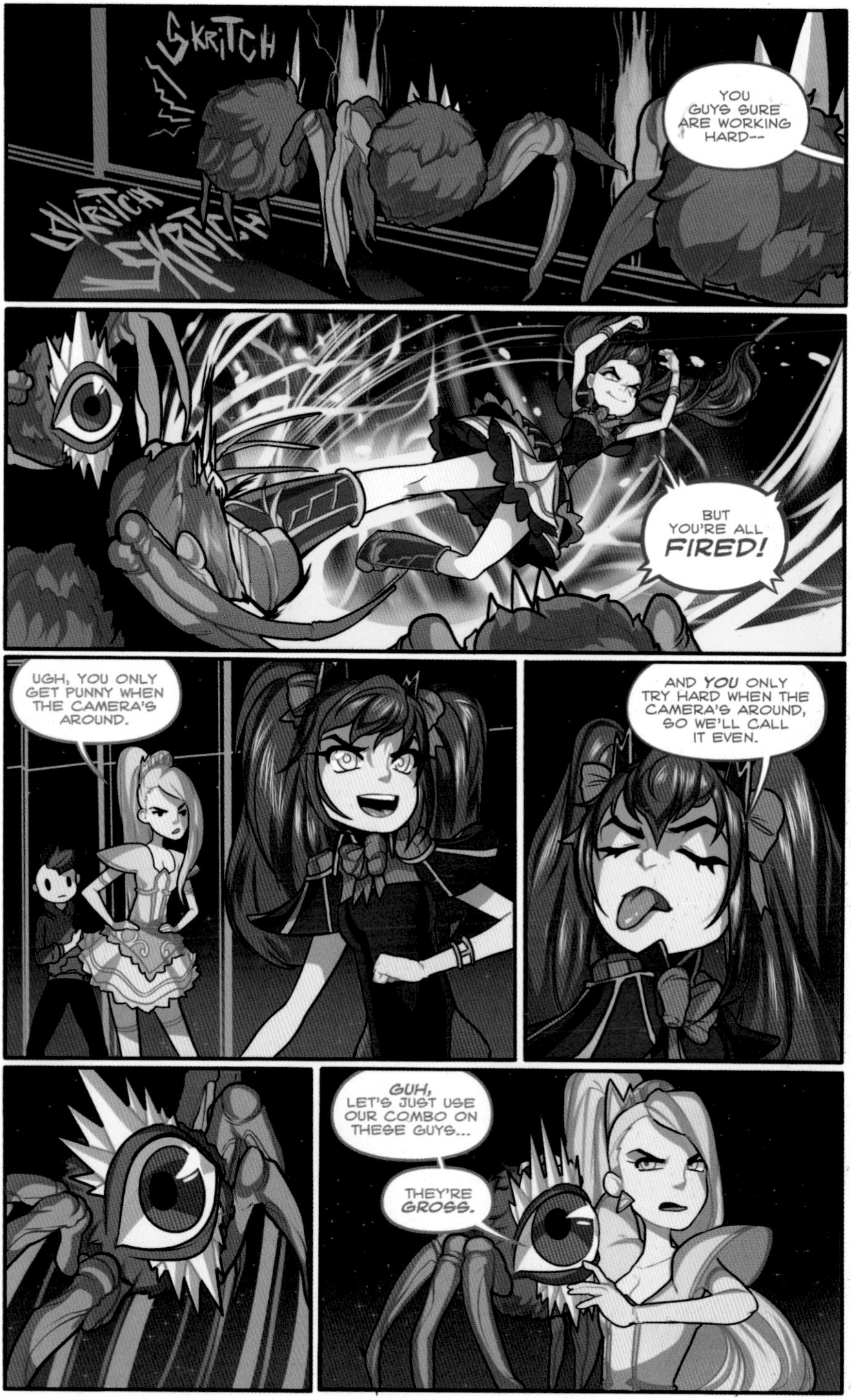
SKRITCH
SKRITCH
SKRITCH
YOU GUYS SURE ARE WORKING HARD--
BUT YOU'RE ALL **FIRED!**
UGH, YOU ONLY GET PUNNY WHEN THE CAMERA'S AROUND.
AND *YOU* ONLY TRY HARD WHEN THE CAMERA'S AROUND, SO WE'LL CALL IT EVEN.
GUH, LET'S JUST USE OUR COMBO ON THESE GUYS...
THEY'RE *GROSS.*

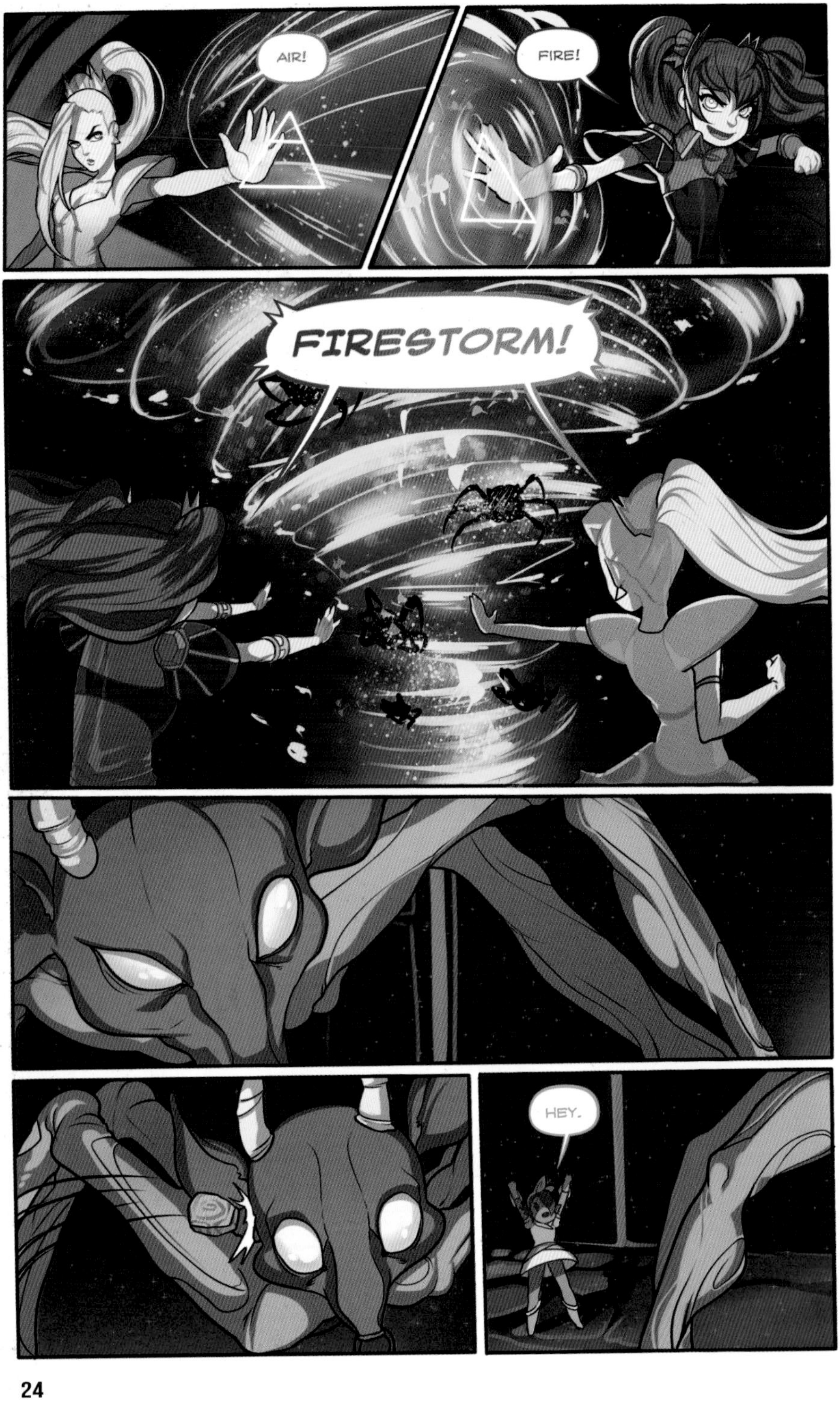
AIR!
FIRE!
FIRESTORM!
HEY.

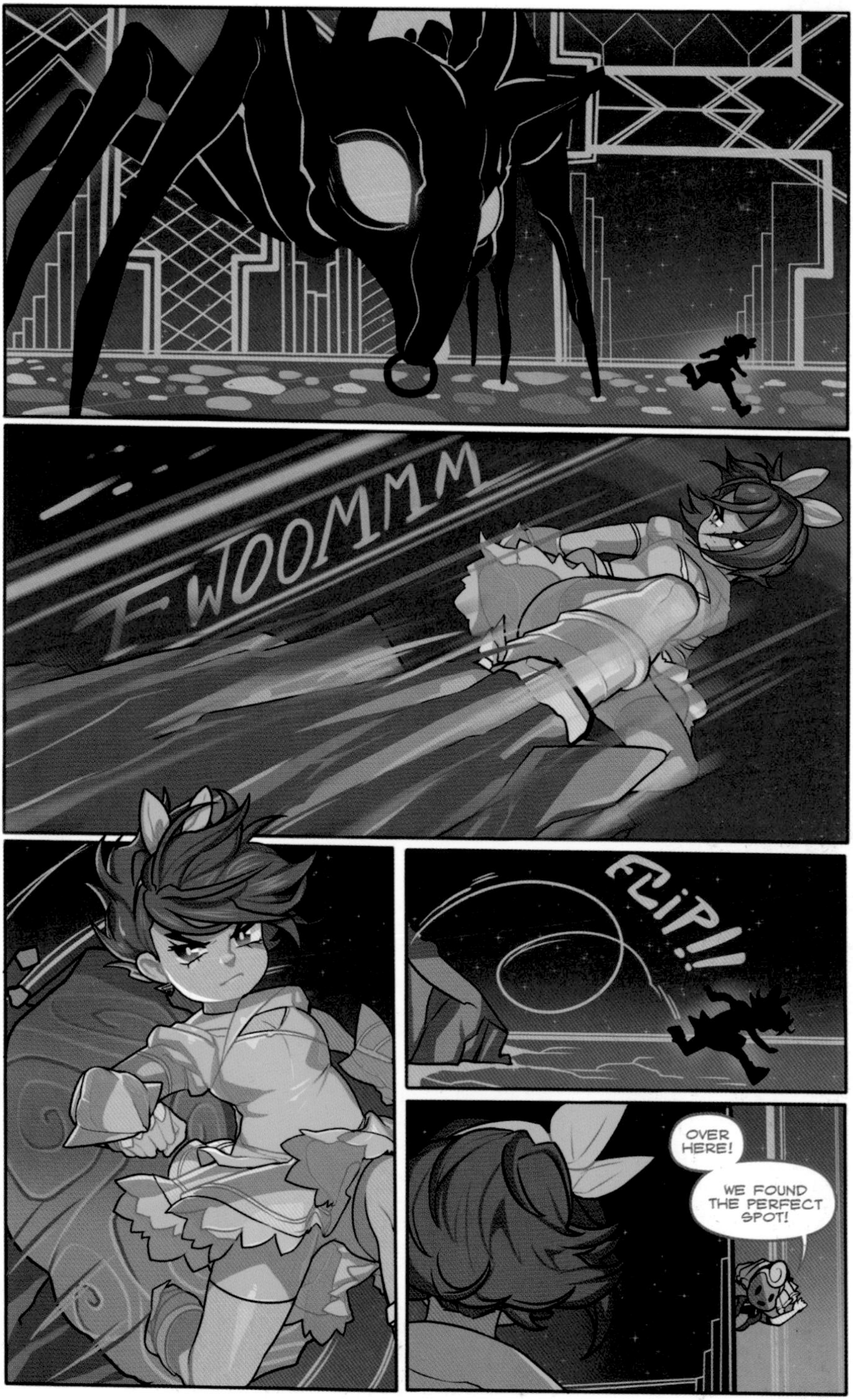
FWOOMMM
FLIP!!!
OVER HERE!
WE FOUND THE PERFECT SPOT!

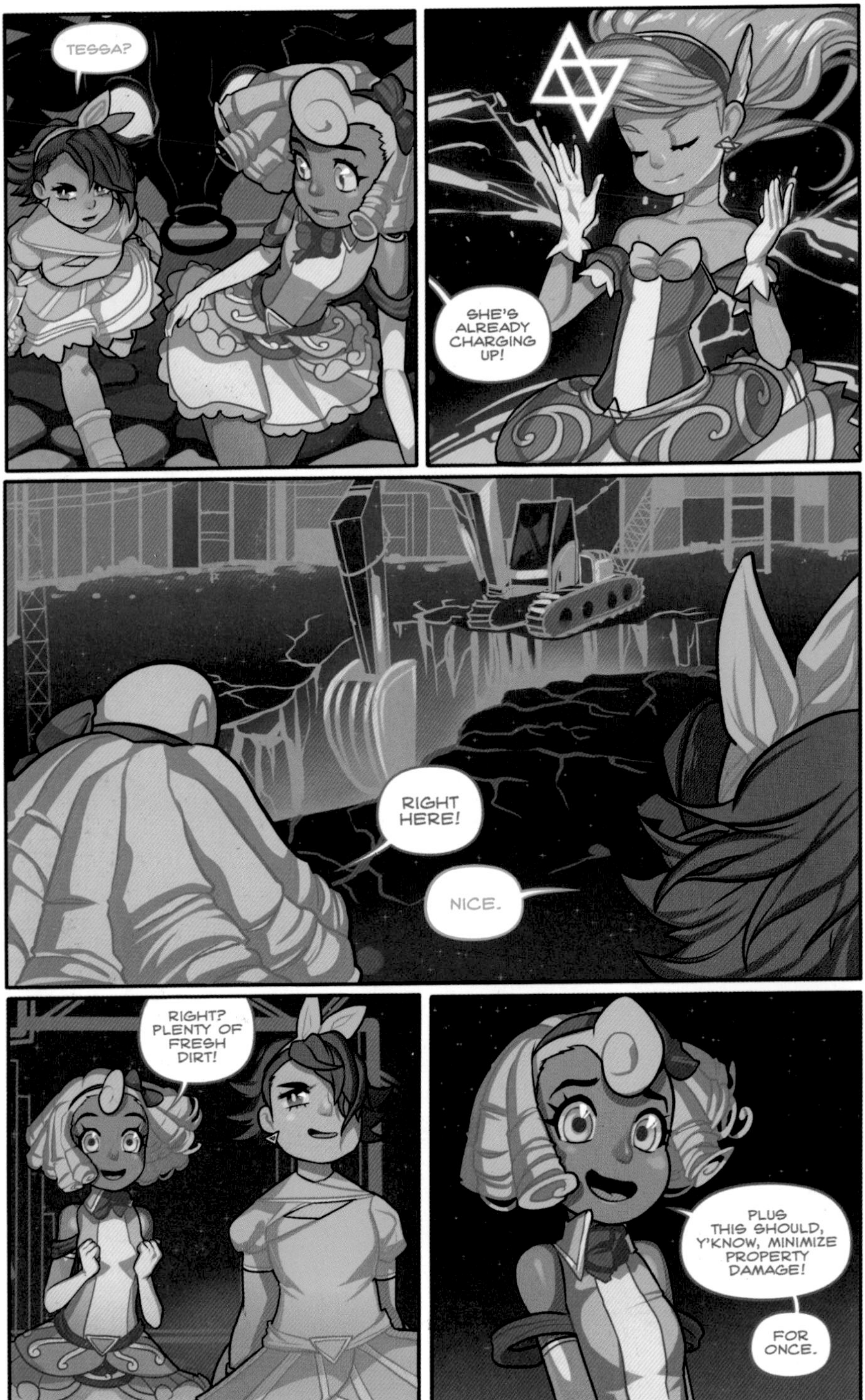
TESSA?
SHE'S ALREADY CHARGING UP!
RIGHT HERE!
NICE.
RIGHT? PLENTY OF FRESH DIRT!
PLUS THIS SHOULD, Y'KNOW, MINIMIZE PROPERTY DAMAGE!
FOR ONCE.

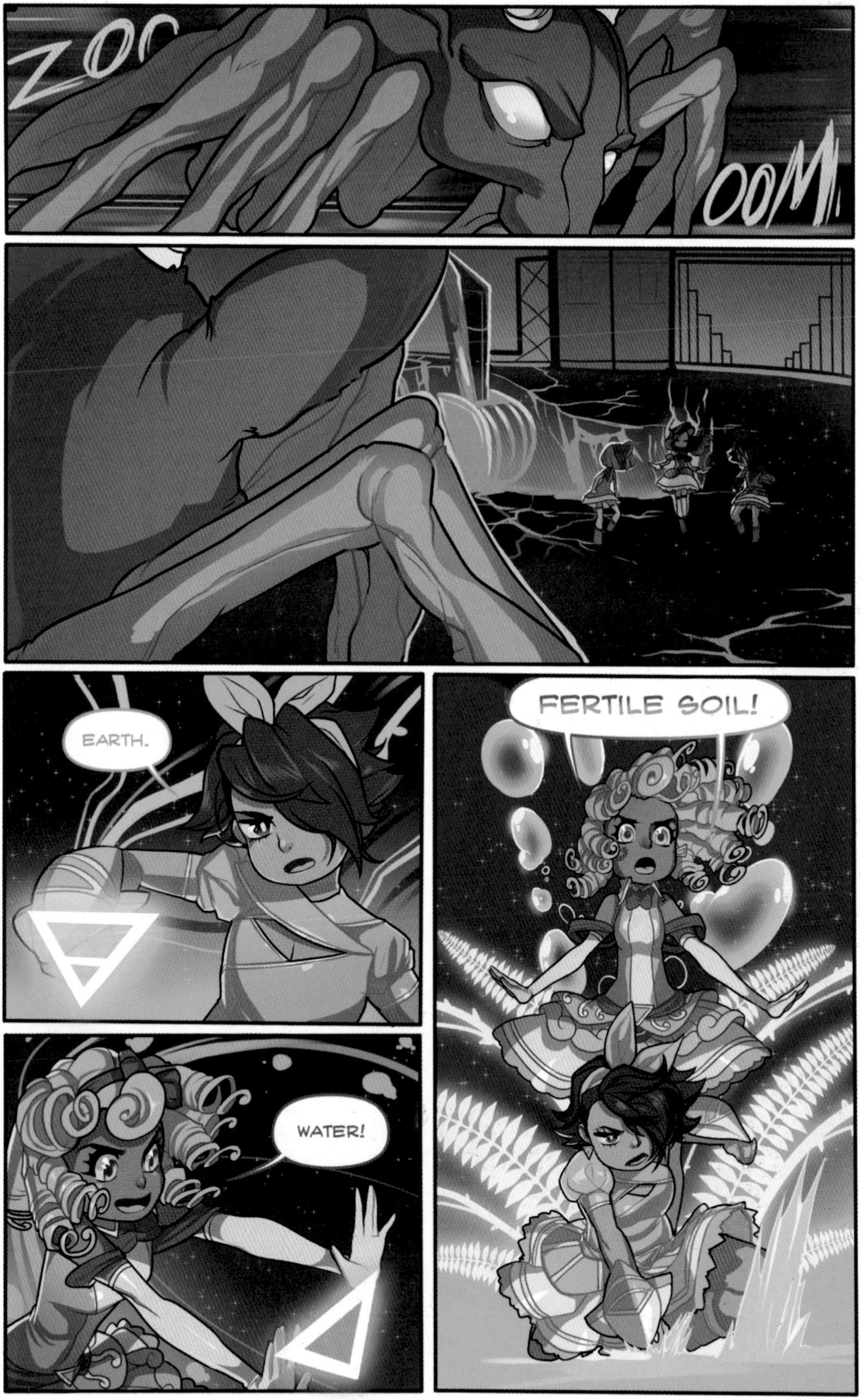
ZOOOOM!
EARTH.
FERTILE SOIL!
WATER!

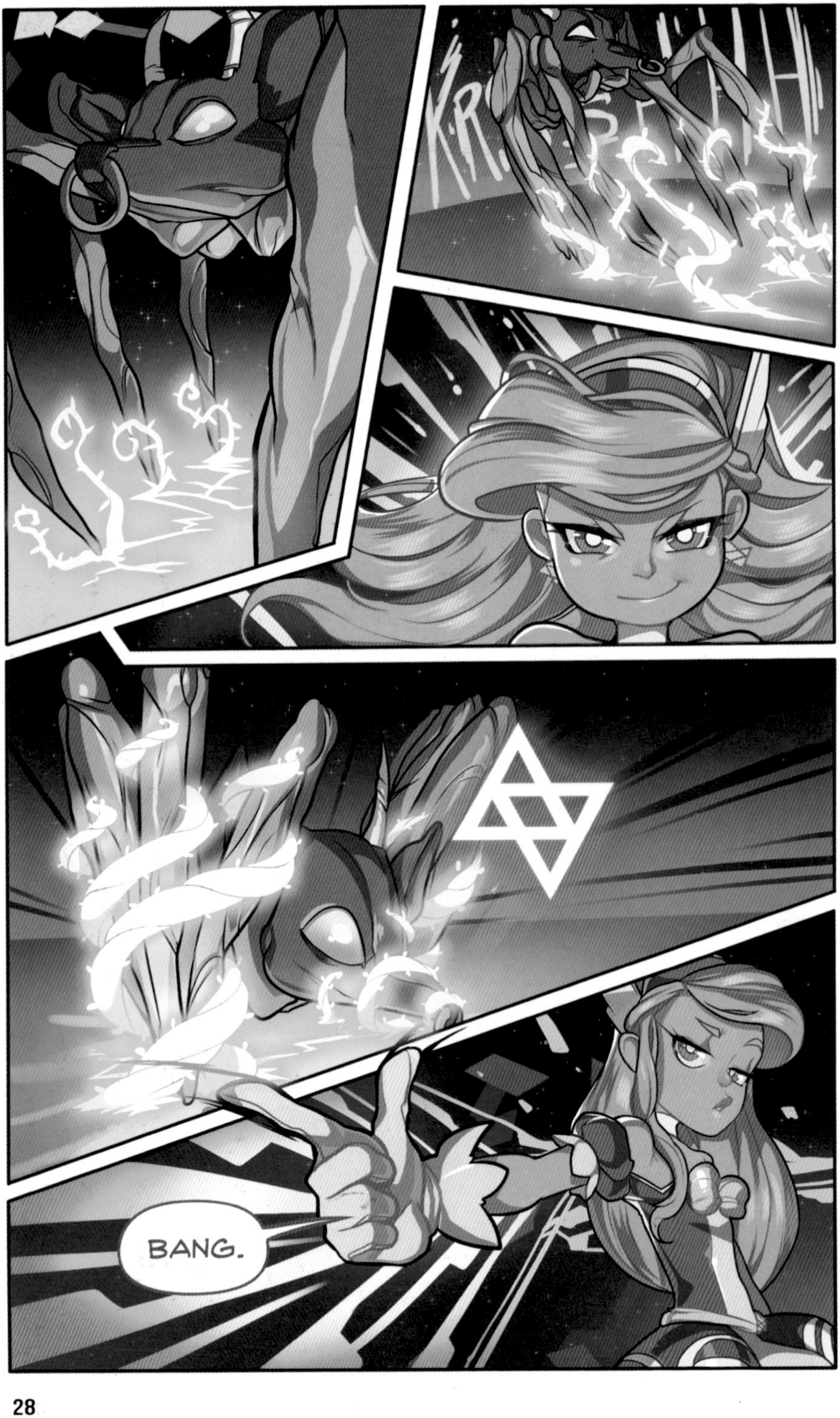
BANG.

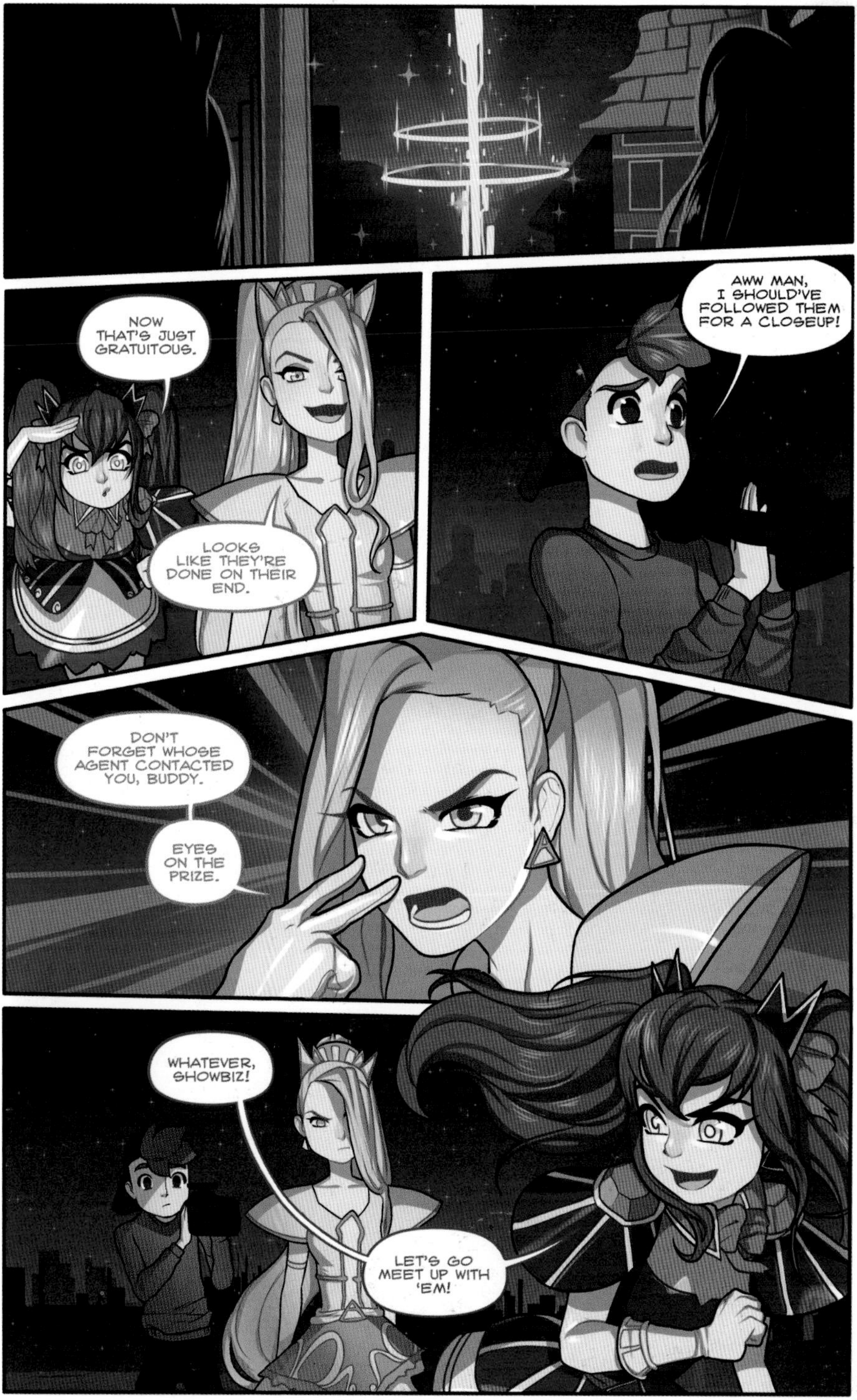
NOW THAT'S JUST GRATUITOUS.
LOOKS LIKE THEY'RE DONE ON THEIR END.
AWW MAN, I SHOULD'VE FOLLOWED THEM FOR A CLOSEUP!
DON'T FORGET WHOSE AGENT CONTACTED YOU, BUDDY.
EYES ON THE PRIZE.
WHATEVER, SHOWBIZ!
LET'S GO MEET UP WITH 'EM!

AT THAT TIME...

...I REALLY THOUGHT THINGS WERE GOING OKAY.

WE HAD OUR PROBLEMS, BUT IT NEVER FELT LIKE WE WERE IN ANY *REAL* DANGER.

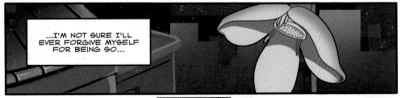

...I'M NOT SURE I'LL EVER FORGIVE MYSELF FOR BEING SO...

COMPLACENT.

END OF CHAPTER 1

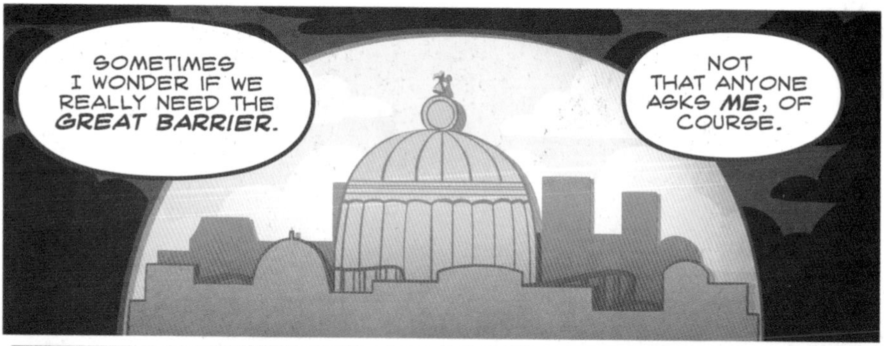
SOMETIMES I WONDER IF WE REALLY NEED THE GREAT BARRIER.
NOT THAT ANYONE ASKS ME, OF COURSE.
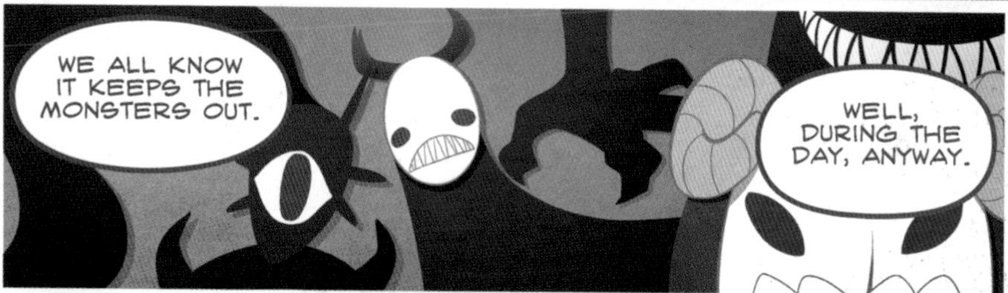
WE ALL KNOW IT KEEPS THE MONSTERS OUT.
WELL, DURING THE DAY, ANYWAY.
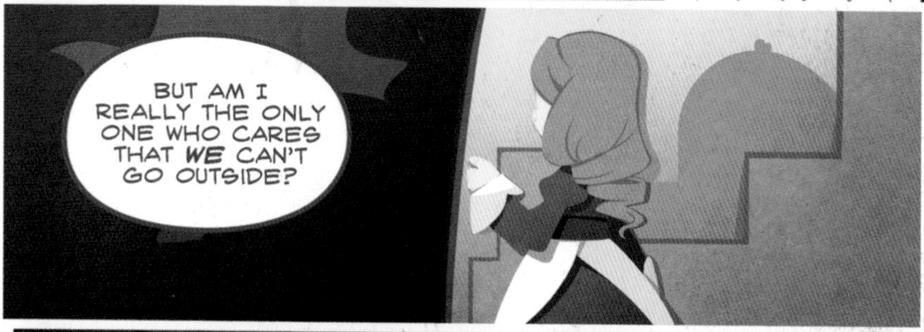
BUT AM I REALLY THE ONLY ONE WHO CARES THAT WE CAN'T GO OUTSIDE?
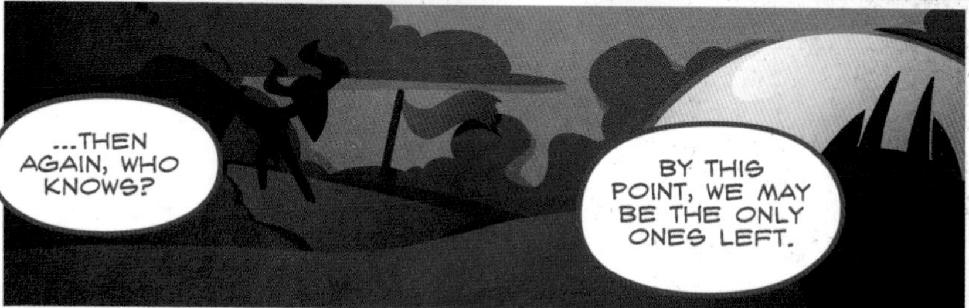
...THEN AGAIN, WHO KNOWS?
BY THIS POINT, WE MAY BE THE ONLY ONES LEFT.
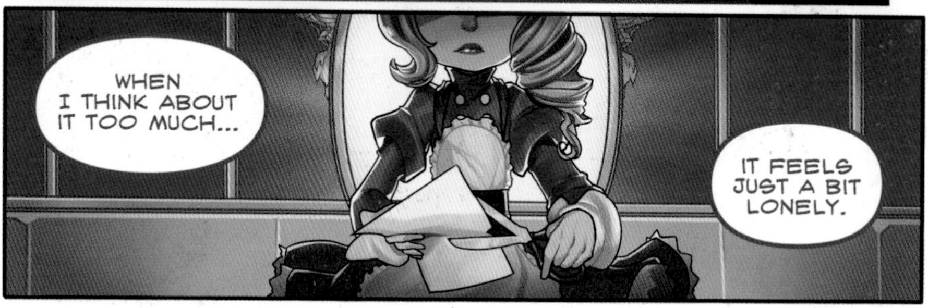
WHEN I THINK ABOUT IT TOO MUCH...
IT FEELS JUST A BIT LONELY.

REGISTER TODAY

REGISTRATION IS EASY AND ***100% FREE!***

Awakening to your new powers can be a confusing and frightening time, but we're here to help!
By registering with the Board of Magical Girls, you'll have access to numerous resources and a personal counselor to help make your transition a smooth one.

FACT!

Registered magical girls are ***70%*** less likely to experience serious injuries or fatalities.

Being a registered magical girl opens up a whole new world of possibilities!
Earn extra money while helping to defend your family and friends!

DON'T WORRY:

-Registration does NOT require you to participate in the nightly monster purge.
-You can also continue to attend your current school if you so choose!

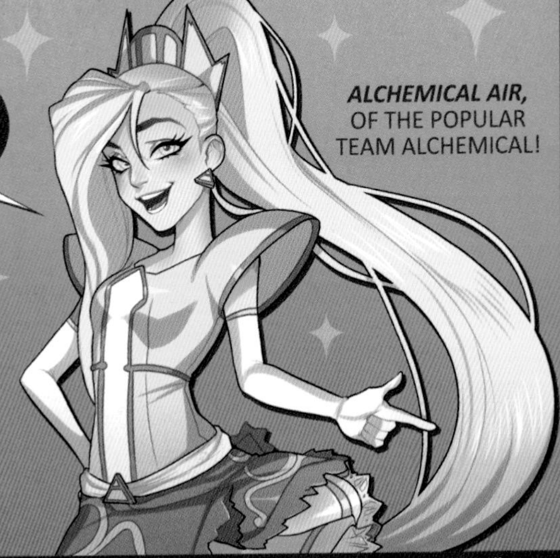
I'M HAPPY TO BE REGISTERED, AND YOU WILL BE TOO!
ALCHEMICAL AIR, OF THE POPULAR TEAM ALCHEMICAL!

Register Today,
and experience the exciting life of a true
MAGICAL GIRL!

Contact us at V.V.V.-IX.VI.VI.IX.

Or talk to your local recruiter!

Magical Girl Registration V.V.V.-IX.VI.VI.IX.

Magical Girl Registration V.V.V.-IX.VI.VI.IX.
Magical Girl Registration V.V.V.-IX.VI.VI.IX.
Magical Girl Registration V.V.V.-IX.VI.VI.IX.
Magical Girl Registration V.V.V.-IX.VI.VI.IX.
Magical Girl Registration V.V.V.-IX.VI.VI.IX.
Magical Girl Registration V.V.V.-IX.VI.VI.IX.
Magical Girl Registration V.V.V.-IX.VI.VI.IX.

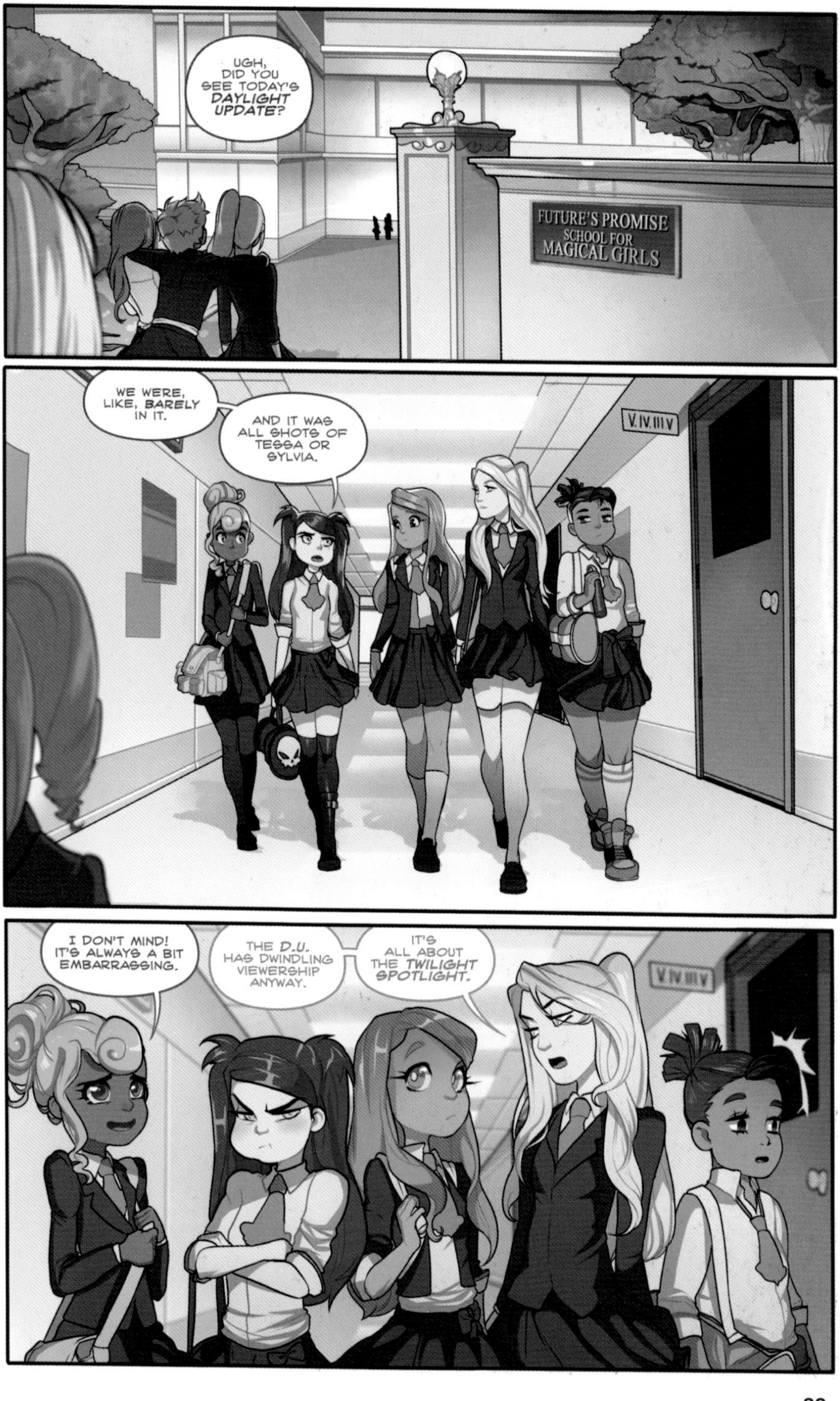
UGH, DID YOU SEE TODAY'S *DAYLIGHT UPDATE*?
FUTURE'S PROMISE SCHOOL FOR MAGICAL GIRLS
WE WERE, LIKE, *BARELY* IN IT.
AND IT WAS ALL SHOTS OF TESSA OR SYLVIA.
V.IV.III.V
I DON'T MIND! IT'S ALWAYS A BIT EMBARRASSING.
THE *D.U.* HAS DWINDLING VIEWERSHIP ANYWAY.
IT'S ALL ABOUT THE *TWILIGHT SPOTLIGHT.*

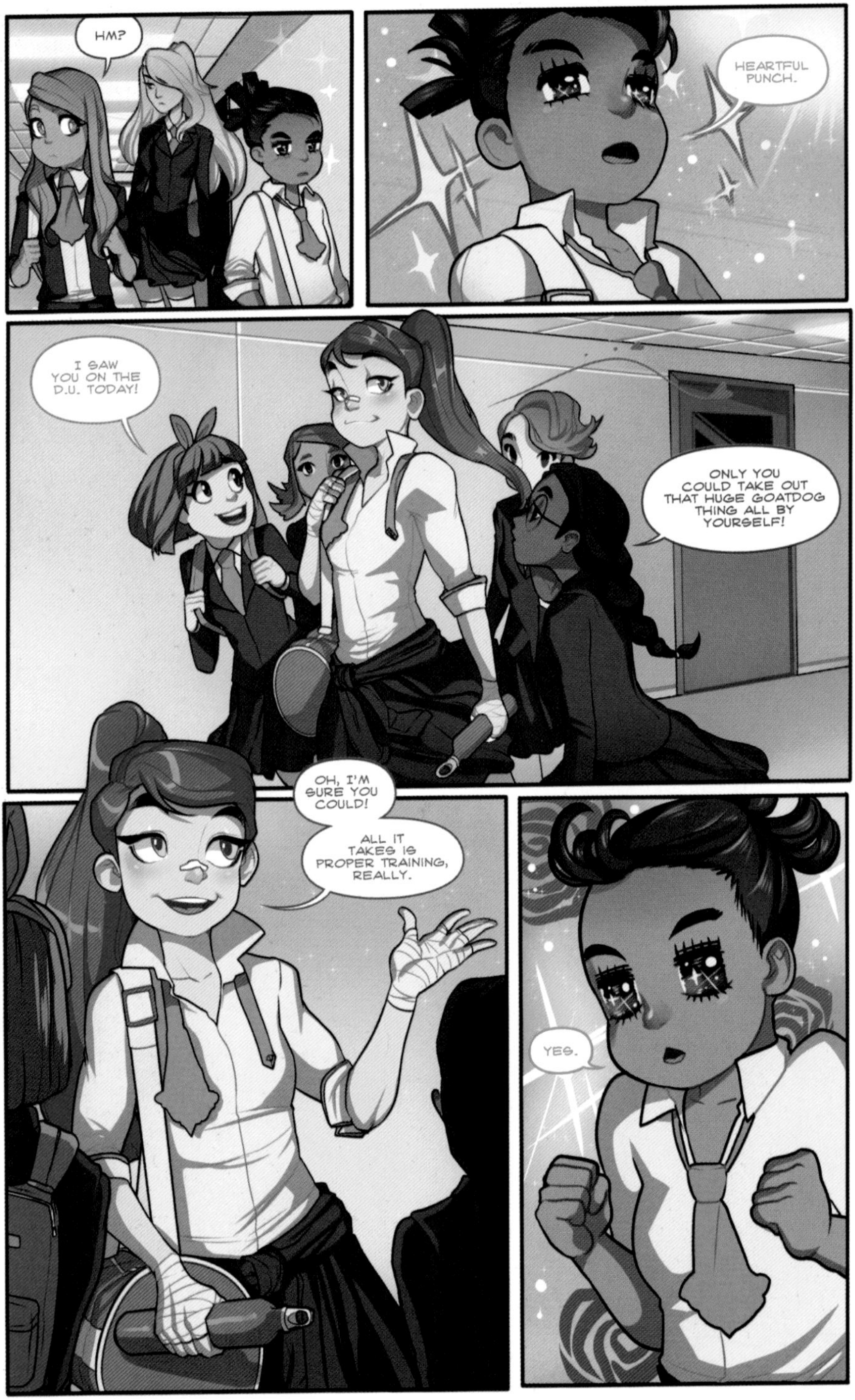
HM?
HEARTFUL PUNCH.
I SAW YOU ON THE D.U. TODAY!
ONLY YOU COULD TAKE OUT THAT HUGE GOATDOG THING ALL BY YOURSELF!
OH, I'M SURE YOU COULD!
ALL IT TAKES IS PROPER TRAINING, REALLY.
YES.

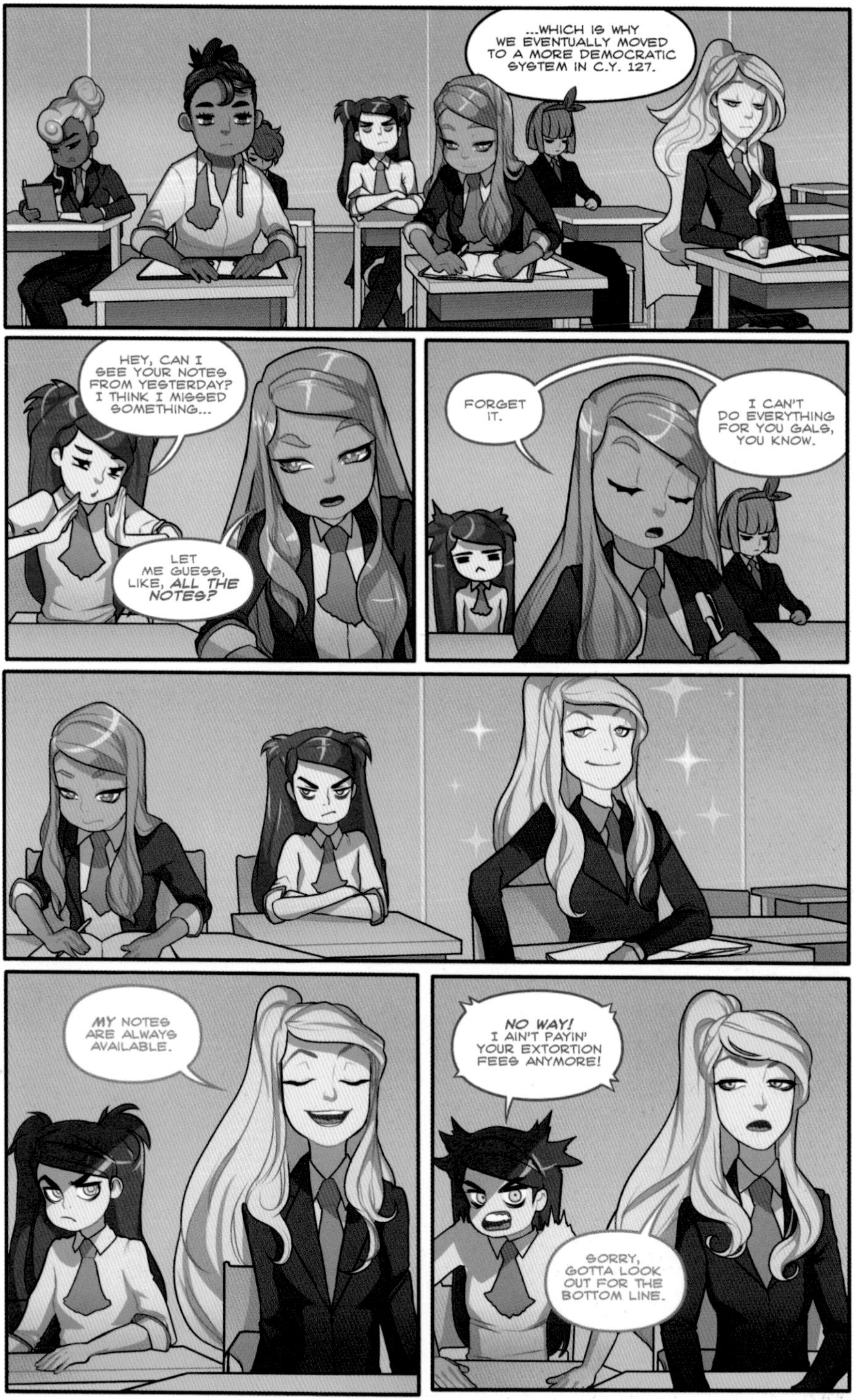
...WHICH IS WHY WE EVENTUALLY MOVED TO A MORE DEMOCRATIC SYSTEM IN C.Y. 127.
HEY, CAN I SEE YOUR NOTES FROM YESTERDAY? I THINK I MISSED SOMETHING...
LET ME GUESS, LIKE, *ALL THE NOTES?*
FORGET IT.
I CAN'T DO EVERYTHING FOR YOU GALS, YOU KNOW.
MY NOTES ARE ALWAYS AVAILABLE.
NO WAY! I AIN'T PAYIN' YOUR EXTORTION FEES ANYMORE!
SORRY, GOTTA LOOK OUT FOR THE BOTTOM LINE.

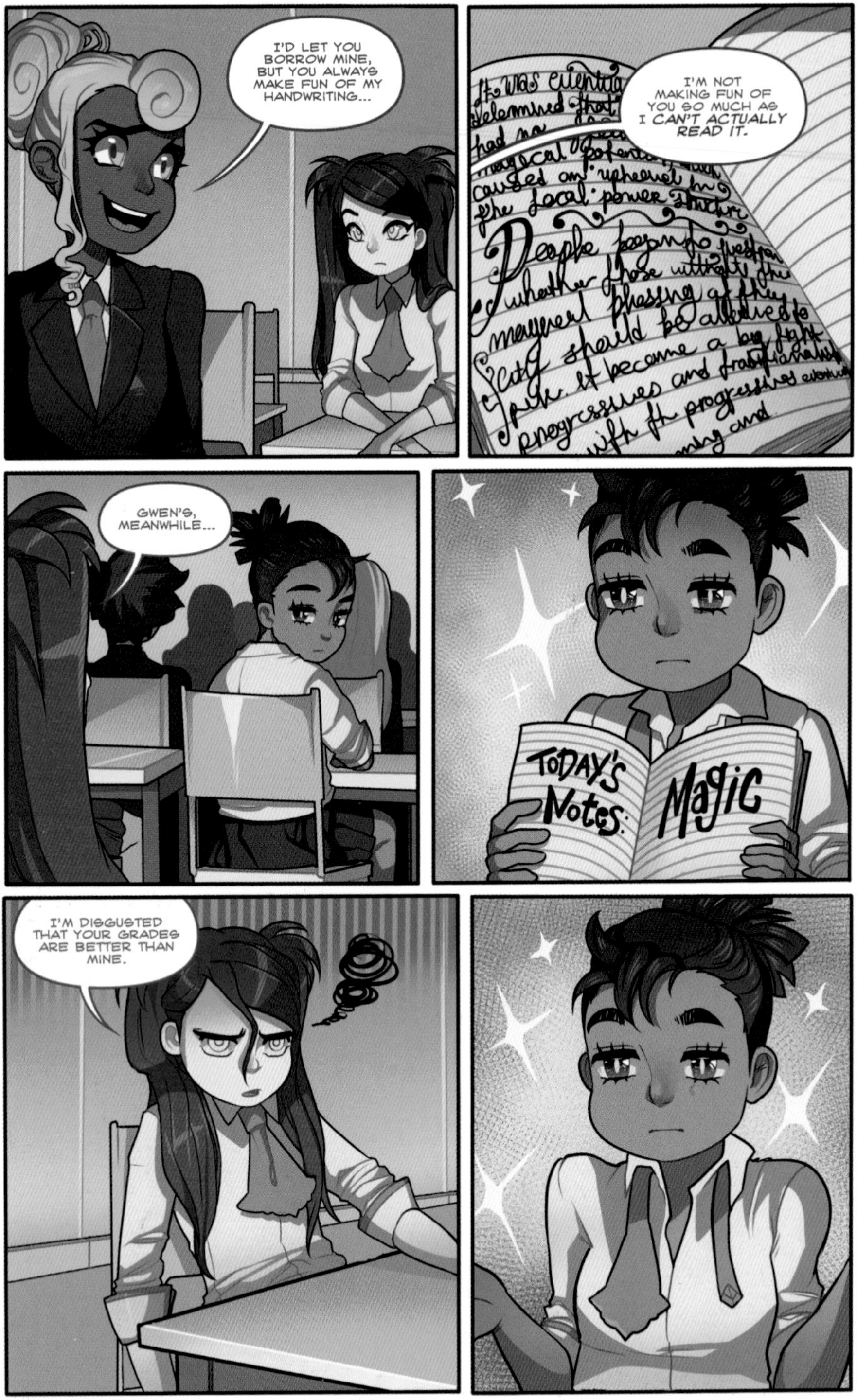
I'D LET YOU BORROW MINE, BUT YOU ALWAYS MAKE FUN OF MY HANDWRITING...
I'M NOT MAKING FUN OF YOU SO MUCH AS I CAN'T ACTUALLY READ IT.
GWEN'S, MEANWHILE...
TODAY'S Notes: Magic
I'M DISGUSTED THAT YOUR GRADES ARE BETTER THAN MINE.

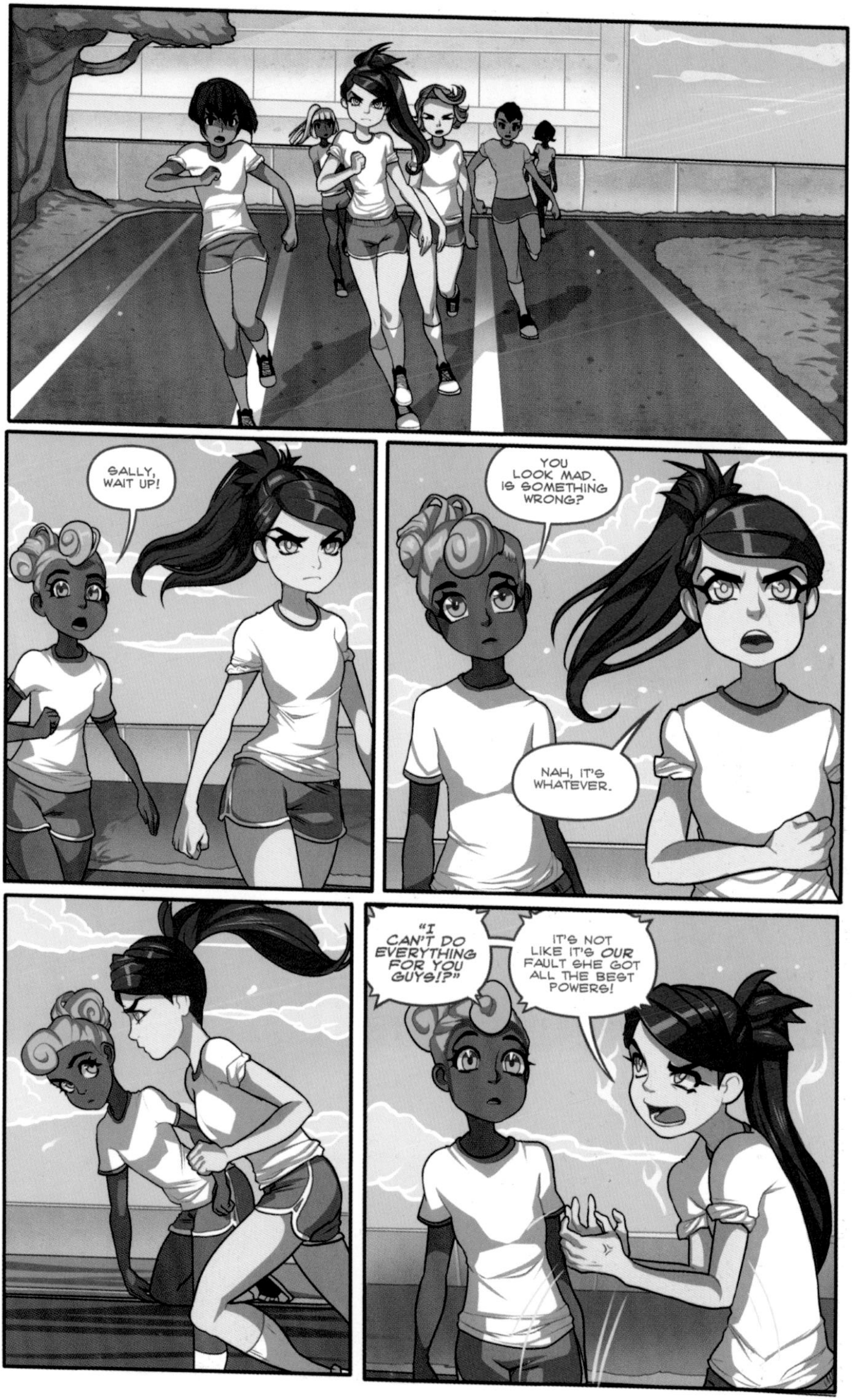
SALLY, WAIT UP!
YOU LOOK MAD. IS SOMETHING WRONG?
NAH, IT'S WHATEVER.
"I CAN'T DO EVERYTHING FOR YOU GUYS!?"
IT'S NOT LIKE IT'S *OUR* FAULT SHE GOT ALL THE BEST POWERS!

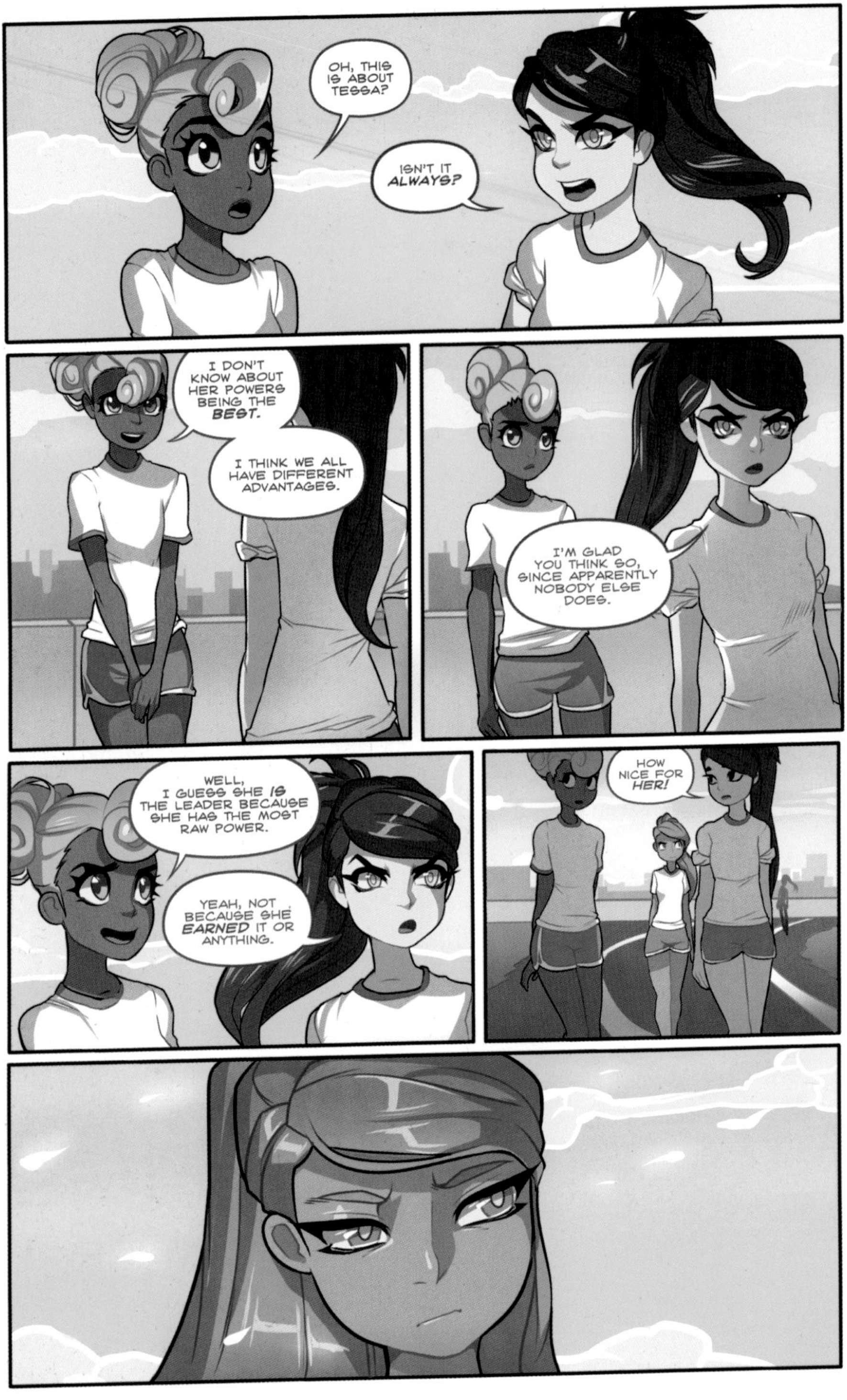

OH, THIS IS ABOUT TESSA?
ISN'T IT ***ALWAYS?***
I DON'T KNOW ABOUT HER POWERS BEING THE ***BEST.***
I THINK WE ALL HAVE DIFFERENT ADVANTAGES.
I'M GLAD YOU THINK SO, SINCE APPARENTLY NOBODY ELSE DOES.
WELL, I GUESS SHE ***IS*** THE LEADER BECAUSE SHE HAS THE MOST RAW POWER.
YEAH, NOT BECAUSE SHE ***EARNED*** IT OR ANYTHING.
HOW NICE FOR ***HER!***

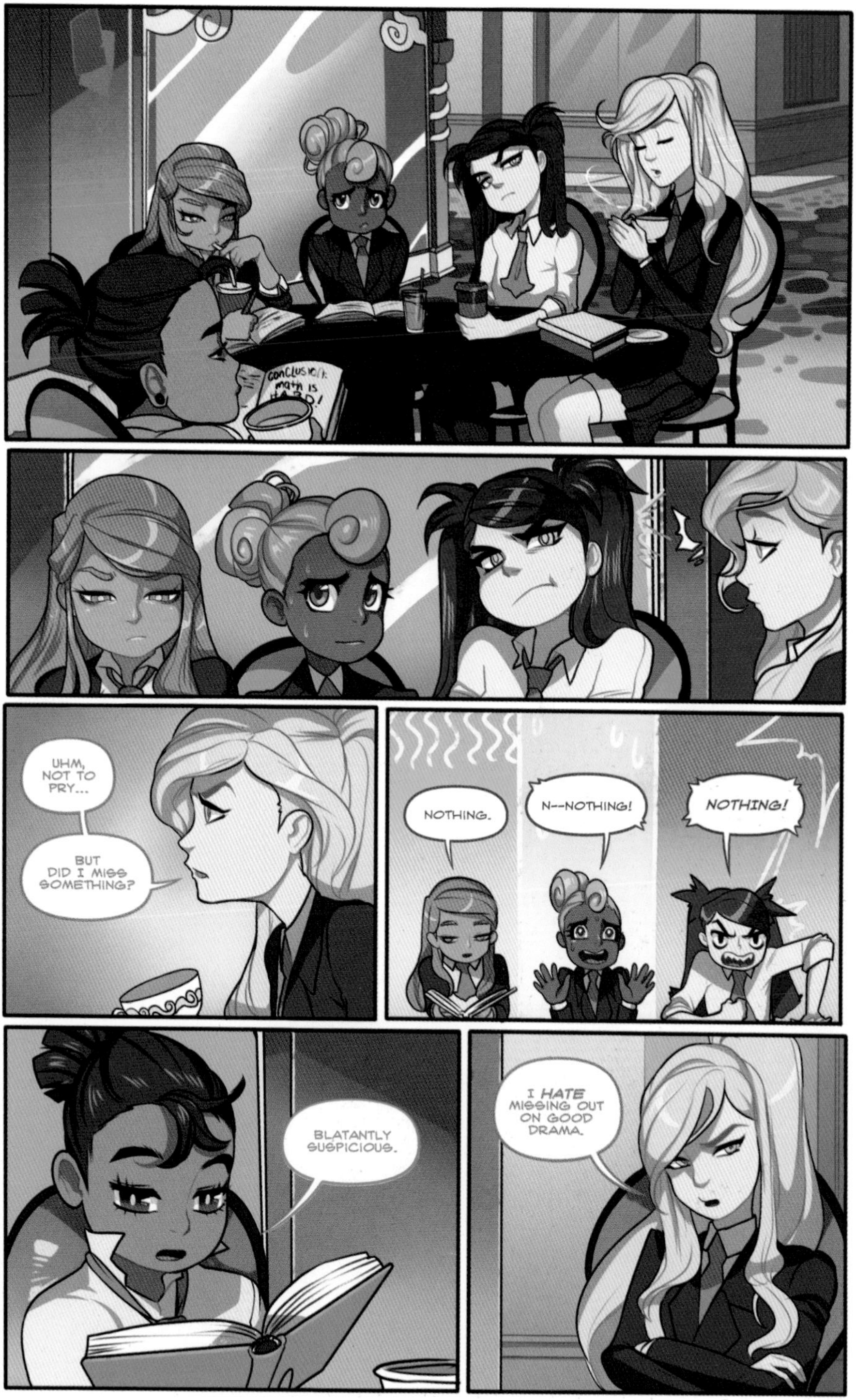

CONCLUSION: math is HARD!
UHM, NOT TO PRY...
BUT DID I MISS SOMETHING?
NOTHING.
N--NOTHING!
NOTHING!
BLATANTLY SUSPICIOUS.
I HATE MISSING OUT ON GOOD DRAMA.

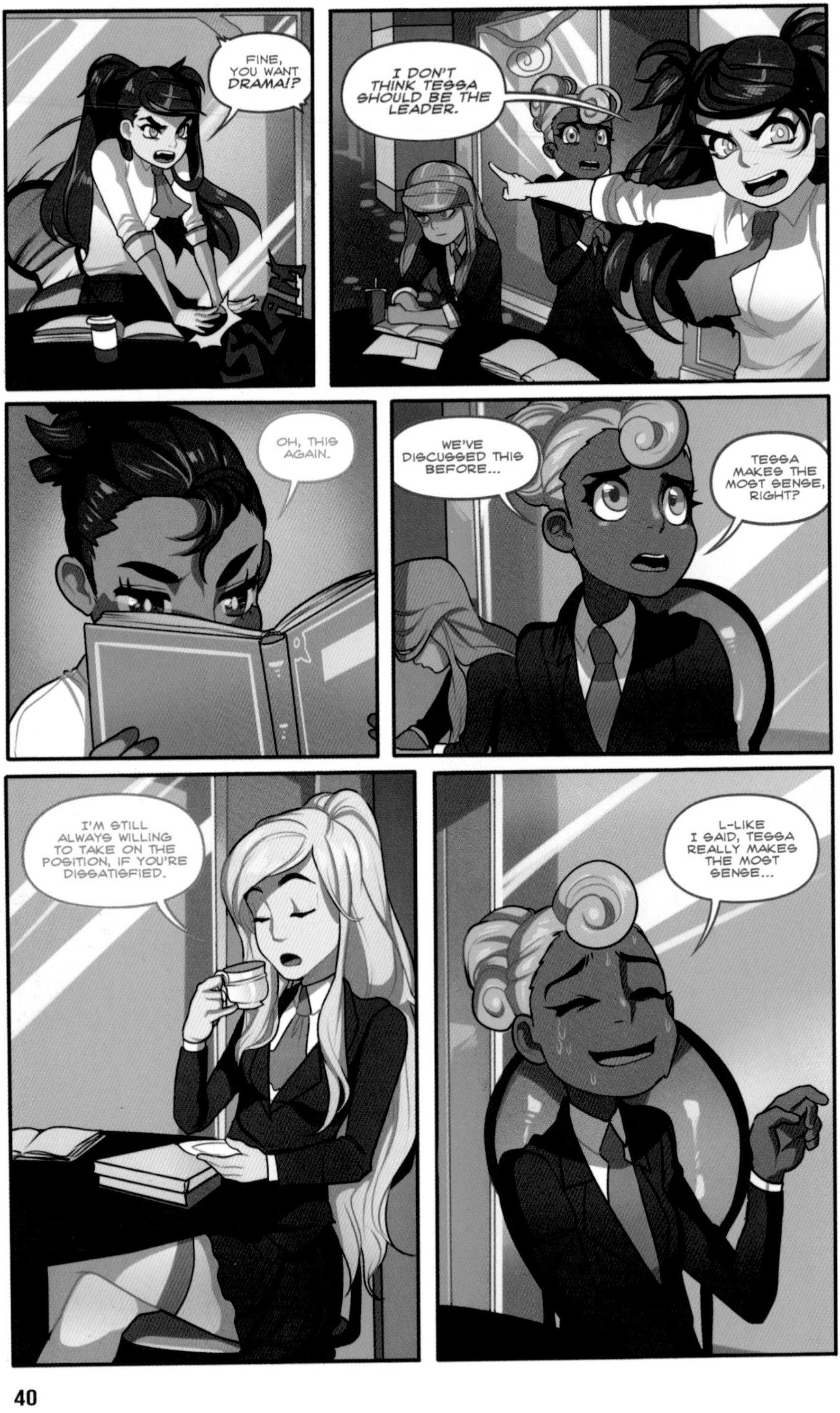
FINE, YOU WANT DRAMA!?
I DON'T THINK TESSA SHOULD BE THE LEADER.
OH, THIS AGAIN.
WE'VE DISCUSSED THIS BEFORE...
TESSA MAKES THE MOST SENSE, RIGHT?
I'M STILL ALWAYS WILLING TO TAKE ON THE POSITION, IF YOU'RE DISSATISFIED.
L-LIKE I SAID, TESSA REALLY MAKES THE MOST SENSE...

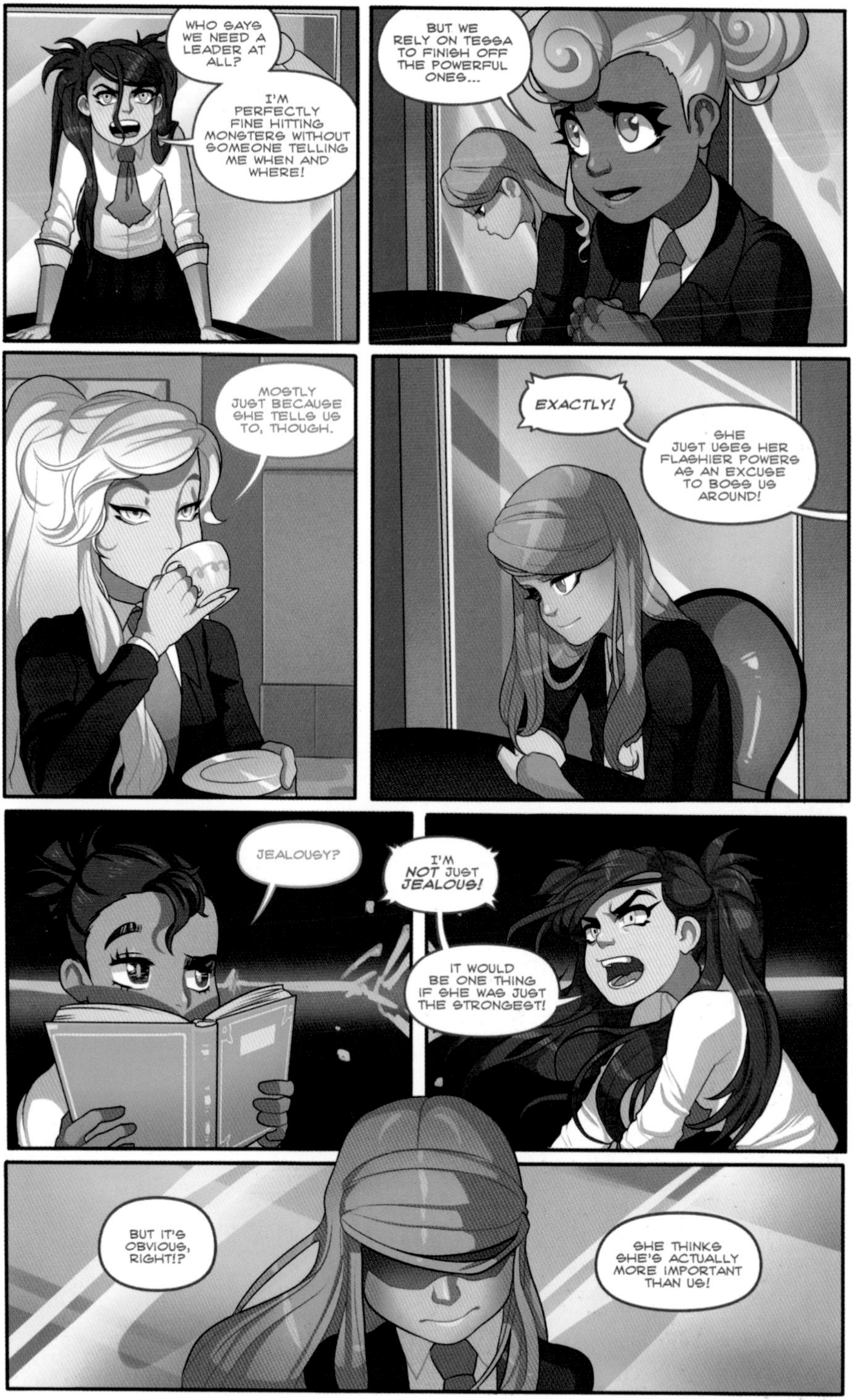

WHO SAYS WE NEED A LEADER AT ALL?
I'M PERFECTLY FINE HITTING MONSTERS WITHOUT SOMEONE TELLING ME WHEN AND WHERE!
BUT WE RELY ON TESSA TO FINISH OFF THE POWERFUL ONES...
MOSTLY JUST BECAUSE SHE TELLS US TO, THOUGH.
EXACTLY!
SHE JUST USES HER FLASHIER POWERS AS AN EXCUSE TO BOSS US AROUND!
JEALOUSY?
I'M NOT JUST JEALOUS!
IT WOULD BE ONE THING IF SHE WAS JUST THE STRONGEST!
BUT IT'S OBVIOUS, RIGHT!?
SHE THINKS SHE'S ACTUALLY MORE IMPORTANT THAN US!

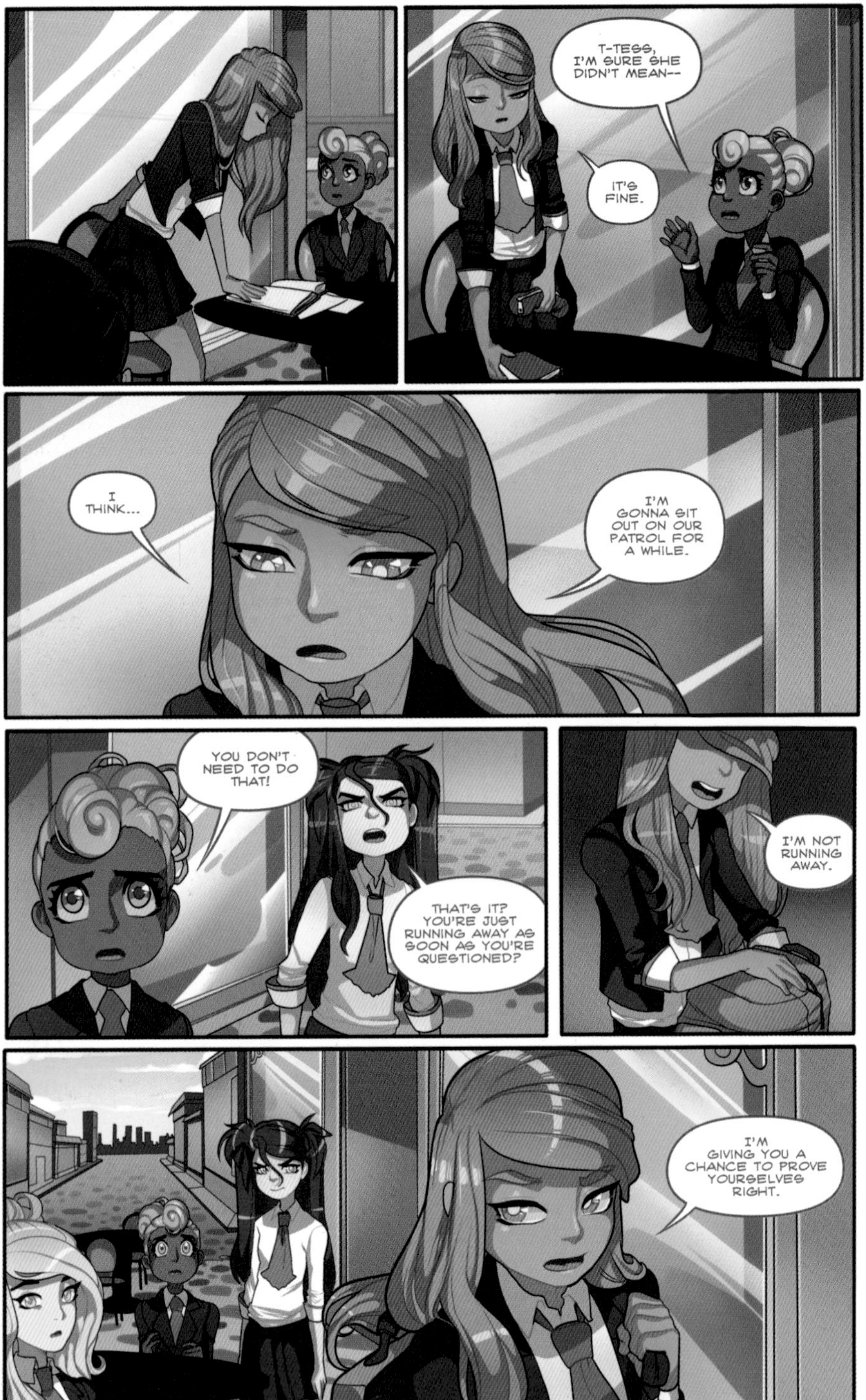
T-TESS, I'M SURE SHE DIDN'T MEAN--
IT'S FINE.
I THINK...
I'M GONNA SIT OUT ON OUR PATROL FOR A WHILE.
YOU DON'T NEED TO DO THAT!
THAT'S IT? YOU'RE JUST RUNNING AWAY AS SOON AS YOU'RE QUESTIONED?
I'M NOT RUNNING AWAY.
I'M GIVING YOU A CHANCE TO PROVE YOURSELVES RIGHT.

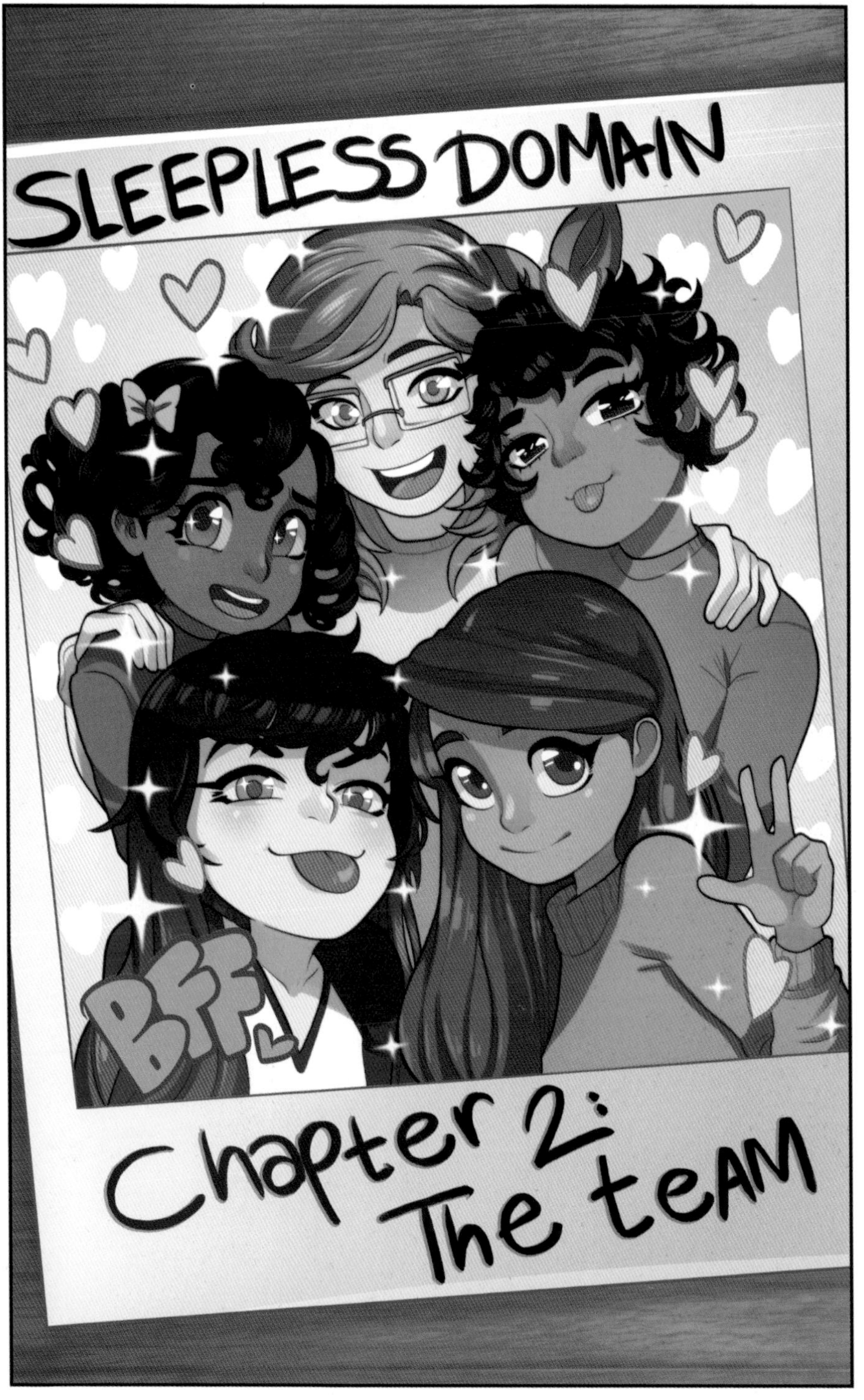
SLEEPLESS DOMAIN
BFF
Chapter 2:
The team

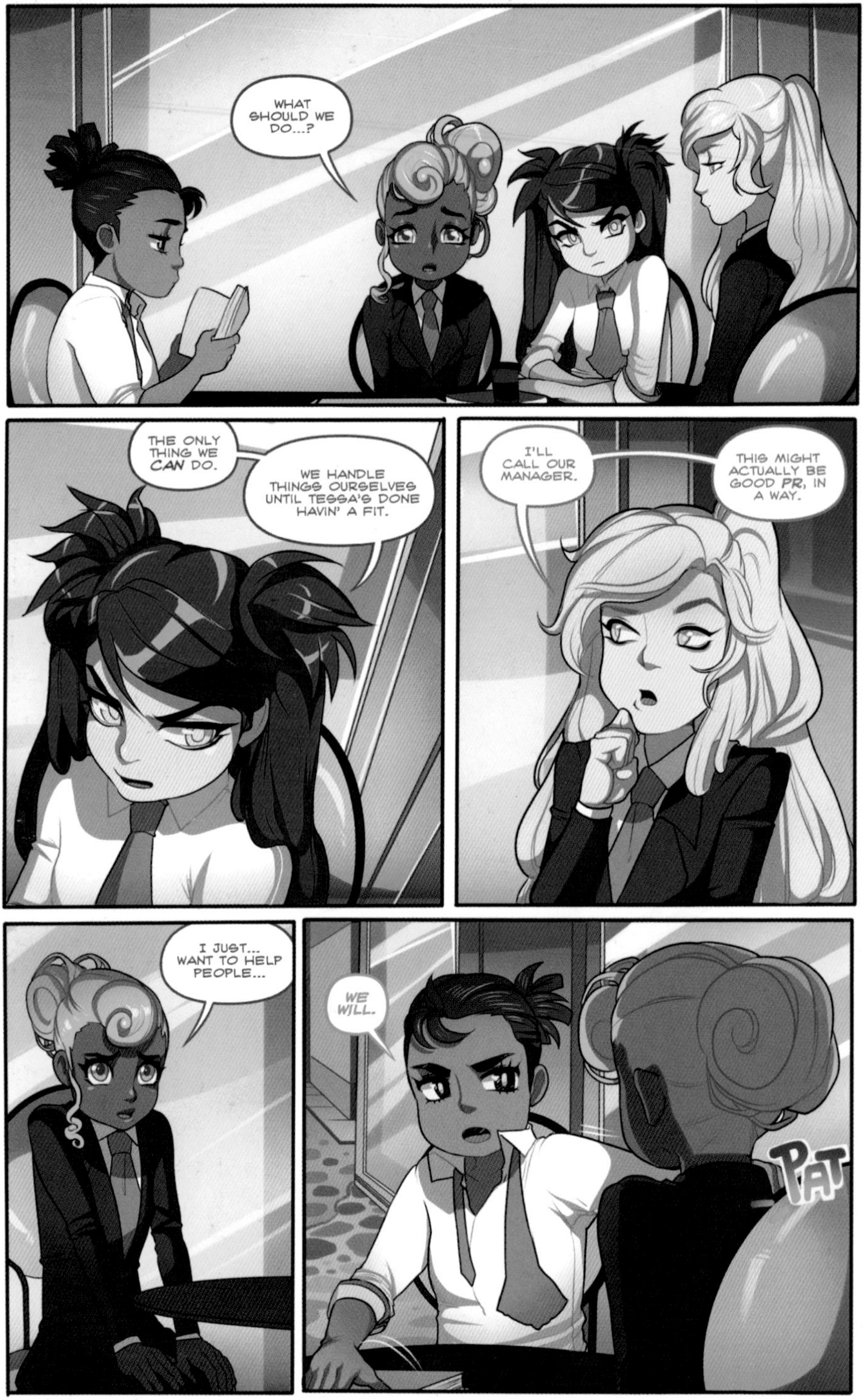
WHAT SHOULD WE DO...?
THE ONLY THING WE CAN DO.
WE HANDLE THINGS OURSELVES UNTIL TESSA'S DONE HAVIN' A FIT.
I'LL CALL OUR MANAGER.
THIS MIGHT ACTUALLY BE GOOD PR, IN A WAY.
I JUST... WANT TO HELP PEOPLE...
WE WILL.
PAT

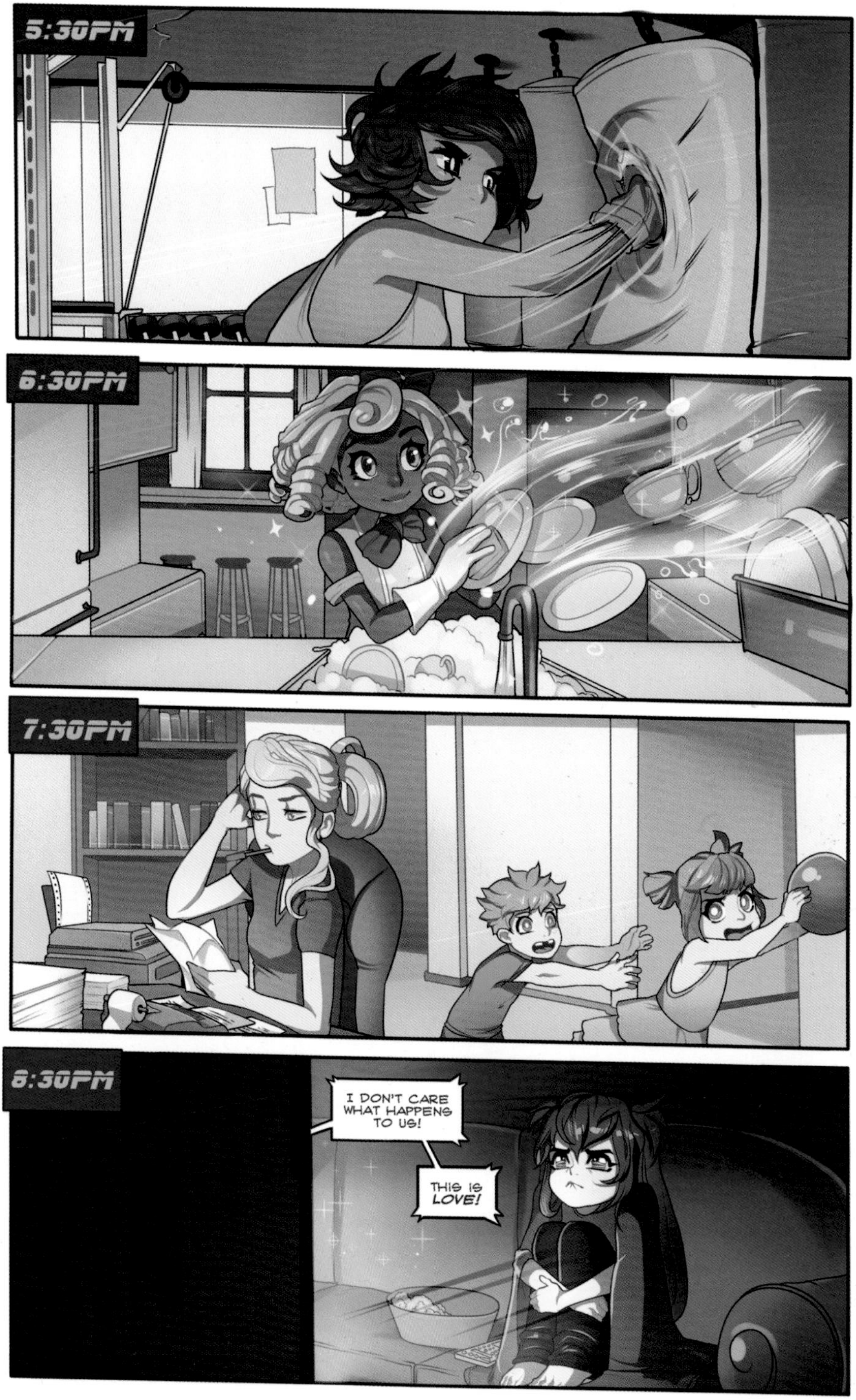
5:30PM
6:30PM
7:30PM
8:30PM
I DON'T CARE WHAT HAPPENS TO US!
THIS IS *LOVE!*

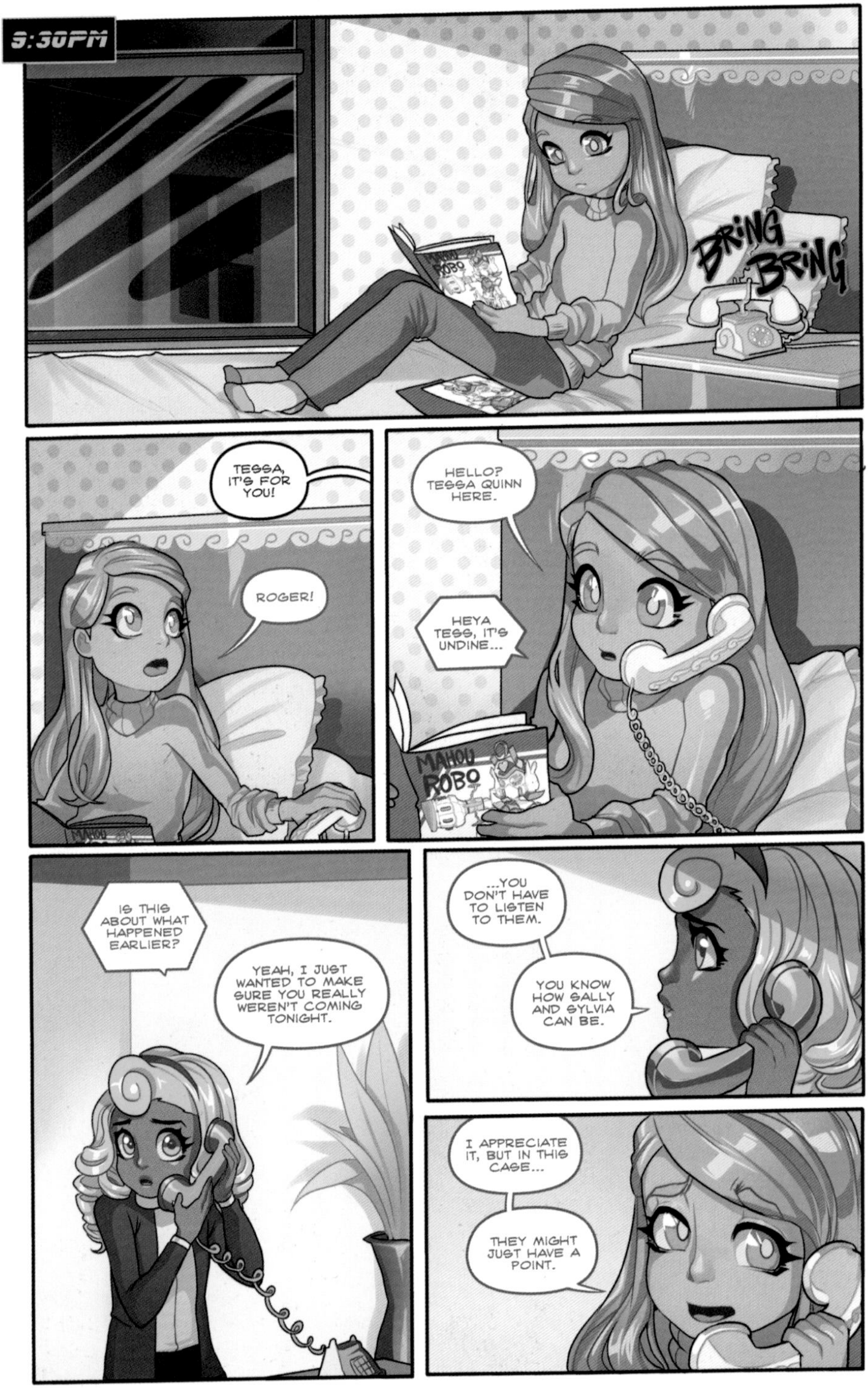
9:30PM
MAHOU ROBO
BRING BRING
TESSA, IT'S FOR YOU!
ROGER!
HELLO? TESSA QUINN HERE.
HEYA TESS, IT'S UNDINE...
MAHOU ROBO
IS THIS ABOUT WHAT HAPPENED EARLIER?
YEAH, I JUST WANTED TO MAKE SURE YOU REALLY WEREN'T COMING TONIGHT.
...YOU DON'T HAVE TO LISTEN TO THEM.
YOU KNOW HOW SALLY AND SYLVIA CAN BE.
I APPRECIATE IT, BUT IN THIS CASE...
THEY MIGHT JUST HAVE A POINT.

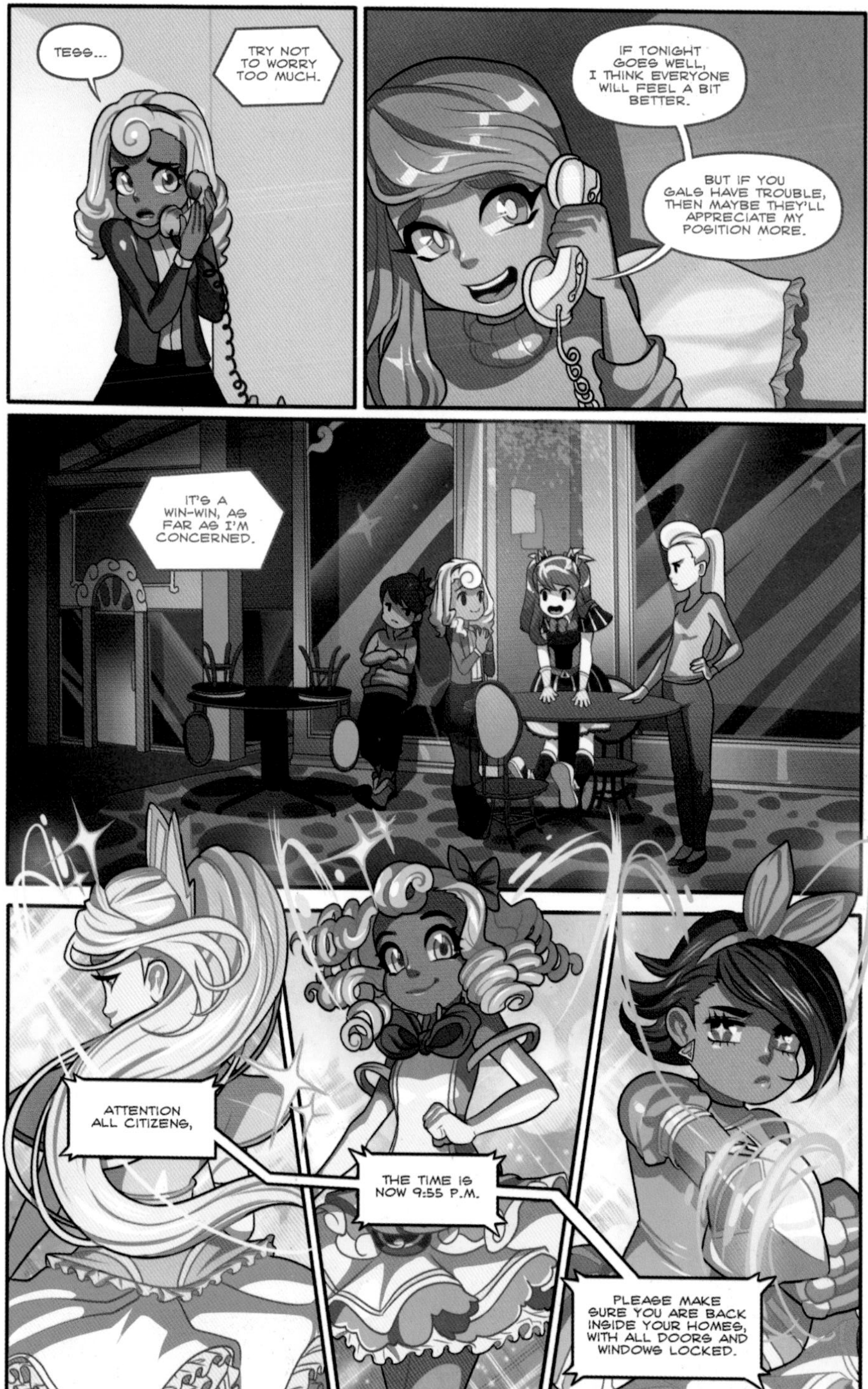
TESS...
TRY NOT TO WORRY TOO MUCH.
IF TONIGHT GOES WELL, I THINK EVERYONE WILL FEEL A BIT BETTER.
BUT IF YOU GALS HAVE TROUBLE, THEN MAYBE THEY'LL APPRECIATE MY POSITION MORE.
IT'S A WIN-WIN, AS FAR AS I'M CONCERNED.
ATTENTION ALL CITIZENS,
THE TIME IS NOW 9:55 P.M.
PLEASE MAKE SURE YOU ARE BACK INSIDE YOUR HOMES, WITH ALL DOORS AND WINDOWS LOCKED.

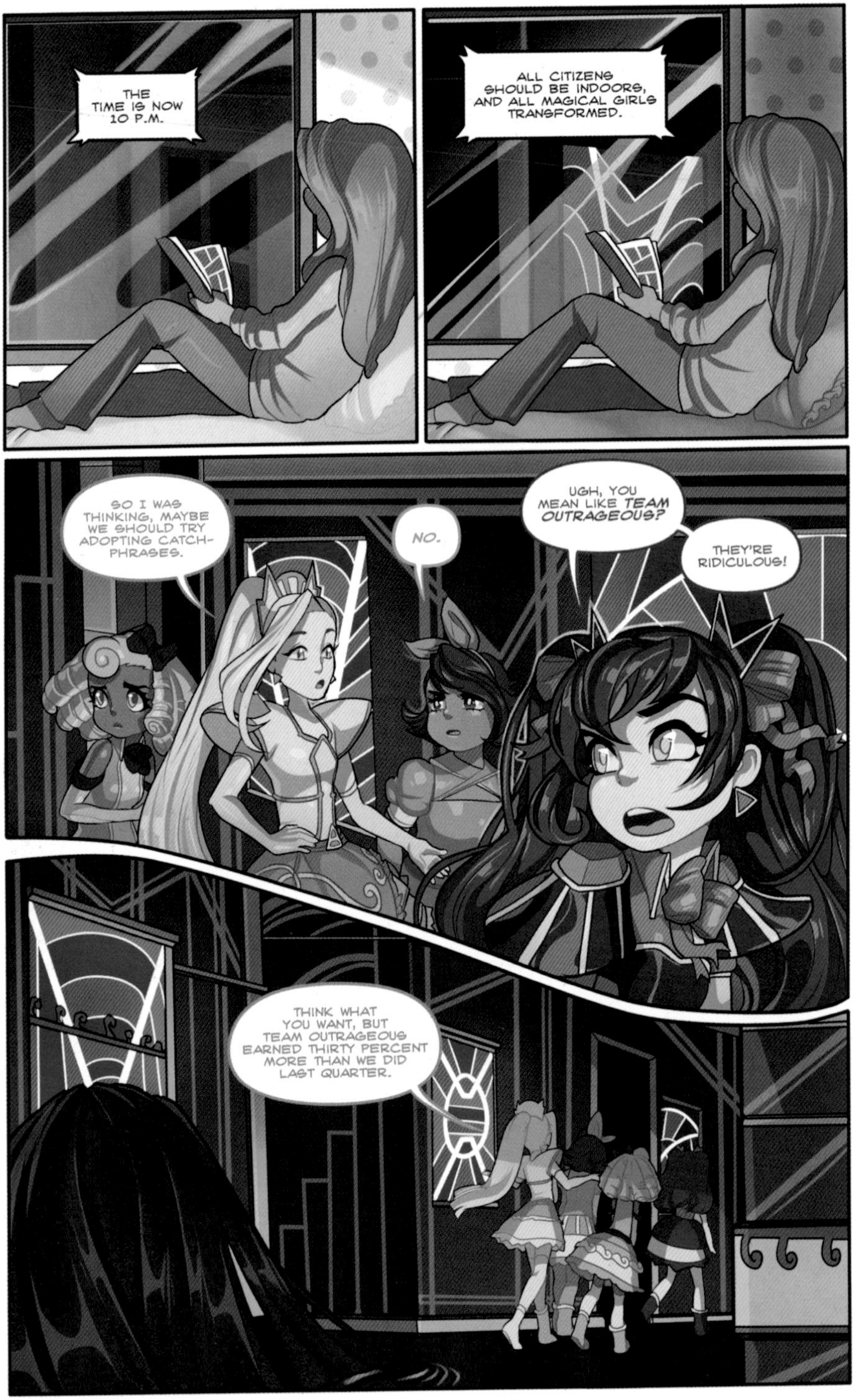
THE TIME IS NOW 10 P.M.
ALL CITIZENS SHOULD BE INDOORS, AND ALL MAGICAL GIRLS TRANSFORMED.
SO I WAS THINKING, MAYBE WE SHOULD TRY ADOPTING CATCH-PHRASES.
NO.
UGH, YOU MEAN LIKE *TEAM OUTRAGEOUS?*
THEY'RE RIDICULOUS!
THINK WHAT YOU WANT, BUT TEAM OUTRAGEOUS EARNED THIRTY PERCENT MORE THAN WE DID LAST QUARTER.

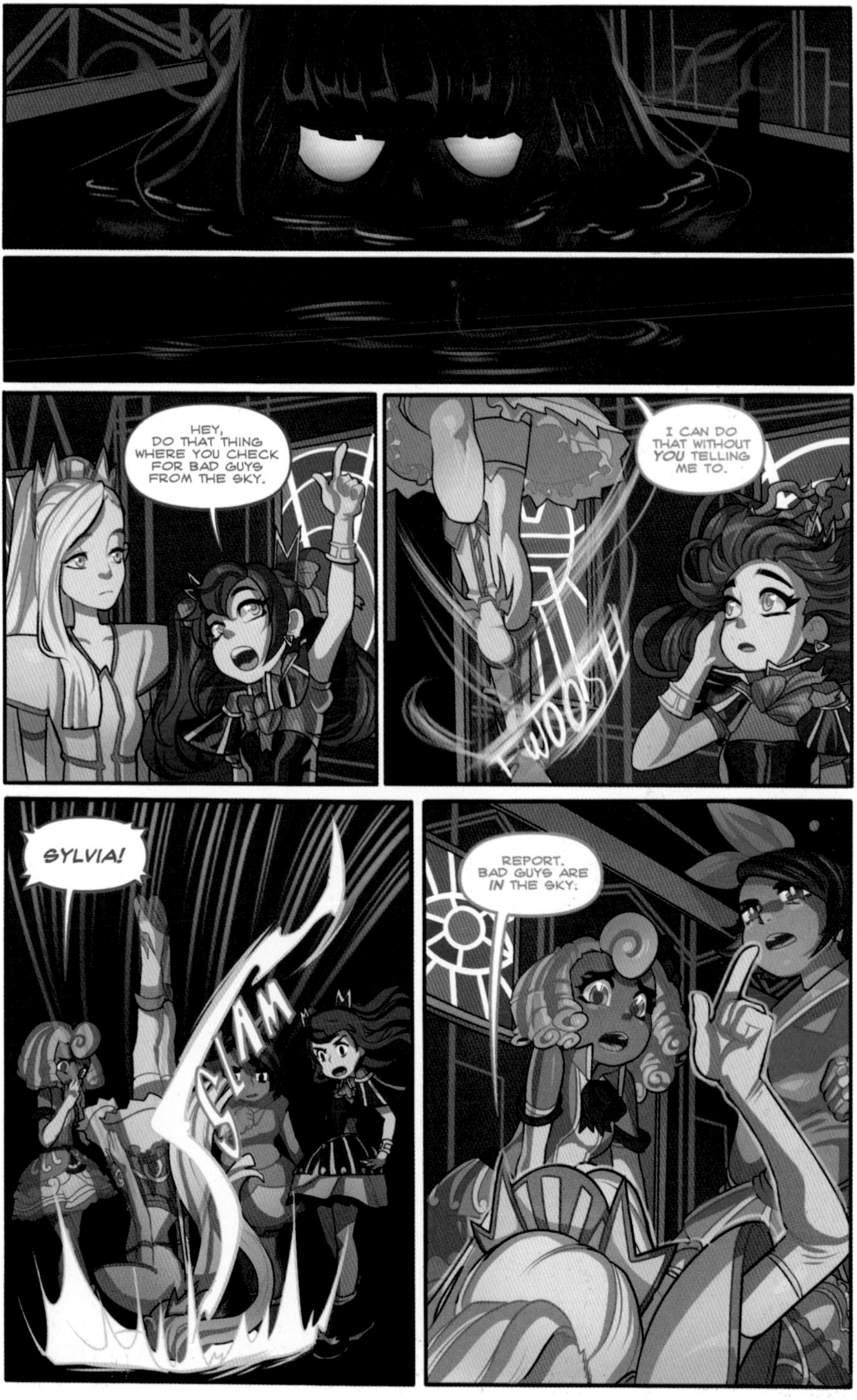
HEY, DO THAT THING WHERE YOU CHECK FOR BAD GUYS FROM THE SKY.
I CAN DO THAT WITHOUT YOU TELLING ME TO.
FWOOSH
SYLVIA!
SLAM
REPORT. BAD GUYS ARE IN THE SKY.

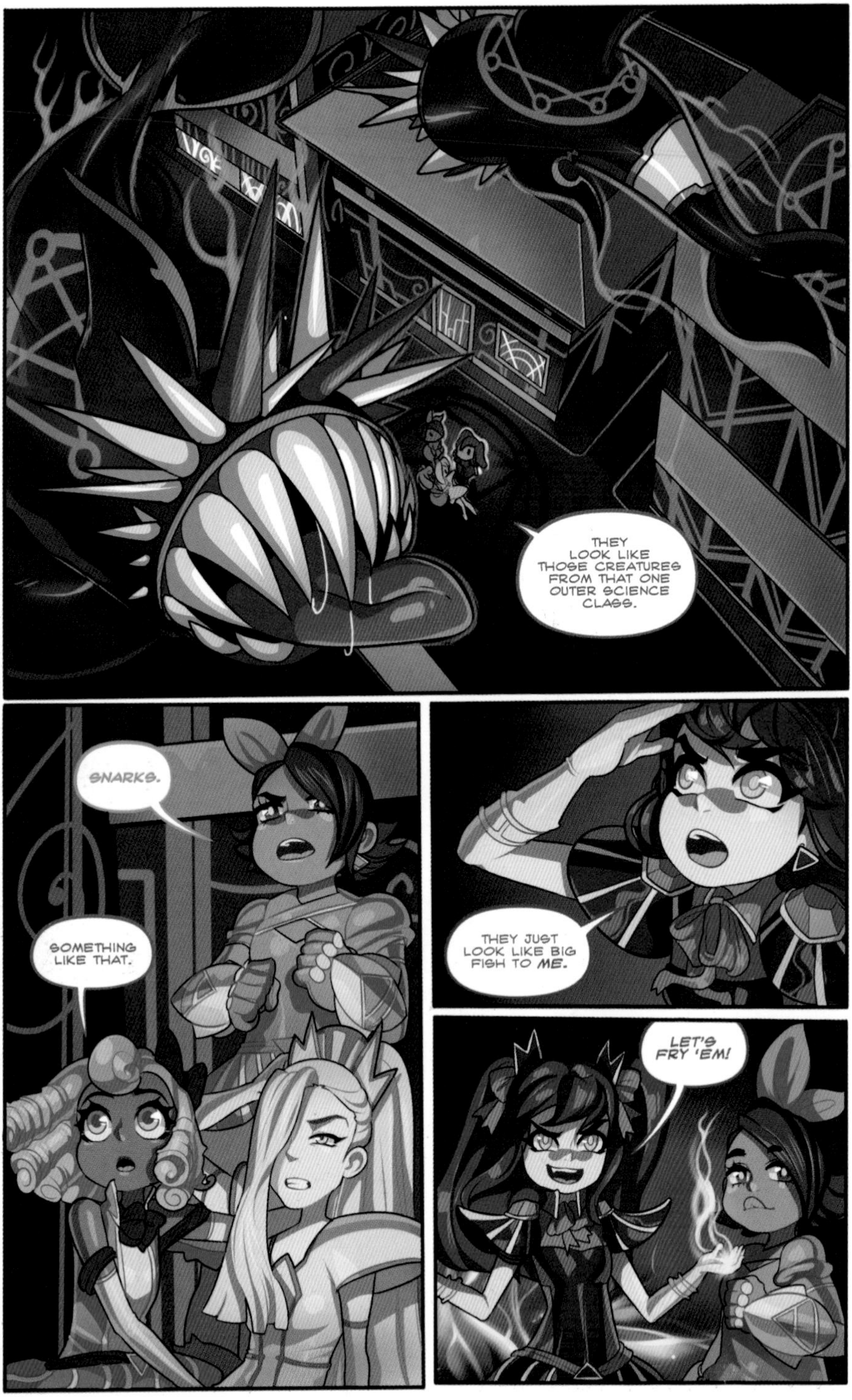
THEY LOOK LIKE THOSE CREATURES FROM THAT ONE OUTER SCIENCE CLASS.
SNARKS.
SOMETHING LIKE THAT.
THEY JUST LOOK LIKE BIG FISH TO *ME*.
LET'S FRY 'EM!

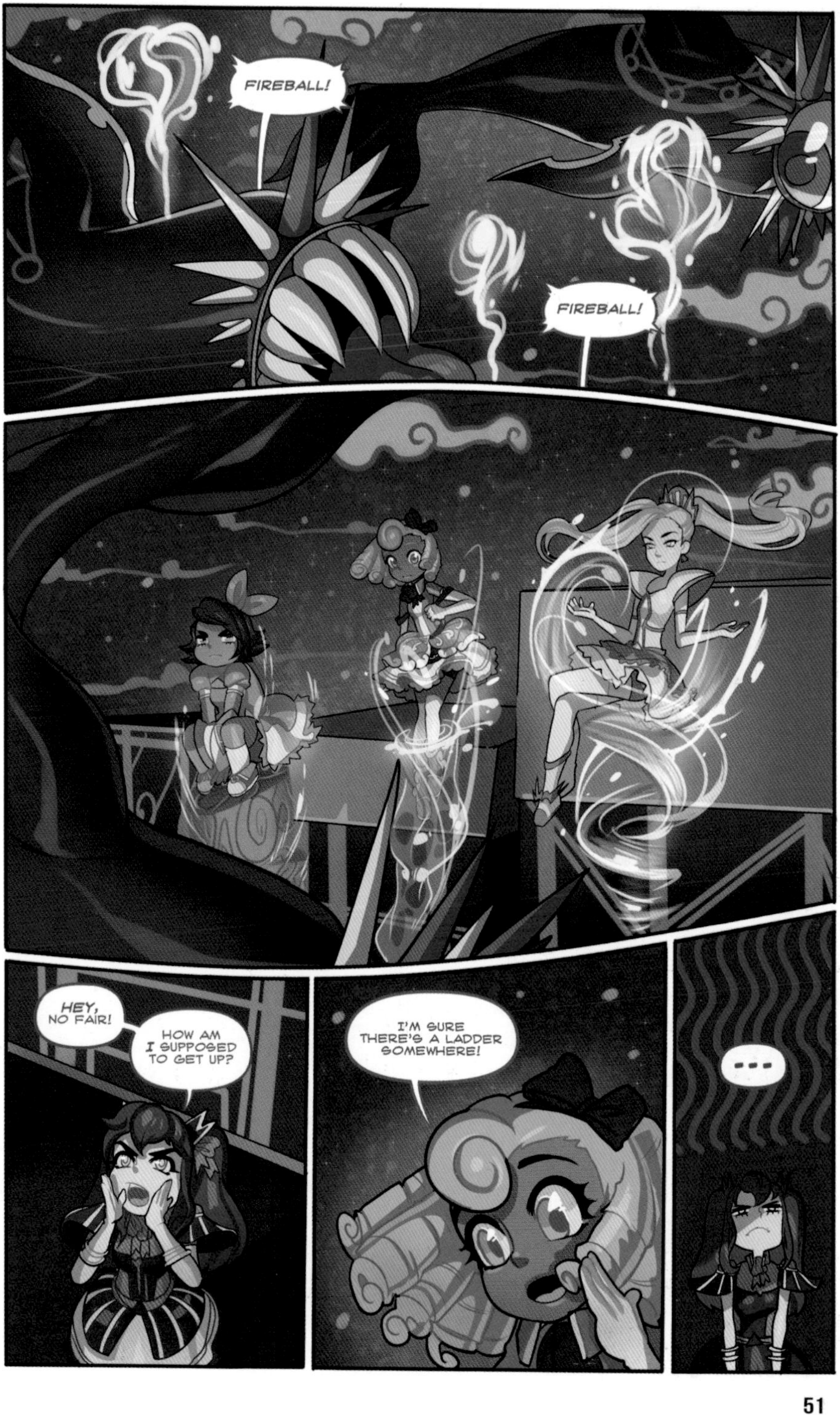
FIREBALL!
FIREBALL!
HEY, NO FAIR!
HOW AM I SUPPOSED TO GET UP?
I'M SURE THERE'S A LADDER SOMEWHERE!
...

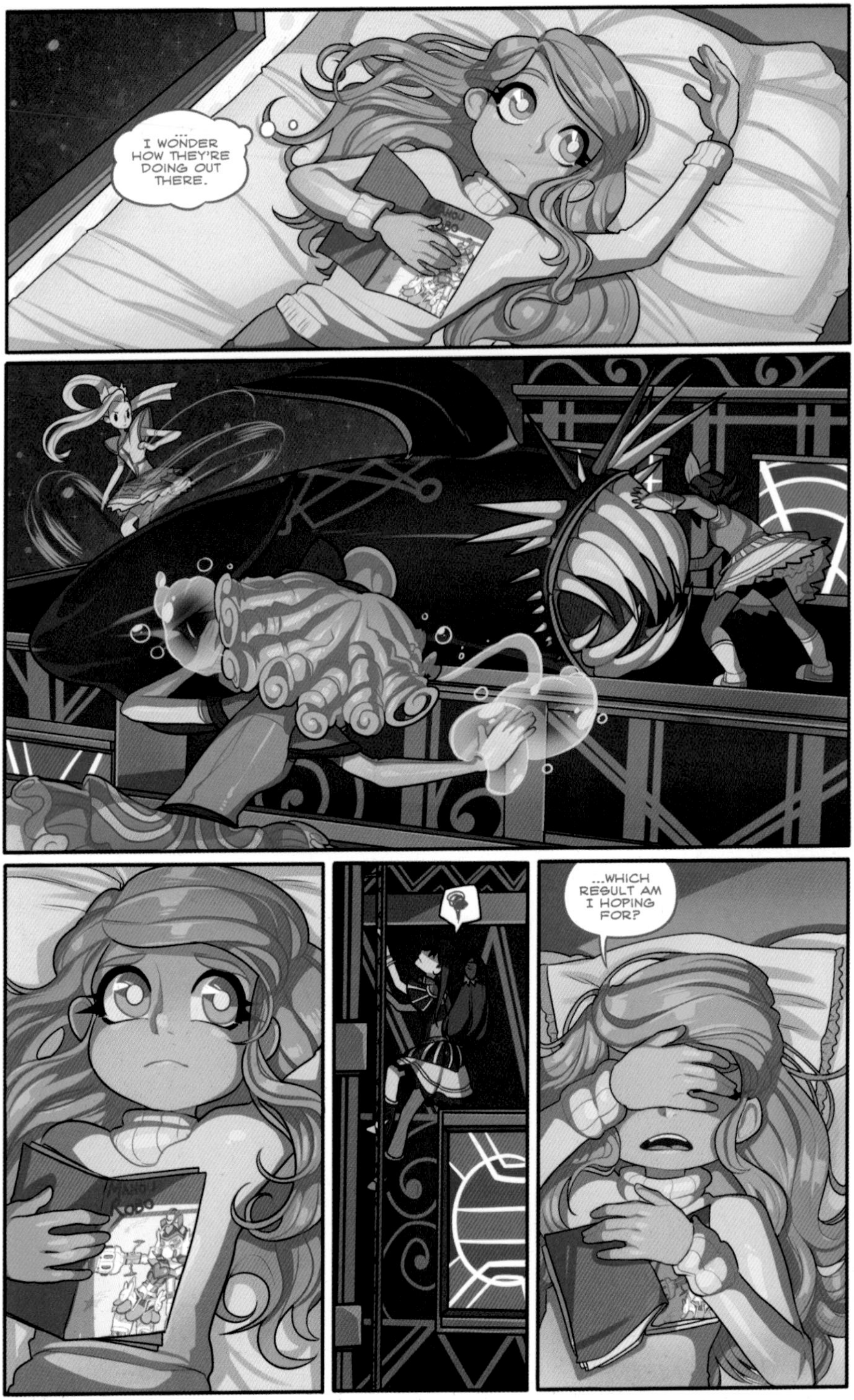
...
I WONDER HOW THEY'RE DOING OUT THERE.
...WHICH RESULT AM I HOPING FOR?

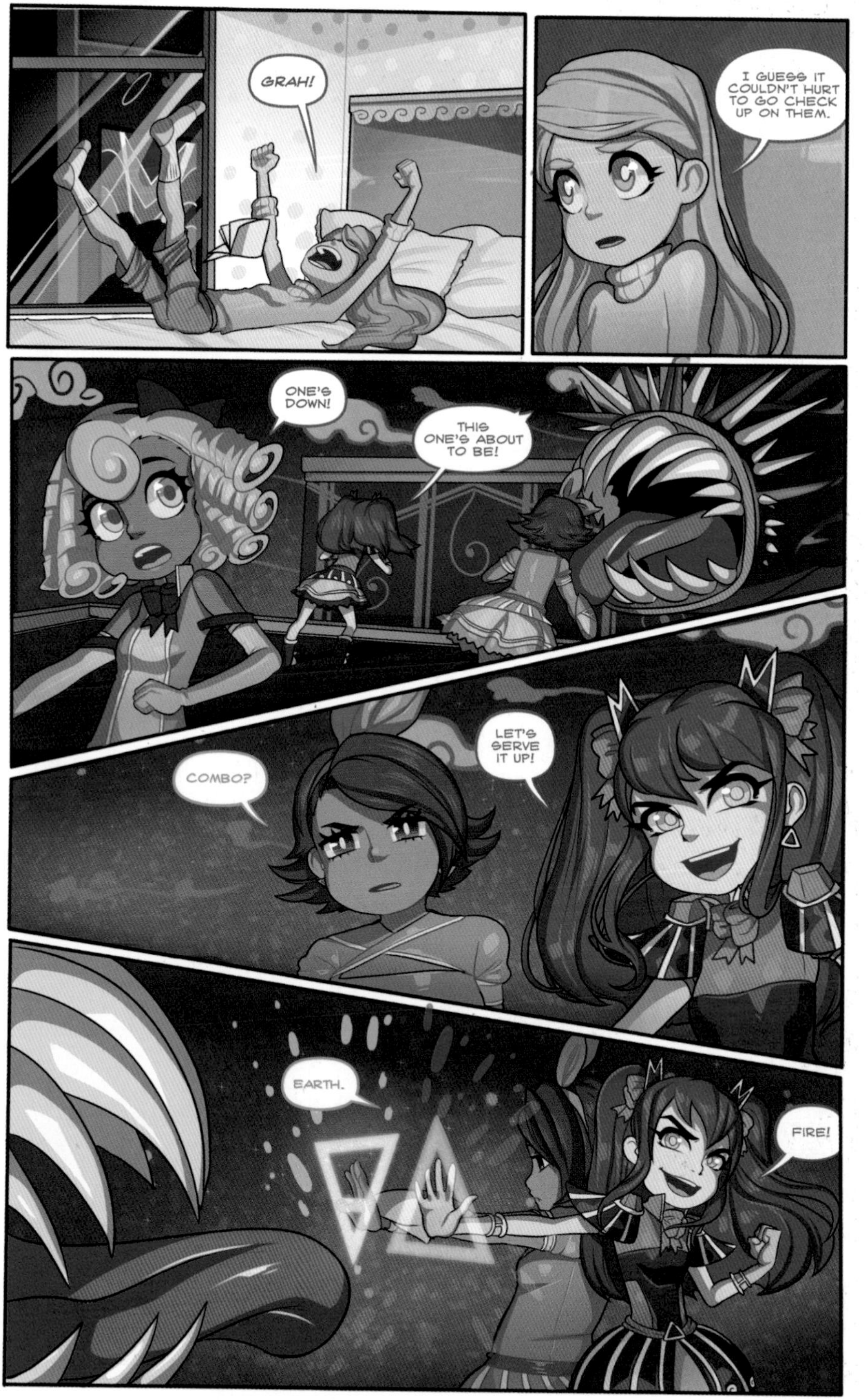

GRAH!
I GUESS IT COULDN'T HURT TO GO CHECK UP ON THEM.
ONE'S DOWN!
THIS ONE'S ABOUT TO BE!
COMBO?
LET'S SERVE IT UP!
EARTH.
FIRE!

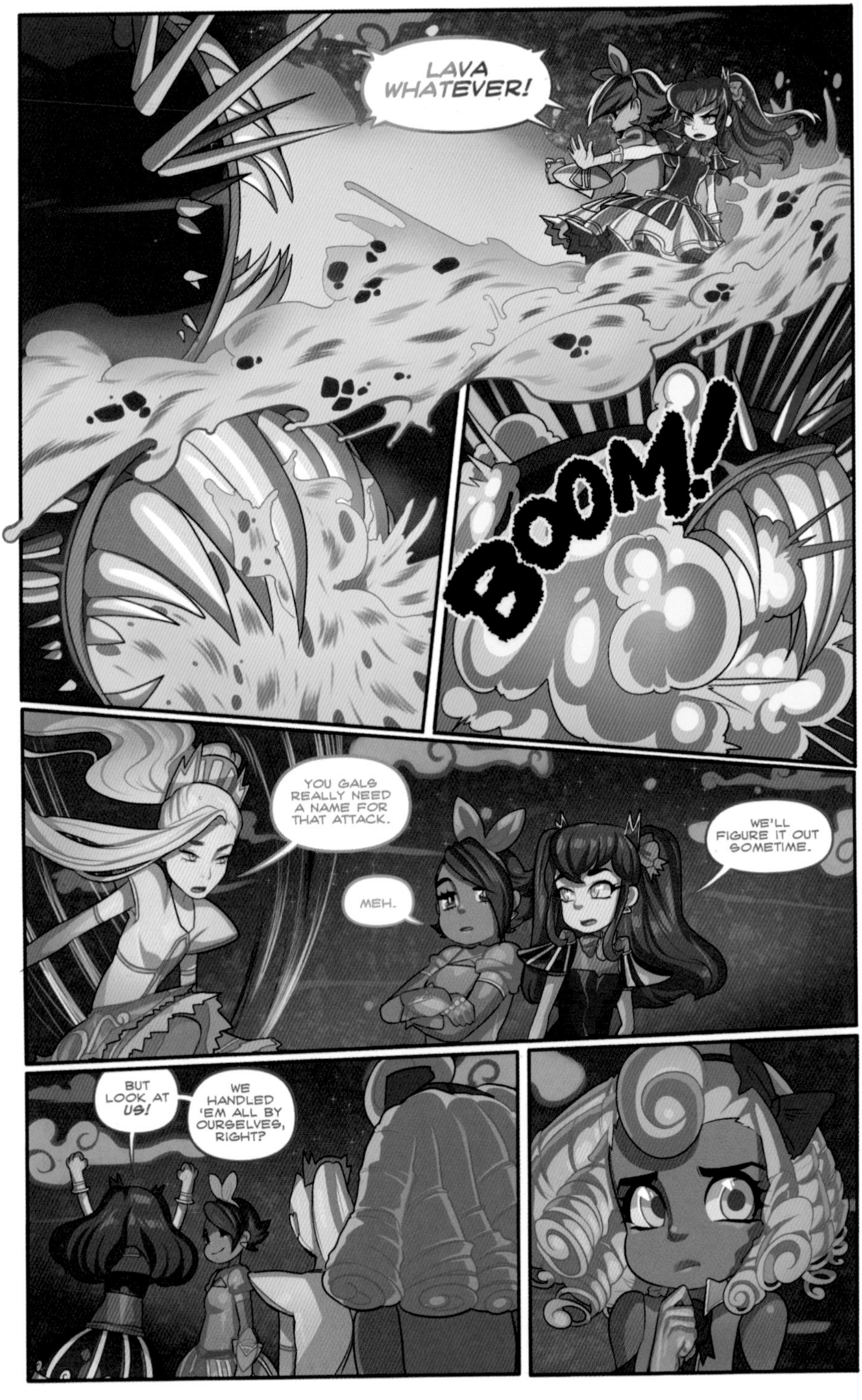
LAVA WHATEVER!
BOOM!
YOU GALS REALLY NEED A NAME FOR THAT ATTACK.
MEH.
WE'LL FIGURE IT OUT SOMETIME.
BUT LOOK AT US!
WE HANDLED 'EM ALL BY OURSELVES, RIGHT?

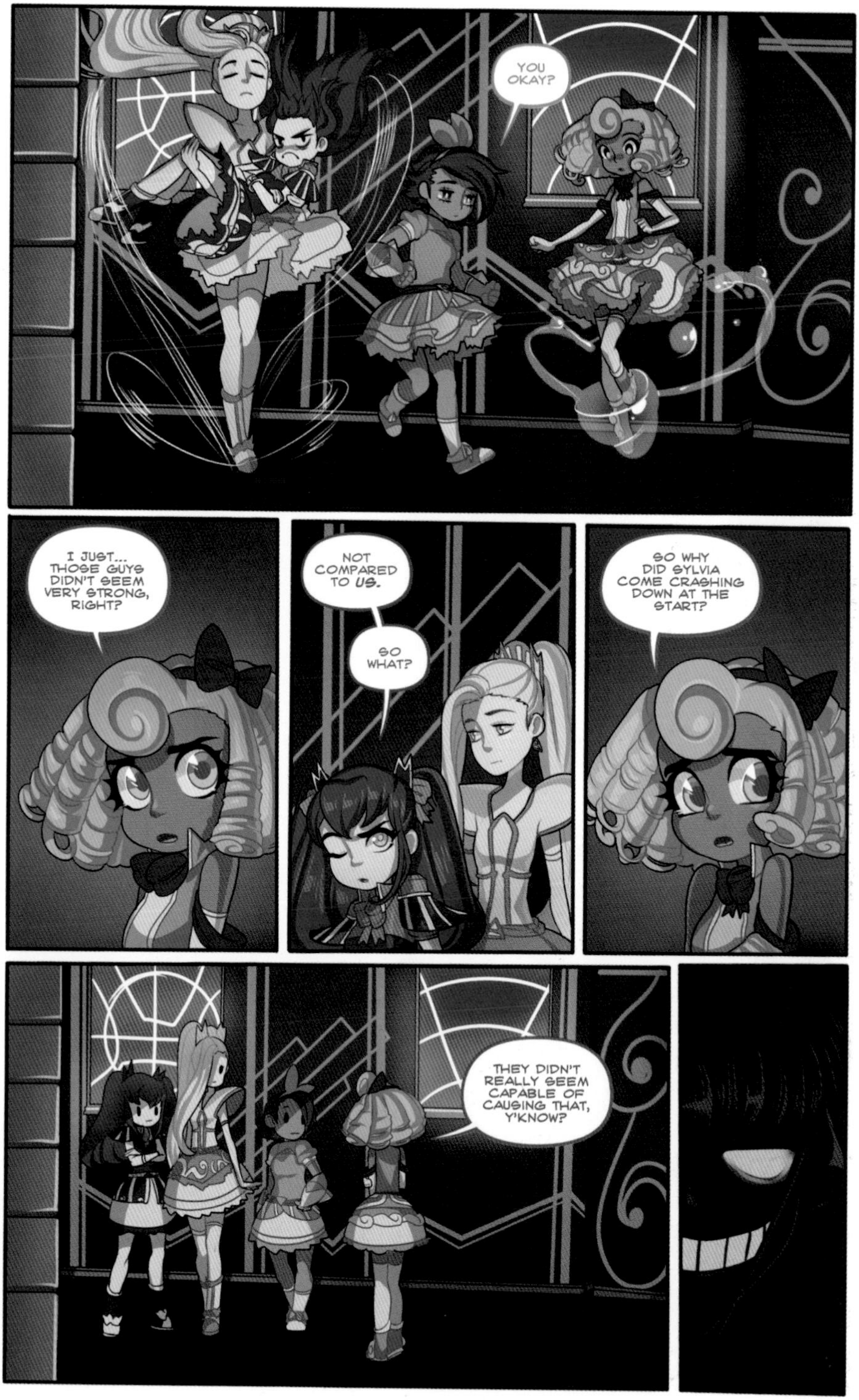
YOU OKAY?
I JUST... THOSE GUYS DIDN'T SEEM VERY STRONG, RIGHT?
NOT COMPARED TO *US.*
SO WHAT?
SO WHY DID SYLVIA COME CRASHING DOWN AT THE START?
THEY DIDN'T REALLY SEEM CAPABLE OF CAUSING THAT, Y'KNOW?

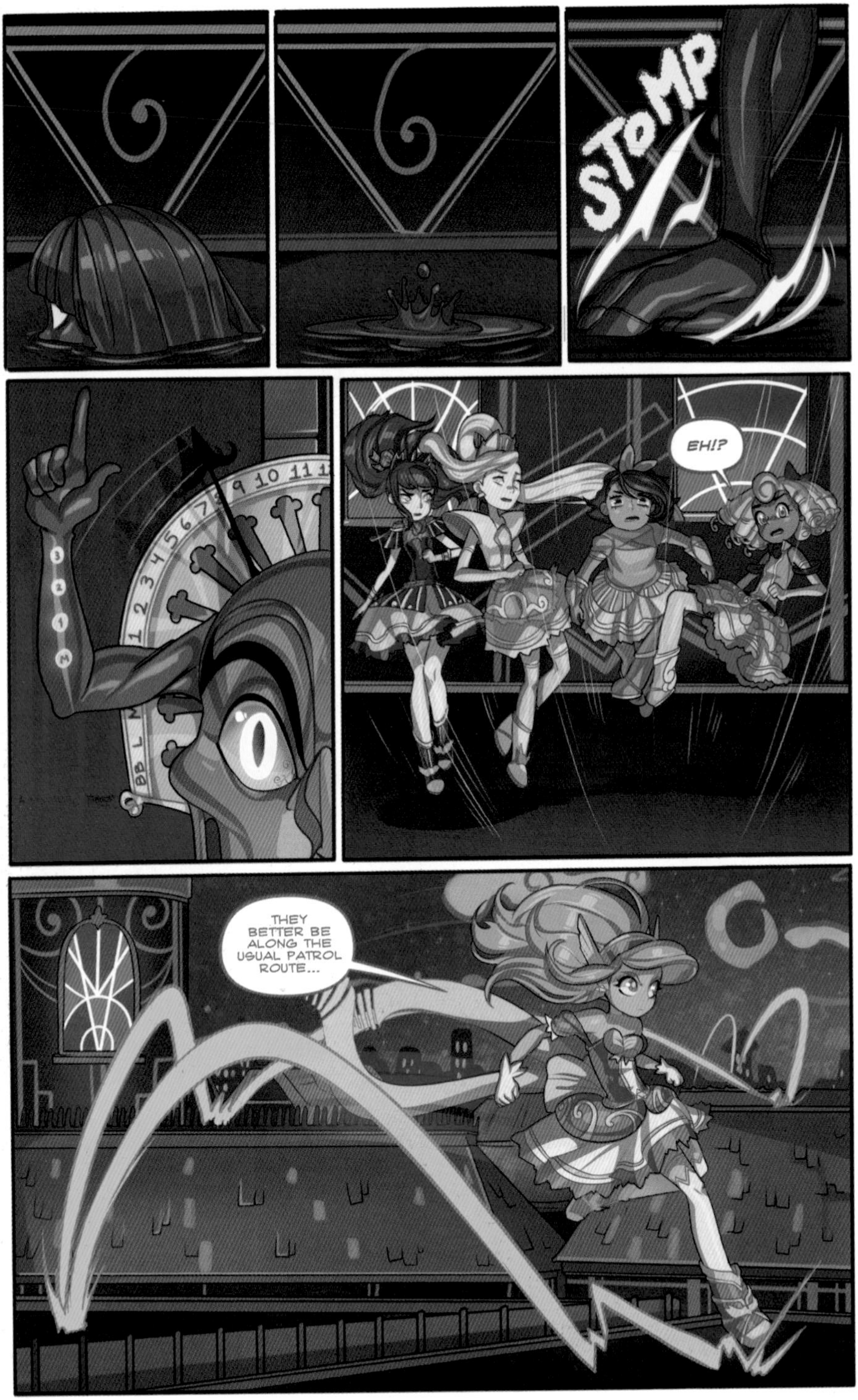
STOMP
EH!?
THEY BETTER BE ALONG THE USUAL PATROL ROUTE...

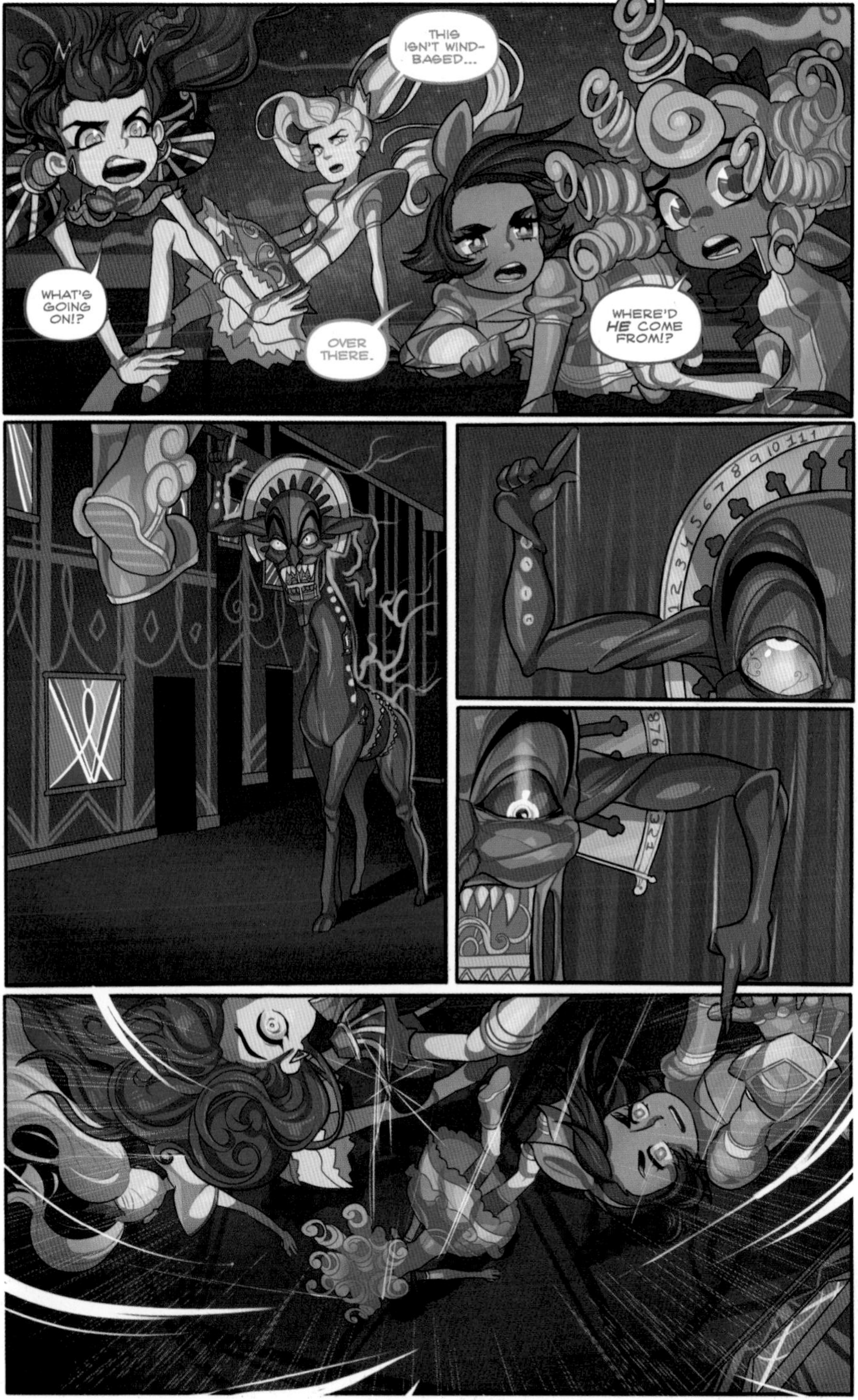
WHAT'S GOING ON!?
THIS ISN'T WIND-BASED...
OVER THERE.
WHERE'D *HE* COME FROM!?

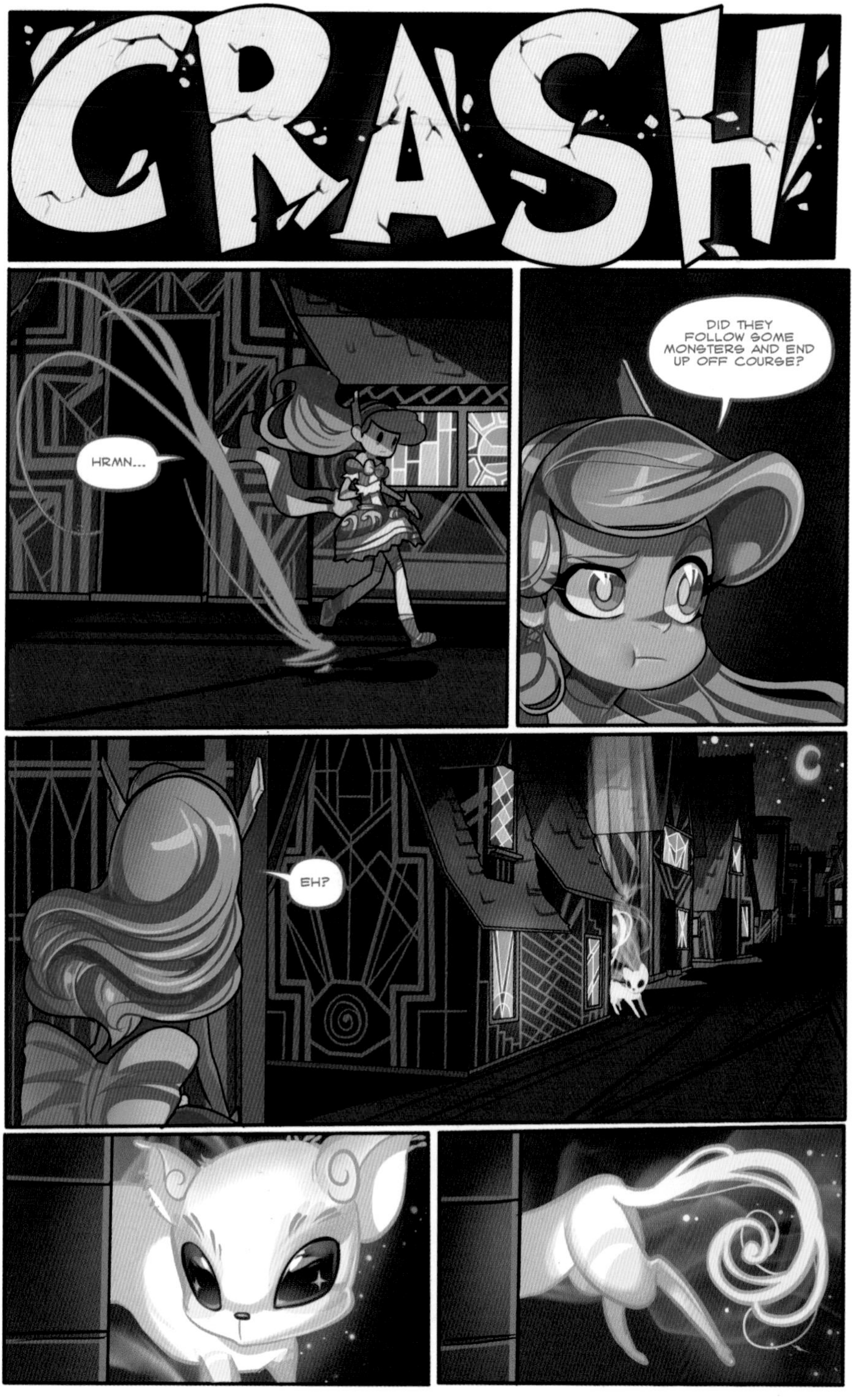
CRASH!
HRMN...
DID THEY FOLLOW SOME MONSTERS AND END UP OFF COURSE?
EH?

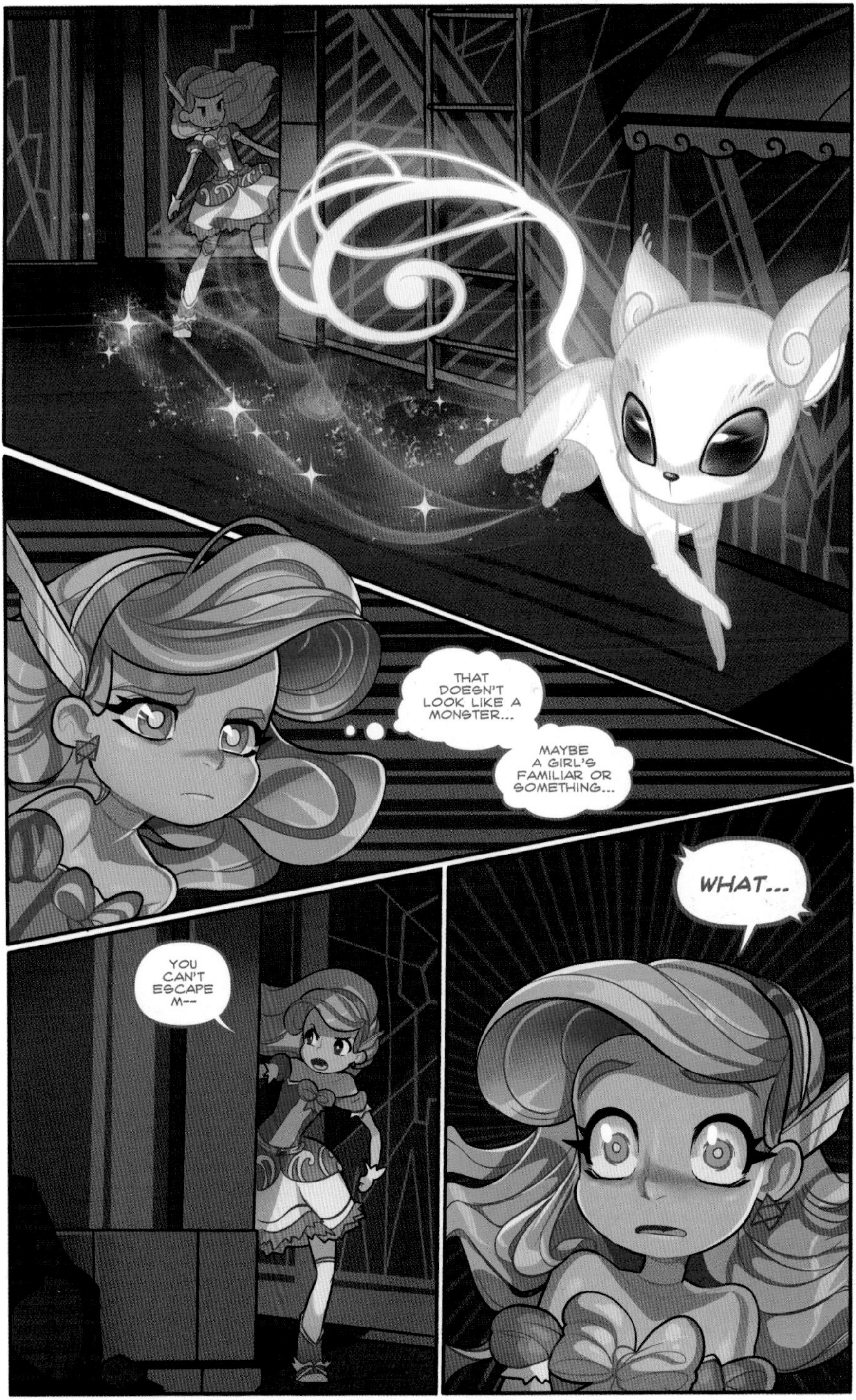
THAT DOESN'T LOOK LIKE A MONSTER...
MAYBE A GIRL'S FAMILIAR OR SOMETHING...
YOU CAN'T ESCAPE M--
WHAT...

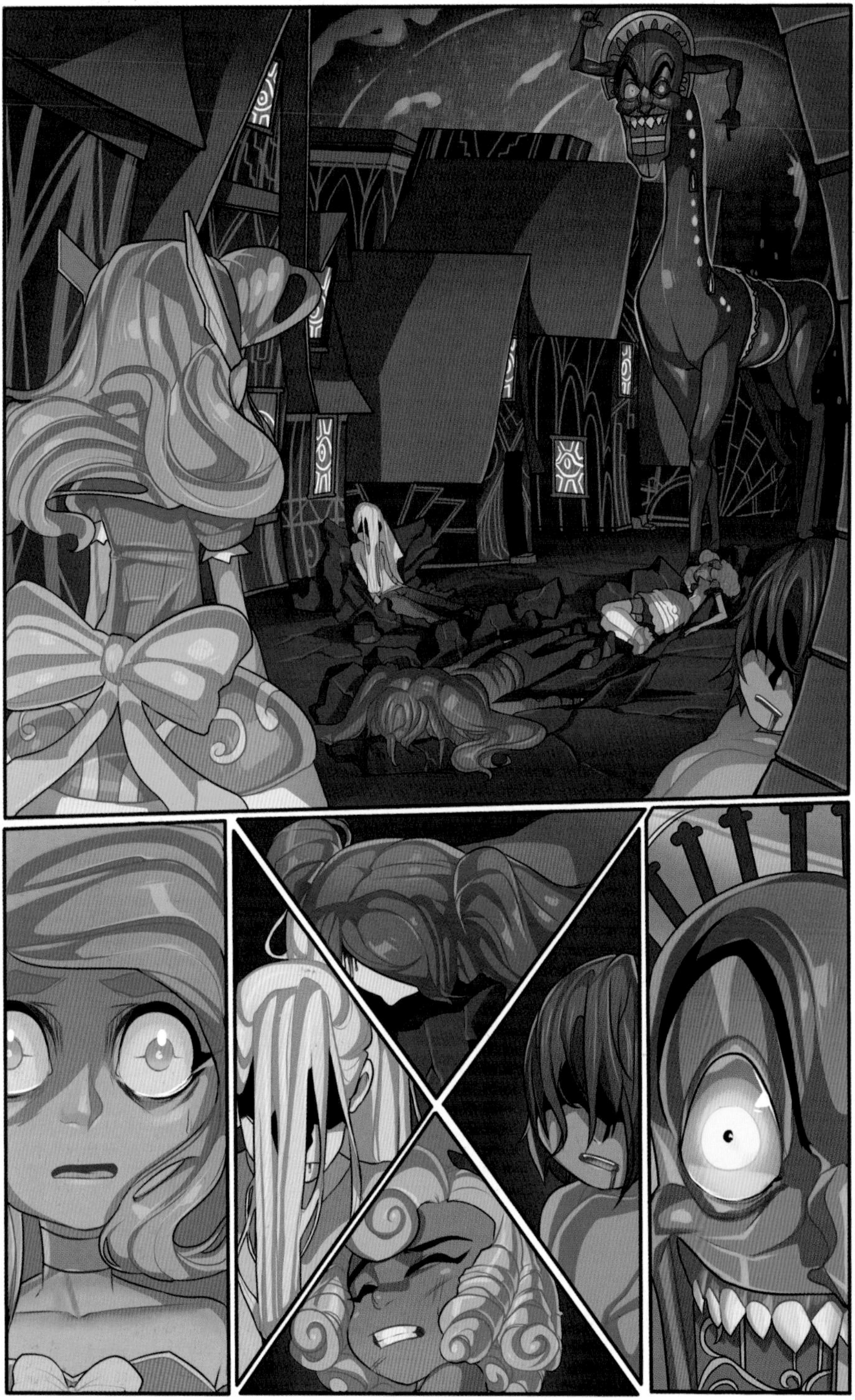

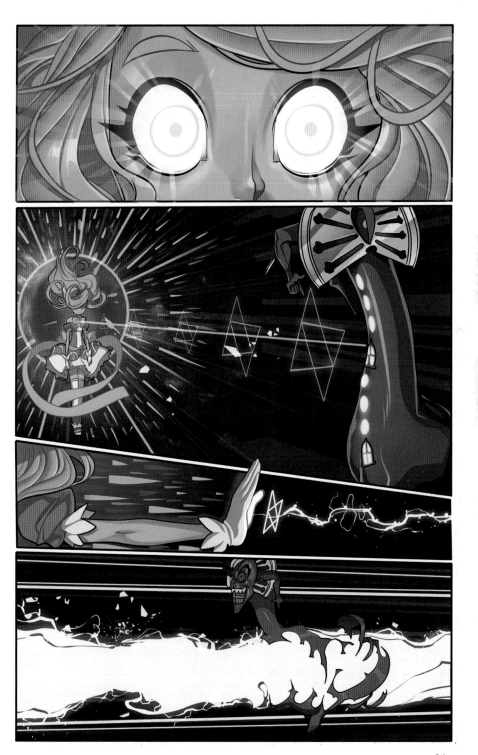

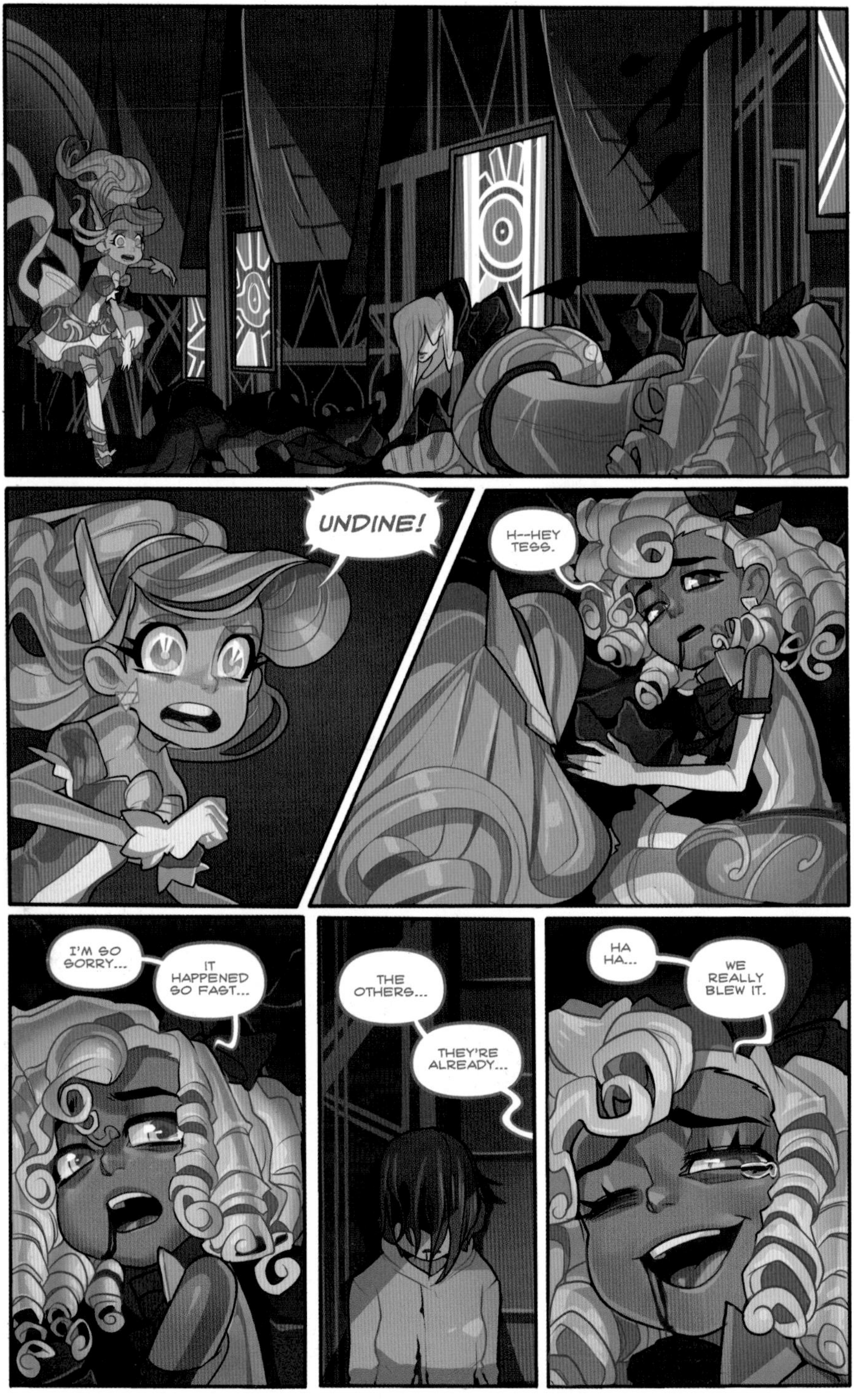
UNDINE!
H--HEY TESS.
I'M SO SORRY...
IT HAPPENED SO FAST...
THE OTHERS...
THEY'RE ALREADY...
HA HA...
WE REALLY BLEW IT.

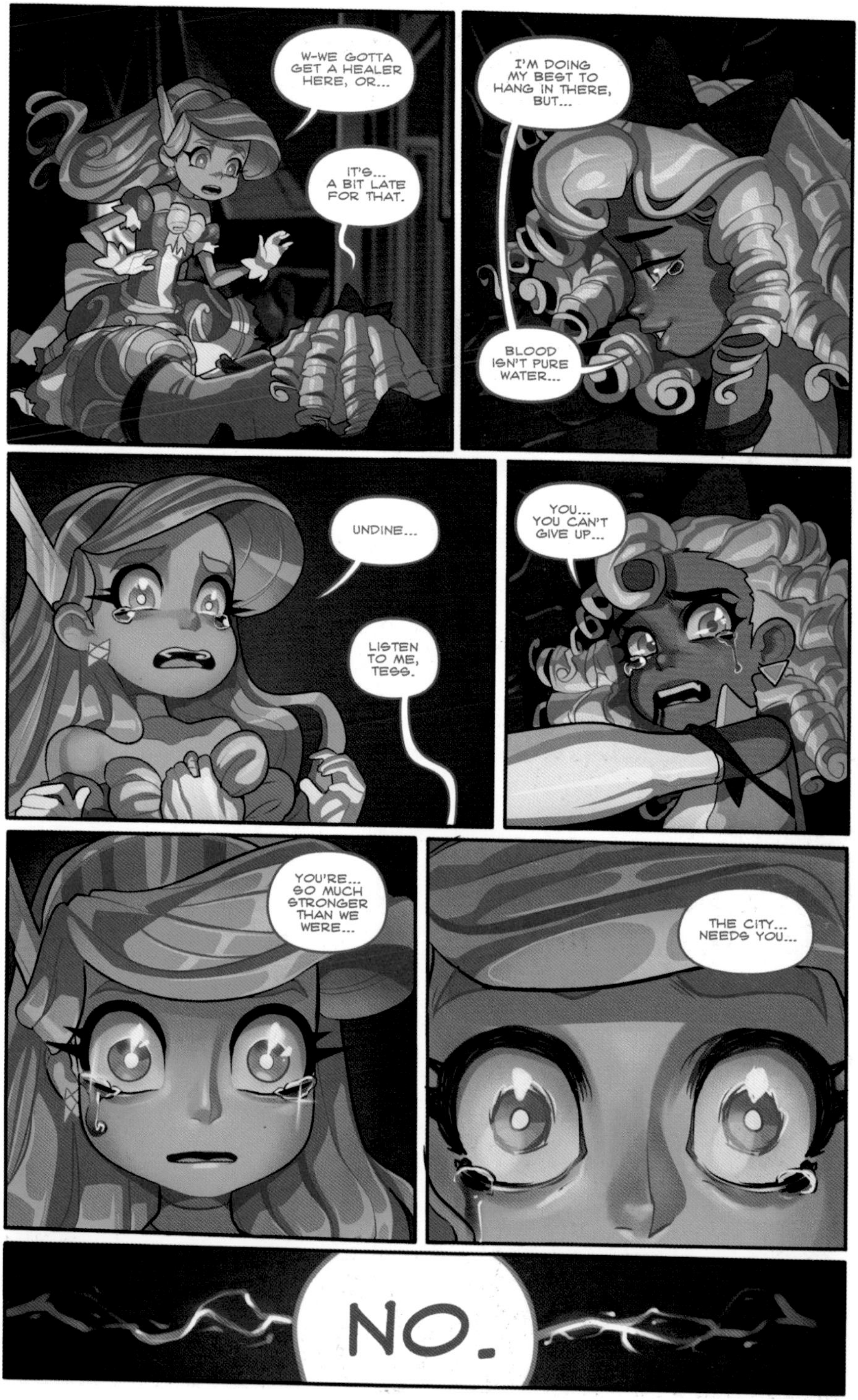

W-WE GOTTA GET A HEALER HERE, OR...
IT'S... A BIT LATE FOR THAT.
I'M DOING MY BEST TO HANG IN THERE, BUT...
BLOOD ISN'T PURE WATER...
UNDINE...
LISTEN TO ME, TESS.
YOU... YOU CAN'T GIVE UP...
YOU'RE... SO MUCH STRONGER THAN WE WERE...
THE CITY... NEEDS YOU...
NO.

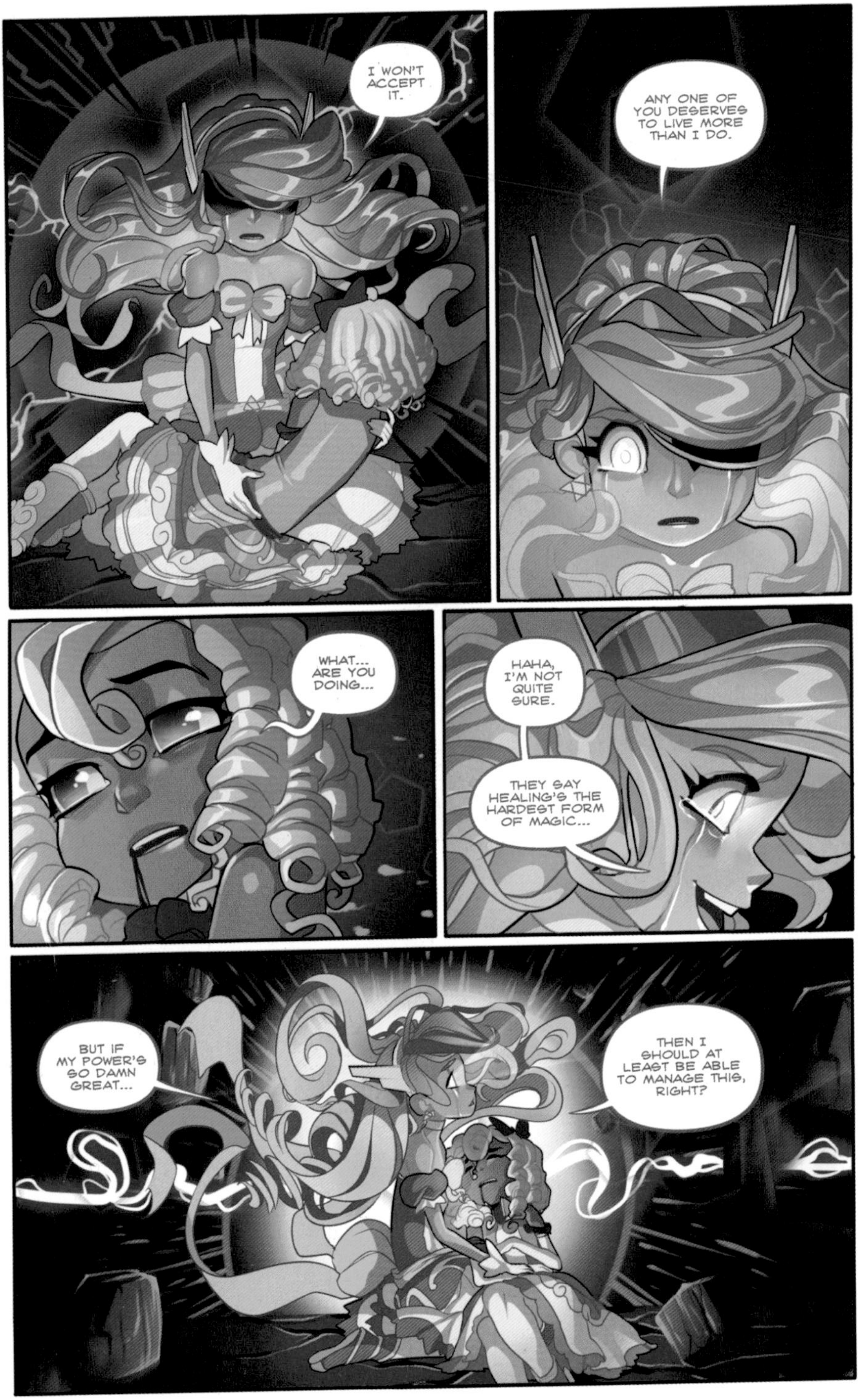
I WON'T ACCEPT IT.
ANY ONE OF YOU DESERVES TO LIVE MORE THAN I DO.
WHAT... ARE YOU DOING...
HAHA, I'M NOT QUITE SURE.
THEY SAY HEALING'S THE HARDEST FORM OF MAGIC...
BUT IF MY POWER'S SO DAMN GREAT...
THEN I SHOULD AT LEAST BE ABLE TO MANAGE THIS, RIGHT?

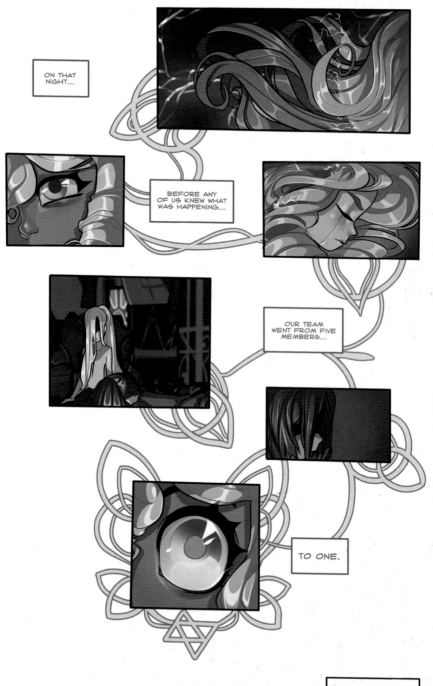

ON THAT NIGHT...

BEFORE ANY OF US KNEW WHAT WAS HAPPENING...

OUR TEAM WENT FROM FIVE MEMBERS...

TO ONE.

END OF CHAPTER 2

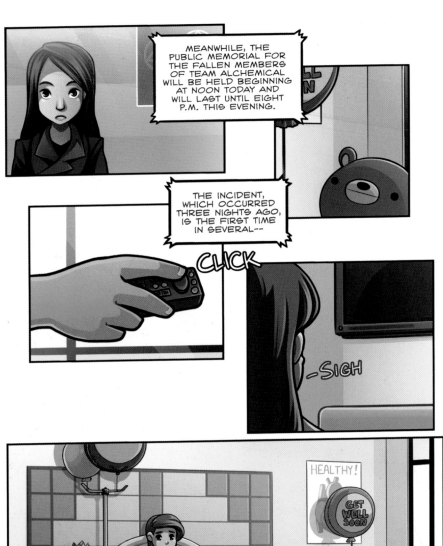

MEANWHILE, THE PUBLIC MEMORIAL FOR THE FALLEN MEMBERS OF TEAM ALCHEMICAL WILL BE HELD BEGINNING AT NOON TODAY AND WILL LAST UNTIL EIGHT P.M. THIS EVENING.

THE INCIDENT, WHICH OCCURRED THREE NIGHTS AGO, IS THE FIRST TIME IN SEVERAL--

CLICK

-SIGH

HEALTHY!

GET WELL SOON

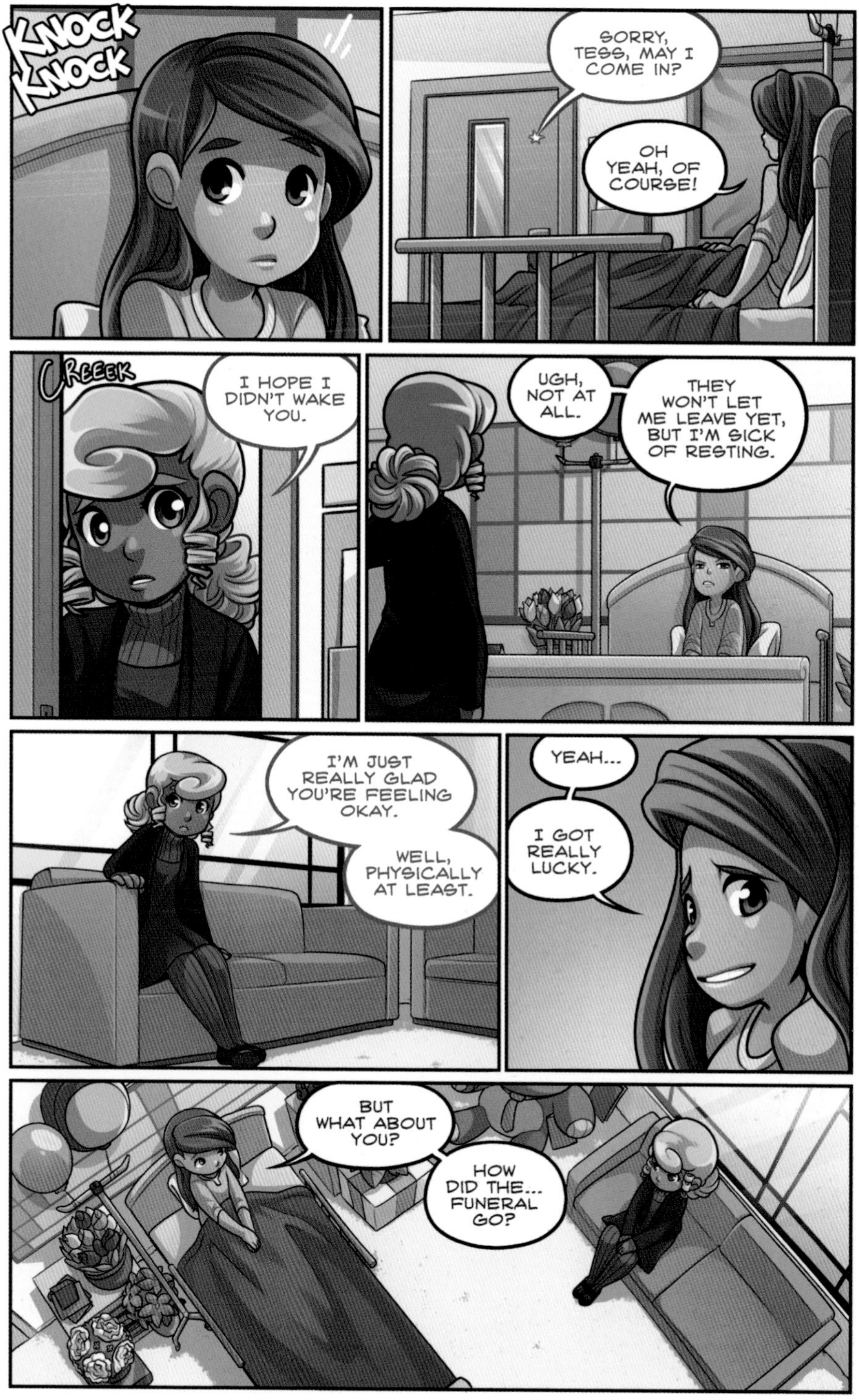
KNOCK KNOCK
SORRY, TESS, MAY I COME IN?
OH YEAH, OF COURSE!
CREEEK
I HOPE I DIDN'T WAKE YOU.
UGH, NOT AT ALL.
THEY WON'T LET ME LEAVE YET, BUT I'M SICK OF RESTING.
I'M JUST REALLY GLAD YOU'RE FEELING OKAY.
WELL, PHYSICALLY AT LEAST.
YEAH...
I GOT REALLY LUCKY.
BUT WHAT ABOUT YOU?
HOW DID THE... FUNERAL GO?

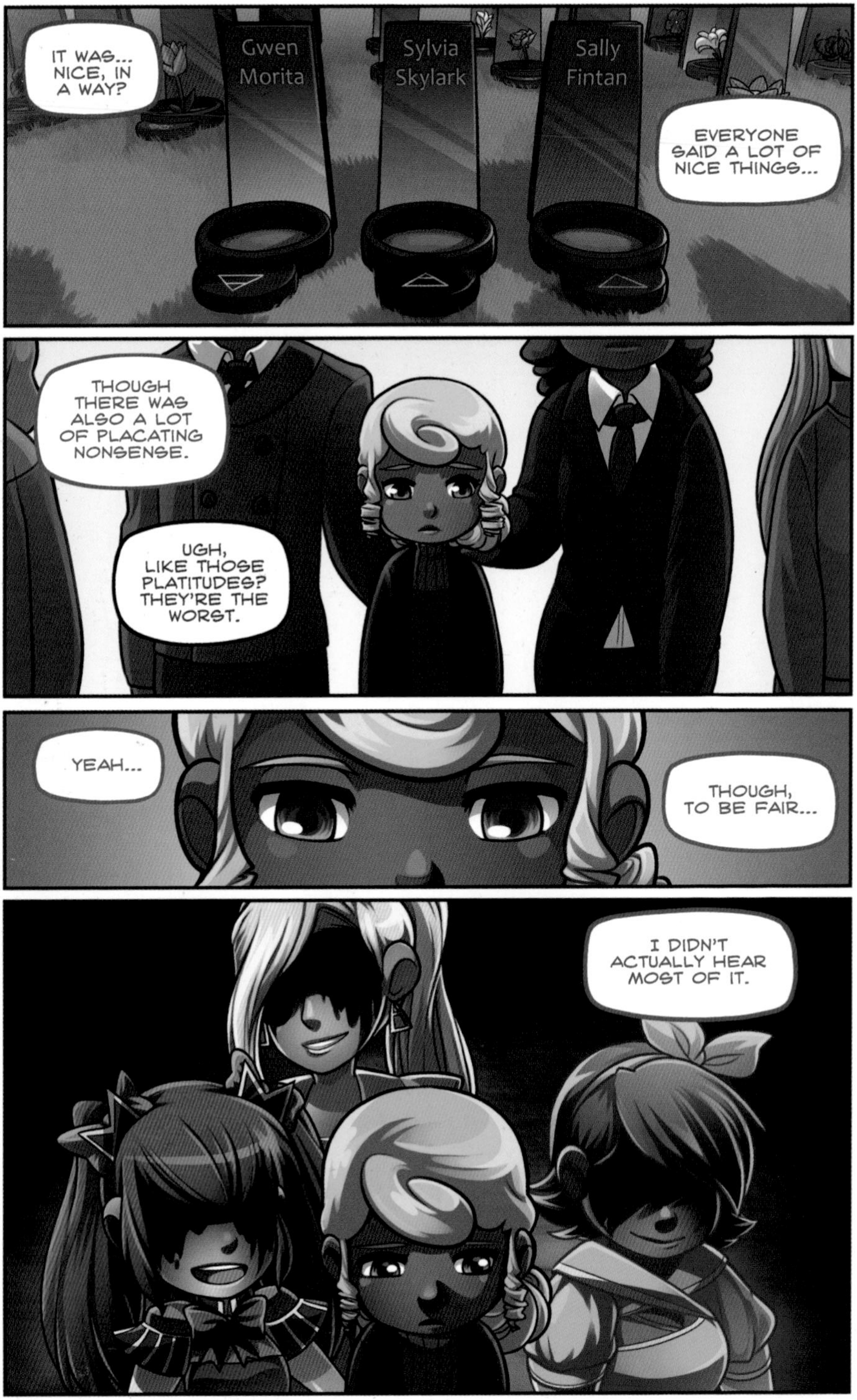
IT WAS... NICE, IN A WAY?
Gwen Morita
Sylvia Skylark
Sally Fintan
EVERYONE SAID A LOT OF NICE THINGS...
THOUGH THERE WAS ALSO A LOT OF PLACATING NONSENSE.
UGH, LIKE THOSE PLATITUDES? THEY'RE THE WORST.
YEAH...
THOUGH, TO BE FAIR...
I DIDN'T ACTUALLY HEAR MOST OF IT.

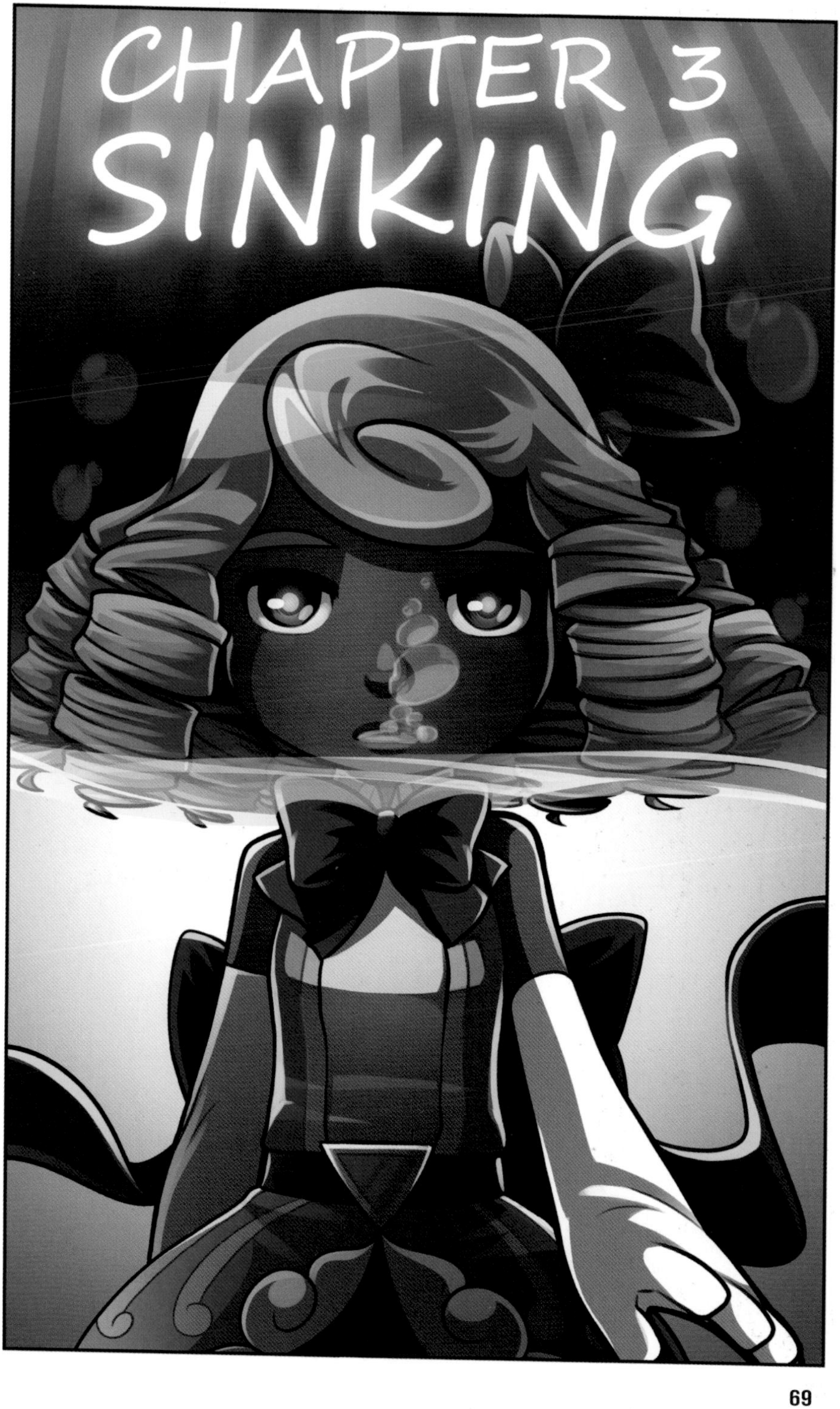
CHAPTER 3
SINKING

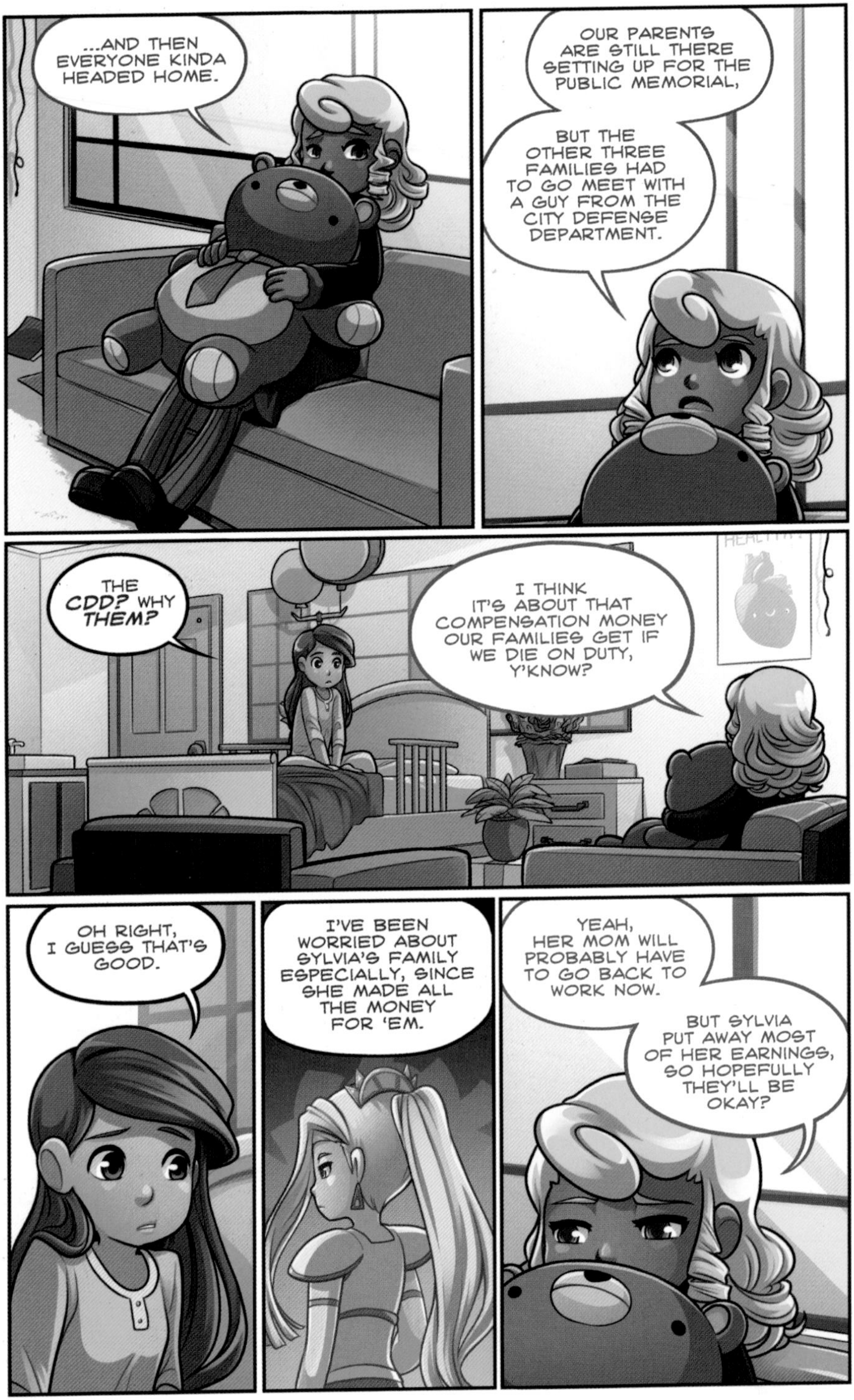
...AND THEN EVERYONE KINDA HEADED HOME.
OUR PARENTS ARE STILL THERE SETTING UP FOR THE PUBLIC MEMORIAL,
BUT THE OTHER THREE FAMILIES HAD TO GO MEET WITH A GUY FROM THE CITY DEFENSE DEPARTMENT.
THE *CDD?* WHY *THEM?*
I THINK IT'S ABOUT THAT COMPENSATION MONEY OUR FAMILIES GET IF WE DIE ON DUTY, Y'KNOW?
OH RIGHT, I GUESS THAT'S GOOD.
I'VE BEEN WORRIED ABOUT SYLVIA'S FAMILY ESPECIALLY, SINCE SHE MADE ALL THE MONEY FOR 'EM.
YEAH, HER MOM WILL PROBABLY HAVE TO GO BACK TO WORK NOW.
BUT SYLVIA PUT AWAY MOST OF HER EARNINGS, SO HOPEFULLY THEY'LL BE OKAY?

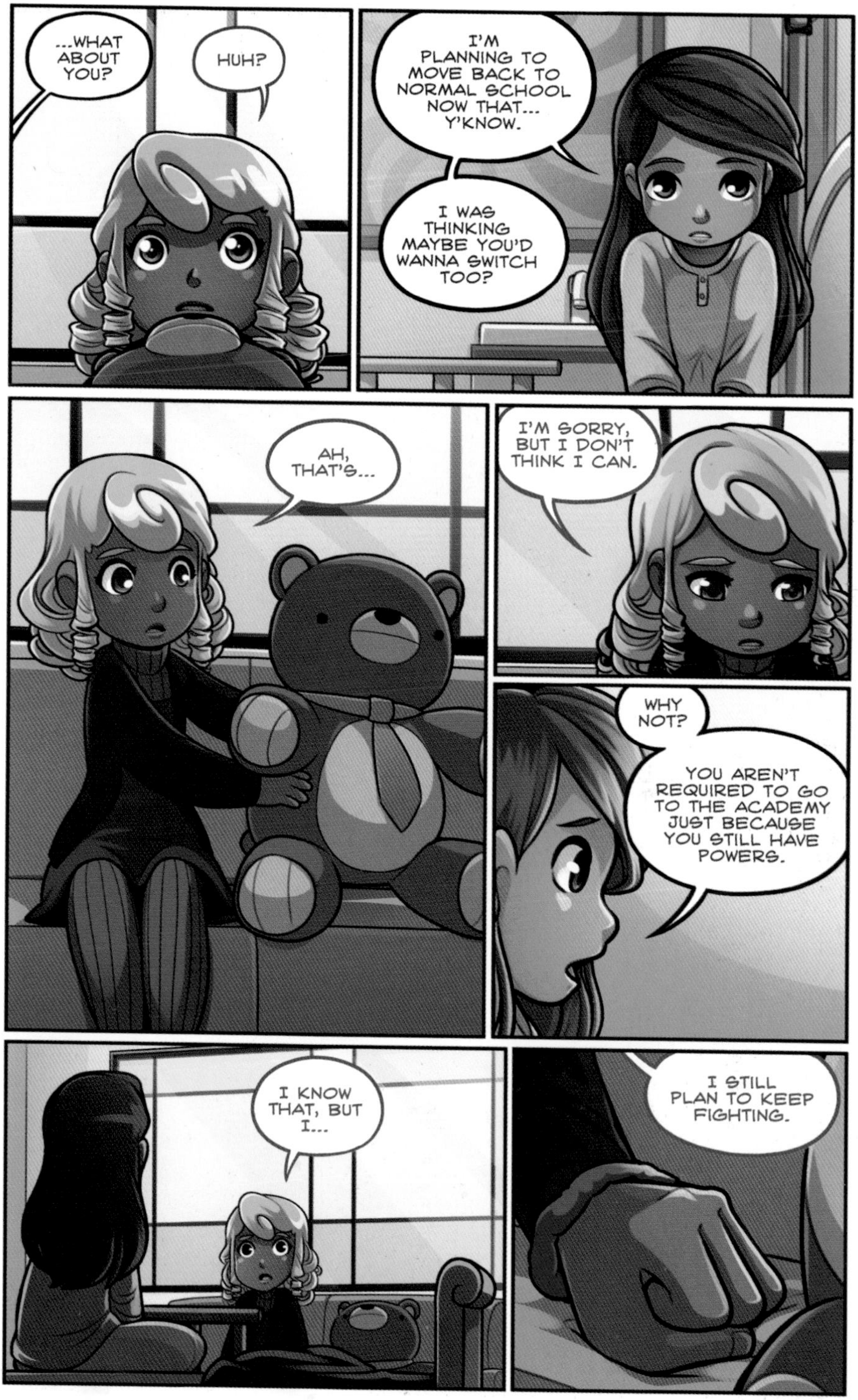
...WHAT ABOUT YOU?
HUH?
I'M PLANNING TO MOVE BACK TO NORMAL SCHOOL NOW THAT... Y'KNOW.
I WAS THINKING MAYBE YOU'D WANNA SWITCH TOO?
AH, THAT'S...
I'M SORRY, BUT I DON'T THINK I CAN.
WHY NOT?
YOU AREN'T REQUIRED TO GO TO THE ACADEMY JUST BECAUSE YOU STILL HAVE POWERS.
I KNOW THAT, BUT I...
I STILL PLAN TO KEEP FIGHTING.

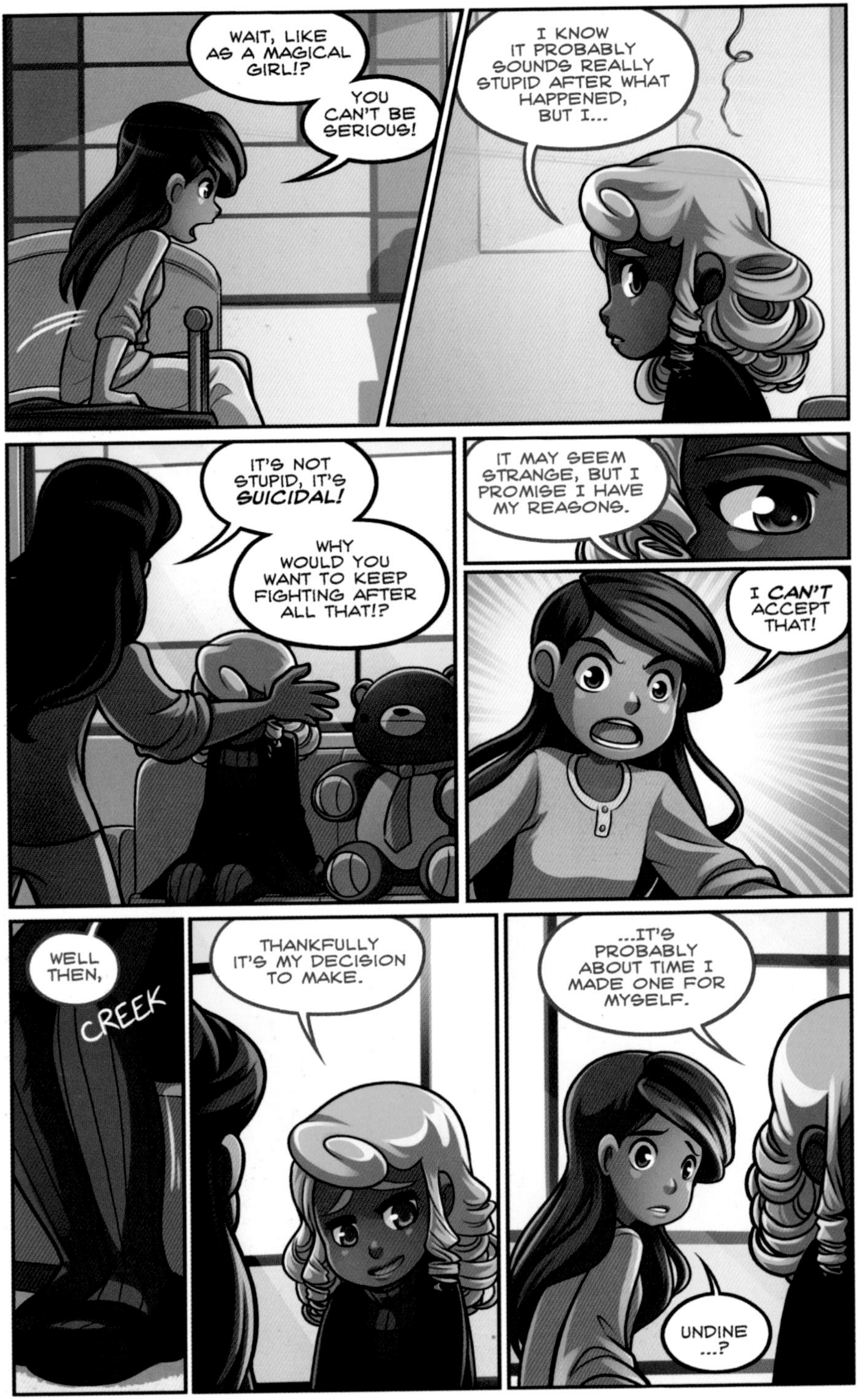
WAIT, LIKE AS A MAGICAL GIRL!?
YOU CAN'T BE SERIOUS!
I KNOW IT PROBABLY SOUNDS REALLY STUPID AFTER WHAT HAPPENED, BUT I...
IT'S NOT STUPID, IT'S *SUICIDAL!*
WHY WOULD YOU WANT TO KEEP FIGHTING AFTER ALL THAT!?
IT MAY SEEM STRANGE, BUT I PROMISE I HAVE MY REASONS.
I *CAN'T* ACCEPT THAT!
WELL THEN,
CREEK
THANKFULLY IT'S MY DECISION TO MAKE.
...IT'S PROBABLY ABOUT TIME I MADE ONE FOR MYSELF.
UNDINE ...?

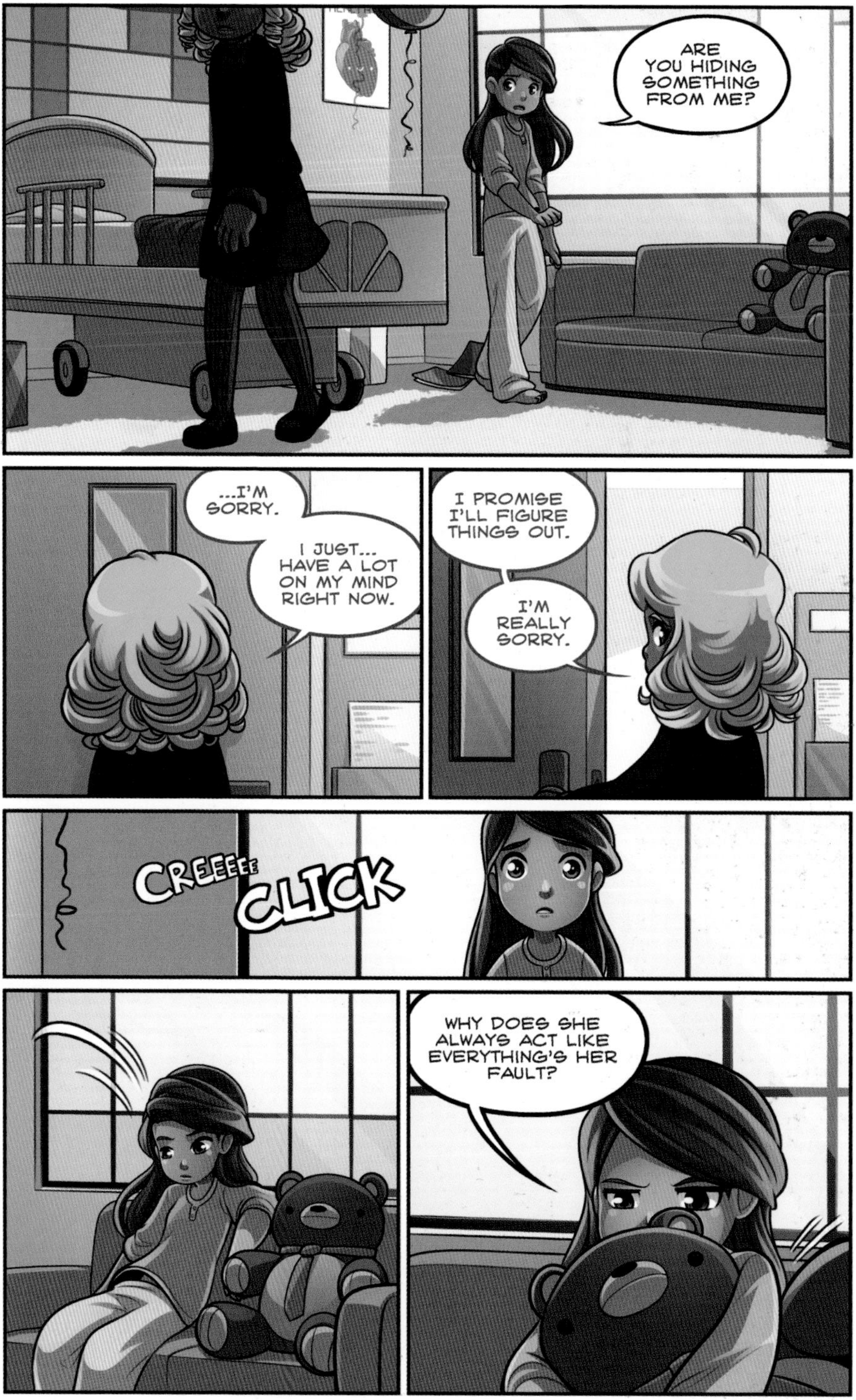
ARE YOU HIDING SOMETHING FROM ME?
...I'M SORRY.
I JUST... HAVE A LOT ON MY MIND RIGHT NOW.
I PROMISE I'LL FIGURE THINGS OUT.
I'M REALLY SORRY.
CREEEEE
CLICK
WHY DOES SHE ALWAYS ACT LIKE EVERYTHING'S HER FAULT?

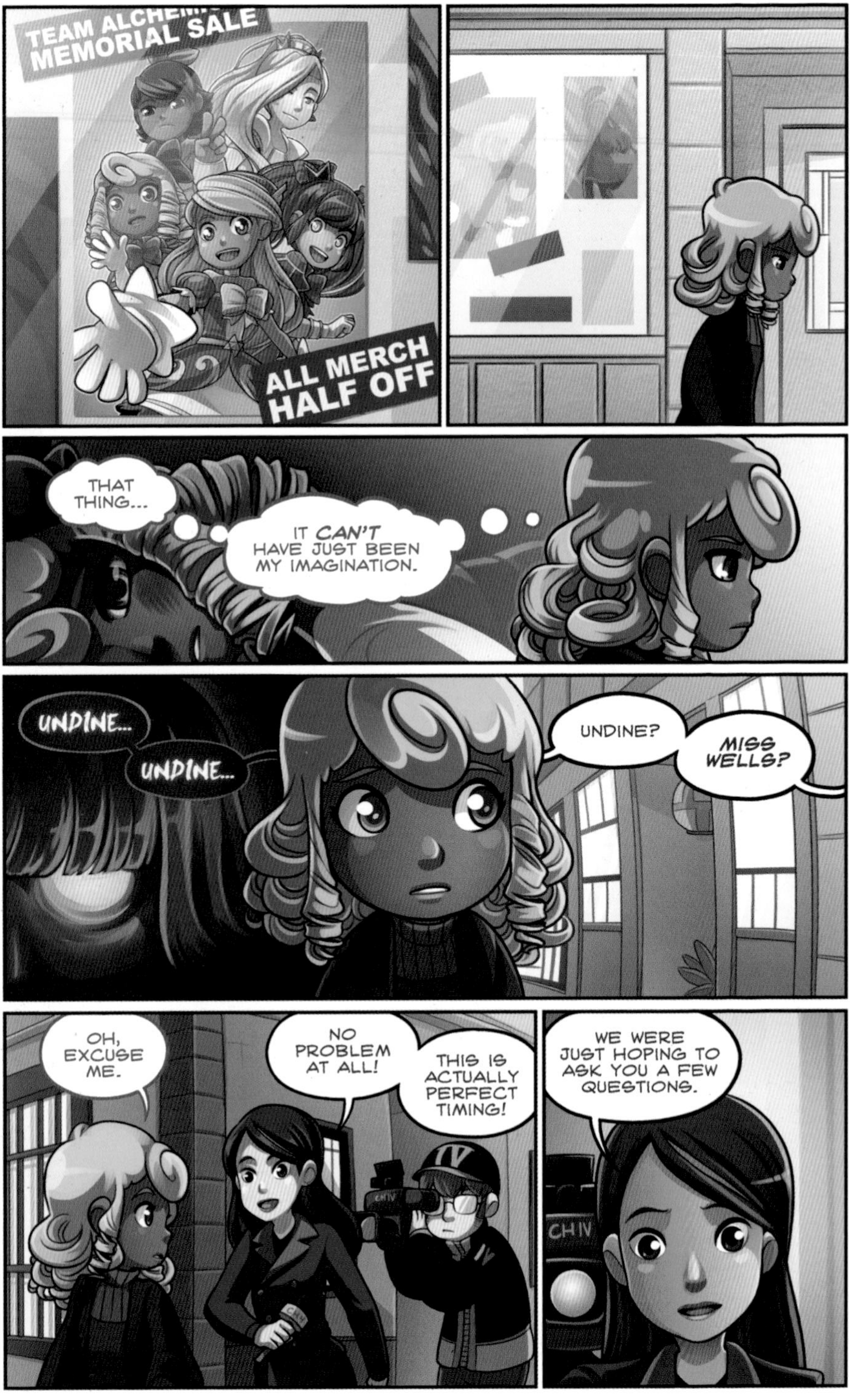
TEAM ALCHEMI...
MEMORIAL SALE
ALL MERCH HALF OFF
THAT THING...
IT CAN'T HAVE JUST BEEN MY IMAGINATION.
UNDINE...
UNDINE...
UNDINE?
MISS WELLS?
OH, EXCUSE ME.
NO PROBLEM AT ALL!
THIS IS ACTUALLY PERFECT TIMING!
TV
CHIV
WE WERE JUST HOPING TO ASK YOU A FEW QUESTIONS.
CHIV

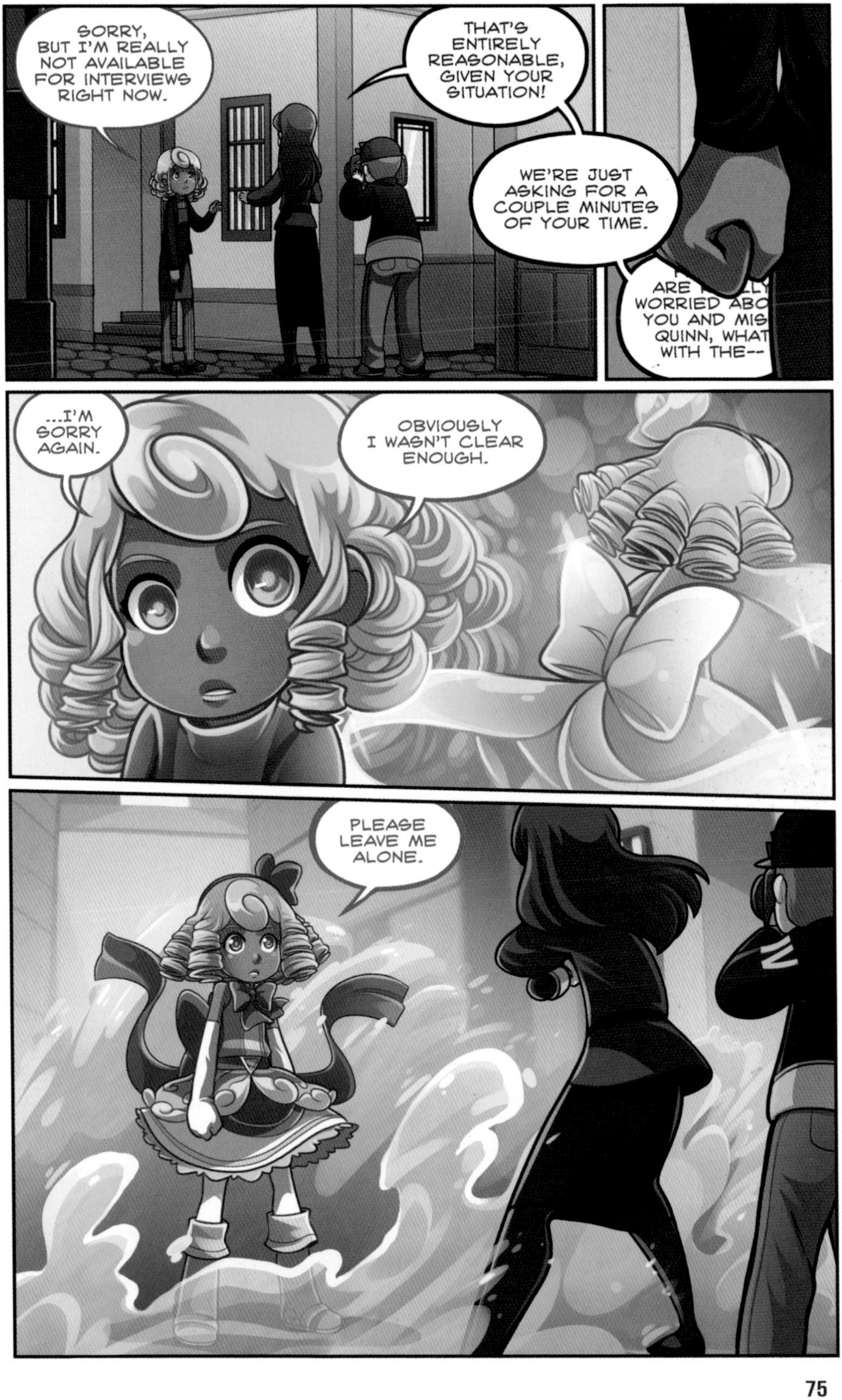
SORRY, BUT I'M REALLY NOT AVAILABLE FOR INTERVIEWS RIGHT NOW.
THAT'S ENTIRELY REASONABLE, GIVEN YOUR SITUATION!
WE'RE JUST ASKING FOR A COUPLE MINUTES OF YOUR TIME.
ARE WORRIED ABO YOU AND MIS QUINN, WHAT WITH THE--
...I'M SORRY AGAIN.
OBVIOUSLY I WASN'T CLEAR ENOUGH.
PLEASE LEAVE ME ALONE.

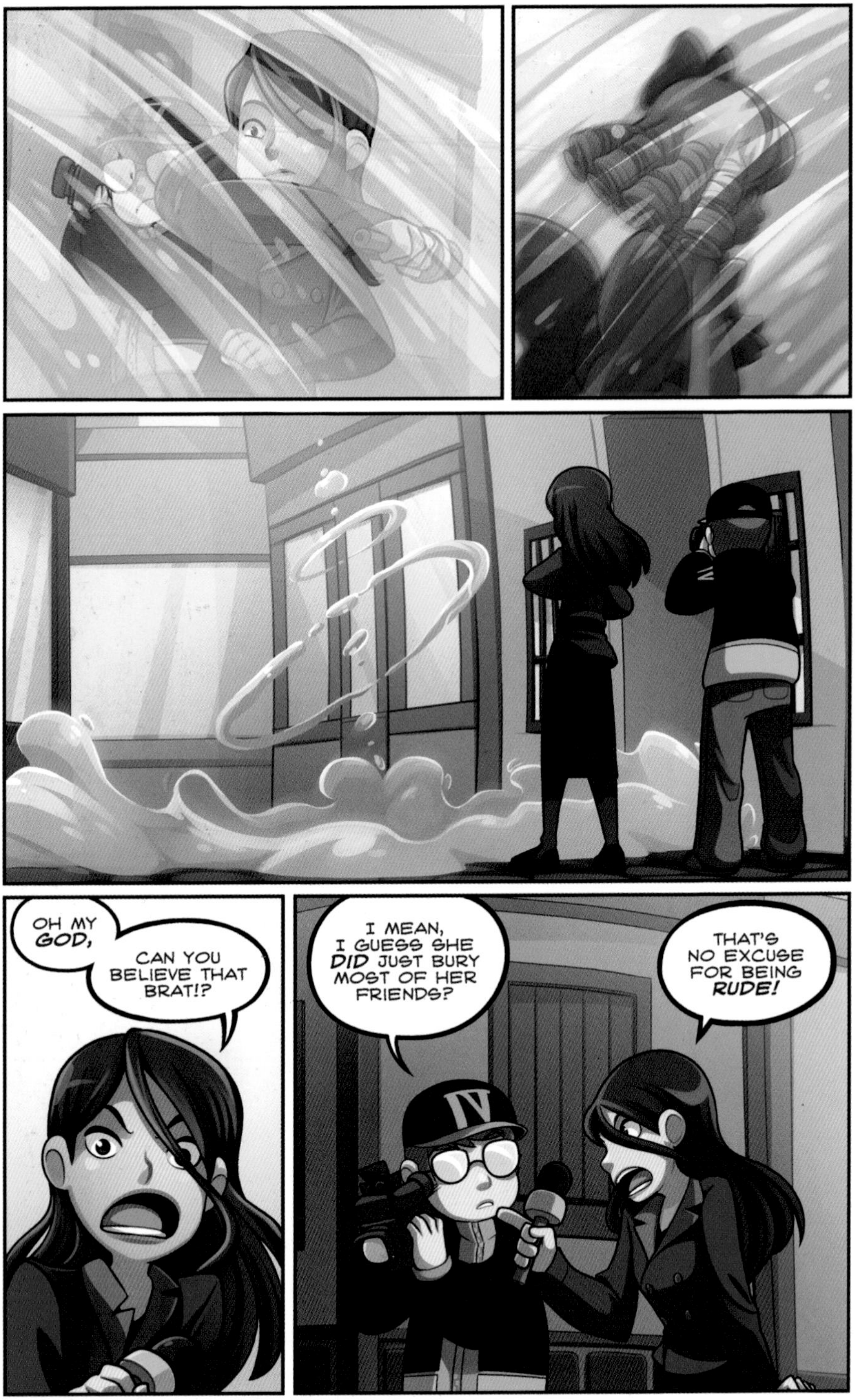
OH MY *GOD*,
CAN YOU BELIEVE THAT BRAT!?
I MEAN, I GUESS SHE *DID* JUST BURY MOST OF HER FRIENDS?
THAT'S NO EXCUSE FOR BEING *RUDE!*

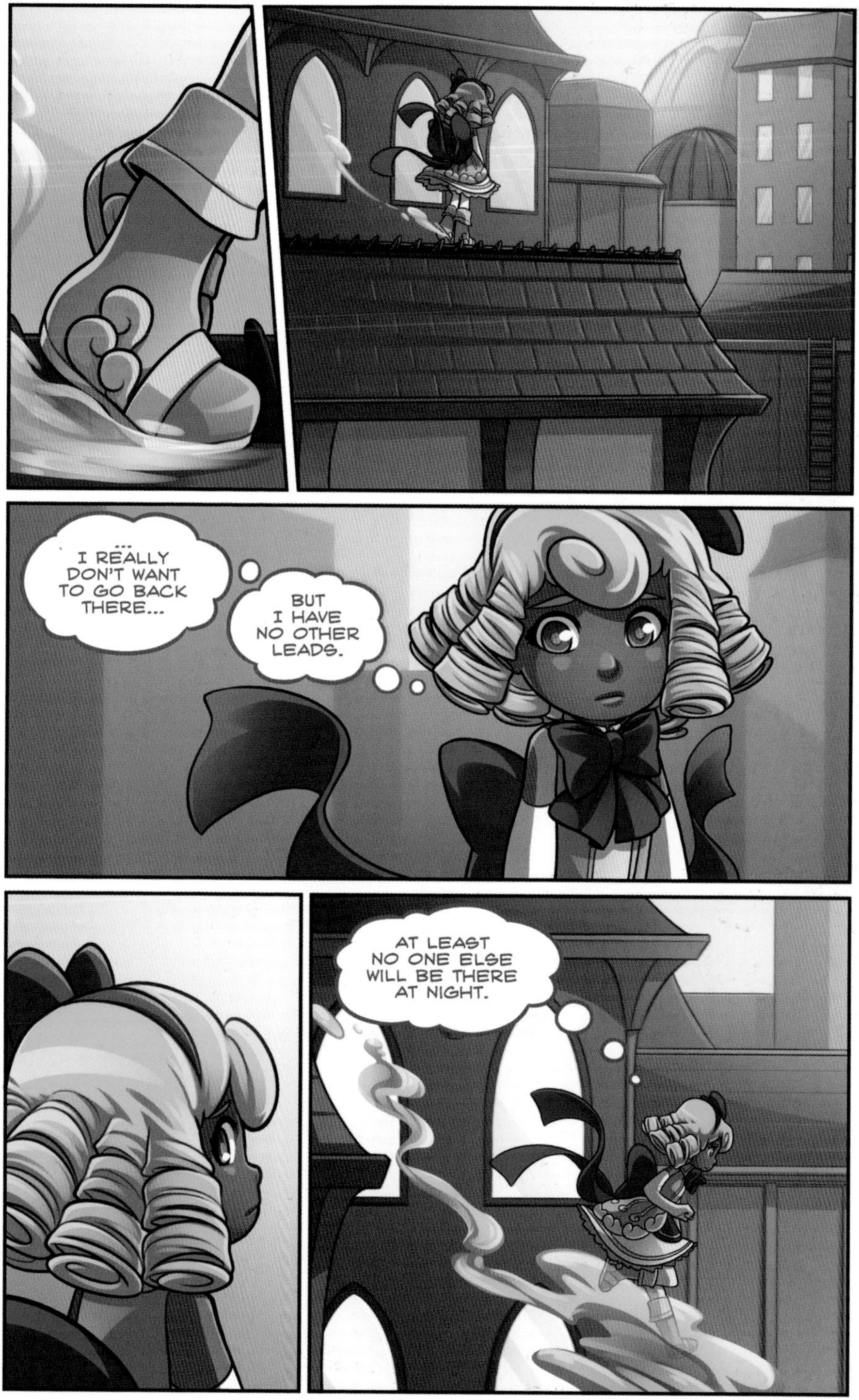

... I REALLY DON'T WANT TO GO BACK THERE...
BUT I HAVE NO OTHER LEADS.
AT LEAST NO ONE ELSE WILL BE THERE AT NIGHT.

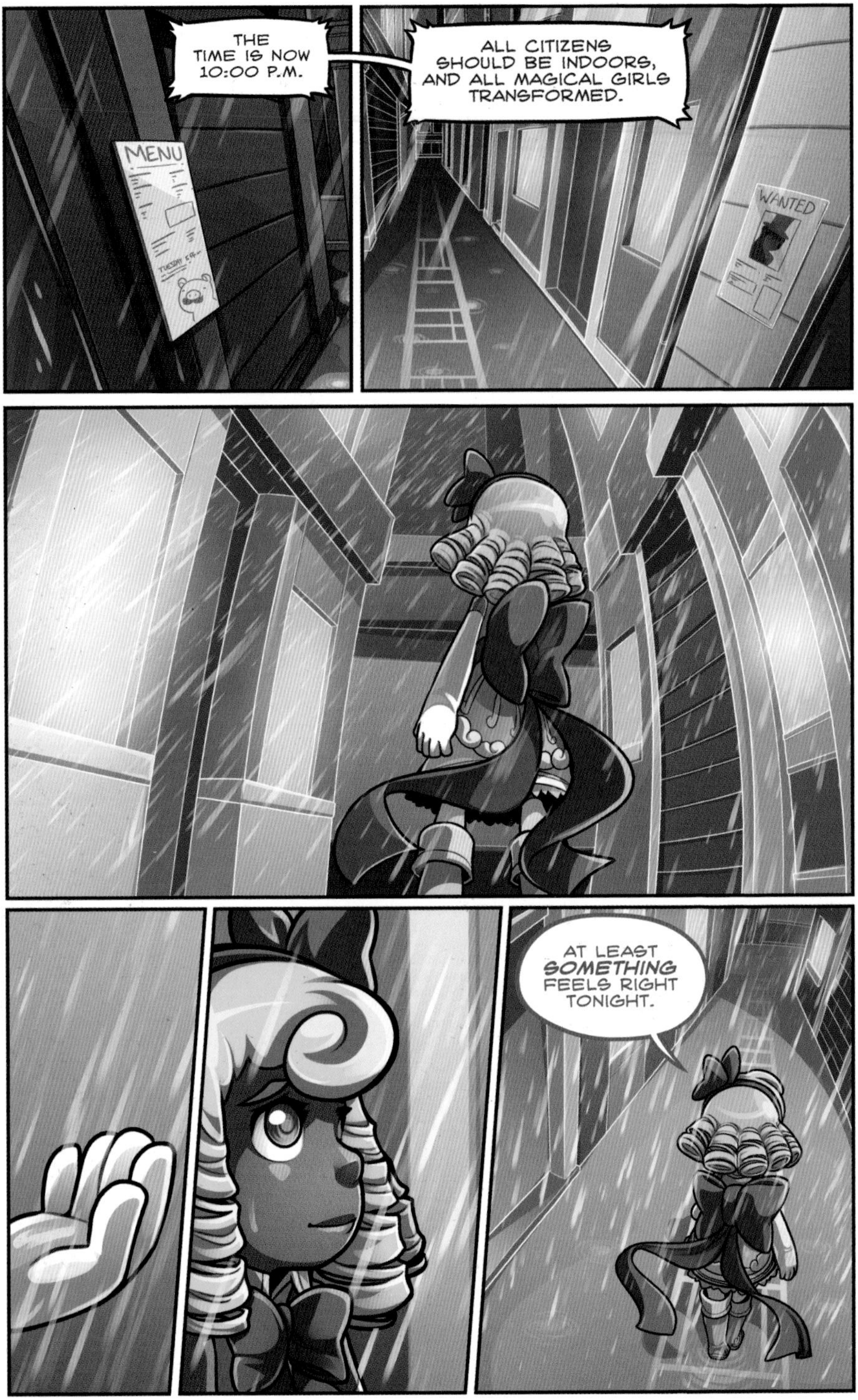
THE TIME IS NOW 10:00 P.M.
ALL CITIZENS SHOULD BE INDOORS, AND ALL MAGICAL GIRLS TRANSFORMED.
MENU
WANTED
AT LEAST *SOMETHING* FEELS RIGHT TONIGHT.

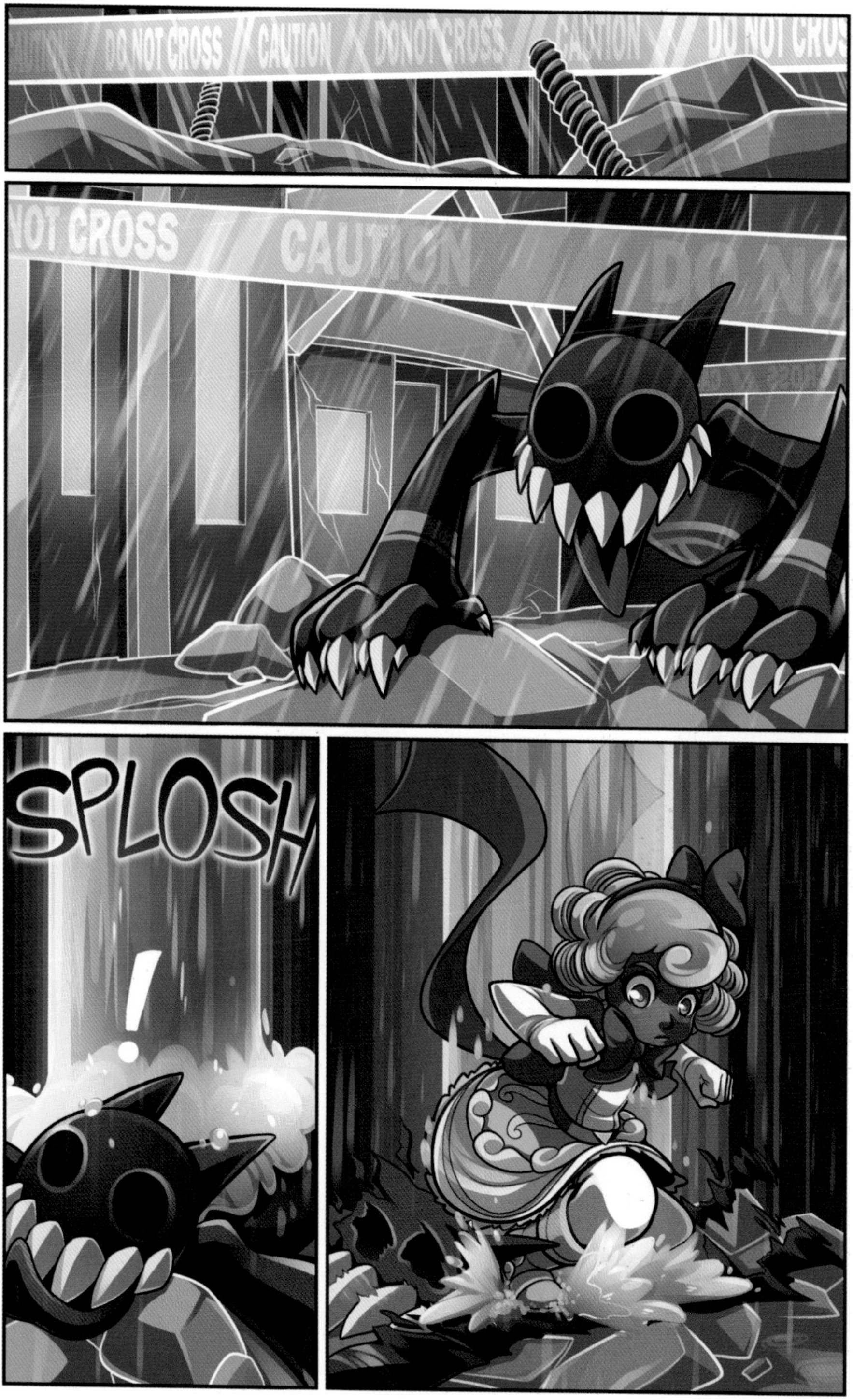
DO NOT CROSS
CAUTION
DO NOT CROSS
CAUTION
DO NOT CROSS
CAUTION
SPLOSH
!

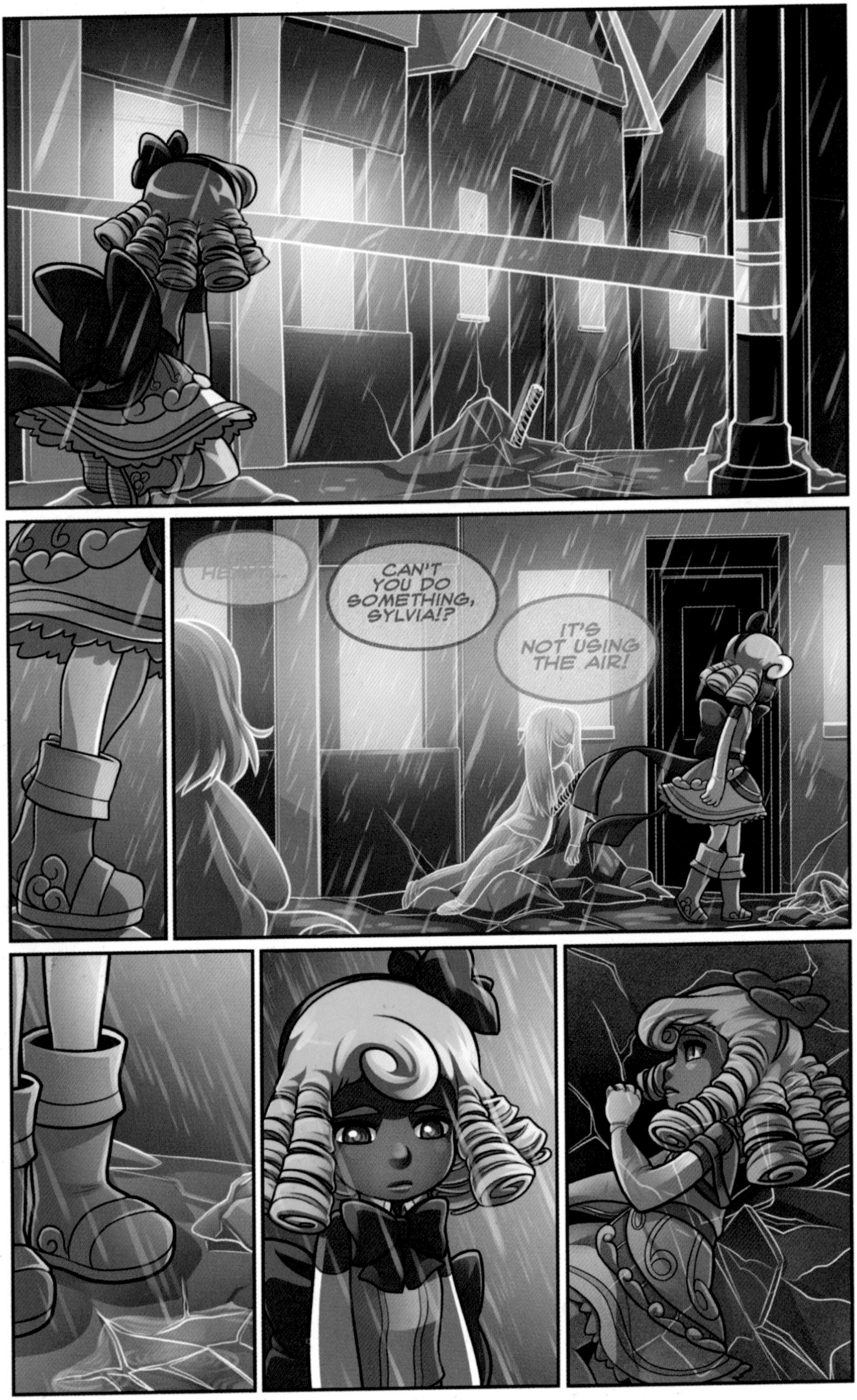
CAN'T YOU DO SOMETHING, SYLVIA!?
IT'S NOT USING THE AIR!

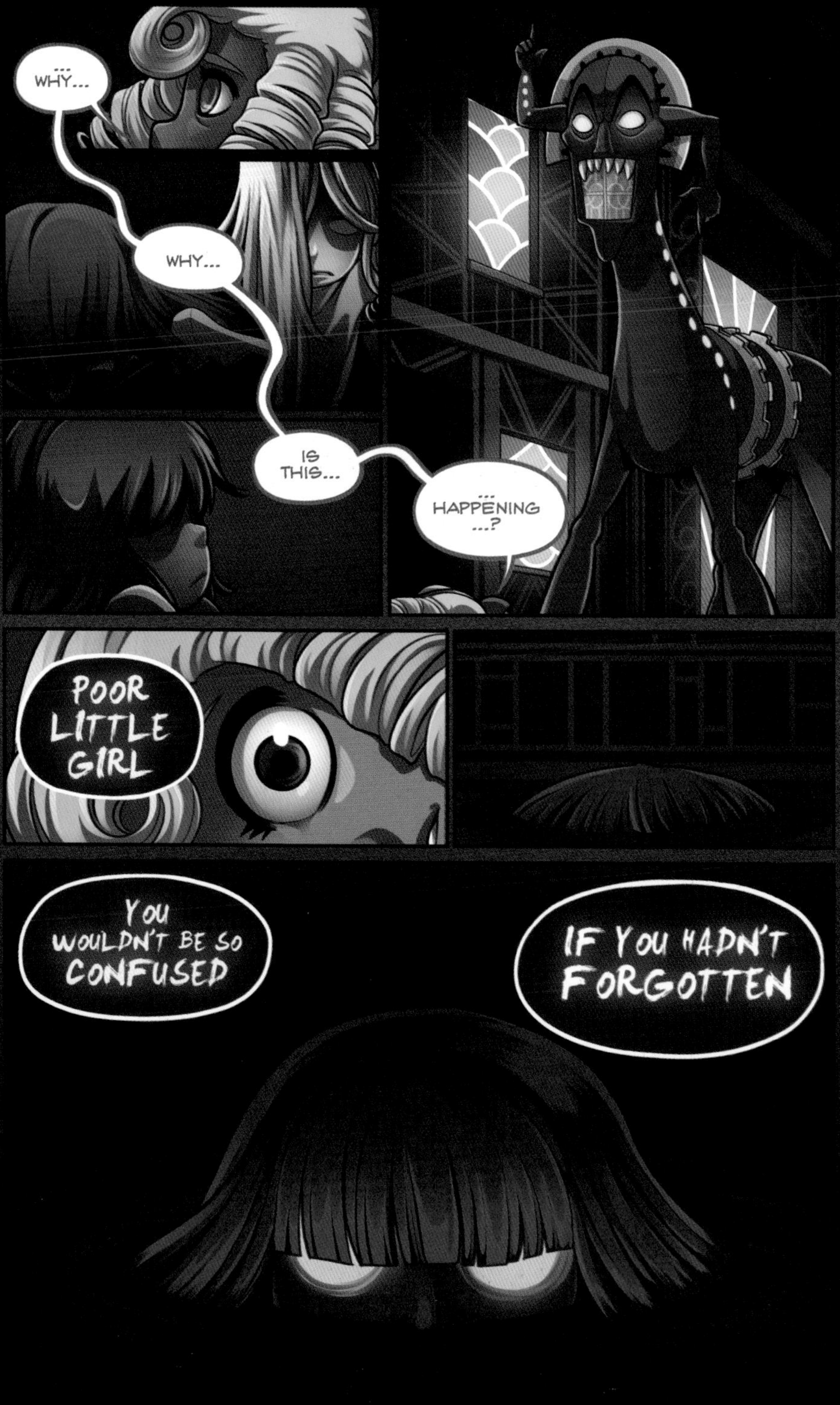

... WHY...
WHY...
IS THIS...
... HAPPENING ...?
POOR LITTLE GIRL
YOU WOULDN'T BE SO CONFUSED
IF YOU HADN'T FORGOTTEN

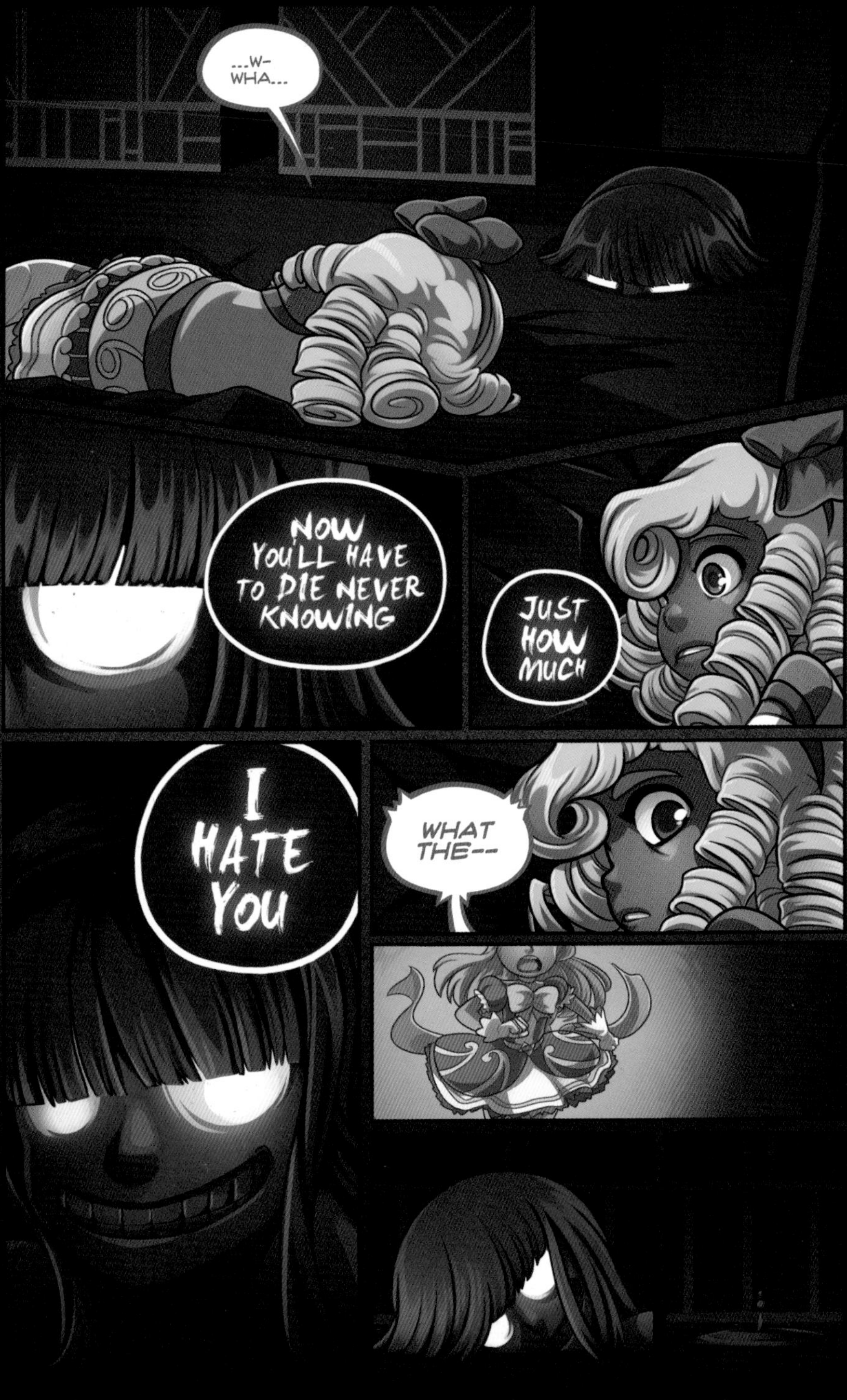
...W-WHA...
NOW YOU'LL HAVE TO DIE NEVER KNOWING
JUST HOW MUCH
I HATE YOU
WHAT THE--

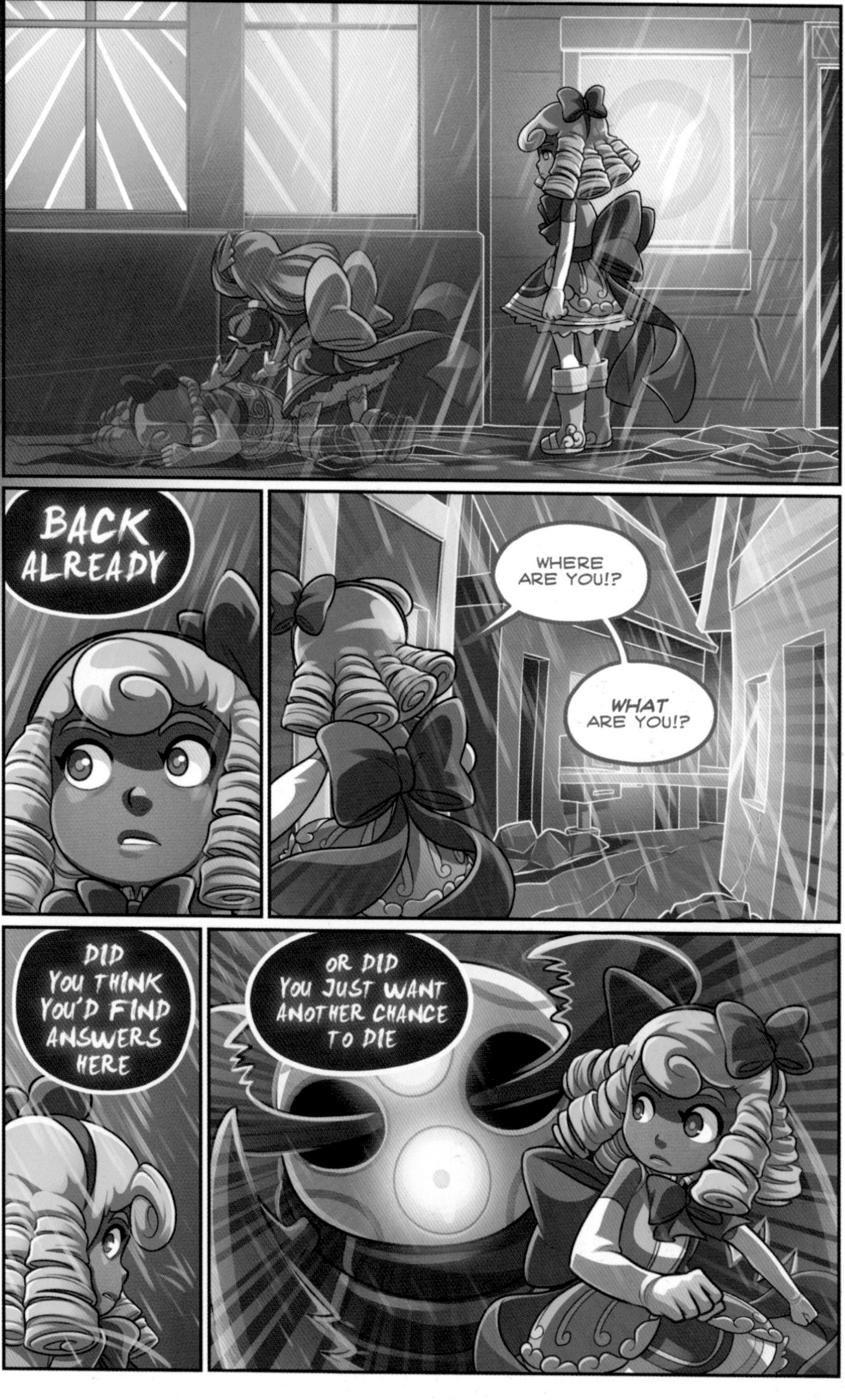
BACK ALREADY
WHERE ARE YOU!?
WHAT ARE YOU!?
DID YOU THINK YOU'D FIND ANSWERS HERE
OR DID YOU JUST WANT ANOTHER CHANCE TO DIE

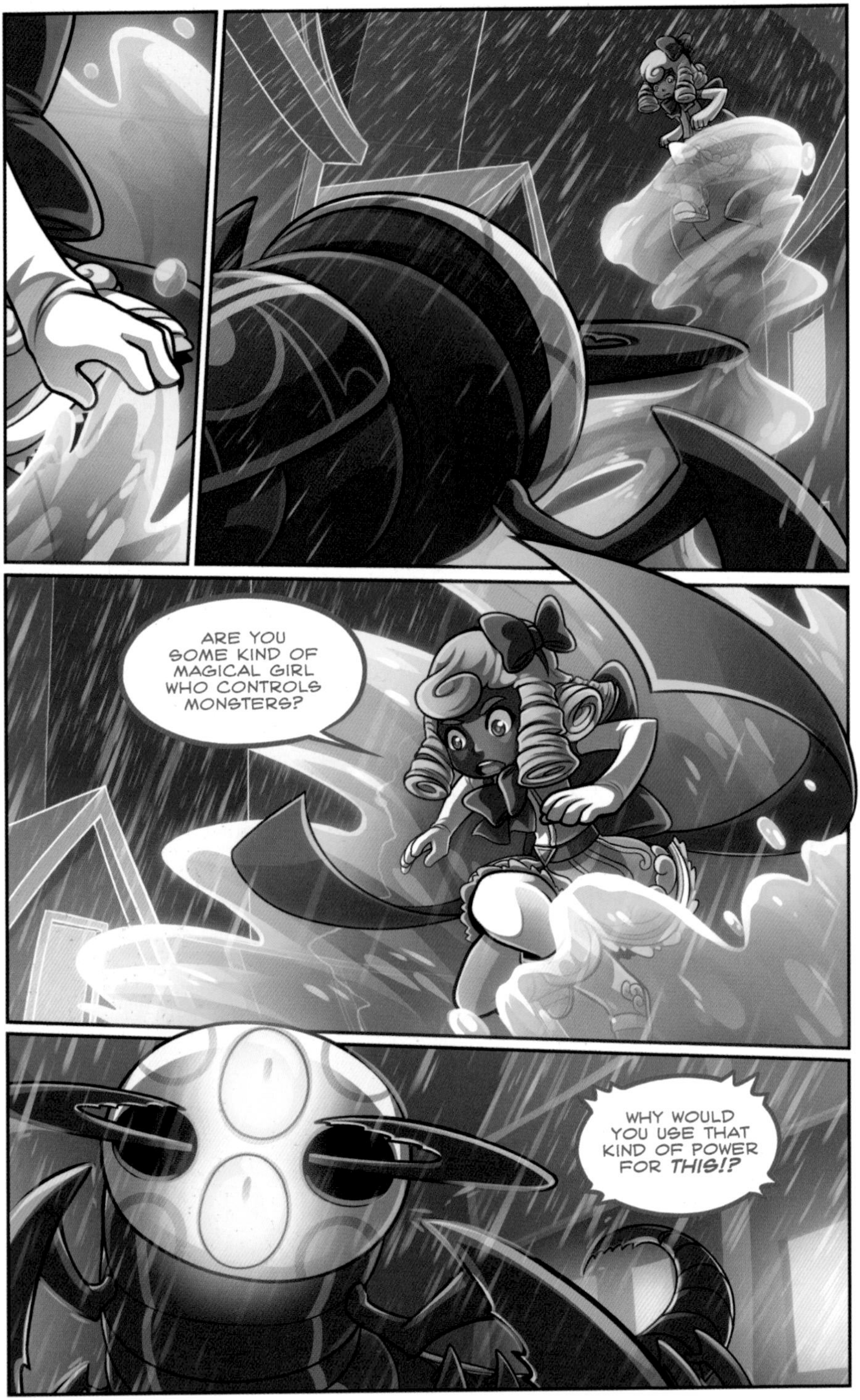
ARE YOU SOME KIND OF MAGICAL GIRL WHO CONTROLS MONSTERS?
WHY WOULD YOU USE THAT KIND OF POWER FOR *THIS!?*

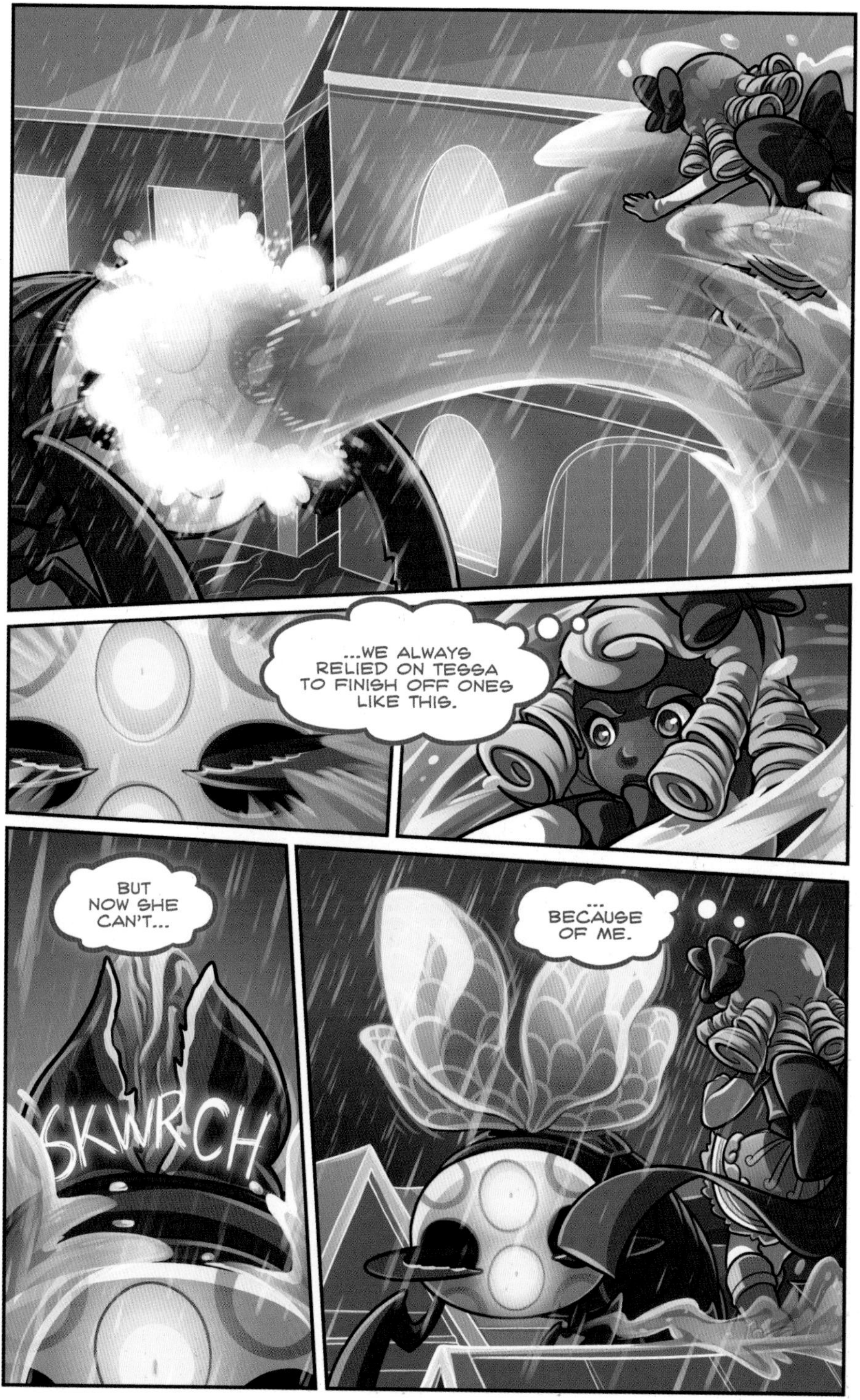
...WE ALWAYS RELIED ON TESSA TO FINISH OFF ONES LIKE THIS.
BUT NOW SHE CAN'T...
SKWRCH
... BECAUSE OF ME.

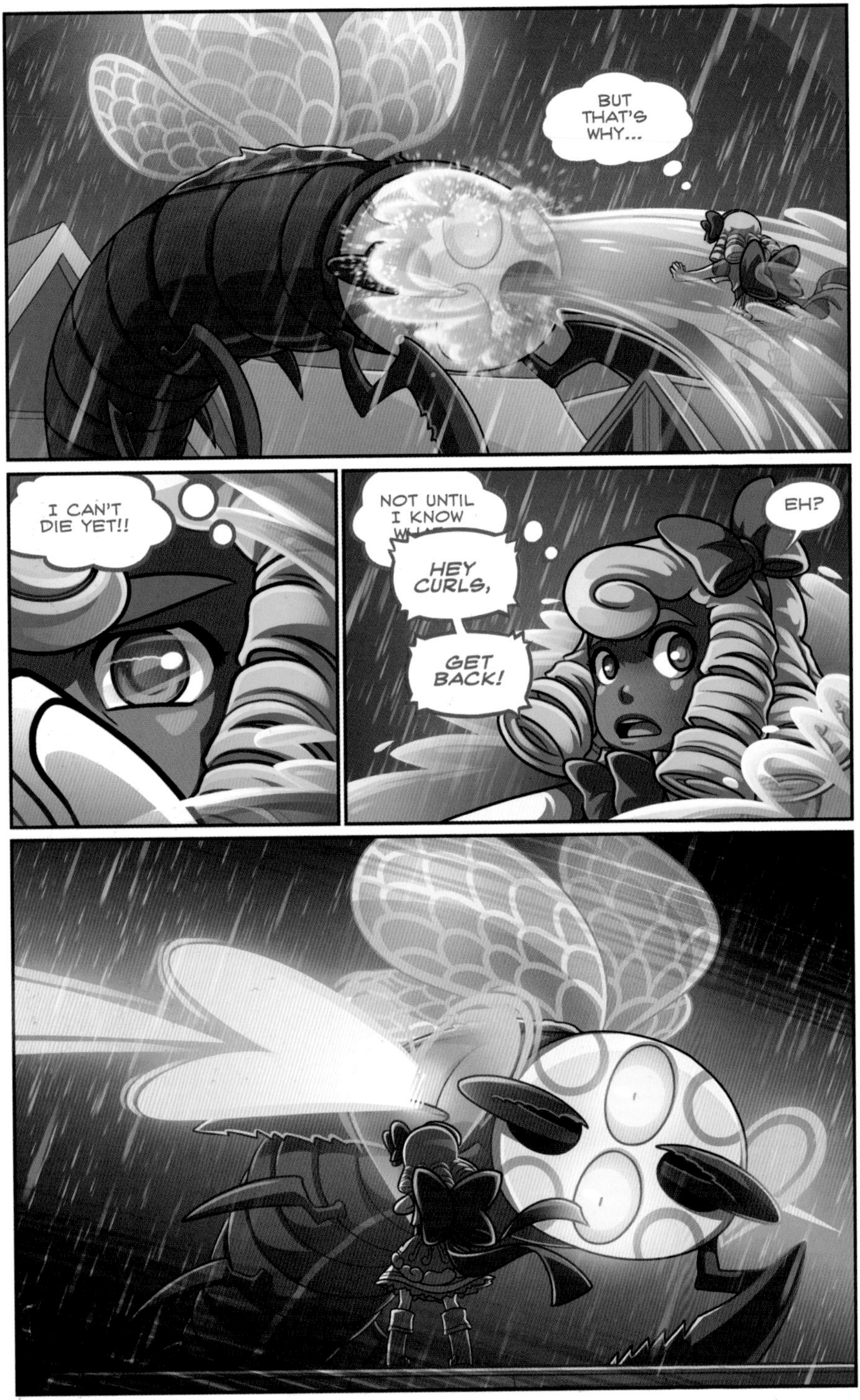
BUT THAT'S WHY...
I CAN'T DIE YET!!
NOT UNTIL I KNOW
HEY CURLS,
GET BACK!
EH?

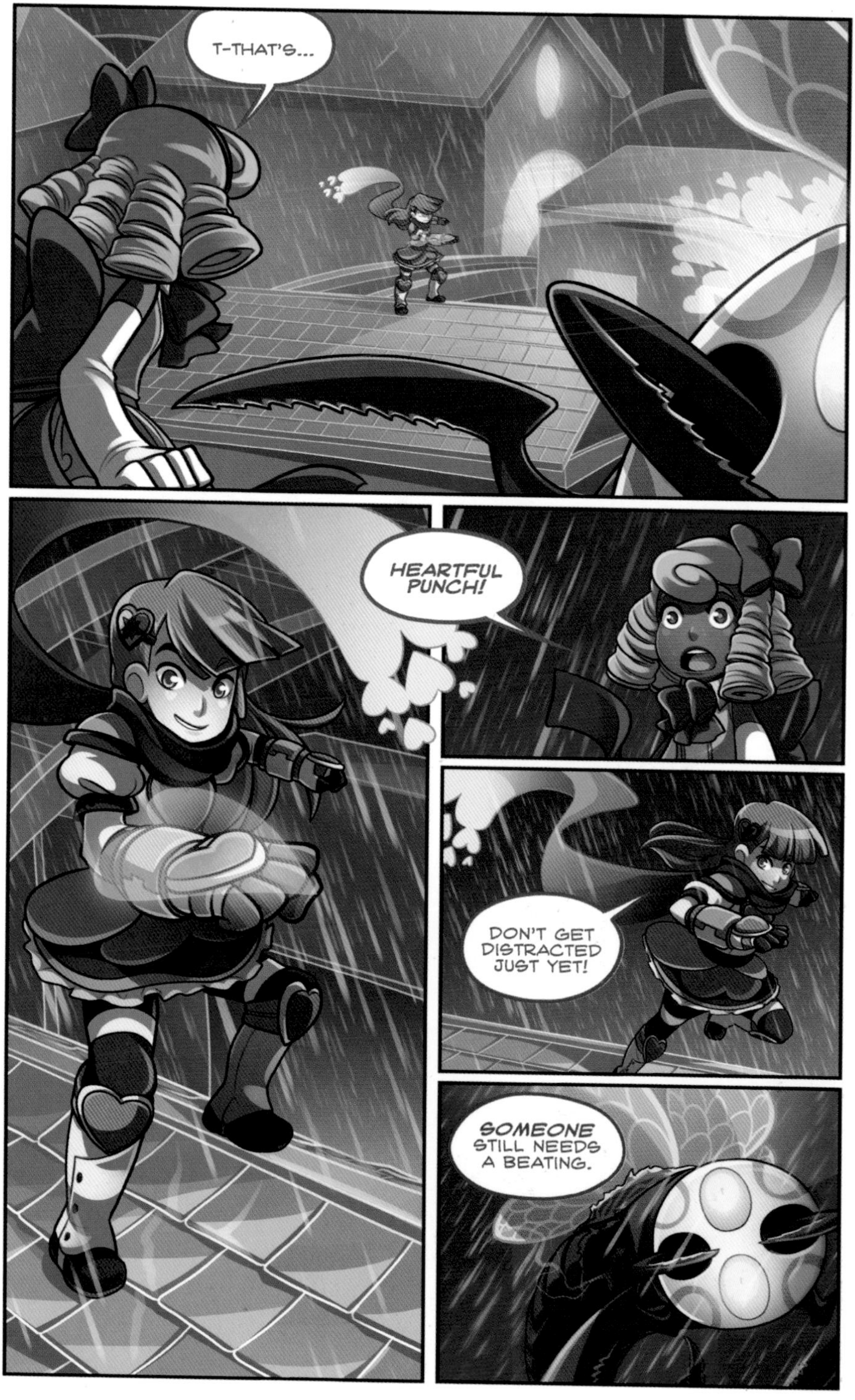
T-THAT'S...
HEARTFUL PUNCH!
DON'T GET DISTRACTED JUST YET!
SOMEONE STILL NEEDS A BEATING.

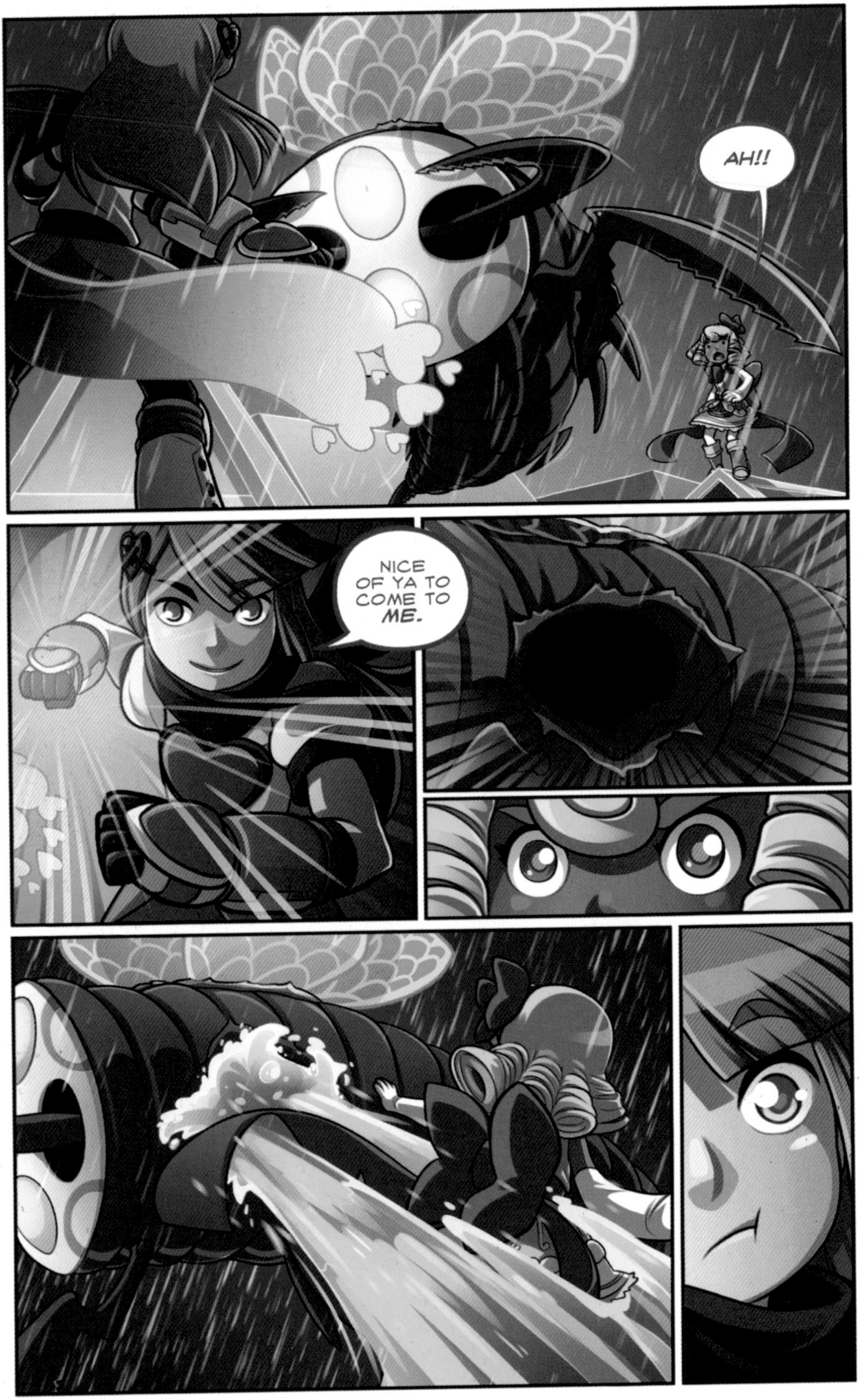
AH!!
NICE OF YA TO COME TO ME.

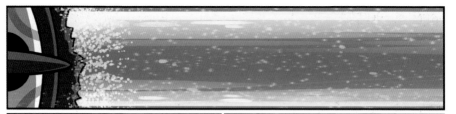

GLORM

SKORSH

SHHHHHHHH

THAT WORKS TOO?

WAIT, SHE MIGHT STILL BE HERE!

SHE?

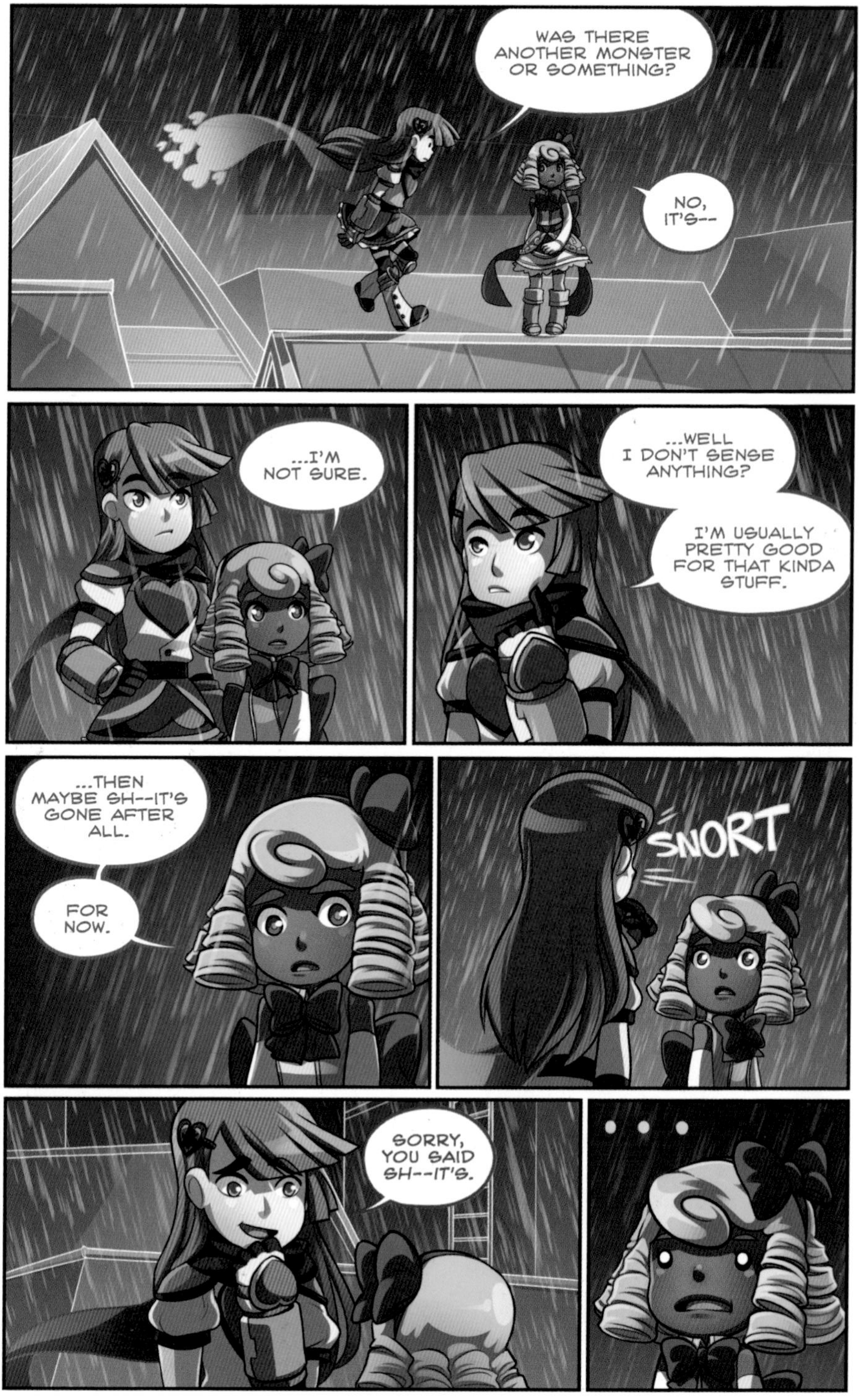
WAS THERE ANOTHER MONSTER OR SOMETHING?
NO, IT'S--
...I'M NOT SURE.
...WELL I DON'T SENSE ANYTHING?
I'M USUALLY PRETTY GOOD FOR THAT KINDA STUFF.
...THEN MAYBE SH--IT'S GONE AFTER ALL.
FOR NOW.
SNORT
SORRY, YOU SAID SH--IT'S.
• • •

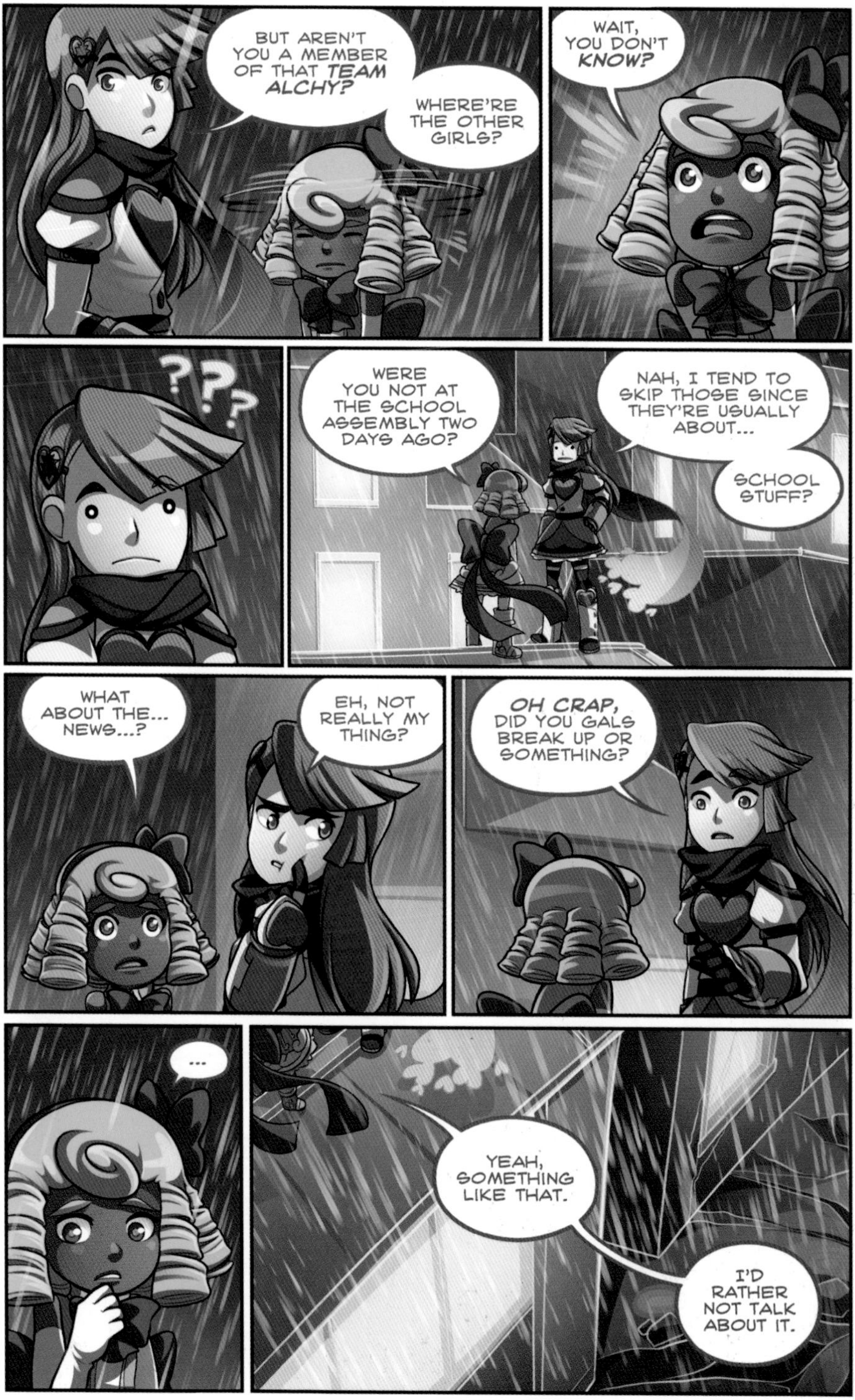
BUT AREN'T YOU A MEMBER OF THAT *TEAM ALCHY?*
WHERE'RE THE OTHER GIRLS?
WAIT, YOU DON'T *KNOW?*
???
WERE YOU NOT AT THE SCHOOL ASSEMBLY TWO DAYS AGO?
NAH, I TEND TO SKIP THOSE SINCE THEY'RE USUALLY ABOUT...
SCHOOL STUFF?
WHAT ABOUT THE... NEWS...?
EH, NOT REALLY MY THING?
OH CRAP, DID YOU GALS BREAK UP OR SOMETHING?
...
YEAH, SOMETHING LIKE THAT.
I'D RATHER NOT TALK ABOUT IT.

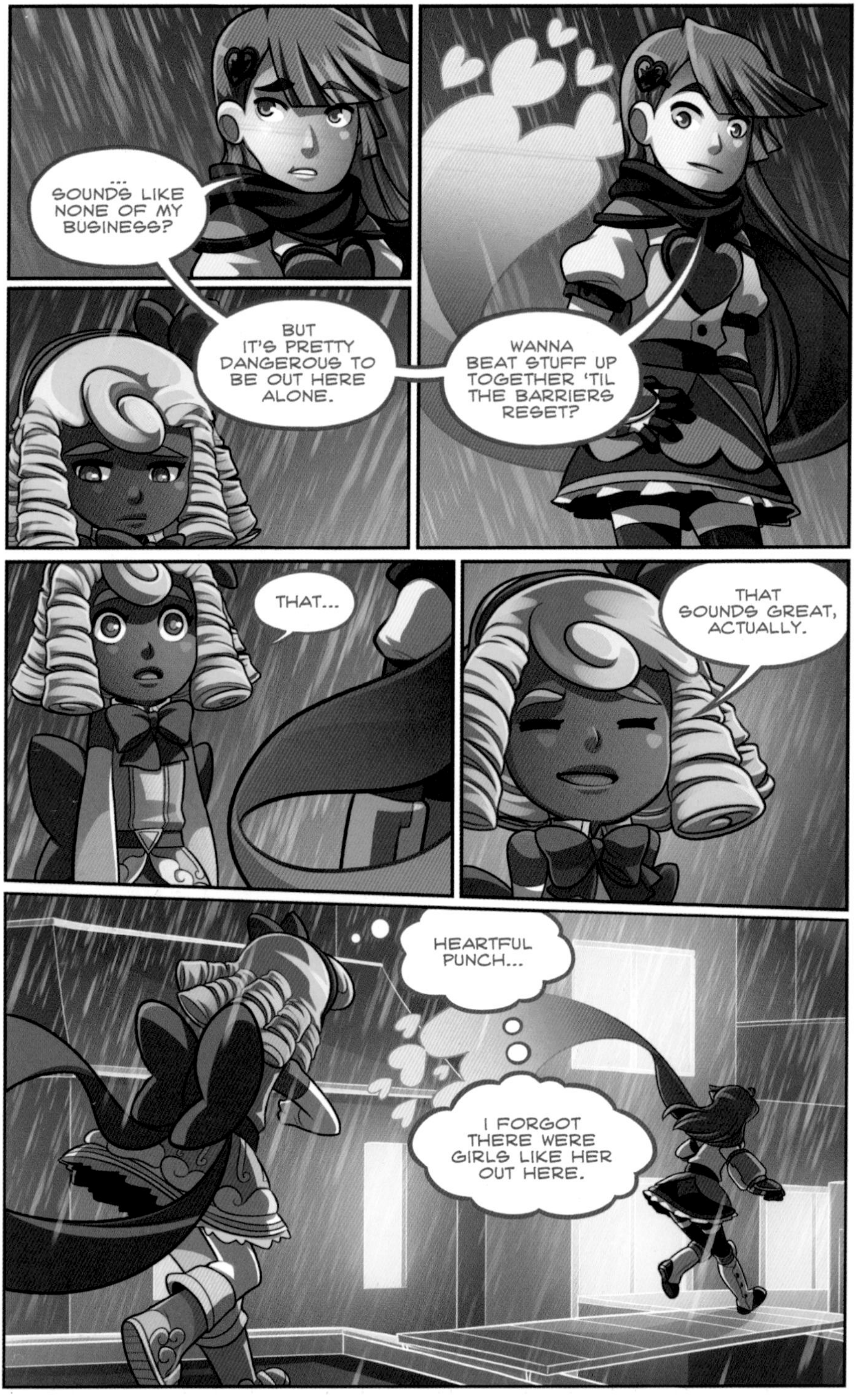
...
SOUNDS LIKE NONE OF MY BUSINESS?
BUT IT'S PRETTY DANGEROUS TO BE OUT HERE ALONE.
WANNA BEAT STUFF UP TOGETHER 'TIL THE BARRIERS RESET?
THAT...
THAT SOUNDS GREAT, ACTUALLY.
HEARTFUL PUNCH...
I FORGOT THERE WERE GIRLS LIKE HER OUT HERE.

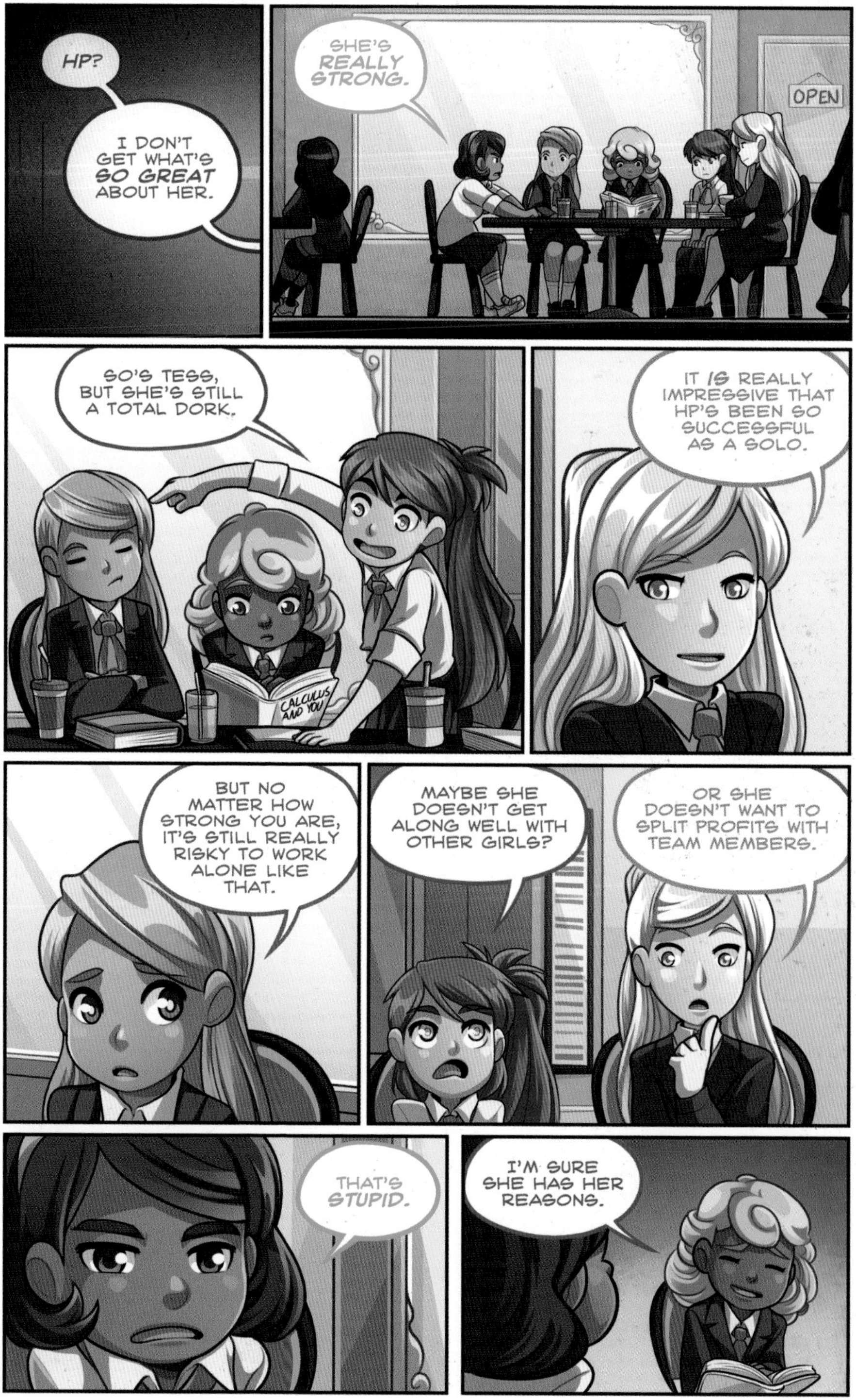
HP?
I DON'T GET WHAT'S SO GREAT ABOUT HER.
SHE'S REALLY STRONG.
OPEN
SO'S TESS, BUT SHE'S STILL A TOTAL DORK.
CALCULUS AND YOU
IT IS REALLY IMPRESSIVE THAT HP'S BEEN SO SUCCESSFUL AS A SOLO.
BUT NO MATTER HOW STRONG YOU ARE, IT'S STILL REALLY RISKY TO WORK ALONE LIKE THAT.
MAYBE SHE DOESN'T GET ALONG WELL WITH OTHER GIRLS?
OR SHE DOESN'T WANT TO SPLIT PROFITS WITH TEAM MEMBERS.
THAT'S STUPID.
I'M SURE SHE HAS HER REASONS.

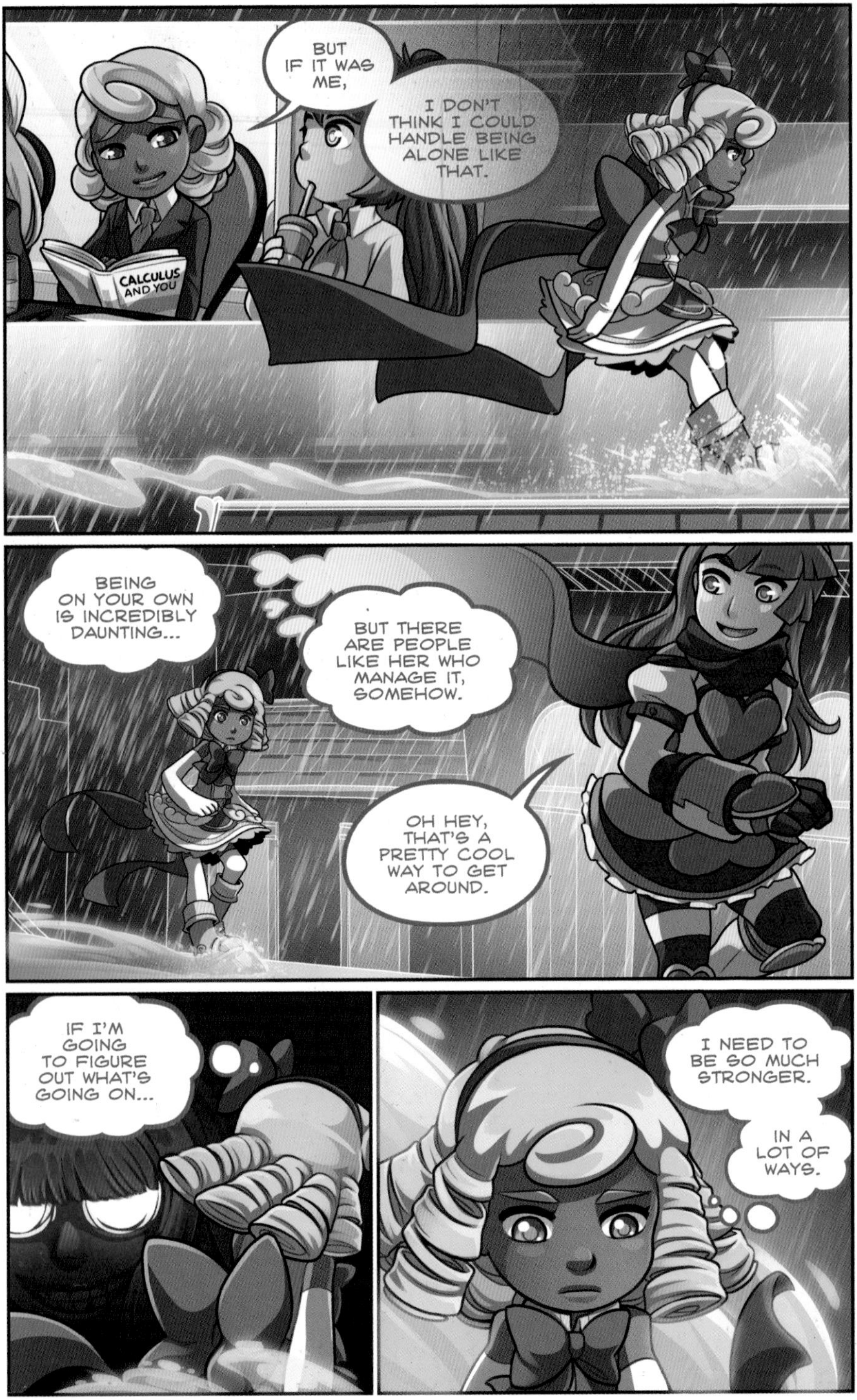

CALCULUS AND YOU
BUT IF IT WAS ME,
I DON'T THINK I COULD HANDLE BEING ALONE LIKE THAT.
BEING ON YOUR OWN IS INCREDIBLY DAUNTING...
BUT THERE ARE PEOPLE LIKE HER WHO MANAGE IT, SOMEHOW.
OH HEY, THAT'S A PRETTY COOL WAY TO GET AROUND.
IF I'M GOING TO FIGURE OUT WHAT'S GOING ON...
I NEED TO BE SO MUCH STRONGER.
IN A LOT OF WAYS.

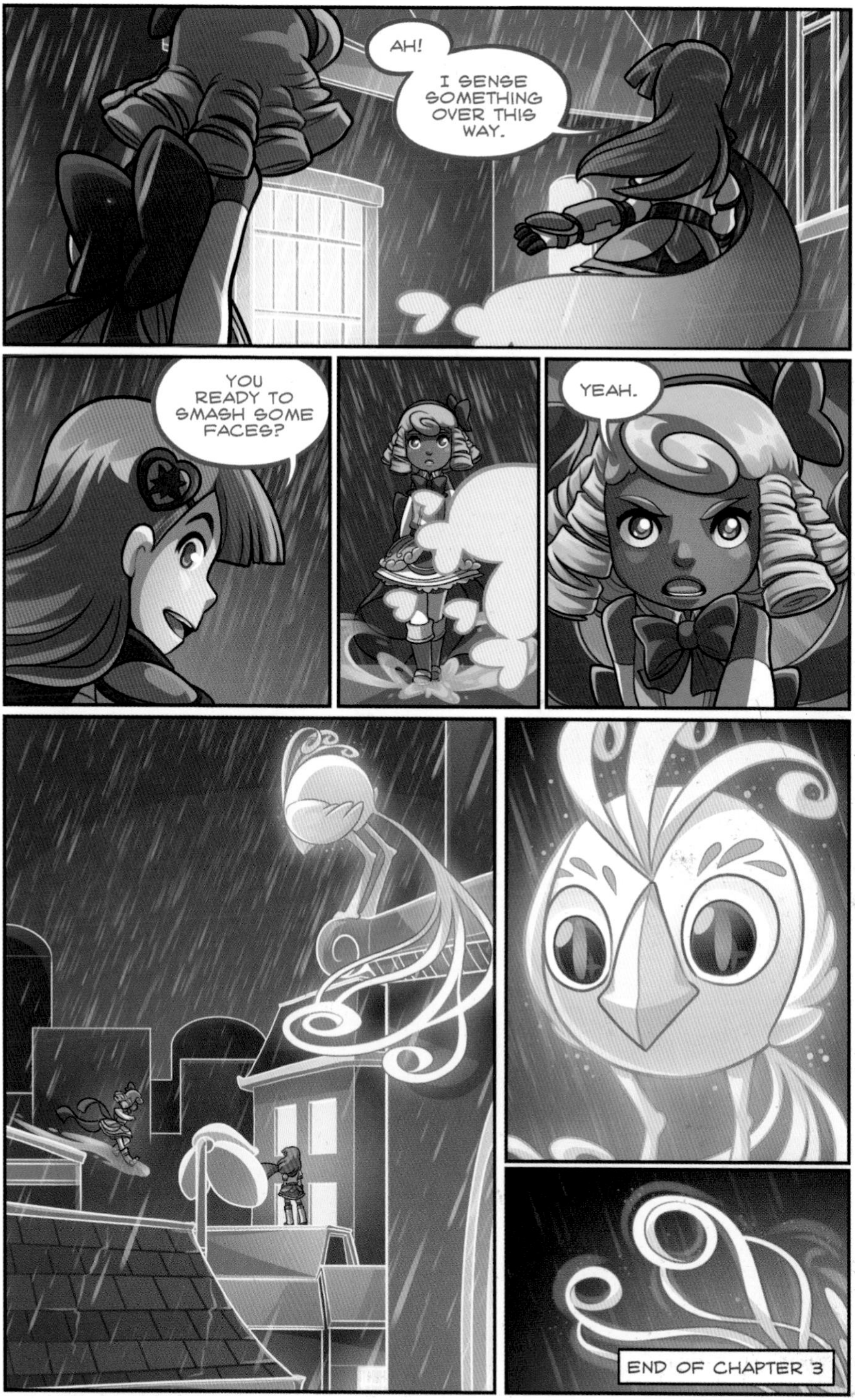
AH!
I SENSE SOMETHING OVER THIS WAY.
YOU READY TO SMASH SOME FACES?
YEAH.
END OF CHAPTER 3

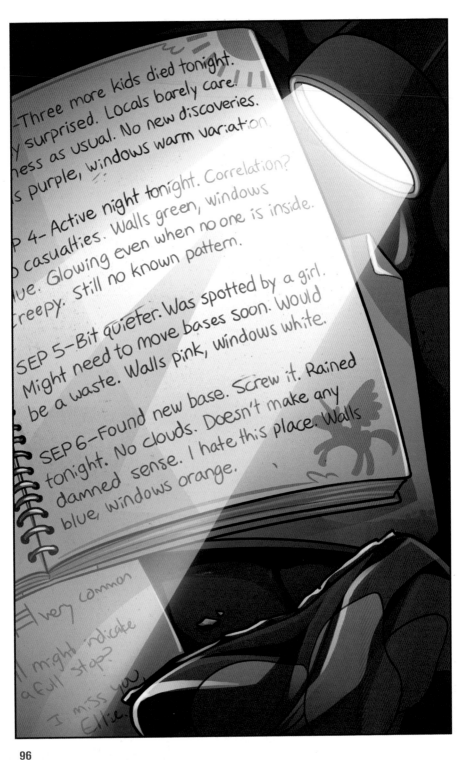

–Three more kids died tonight. y surprised. Locals barely care! ness as usual. No new discoveries. s purple, windows warm variation

P 4– Active night tonight. Correlation? D casualties. Walls green, windows ue. Glowing even when no one is inside. reepy. Still no known pattern.

SEP 5– Bit quieter. Was spotted by a girl. Might need to move bases soon. Would be a waste. Walls pink, windows white.

SEP 6– Found new base. Screw it. Rained tonight. No clouds. Doesn't make any damned sense. I hate this place. Walls blue, windows orange.

very common

might indicate a full stop?

I miss you, Ellie.

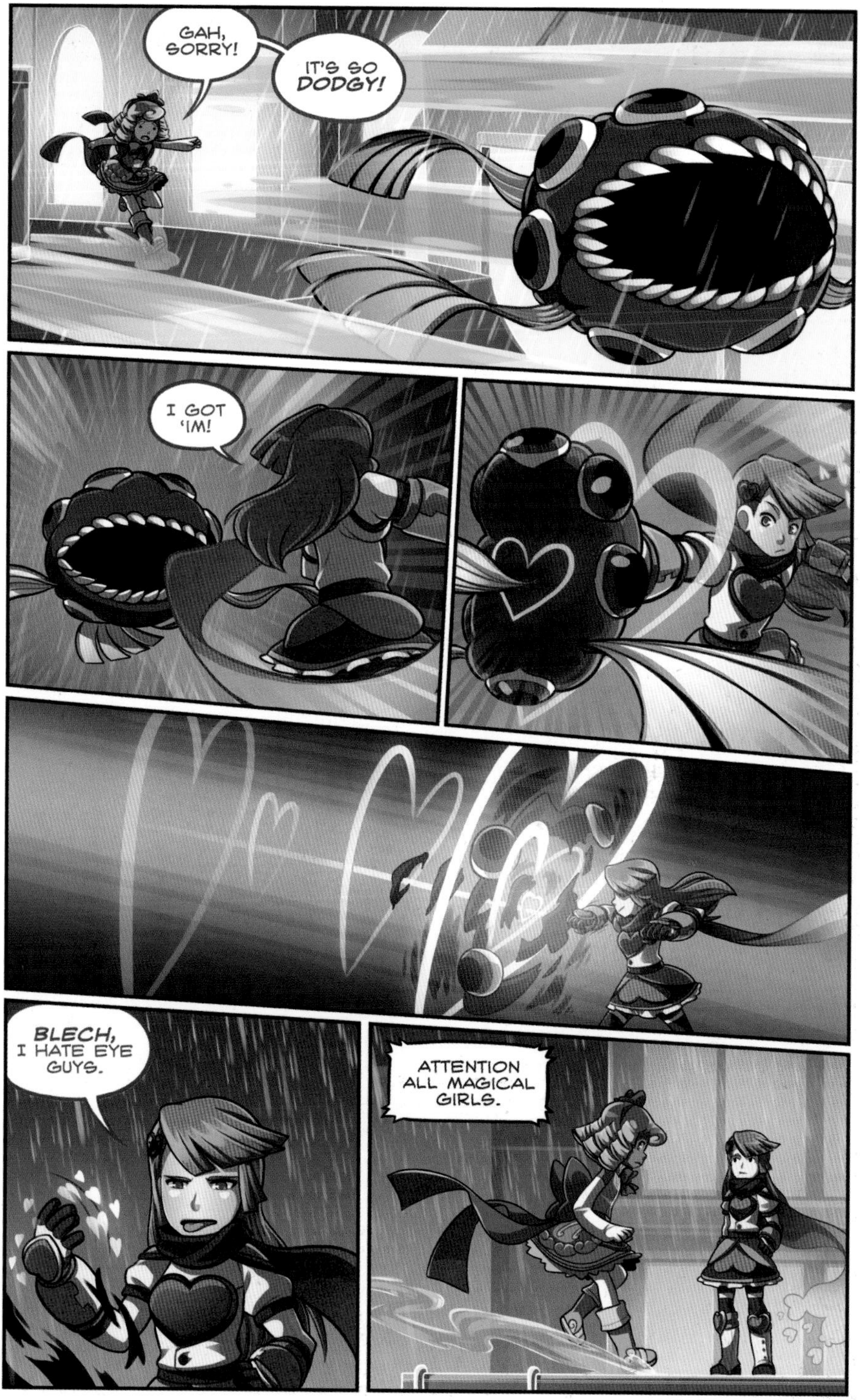
GAH, SORRY!
IT'S SO DODGY!
I GOT 'IM!
BLECH, I HATE EYE GUYS.
ATTENTION ALL MAGICAL GIRLS.

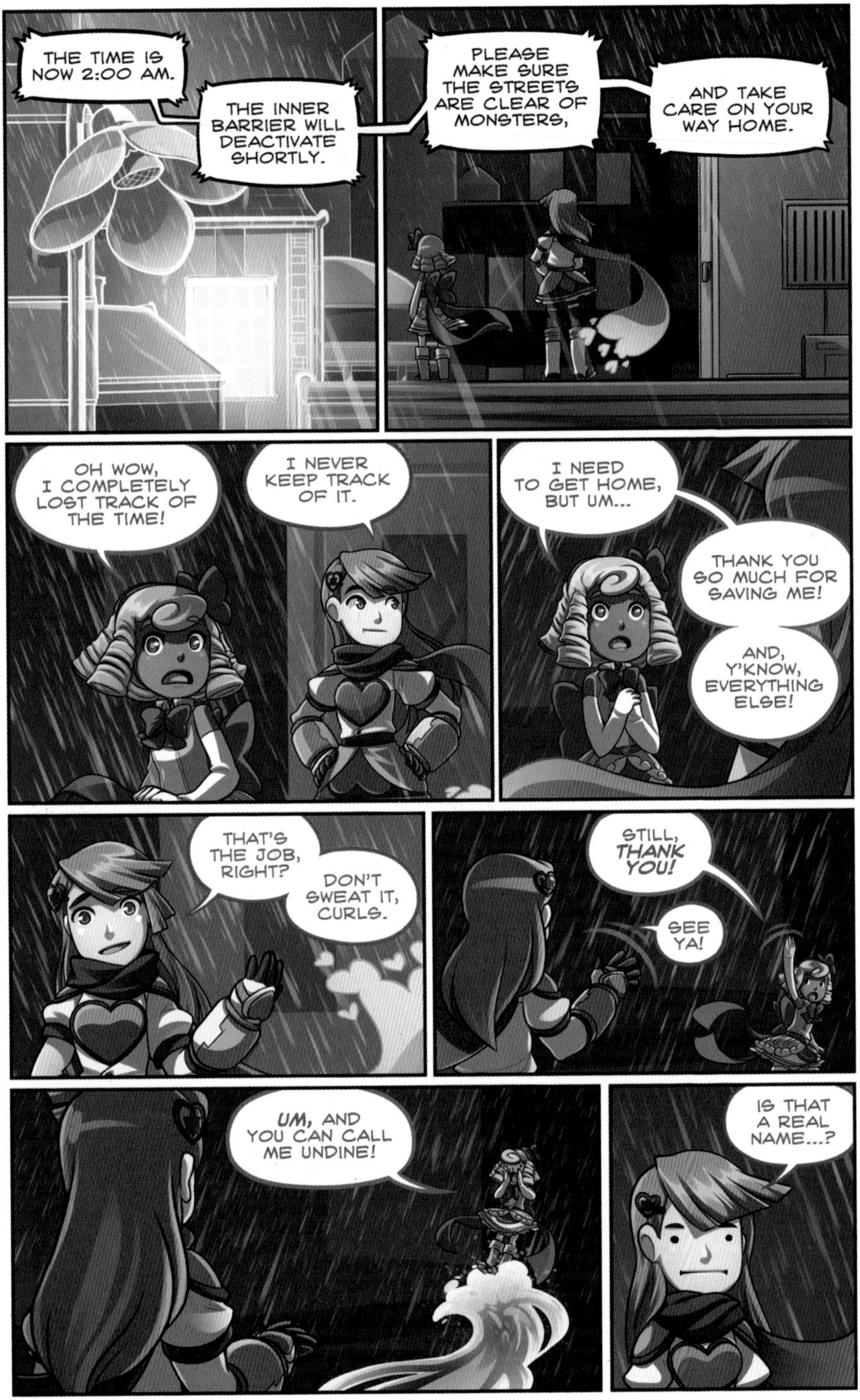
THE TIME IS NOW 2:00 AM.
THE INNER BARRIER WILL DEACTIVATE SHORTLY.
PLEASE MAKE SURE THE STREETS ARE CLEAR OF MONSTERS,
AND TAKE CARE ON YOUR WAY HOME.
OH WOW, I COMPLETELY LOST TRACK OF THE TIME!
I NEVER KEEP TRACK OF IT.
I NEED TO GET HOME, BUT UM...
THANK YOU SO MUCH FOR SAVING ME!
AND, Y'KNOW, EVERYTHING ELSE!
THAT'S THE JOB, RIGHT?
DON'T SWEAT IT, CURLS.
STILL, *THANK YOU!*
SEE YA!
UM, AND YOU CAN CALL ME UNDINE!
IS THAT A REAL NAME...?

CHAPTER 4
TREADING WATER

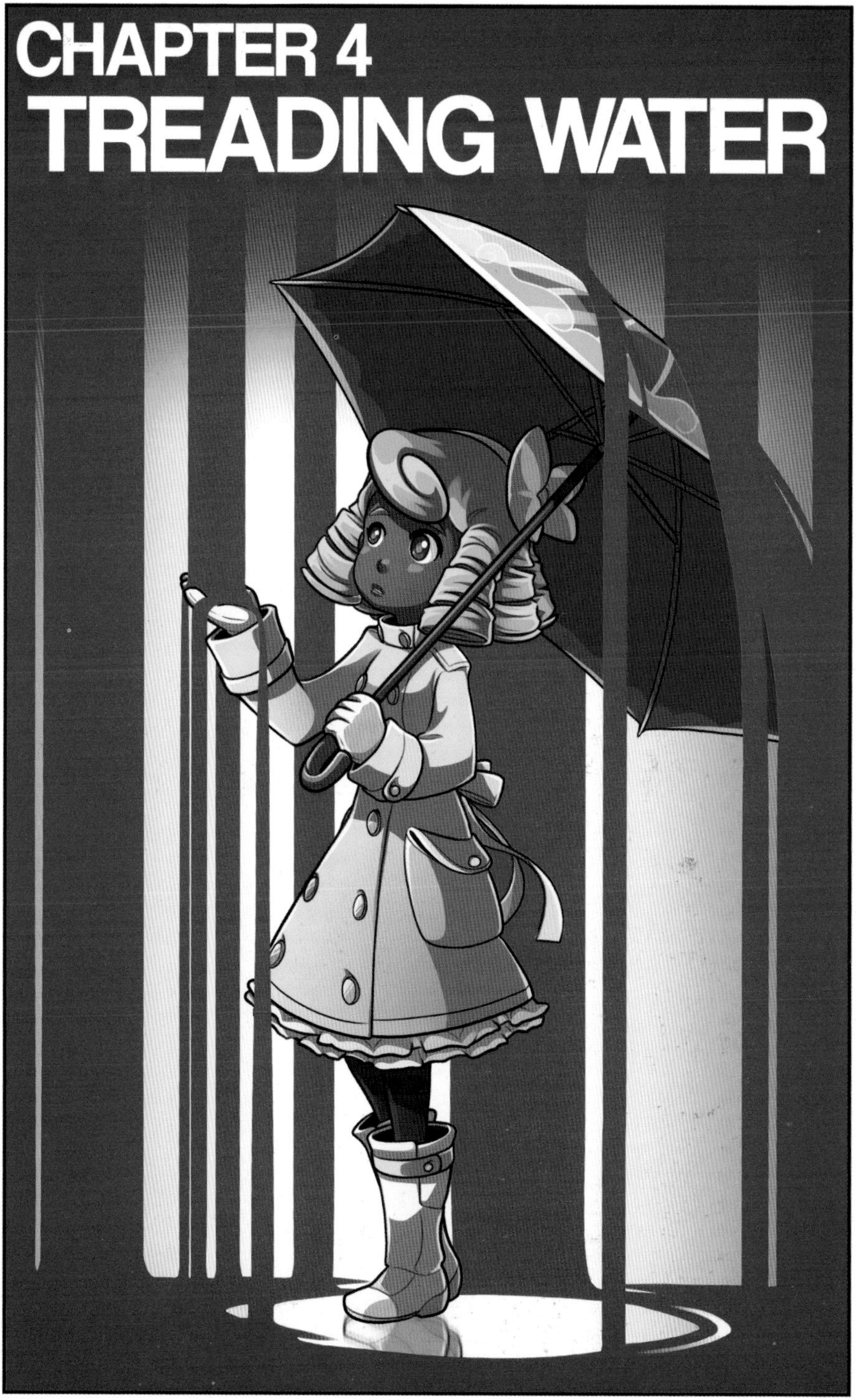

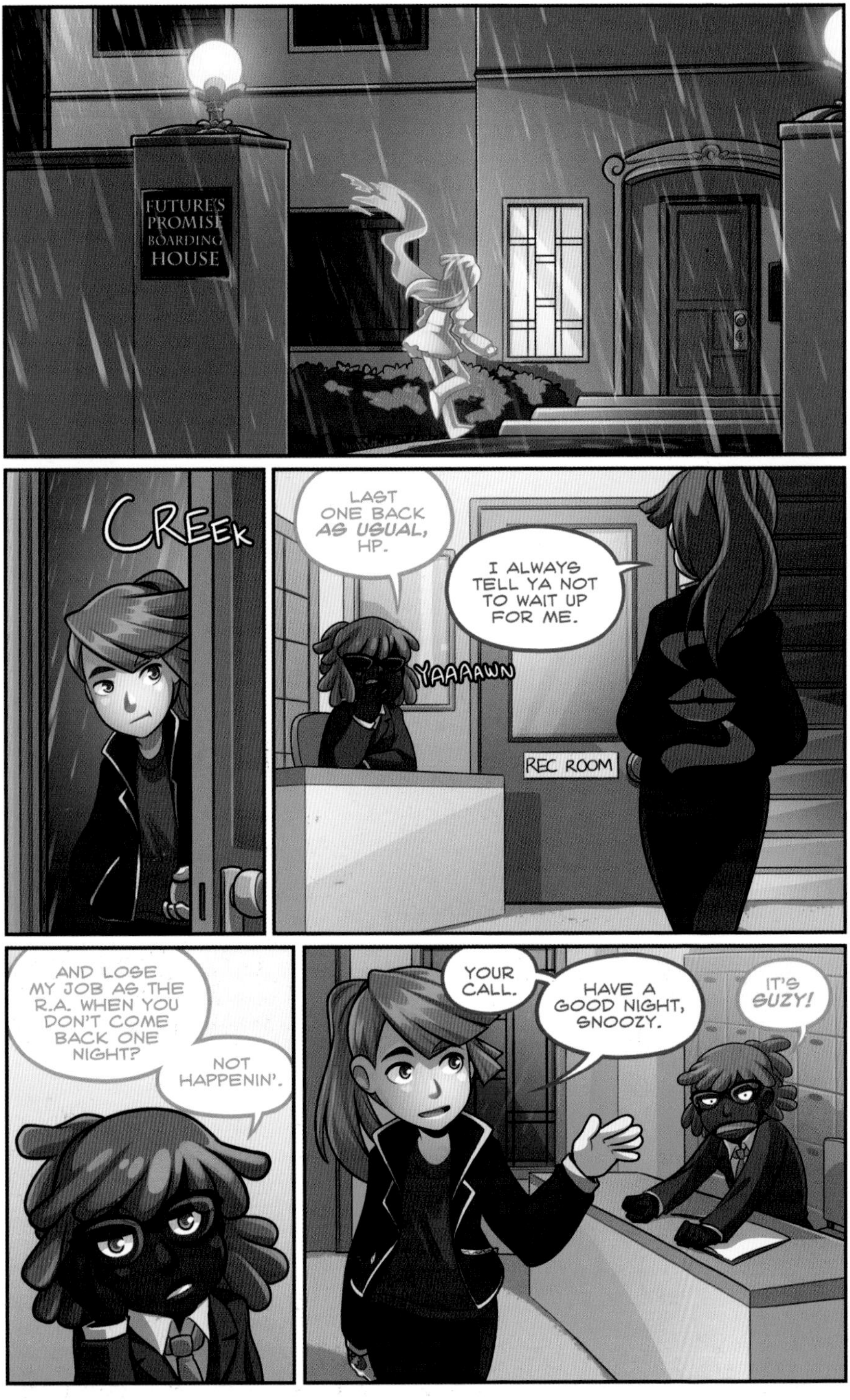
FUTURE'S PROMISE BOARDING HOUSE
CREEK
LAST ONE BACK AS USUAL, HP.
YAAAAWN
I ALWAYS TELL YA NOT TO WAIT UP FOR ME.
REC ROOM
AND LOSE MY JOB AS THE R.A. WHEN YOU DON'T COME BACK ONE NIGHT?
NOT HAPPENIN'.
YOUR CALL.
HAVE A GOOD NIGHT, SNOOZY.
IT'S SUZY!

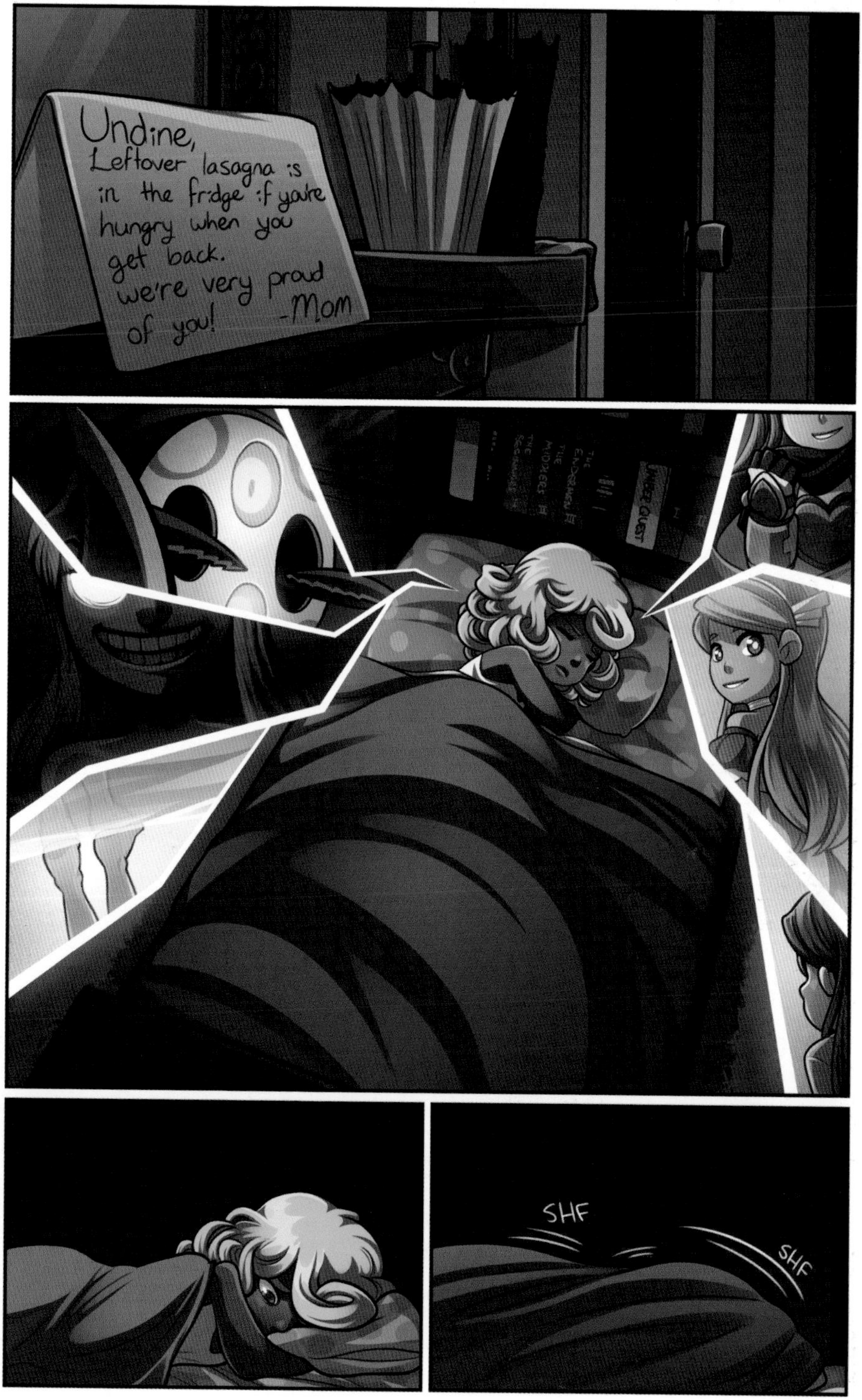
Undine,
Leftover lasagna is in the fridge if you're hungry when you get back.
We're very proud of you! -Mom
SHF
SHF

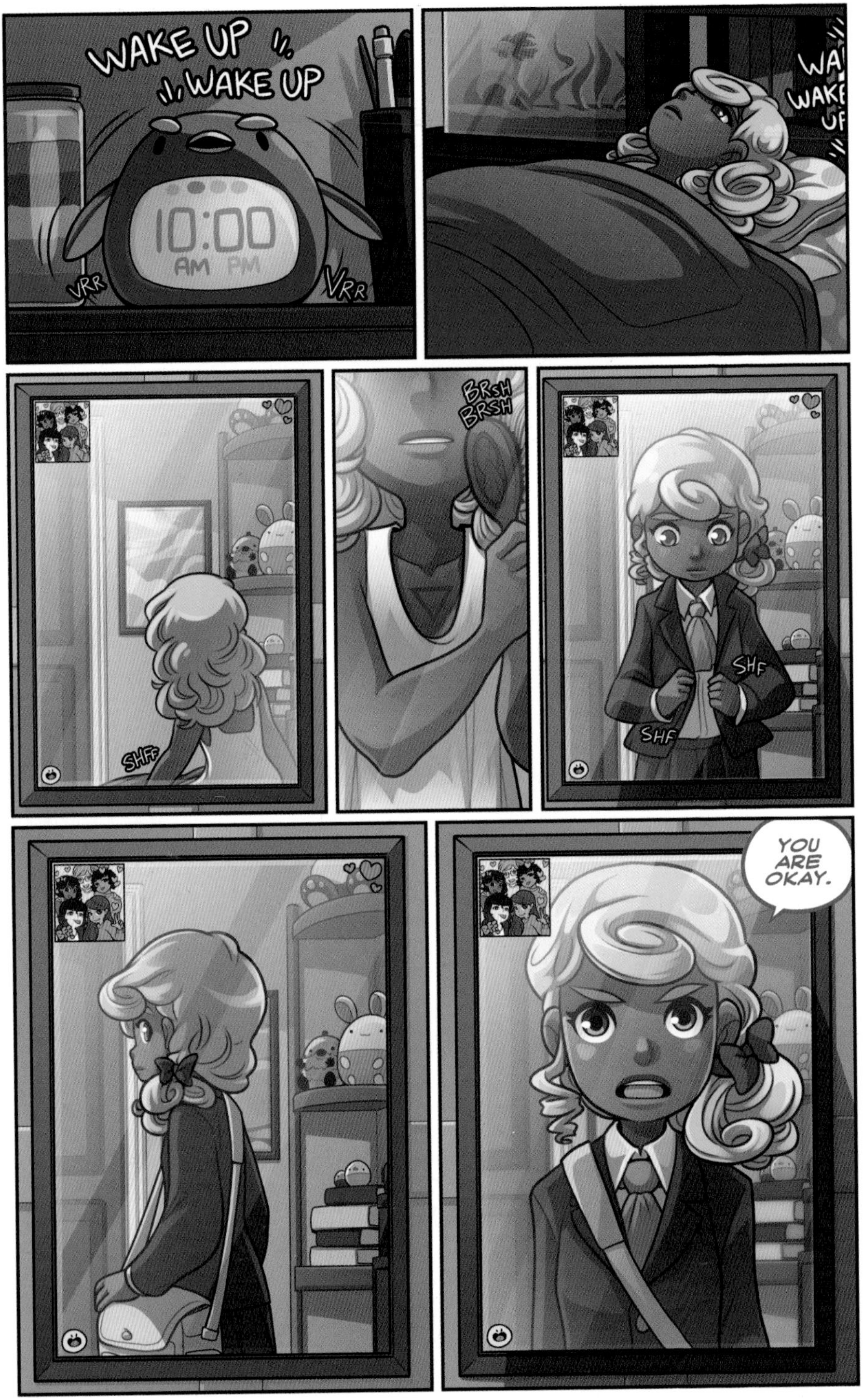
WAKE UP
WAKE UP
10:00
AM PM
VRR
VRR
WAKE UP
BRSH BRSH
SHFF
SHF
SHF
YOU ARE OKAY.

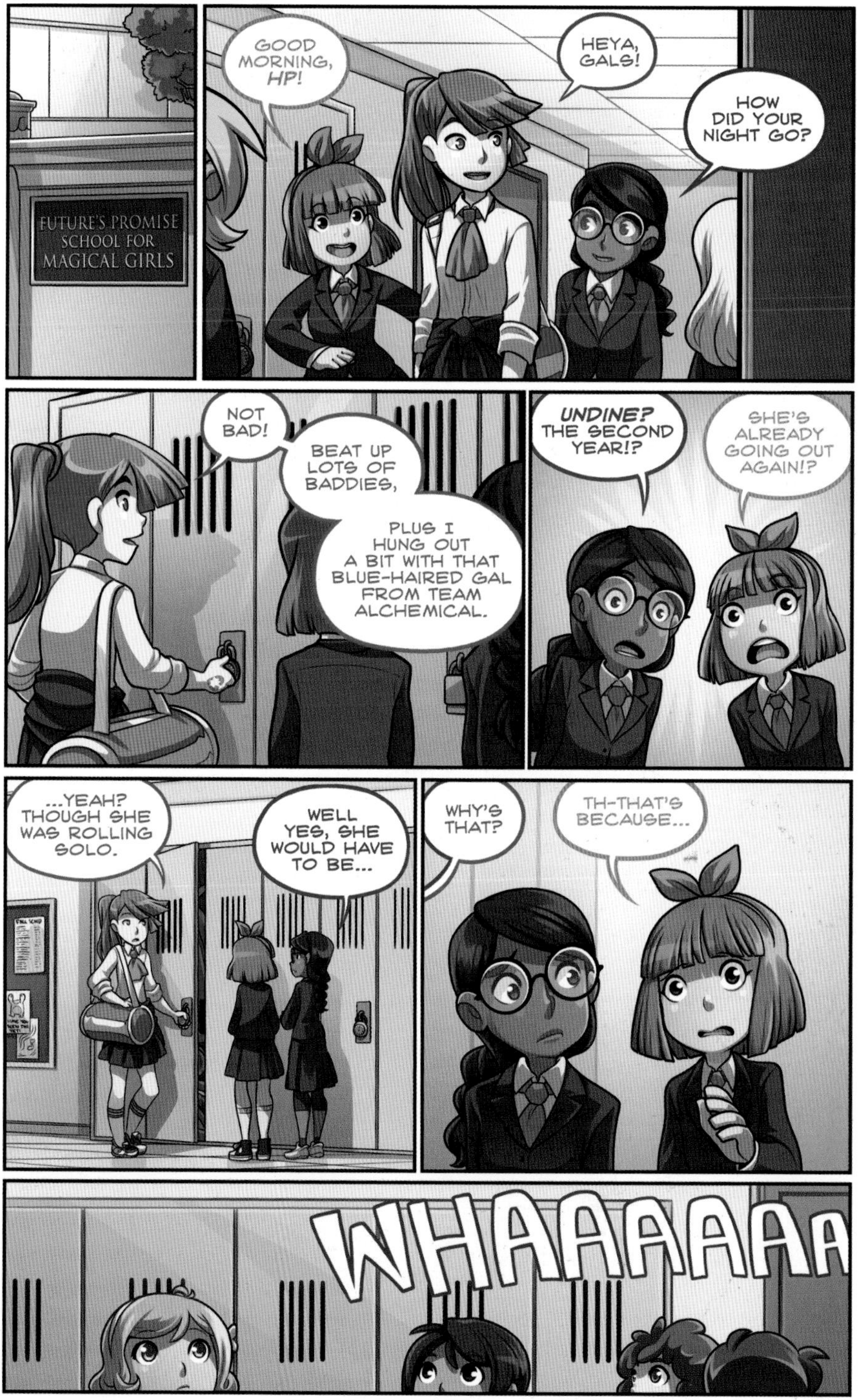
FUTURE'S PROMISE SCHOOL FOR MAGICAL GIRLS
GOOD MORNING, HP!
HEYA, GALS!
HOW DID YOUR NIGHT GO?
NOT BAD!
BEAT UP LOTS OF BADDIES,
PLUS I HUNG OUT A BIT WITH THAT BLUE-HAIRED GAL FROM TEAM ALCHEMICAL.
UNDINE? THE SECOND YEAR!?
SHE'S ALREADY GOING OUT AGAIN!?
...YEAH? THOUGH SHE WAS ROLLING SOLO.
WELL YES, SHE WOULD HAVE TO BE...
WHY'S THAT?
TH-THAT'S BECAUSE...
WHAAAAAAA

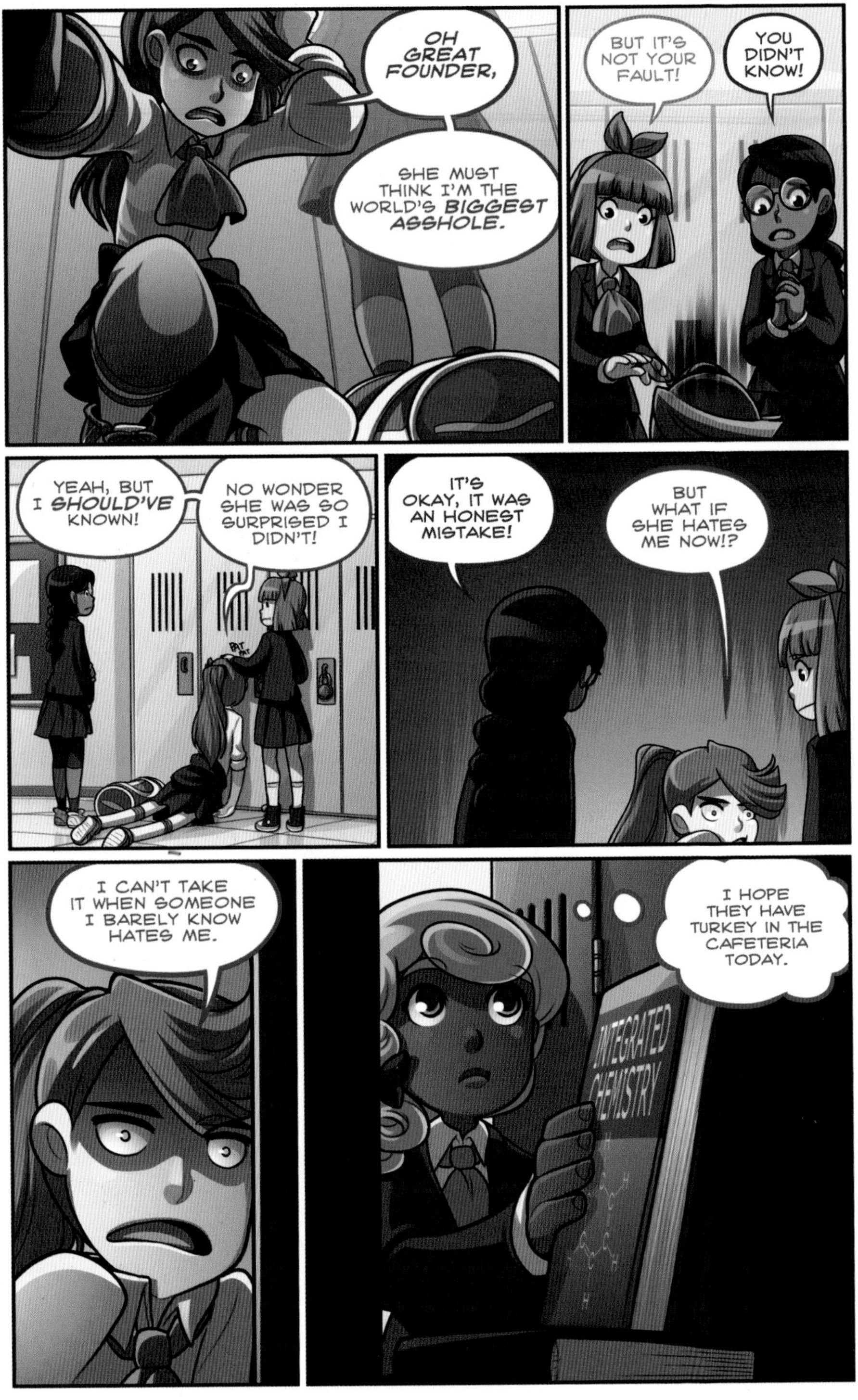
OH GREAT FOUNDER,
SHE MUST THINK I'M THE WORLD'S BIGGEST ASSHOLE.
BUT IT'S NOT YOUR FAULT!
YOU DIDN'T KNOW!
YEAH, BUT I SHOULD'VE KNOWN!
NO WONDER SHE WAS SO SURPRISED I DIDN'T!
PAT PAT
IT'S OKAY, IT WAS AN HONEST MISTAKE!
BUT WHAT IF SHE HATES ME NOW!?
I CAN'T TAKE IT WHEN SOMEONE I BARELY KNOW HATES ME.
I HOPE THEY HAVE TURKEY IN THE CAFETERIA TODAY.
INTEGRATED CHEMISTRY

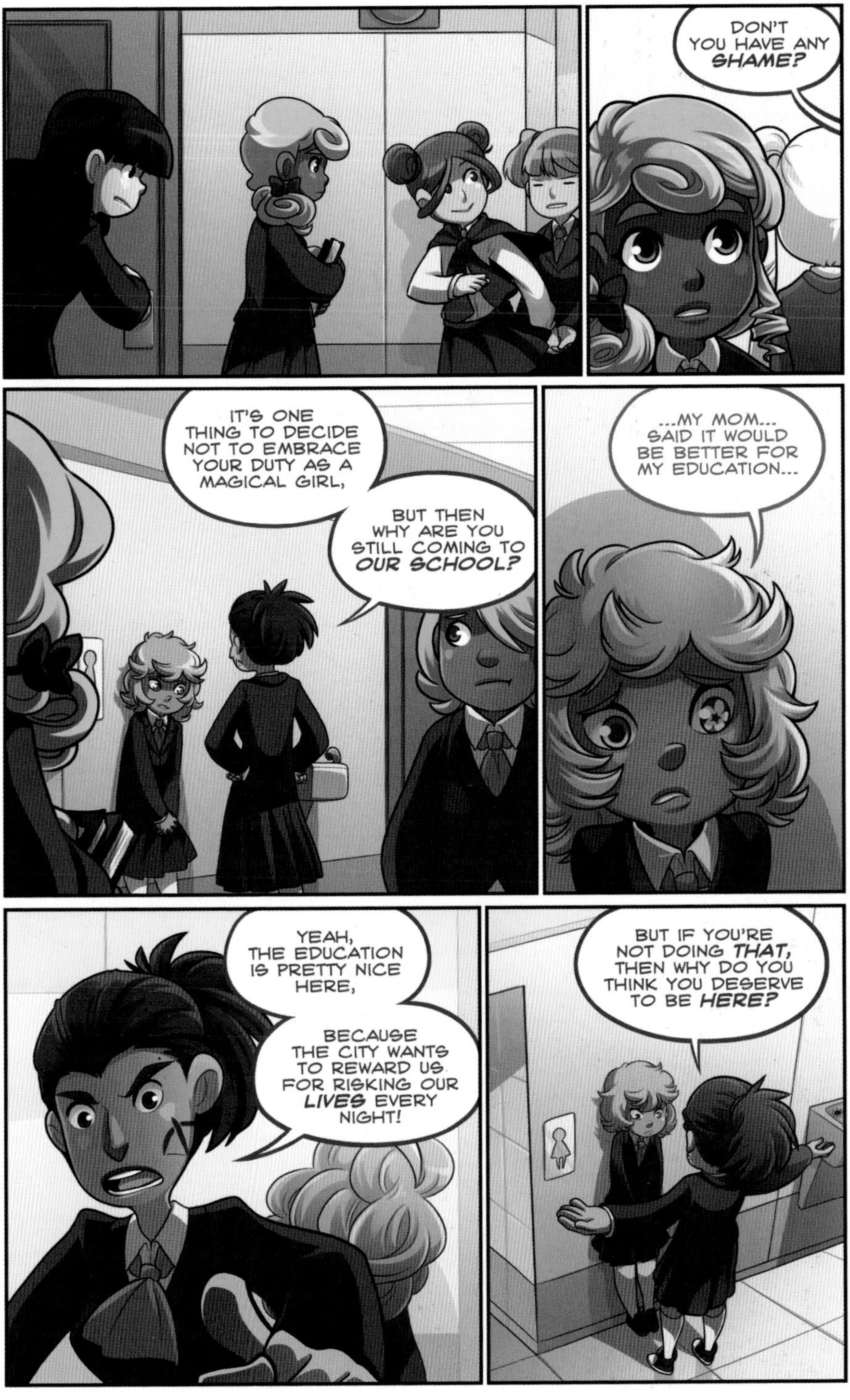
DON'T YOU HAVE ANY ***SHAME?***
IT'S ONE THING TO DECIDE NOT TO EMBRACE YOUR DUTY AS A MAGICAL GIRL,
BUT THEN WHY ARE YOU STILL COMING TO ***OUR SCHOOL?***
...MY MOM... SAID IT WOULD BE BETTER FOR MY EDUCATION...
YEAH, THE EDUCATION IS PRETTY NICE HERE,
BECAUSE THE CITY WANTS TO REWARD US FOR RISKING OUR ***LIVES*** EVERY NIGHT!
BUT IF YOU'RE NOT DOING ***THAT,*** THEN WHY DO YOU THINK YOU DESERVE TO BE ***HERE?***

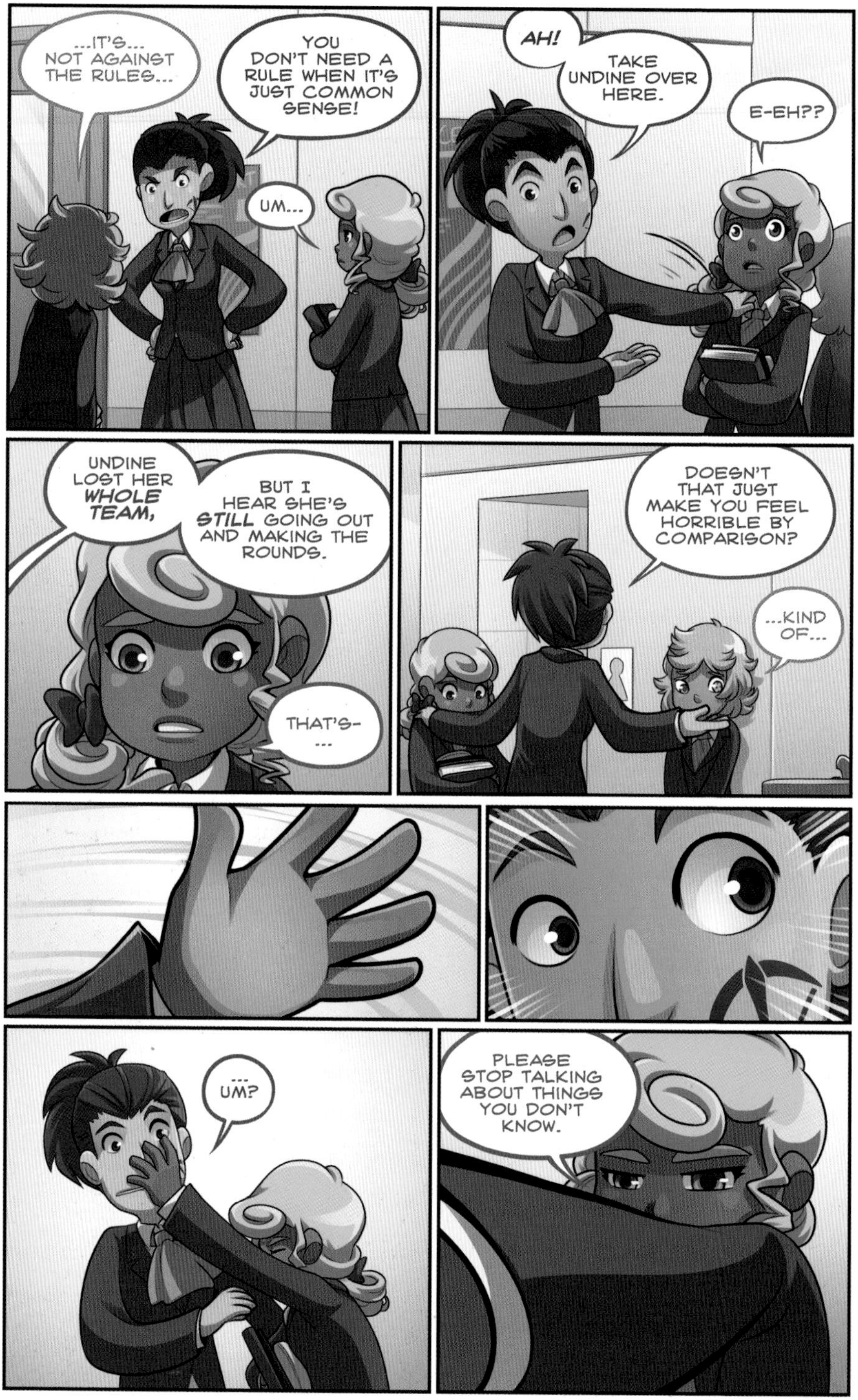
...IT'S... NOT AGAINST THE RULES...
YOU DON'T NEED A RULE WHEN IT'S JUST COMMON SENSE!
UM...
AH!
TAKE UNDINE OVER HERE.
E-EH??
UNDINE LOST HER *WHOLE TEAM,*
BUT I HEAR SHE'S **STILL** GOING OUT AND MAKING THE ROUNDS.
THAT'S- ...
DOESN'T THAT JUST MAKE YOU FEEL HORRIBLE BY COMPARISON?
...KIND OF...
... UM?
PLEASE STOP TALKING ABOUT THINGS YOU DON'T KNOW.

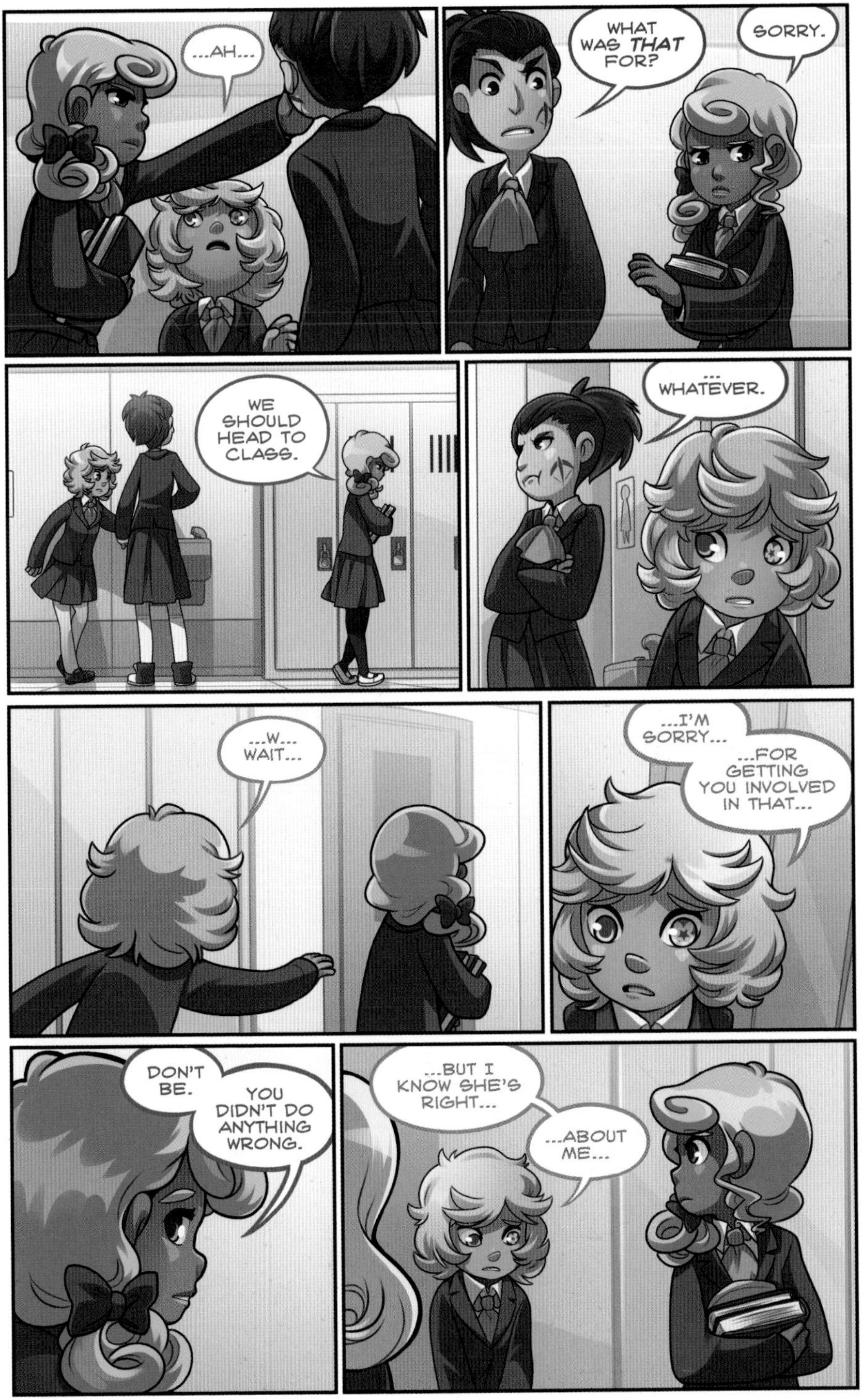
...AH...
WHAT WAS THAT FOR?
SORRY.
WE SHOULD HEAD TO CLASS.
... WHATEVER.
...W... WAIT...
...I'M SORRY...
...FOR GETTING YOU INVOLVED IN THAT...
DON'T BE.
YOU DIDN'T DO ANYTHING WRONG.
...BUT I KNOW SHE'S RIGHT...
...ABOUT ME...

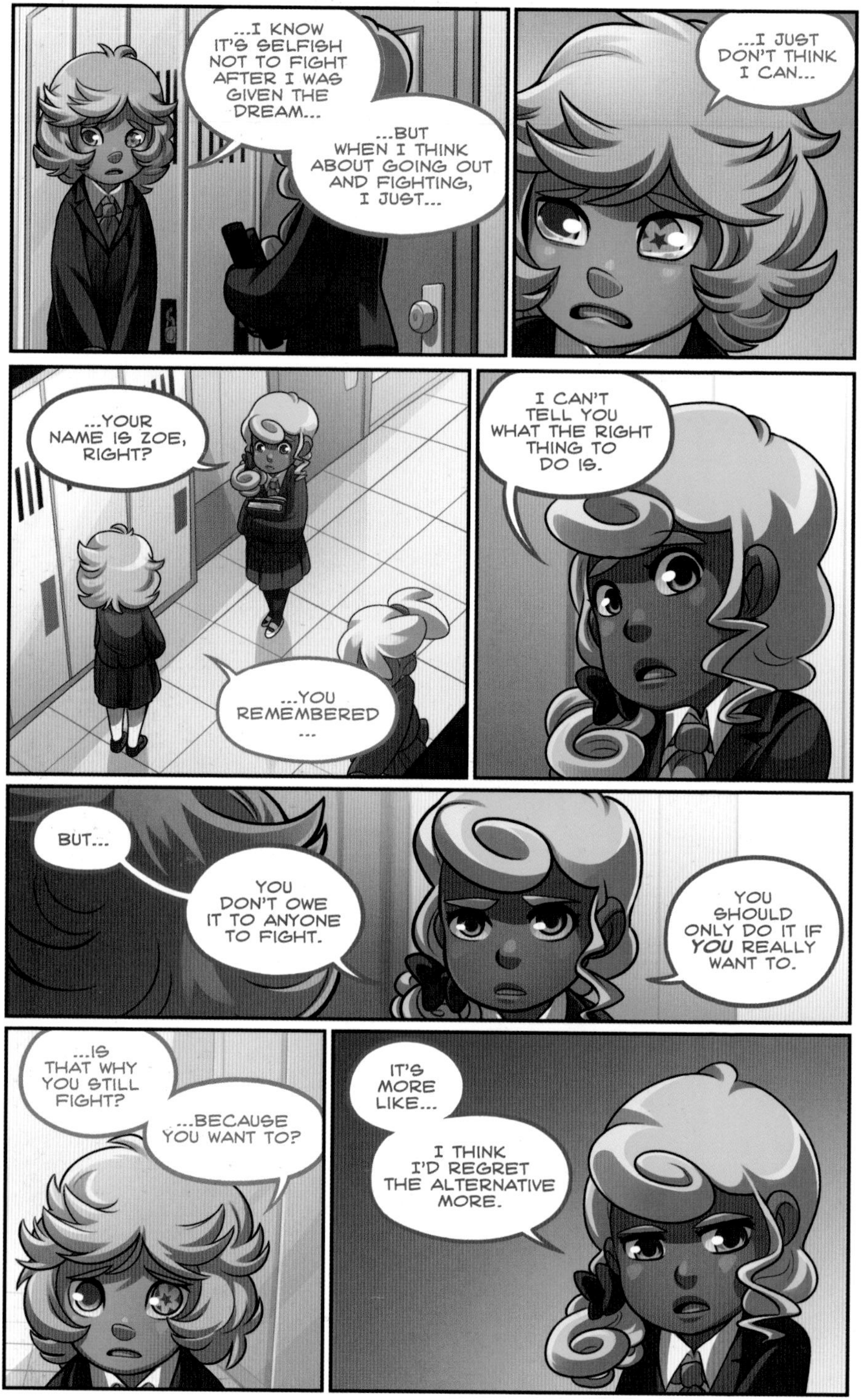

...I KNOW IT'S SELFISH NOT TO FIGHT AFTER I WAS GIVEN THE DREAM...
...BUT WHEN I THINK ABOUT GOING OUT AND FIGHTING, I JUST...
...I JUST DON'T THINK I CAN...
...YOUR NAME IS ZOE, RIGHT?
...YOU REMEMBERED...
I CAN'T TELL YOU WHAT THE RIGHT THING TO DO IS.
BUT...
YOU DON'T OWE IT TO ANYONE TO FIGHT.
YOU SHOULD ONLY DO IT IF *YOU* REALLY WANT TO.
...IS THAT WHY YOU STILL FIGHT?
...BECAUSE YOU WANT TO?
IT'S MORE LIKE...
I THINK I'D REGRET THE ALTERNATIVE MORE.

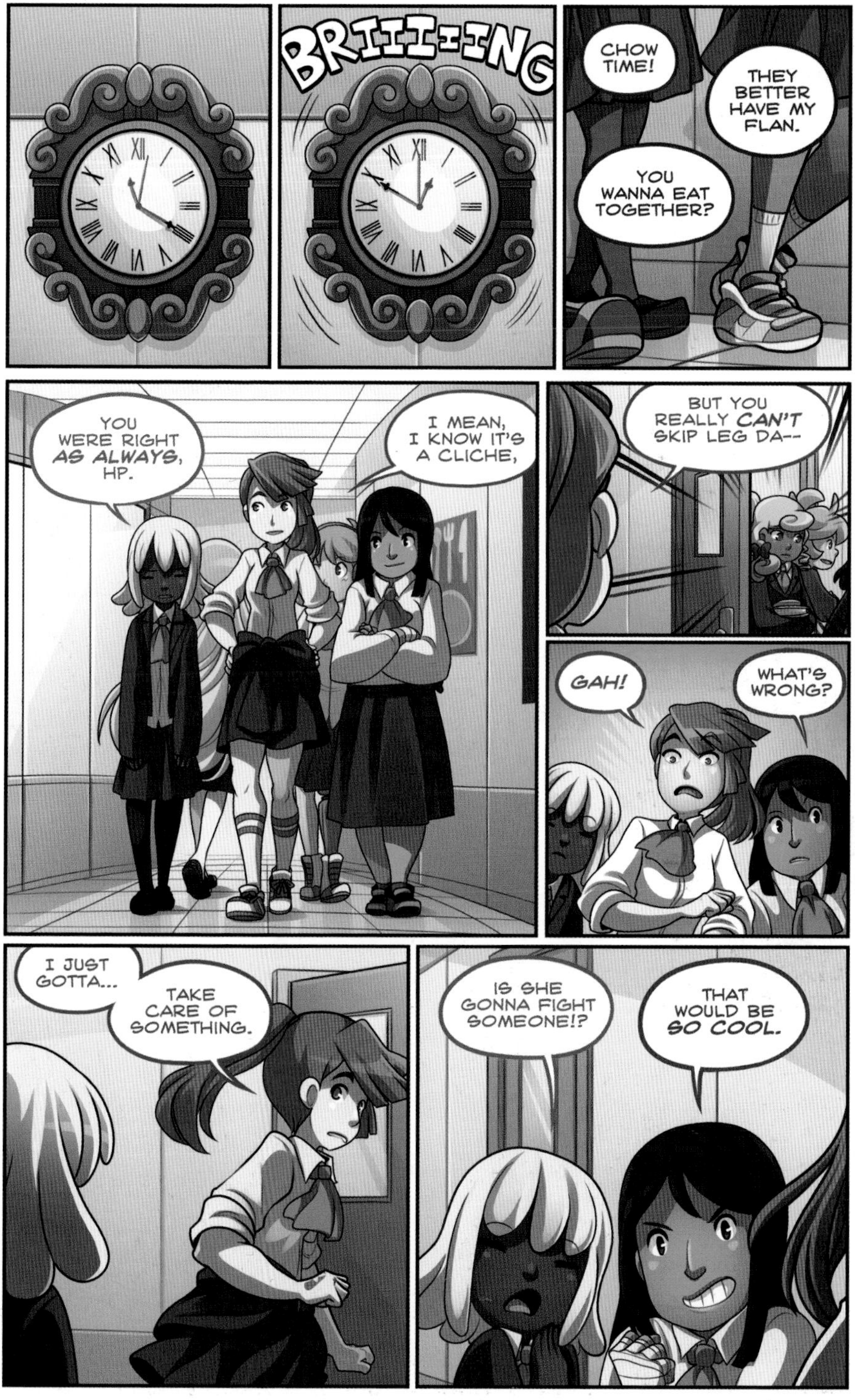
BRIIIIING
CHOW TIME!
THEY BETTER HAVE MY FLAN.
YOU WANNA EAT TOGETHER?
YOU WERE RIGHT AS ALWAYS, HP.
I MEAN, I KNOW IT'S A CLICHE,
BUT YOU REALLY CAN'T SKIP LEG DA--
GAH!
WHAT'S WRONG?
I JUST GOTTA...
TAKE CARE OF SOMETHING.
IS SHE GONNA FIGHT SOMEONE!?
THAT WOULD BE SO COOL.

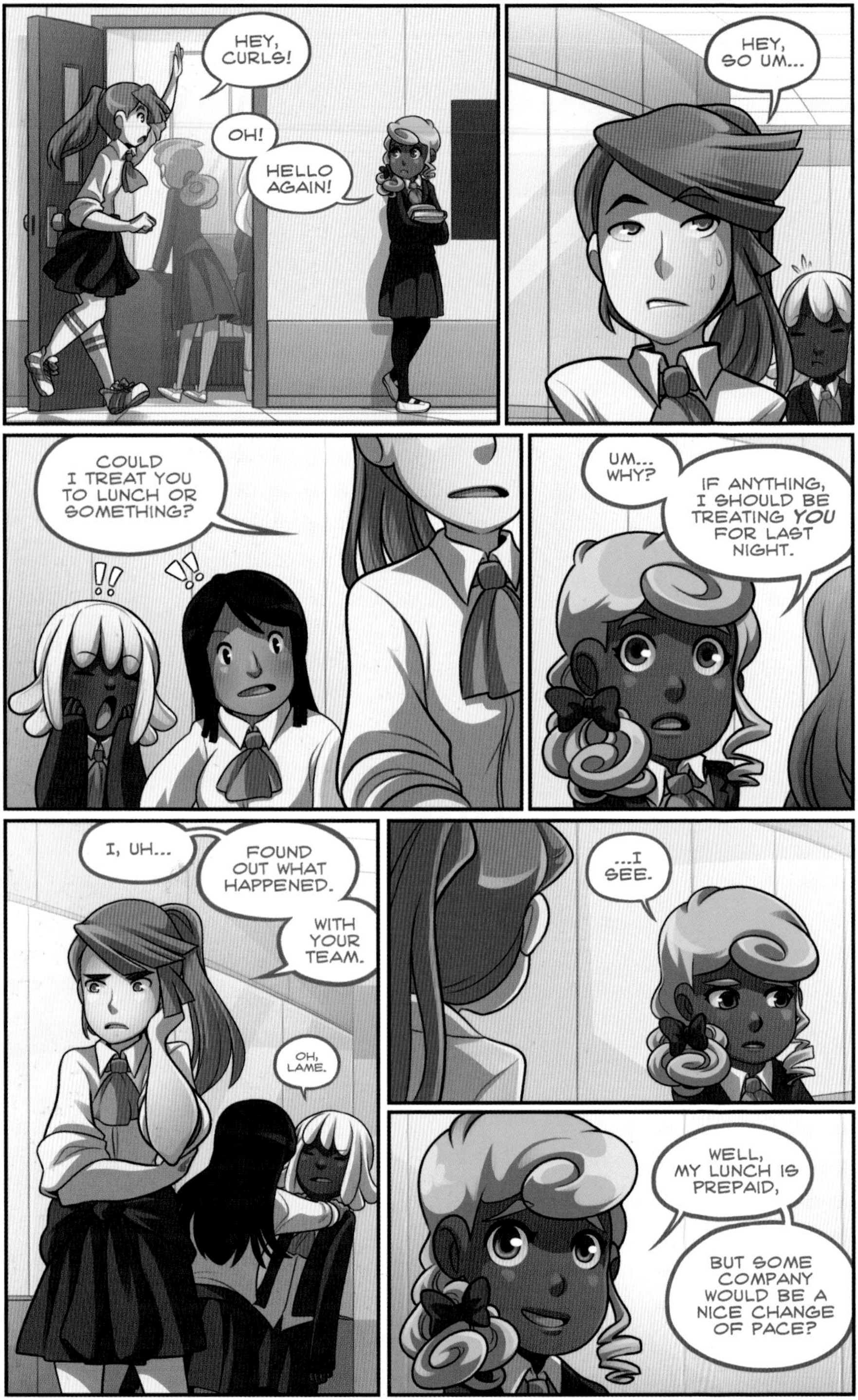
HEY, CURLS!
OH!
HELLO AGAIN!
HEY, SO UM...
COULD I TREAT YOU TO LUNCH OR SOMETHING?
!!
!!
UM... WHY?
IF ANYTHING, I SHOULD BE TREATING *YOU* FOR LAST NIGHT.
I, UH...
FOUND OUT WHAT HAPPENED.
WITH YOUR TEAM.
OH, LAME.
...I SEE.
WELL, MY LUNCH IS PREPAID,
BUT SOME COMPANY WOULD BE A NICE CHANGE OF PACE?

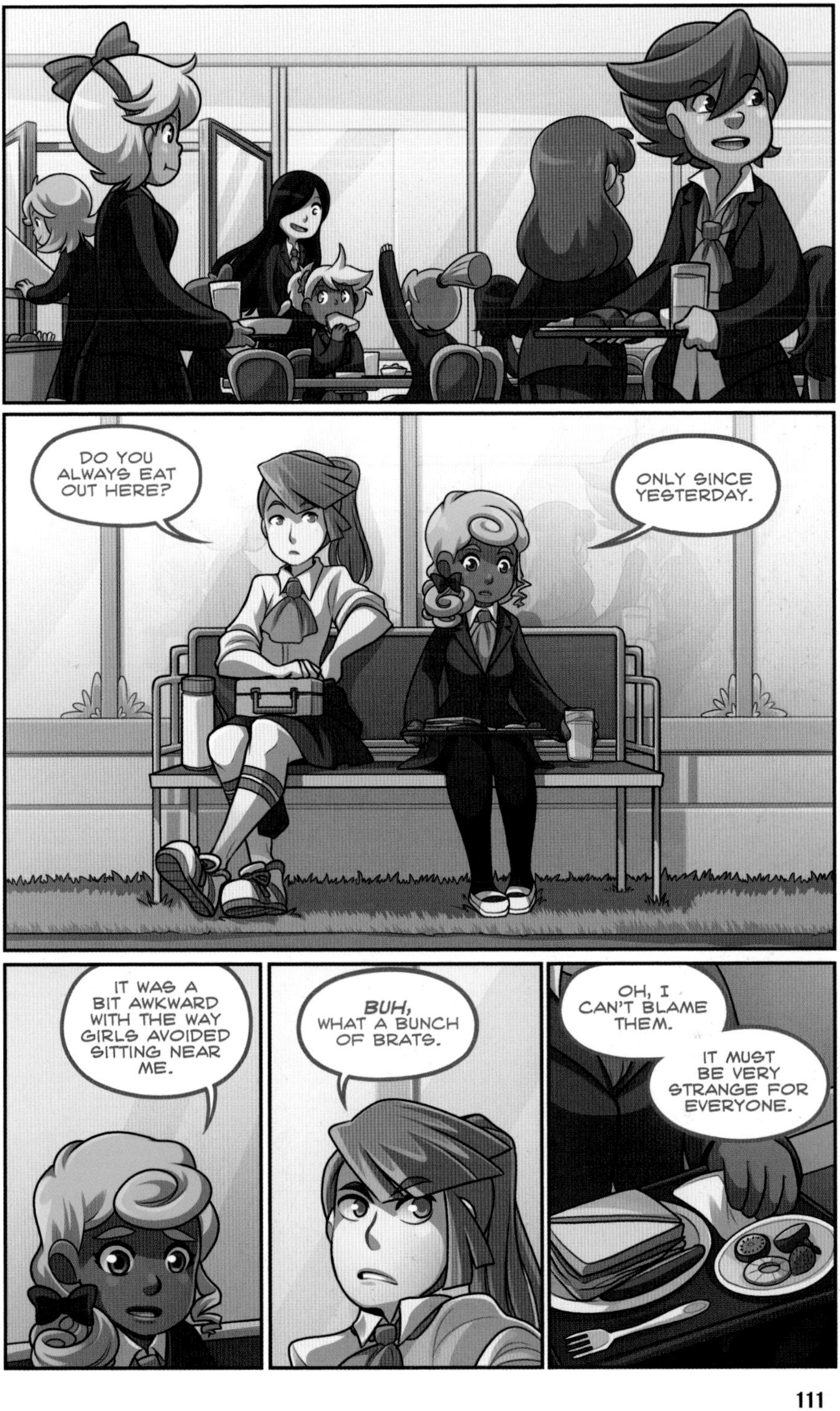
DO YOU ALWAYS EAT OUT HERE?
ONLY SINCE YESTERDAY.
IT WAS A BIT AWKWARD WITH THE WAY GIRLS AVOIDED SITTING NEAR ME.
BUH, WHAT A BUNCH OF BRATS.
OH, I CAN'T BLAME THEM.
IT MUST BE VERY STRANGE FOR EVERYONE.

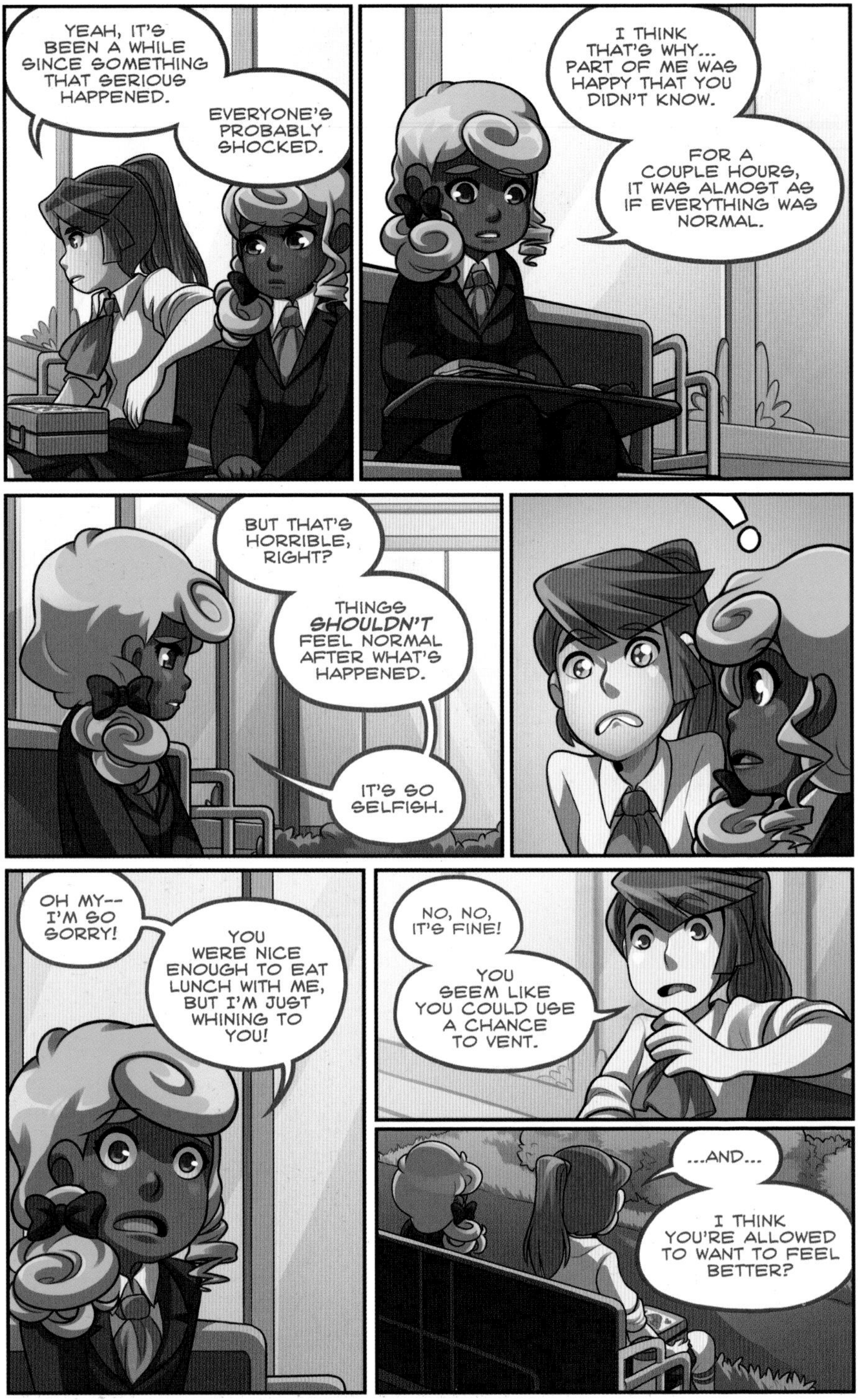
YEAH, IT'S BEEN A WHILE SINCE SOMETHING THAT SERIOUS HAPPENED.
EVERYONE'S PROBABLY SHOCKED.
I THINK THAT'S WHY... PART OF ME WAS HAPPY THAT YOU DIDN'T KNOW.
FOR A COUPLE HOURS, IT WAS ALMOST AS IF EVERYTHING WAS NORMAL.
BUT THAT'S HORRIBLE, RIGHT?
THINGS *SHOULDN'T* FEEL NORMAL AFTER WHAT'S HAPPENED.
IT'S SO SELFISH.
!
OH MY-- I'M SO SORRY!
YOU WERE NICE ENOUGH TO EAT LUNCH WITH ME, BUT I'M JUST WHINING TO YOU!
NO, NO, IT'S FINE!
YOU SEEM LIKE YOU COULD USE A CHANCE TO VENT.
...AND...
I THINK YOU'RE ALLOWED TO WANT TO FEEL BETTER?

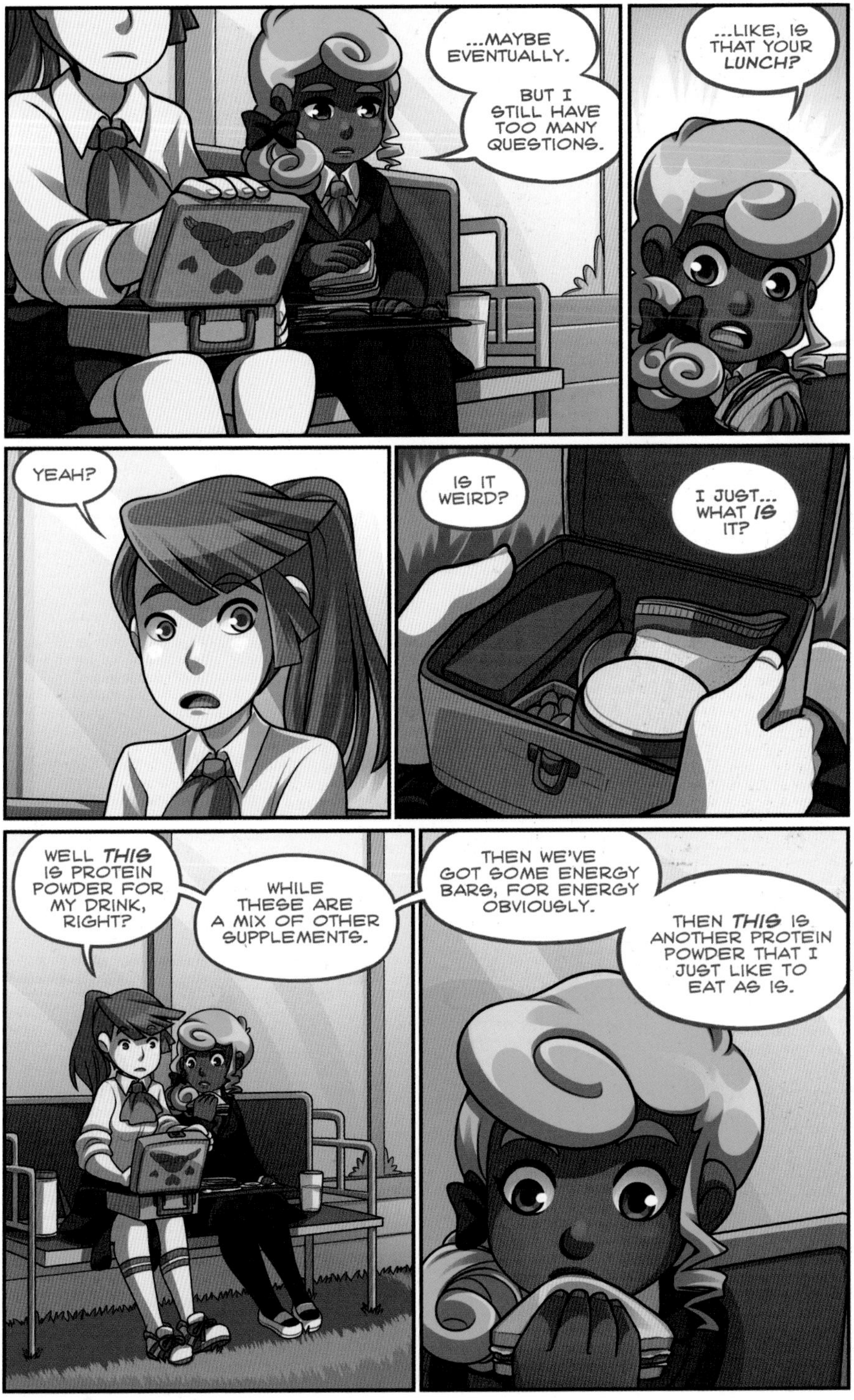
...MAYBE EVENTUALLY.
BUT I STILL HAVE TOO MANY QUESTIONS.
...LIKE, IS THAT YOUR *LUNCH?*
YEAH?
IS IT WEIRD?
I JUST... WHAT *IS* IT?
WELL *THIS* IS PROTEIN POWDER FOR MY DRINK, RIGHT?
WHILE THESE ARE A MIX OF OTHER SUPPLEMENTS.
THEN WE'VE GOT SOME ENERGY BARS, FOR ENERGY OBVIOUSLY.
THEN *THIS* IS ANOTHER PROTEIN POWDER THAT I JUST LIKE TO EAT AS IS.

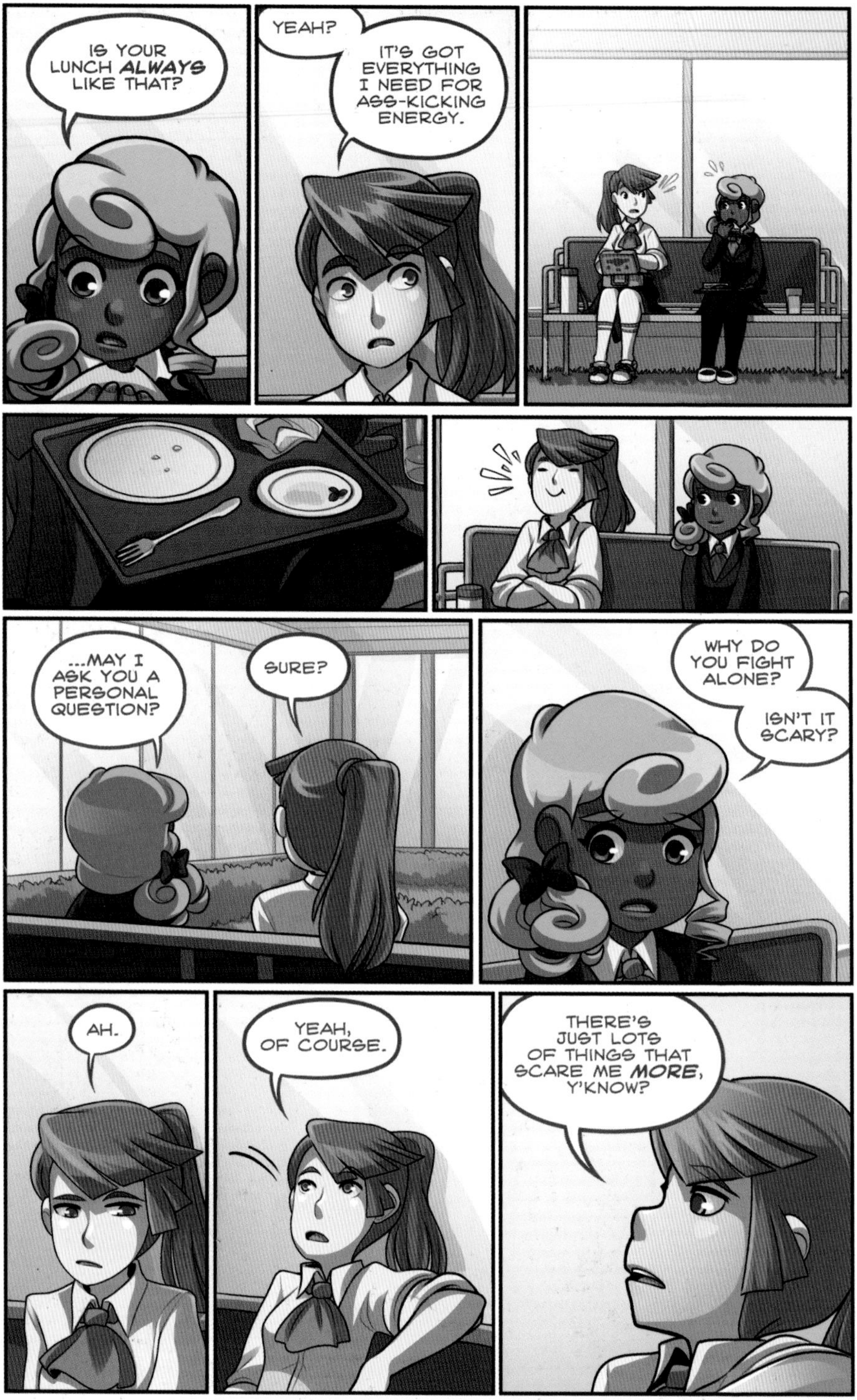

IS YOUR LUNCH **ALWAYS** LIKE THAT?
YEAH?
IT'S GOT EVERYTHING I NEED FOR ASS-KICKING ENERGY.
...MAY I ASK YOU A PERSONAL QUESTION?
SURE?
WHY DO YOU FIGHT ALONE?
ISN'T IT SCARY?
AH.
YEAH, OF COURSE.
THERE'S JUST LOTS OF THINGS THAT SCARE ME **MORE**, Y'KNOW?

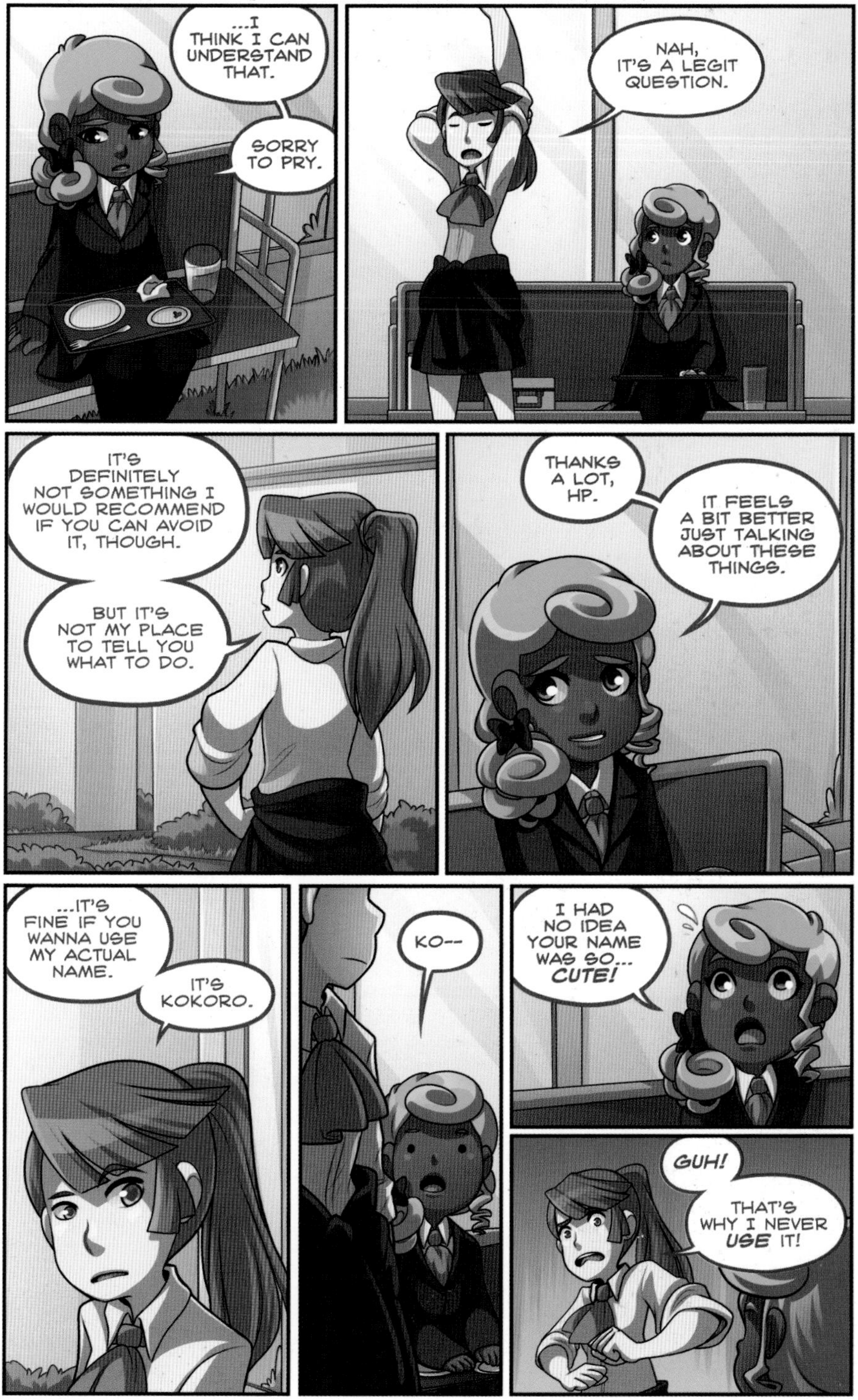
...I THINK I CAN UNDERSTAND THAT.
SORRY TO PRY.
NAH, IT'S A LEGIT QUESTION.
IT'S DEFINITELY NOT SOMETHING I WOULD RECOMMEND IF YOU CAN AVOID IT, THOUGH.
BUT IT'S NOT MY PLACE TO TELL YOU WHAT TO DO.
THANKS A LOT, HP.
IT FEELS A BIT BETTER JUST TALKING ABOUT THESE THINGS.
...IT'S FINE IF YOU WANNA USE MY ACTUAL NAME.
IT'S KOKORO.
KO--
I HAD NO IDEA YOUR NAME WAS SO... *CUTE!*
GUH!
THAT'S WHY I NEVER *USE* IT!

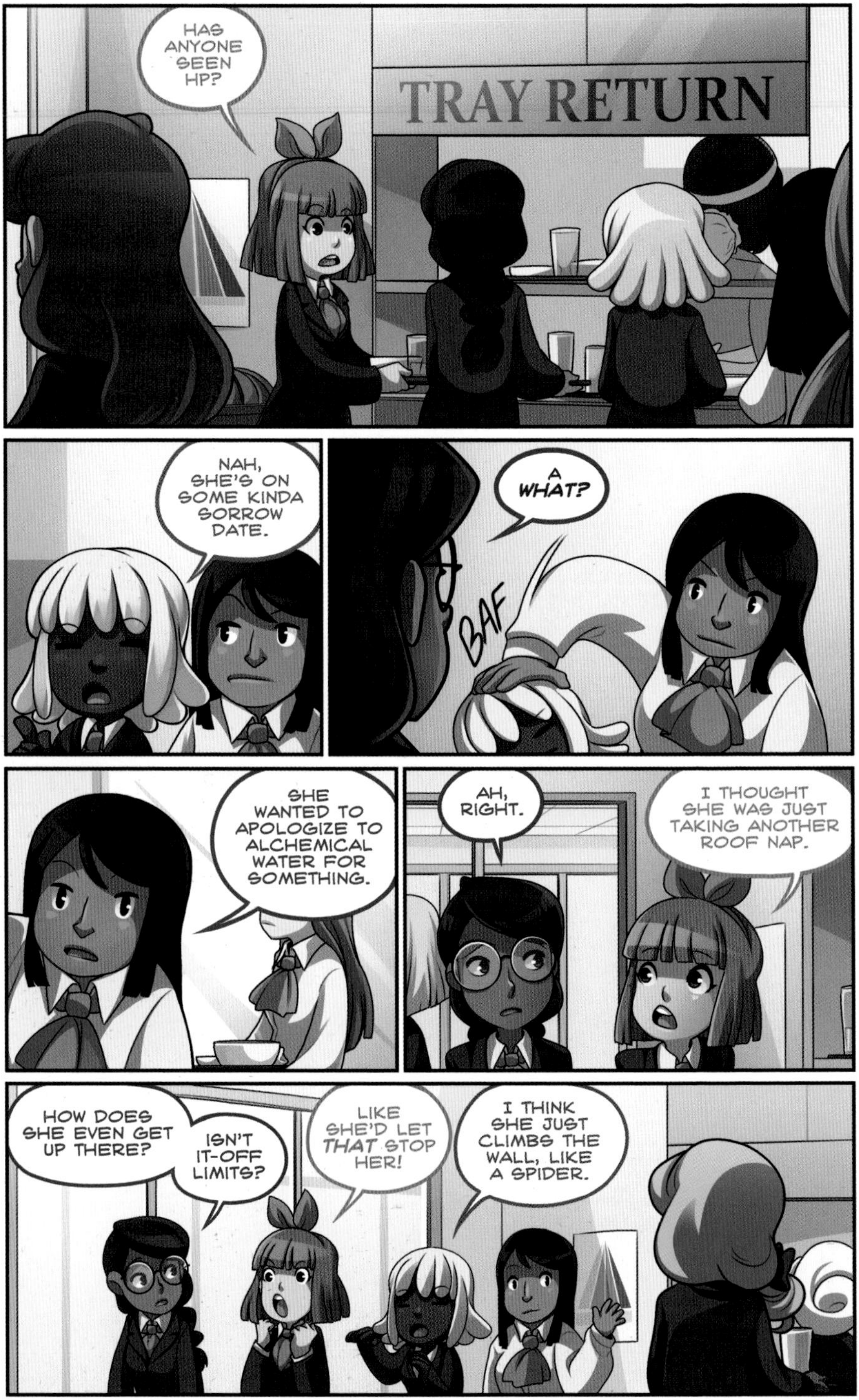
TRAY RETURN
HAS ANYONE SEEN HP?
NAH, SHE'S ON SOME KINDA SORROW DATE.
A *WHAT?*
BAF
SHE WANTED TO APOLOGIZE TO ALCHEMICAL WATER FOR SOMETHING.
AH, RIGHT.
I THOUGHT SHE WAS JUST TAKING ANOTHER ROOF NAP.
HOW DOES SHE EVEN GET UP THERE?
ISN'T IT-OFF LIMITS?
LIKE SHE'D LET *THAT* STOP HER!
I THINK SHE JUST CLIMBS THE WALL, LIKE A SPIDER.

BRIIING

OKAY, GIRLS, DON'T FORGET YOUR HOMEWORK.

AND BE SAFE OUT THERE TONIGHT.

HEY.

OH, TESS!

FUTURE'S PROMISE SCHOOL FOR GIRLS

FUTURE ...OOL FOR AL GIRL

DON'T LOOK SO SURPRISED.

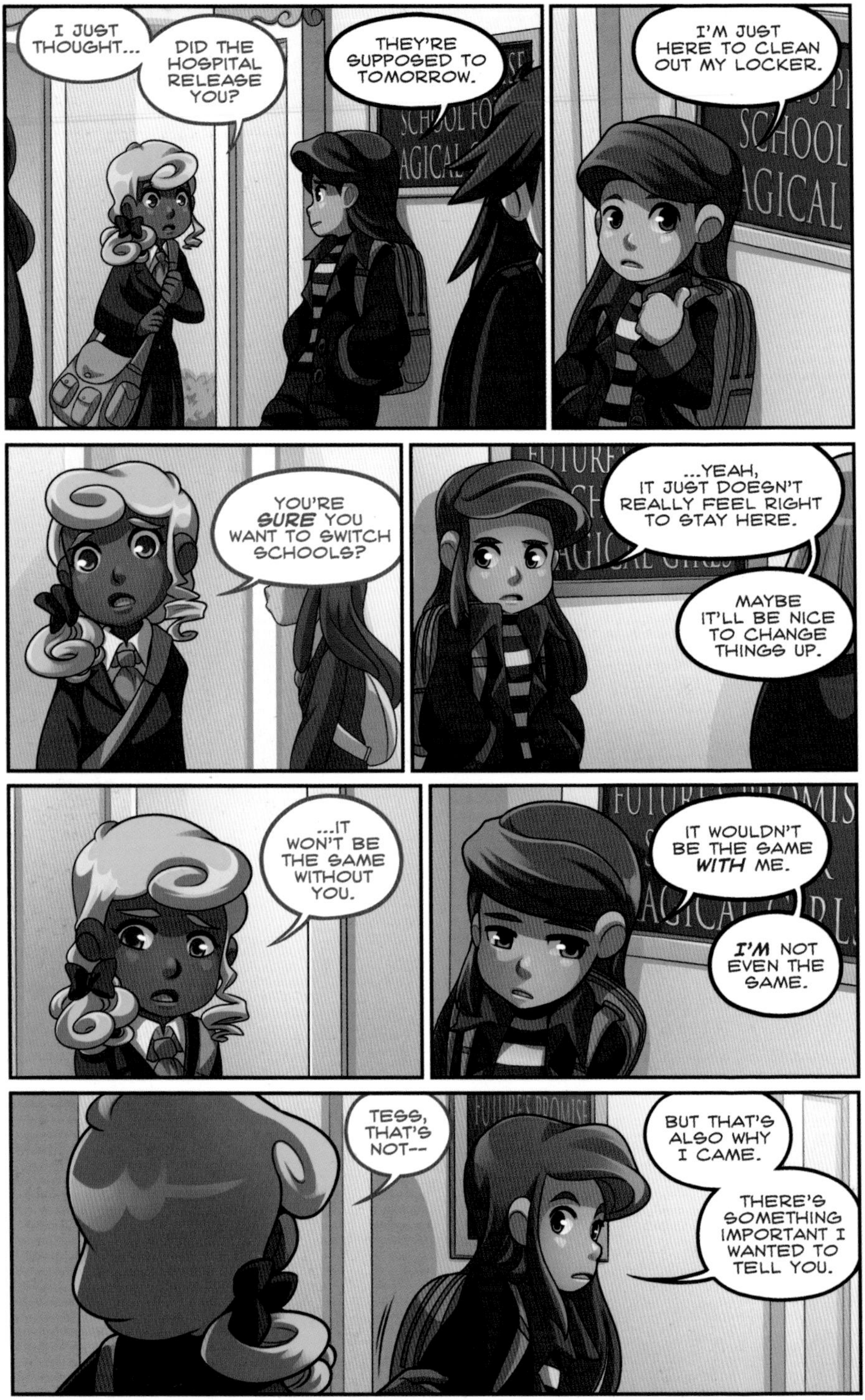
I JUST THOUGHT...
DID THE HOSPITAL RELEASE YOU?
THEY'RE SUPPOSED TO TOMORROW.
I'M JUST HERE TO CLEAN OUT MY LOCKER.
YOU'RE *SURE* YOU WANT TO SWITCH SCHOOLS?
...YEAH, IT JUST DOESN'T REALLY FEEL RIGHT TO STAY HERE.
MAYBE IT'LL BE NICE TO CHANGE THINGS UP.
...IT WON'T BE THE SAME WITHOUT YOU.
IT WOULDN'T BE THE SAME *WITH* ME.
I'M NOT EVEN THE SAME.
TESS, THAT'S NOT--
BUT THAT'S ALSO WHY I CAME.
THERE'S SOMETHING IMPORTANT I WANTED TO TELL YOU.

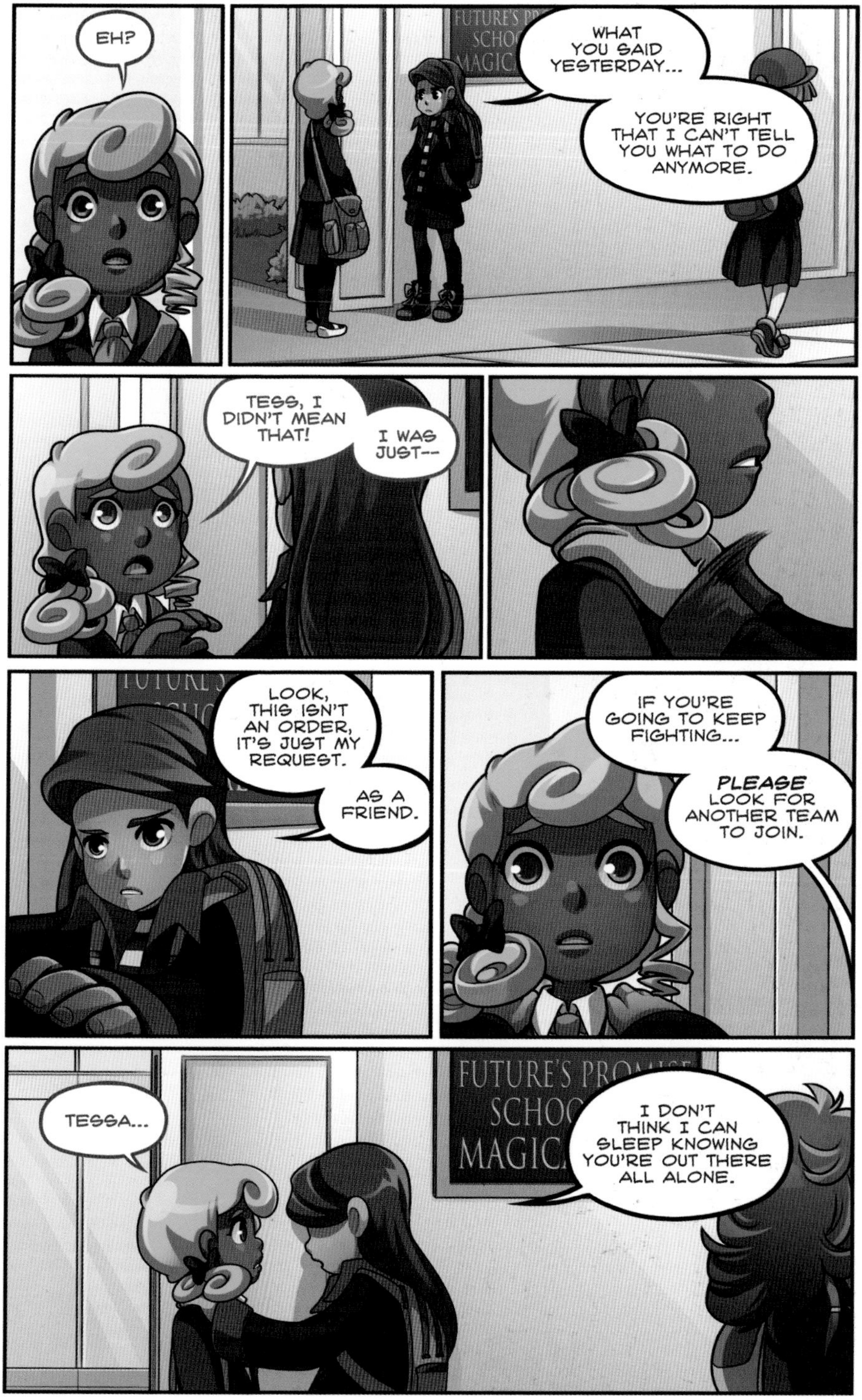
EH?
WHAT YOU SAID YESTERDAY...
YOU'RE RIGHT THAT I CAN'T TELL YOU WHAT TO DO ANYMORE.
FUTURE'S PROMISE SCHOOL MAGICAL
TESS, I DIDN'T MEAN THAT!
I WAS JUST--
LOOK, THIS ISN'T AN ORDER, IT'S JUST MY REQUEST.
AS A FRIEND.
IF YOU'RE GOING TO KEEP FIGHTING...
PLEASE LOOK FOR ANOTHER TEAM TO JOIN.
TESSA...
I DON'T THINK I CAN SLEEP KNOWING YOU'RE OUT THERE ALL ALONE.

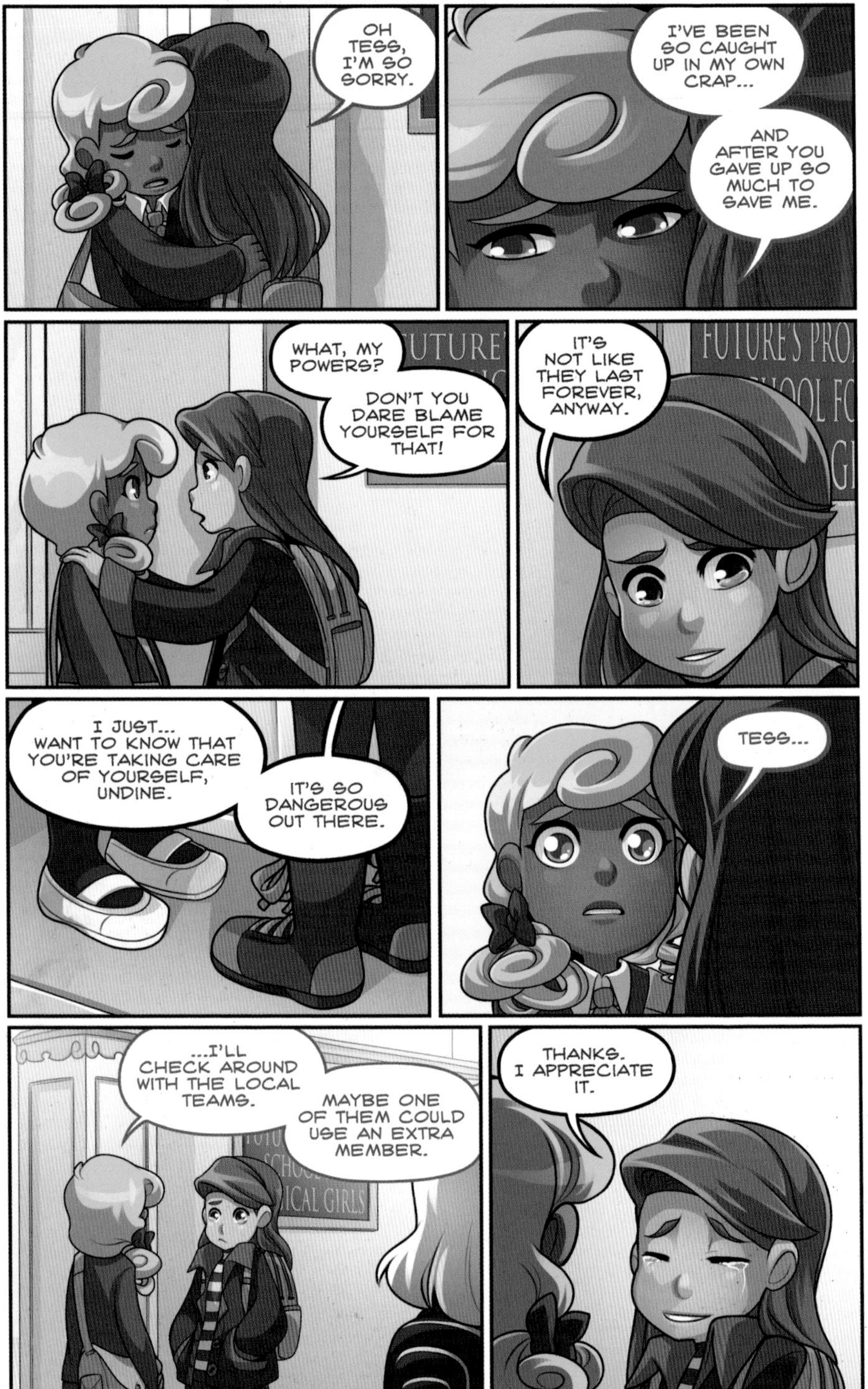
OH TESS, I'M SO SORRY.
I'VE BEEN SO CAUGHT UP IN MY OWN CRAP...
AND AFTER YOU GAVE UP SO MUCH TO SAVE ME.
WHAT, MY POWERS?
DON'T YOU DARE BLAME YOURSELF FOR THAT!
IT'S NOT LIKE THEY LAST FOREVER, ANYWAY.
I JUST... WANT TO KNOW THAT YOU'RE TAKING CARE OF YOURSELF, UNDINE.
IT'S SO DANGEROUS OUT THERE.
TESS...
...I'LL CHECK AROUND WITH THE LOCAL TEAMS.
MAYBE ONE OF THEM COULD USE AN EXTRA MEMBER.
THANKS. I APPRECIATE IT.

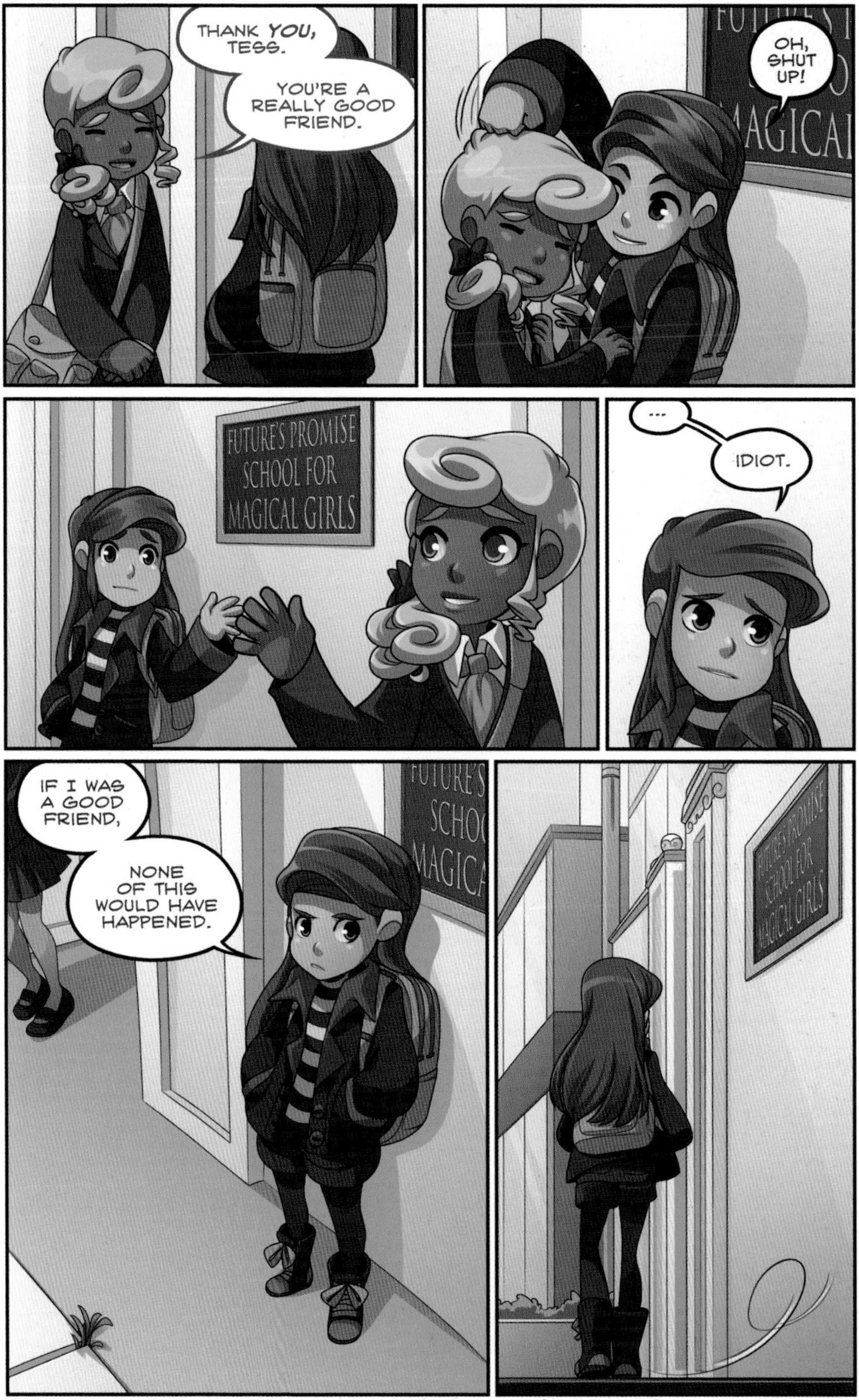
THANK YOU, TESS.
YOU'RE A REALLY GOOD FRIEND.
OH, SHUT UP!
FUTURE'S PROMISE SCHOOL FOR MAGICAL GIRLS
...
IDIOT.
IF I WAS A GOOD FRIEND,
NONE OF THIS WOULD HAVE HAPPENED.
FUTURE'S PROMISE SCHOOL FOR MAGICAL GIRLS

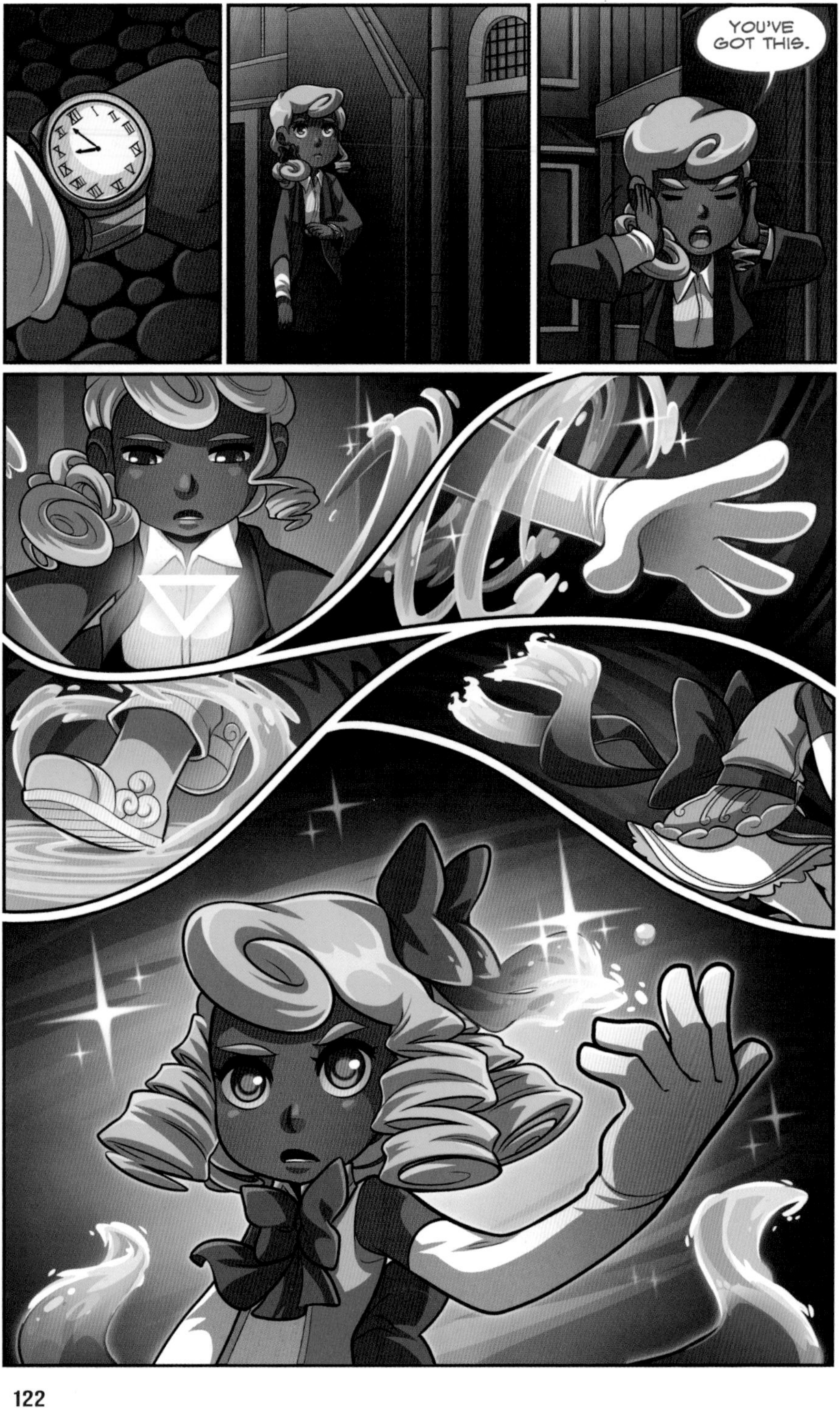
YOU'VE GOT THIS.

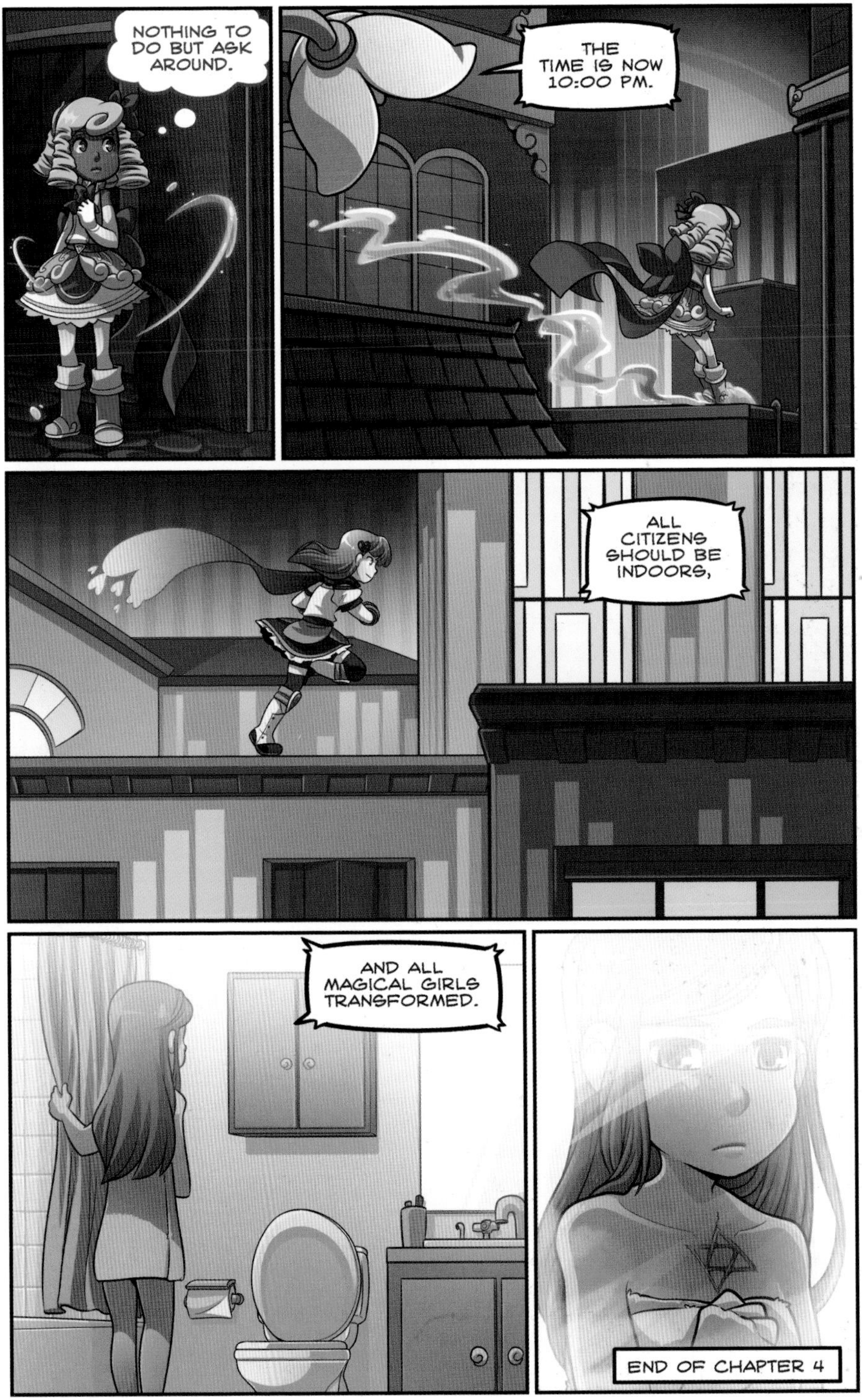
NOTHING TO DO BUT ASK AROUND.
THE TIME IS NOW 10:00 PM.
ALL CITIZENS SHOULD BE INDOORS,
AND ALL MAGICAL GIRLS TRANSFORMED.
END OF CHAPTER 4

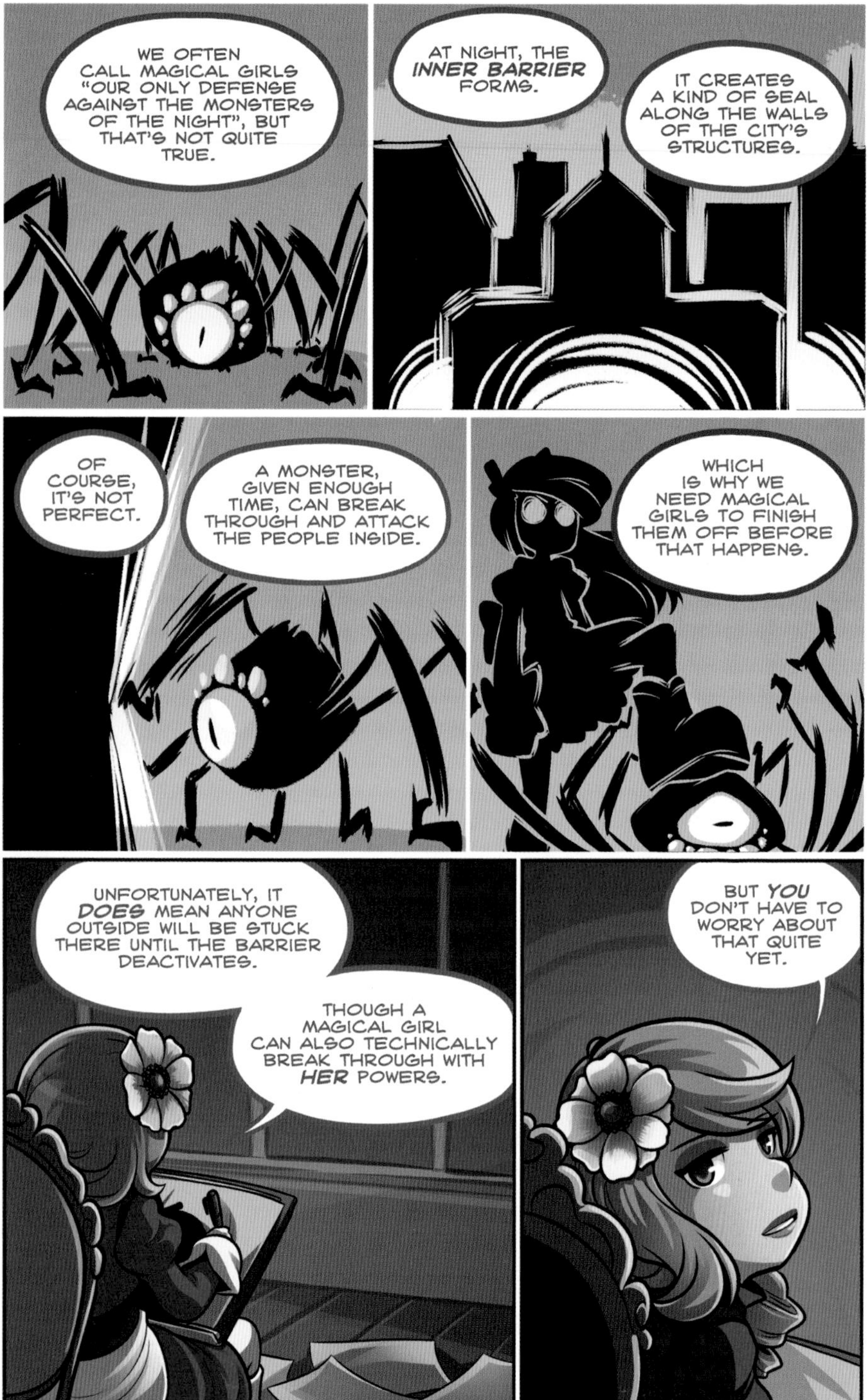
WE OFTEN CALL MAGICAL GIRLS "OUR ONLY DEFENSE AGAINST THE MONSTERS OF THE NIGHT", BUT THAT'S NOT QUITE TRUE.
AT NIGHT, THE ***INNER BARRIER*** FORMS.
IT CREATES A KIND OF SEAL ALONG THE WALLS OF THE CITY'S STRUCTURES.
OF COURSE, IT'S NOT PERFECT.
A MONSTER, GIVEN ENOUGH TIME, CAN BREAK THROUGH AND ATTACK THE PEOPLE INSIDE.
WHICH IS WHY WE NEED MAGICAL GIRLS TO FINISH THEM OFF BEFORE THAT HAPPENS.
UNFORTUNATELY, IT ***DOES*** MEAN ANYONE OUTSIDE WILL BE STUCK THERE UNTIL THE BARRIER DEACTIVATES.
THOUGH A MAGICAL GIRL CAN ALSO TECHNICALLY BREAK THROUGH WITH ***HER*** POWERS.
BUT ***YOU*** DON'T HAVE TO WORRY ABOUT THAT QUITE YET.

TO BE CONTINUED...

SLEEPLESS
DOMAIN

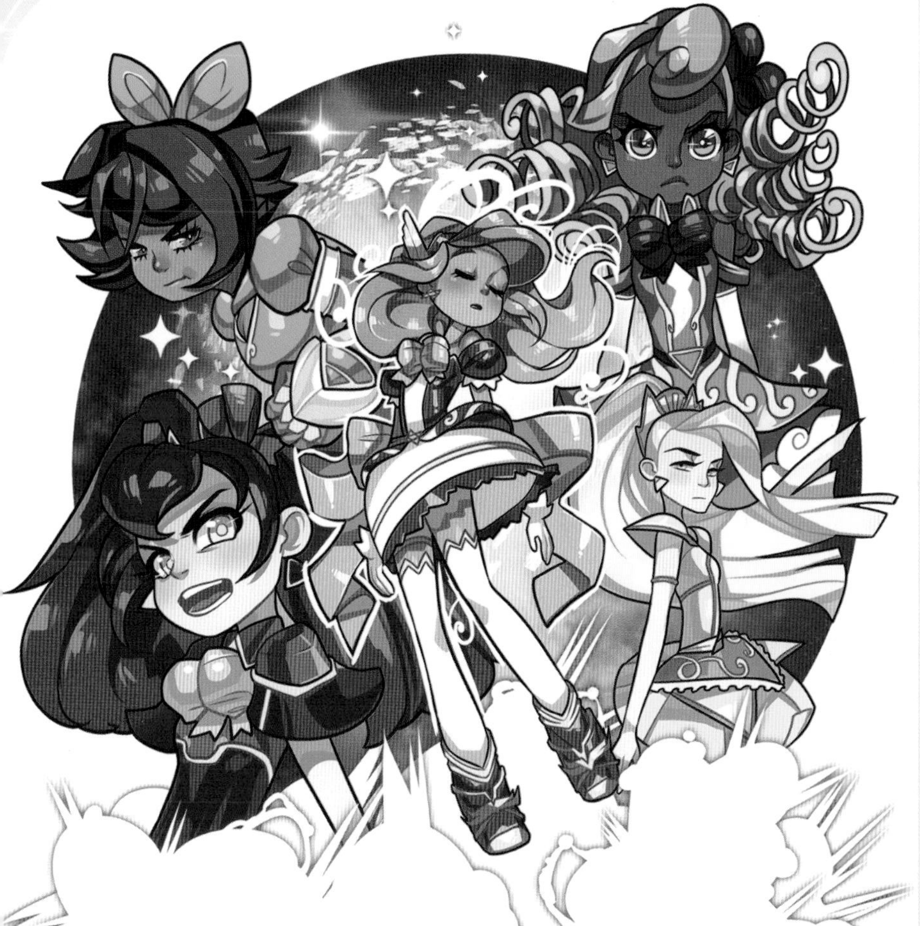

CONCEPTS AND COMMENTARY

INITIAL CONCEPTION

Greetings, everyone, and thank you for reading the first volume of *Sleepless Domain*! Here, you'll find a bit of extra concept work and commentary explaining the process that led to *Sleepless Domain*'s current form. This comic had a lot more initial planning than most things I've done before, so I actually have quite a bit to share!

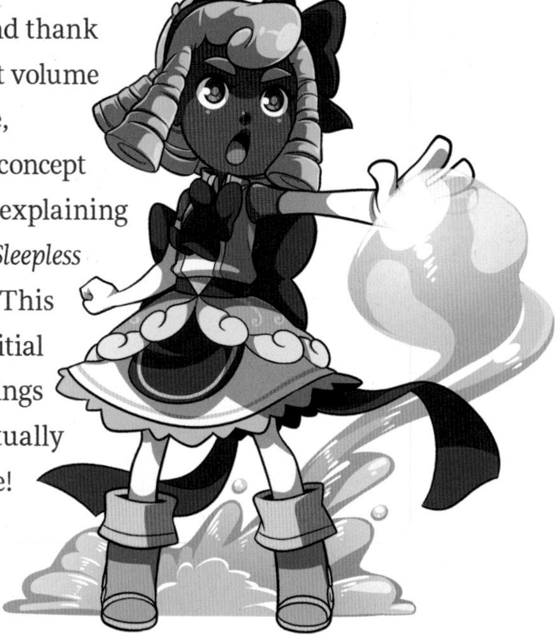

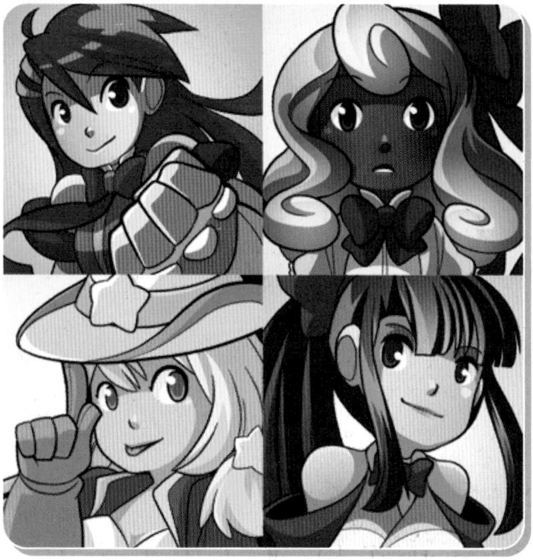

To the left, you'll see a group of four weirdos, two of whom look pretty close to Undine and Kokoro. There were doodled as I was first coming up with the story that would eventually morph into *Sleepless Domain*.

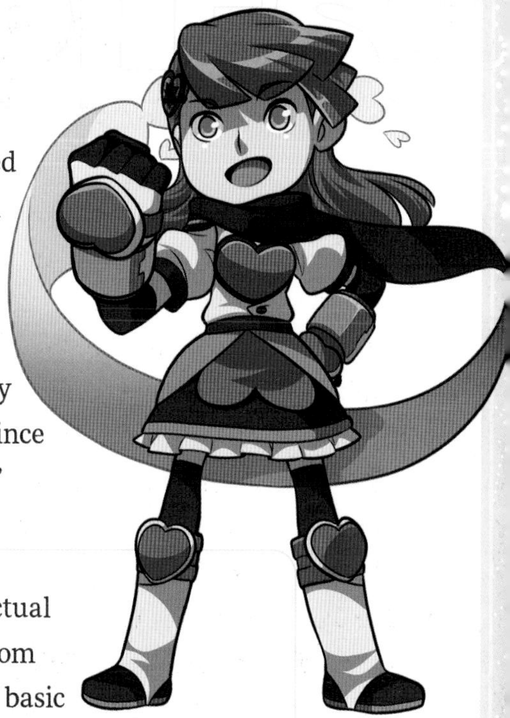

Believe it or not, I initially pitched SD as a "magical girl elimination reality show," like Survivor but for magical girls. Undine was going to be the water member of her team back home, who nobody thought had much of a chance, since she was "just the water member."

Obviously, *Sleepless Domain*'s actual setup became very different from that initial pitch! But Undine's basic concept as a character remained, along with the idea of her having a cool pink punchy girl as a main ally.

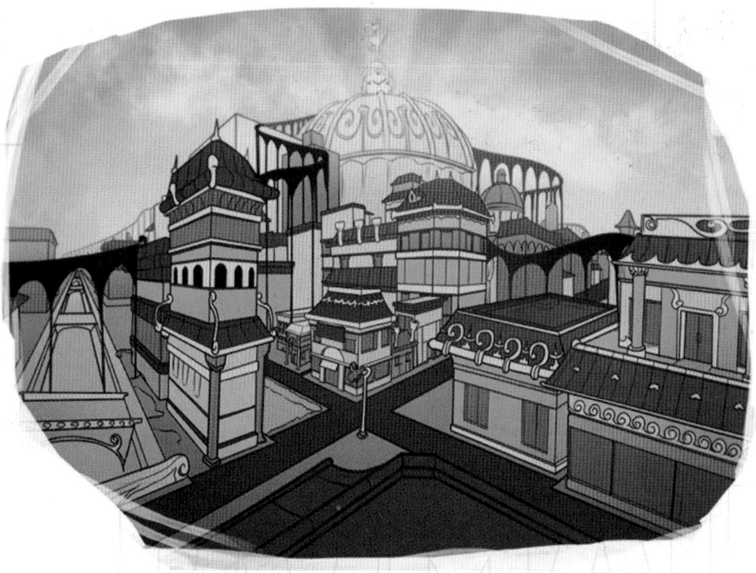

To the right is one of Oscar's initial concepts for the city. Nowadays, I do most of the work on *Sleepless Domain* myself, but much of the setup was a result of a lot of back-and-forth brainstorming between myself and Oscar, along with Isabelle and Jojo of Hiveworks. Everyone brought a lot of ideas to the table, and I'm incredibly happy with how the actual comic turned out!

Most of the concept art was done by Oscar, though I did some too, when I had a specific idea in mind! This was my concept for the night in Chapter 2, since I wanted it to feel extra weird and dramatic.

TESSA

Tessa definitely went through the most iterations by far. We wanted something that screamed "typical main character" without being too generic.

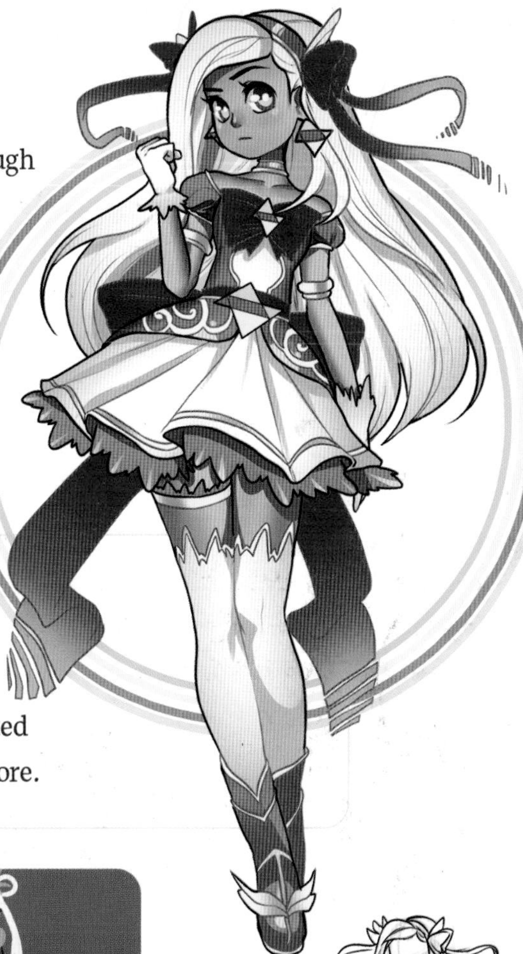

As you can see, her initial "completed" design was a bit more complex and incorporated the other girls' colors more.

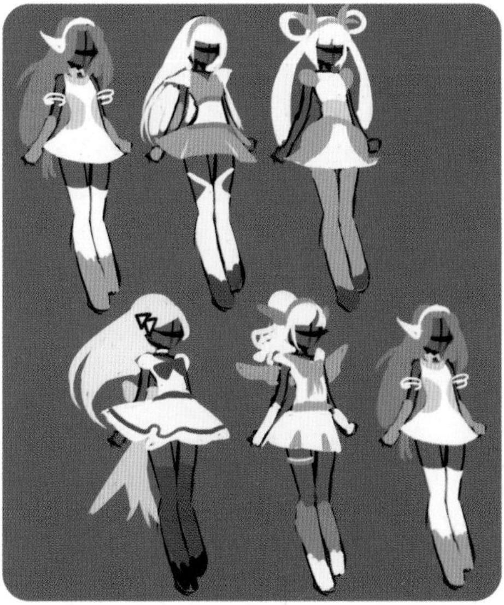

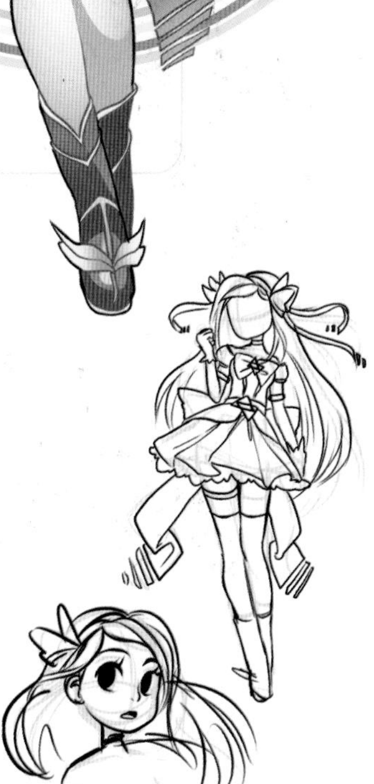

All the designs ended up getting a bit simplified between their initial conception and the comic itself, since comics require you to draw everyone a bajillion times.

I still have a soft spot for the white hair, though.

To the right is a version that still used some of the rainbow elements, while getting closer to her eventual design. She feels a bit more fancy and mysterious in these old concepts! But like all of my characters, she ended up being a huge dork.

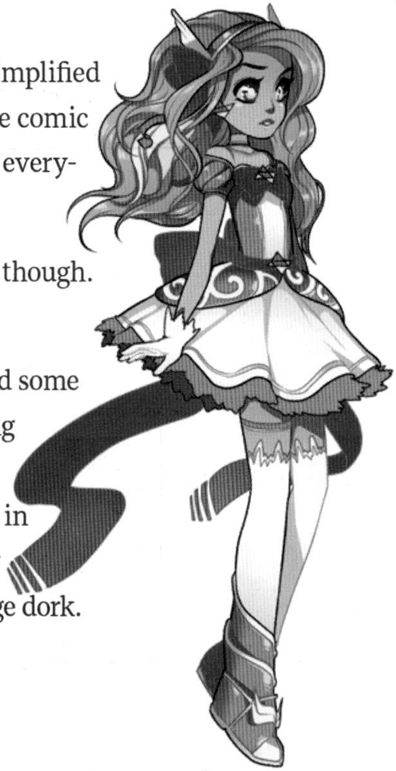

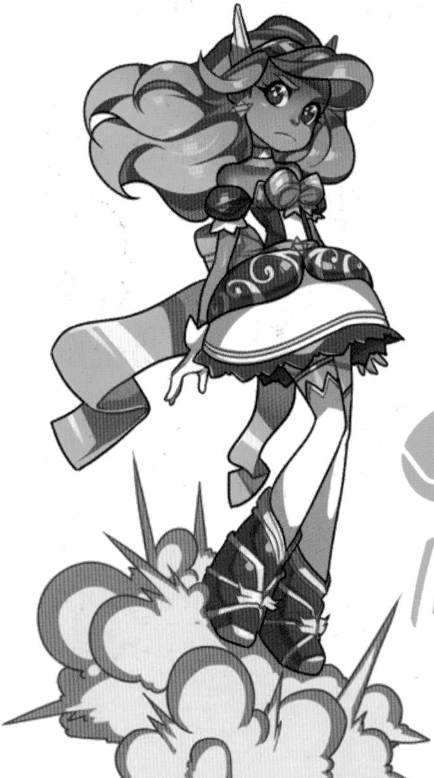

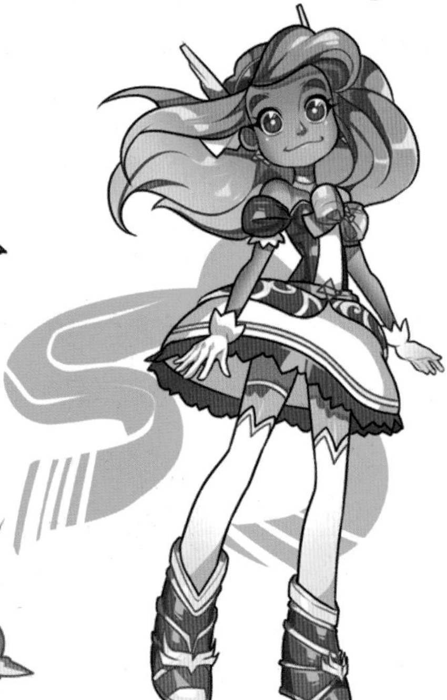

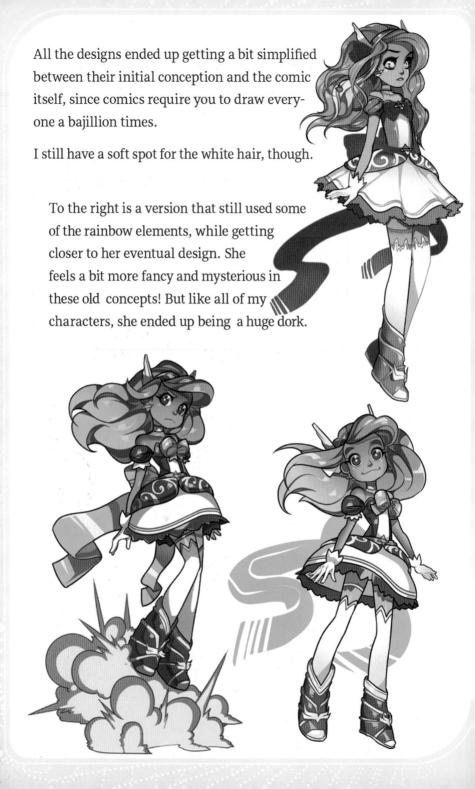

I never appreciated *The Little Mermaid's* mysterious, unknowable bang flip until I tried drawing Tessa. It's a hairdo that only a magical girl could manage.

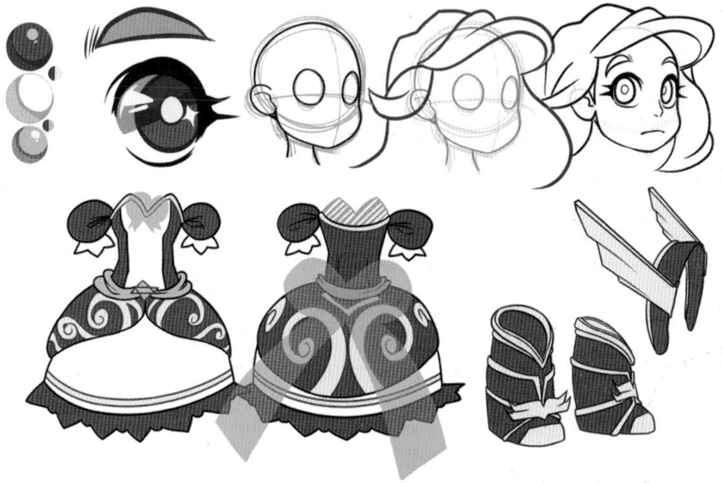

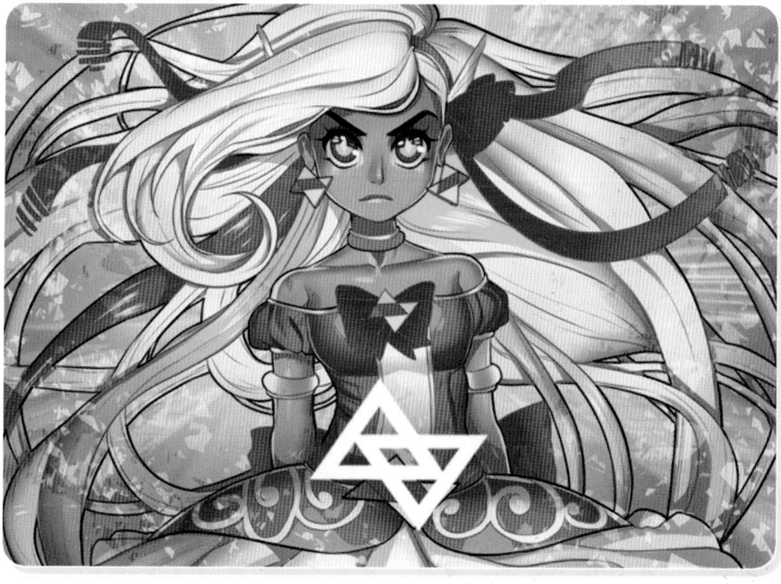

UNDINE

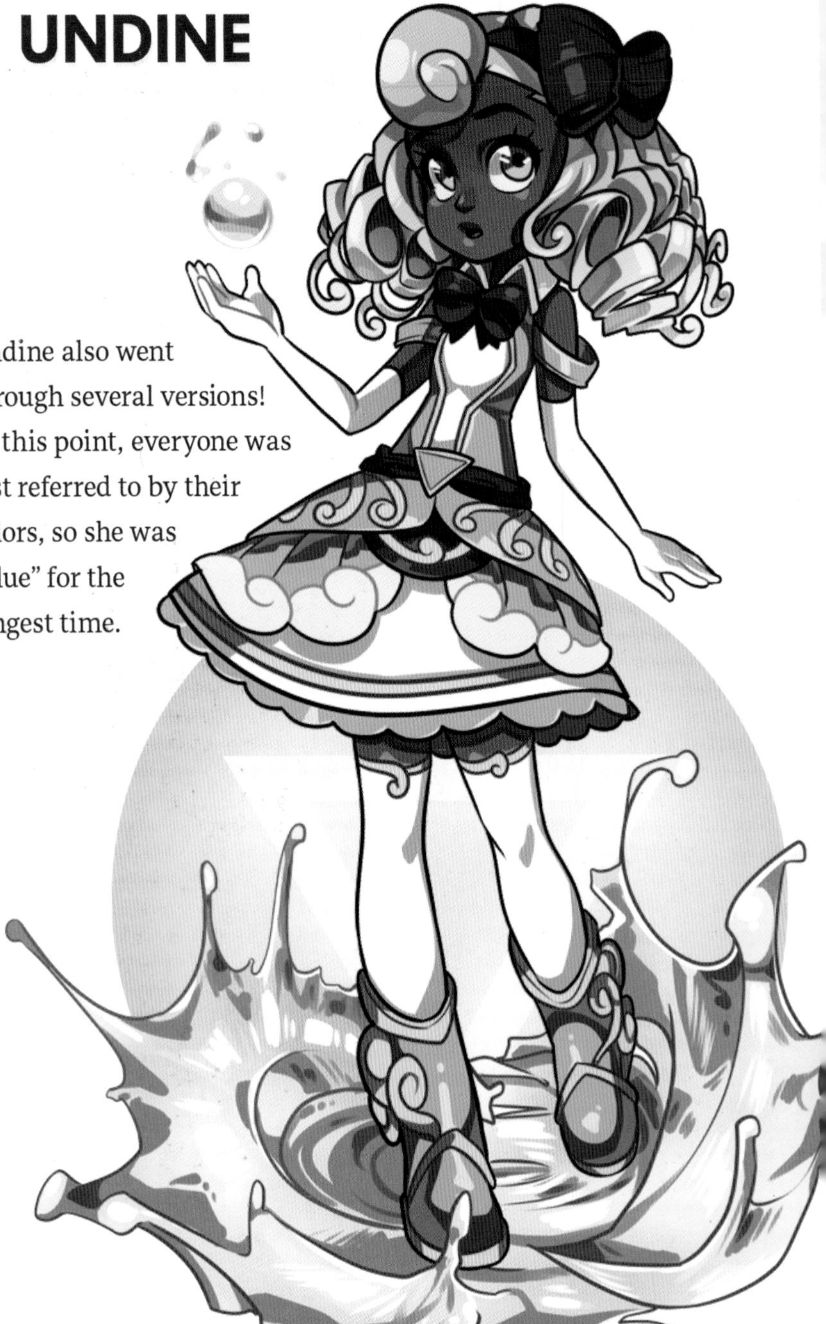

Undine also went through several versions! At this point, everyone was just referred to by their colors, so she was "Blue" for the longest time.

Obviously, her transformed hair ended up as a more simplified princess curl kind of situation, which I'm honestly grateful for. I would have had a heck of a time drawing this hair after I took over art duties, ha ha! Though I still like to play a lot with how she wears her hair when she's not transformed.

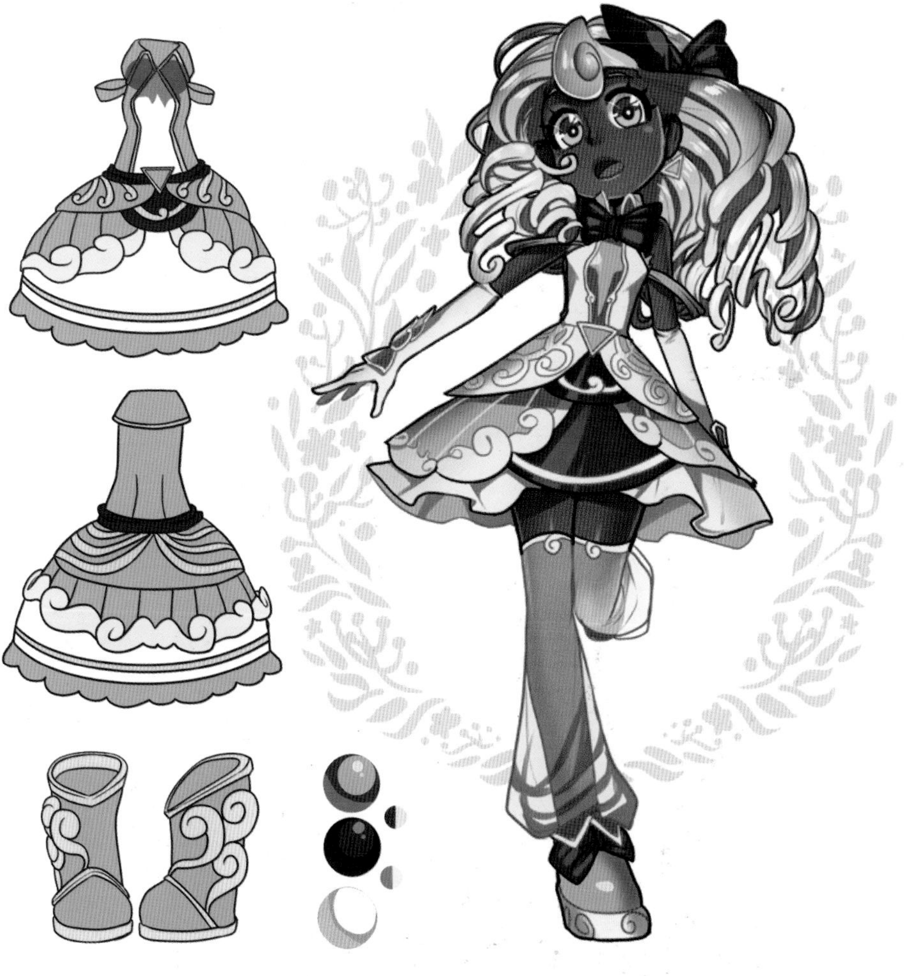

SALLY

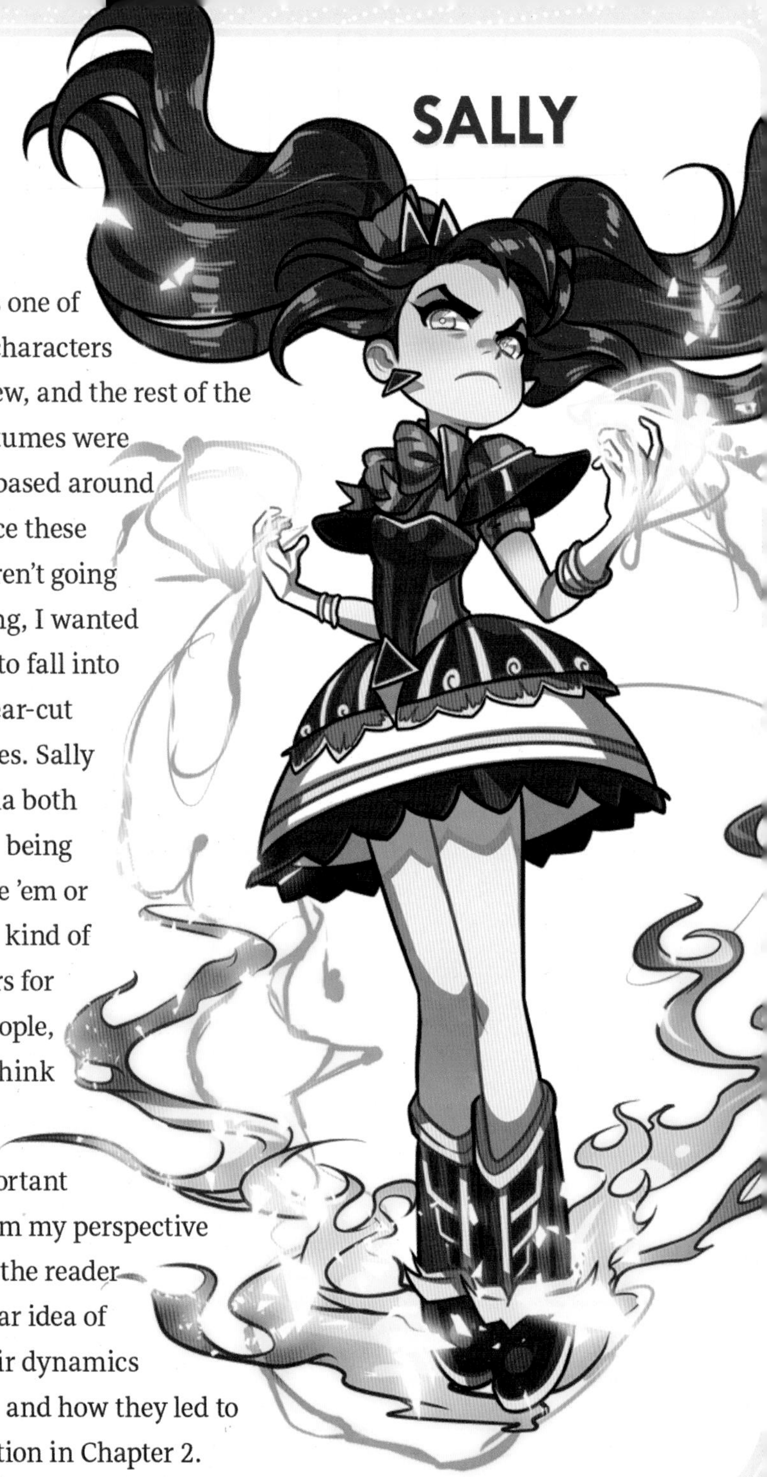

Sally was one of the first characters Oscar drew, and the rest of the girls' costumes were actually based around hers. Since these three weren't going to last long, I wanted them all to fall into pretty clear-cut archetypes. Sally and Sylvia both ended up being very "love 'em or hate 'em" kind of characters for lots of people, which I think is good!

The important thing from my perspective was that the reader had a clear idea of what their dynamics were like and how they led to the situation in Chapter 2.

SYLVIA

Sylvia was the kind of character I rarely write or draw, as a tomboy geek myself. Oscar really brought that fashionista energy to her design in a way I wouldn't have been able to!

Some people were confused by her color being yellow when she's the air-using member, but obviously, air doesn't actually have a color, ha ha! So anything goes! But I did realize later that *Avatar: The Last Airbender* also chose yellow for their air people. I think it's just more fun than having variants of blue on the same team.

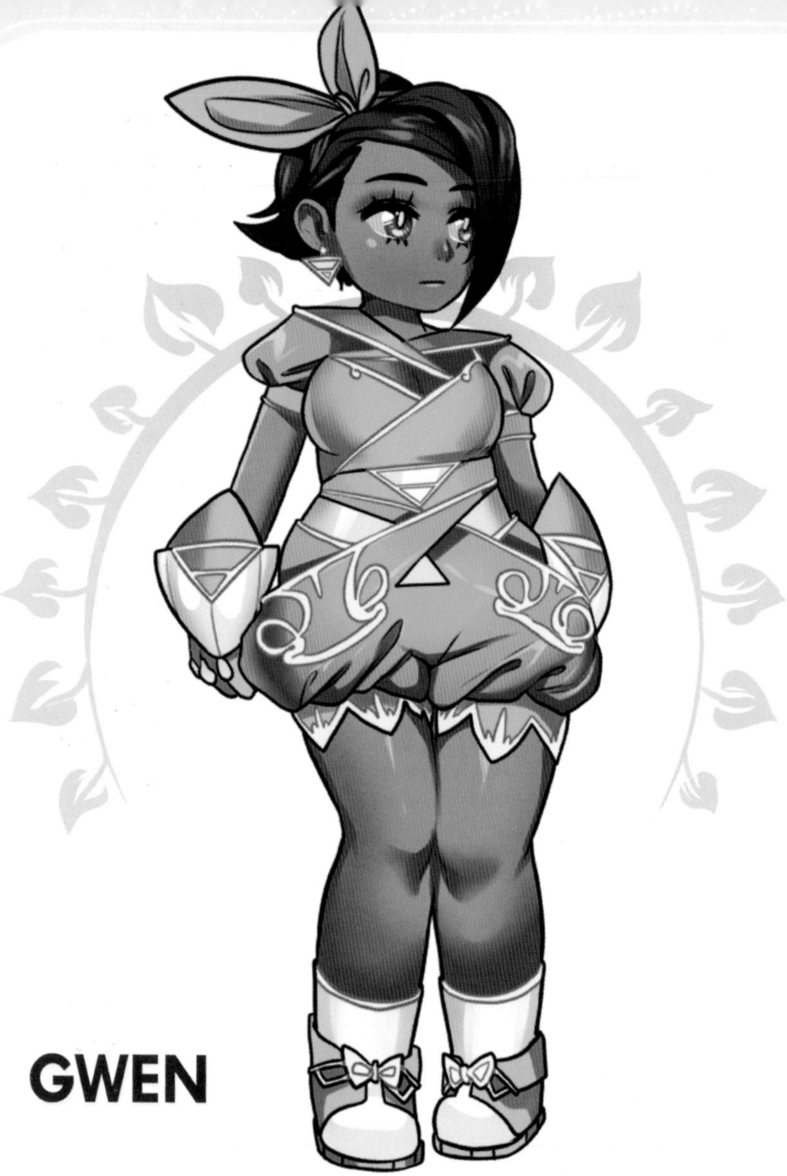

GWEN

Surprise! Gwen almost had…poofy shorts! But as she's the slightly heavier member of the team, I didn't want her to be the only one without a skirt. It did make some sense for general sporty nature, though. Gwen was a pretty simple character, but a lot of people liked her! I'm sorry about the whole "killing her" thing!

She's basically about as earth-element-person as you can be, but it turns out, I also like that kind of character a lot, so I'm sorry, Gwen! I miss you, too! I'm sure there's an alternate universe somewhere in which you survived and kicked everyone's butt that needed kicking.

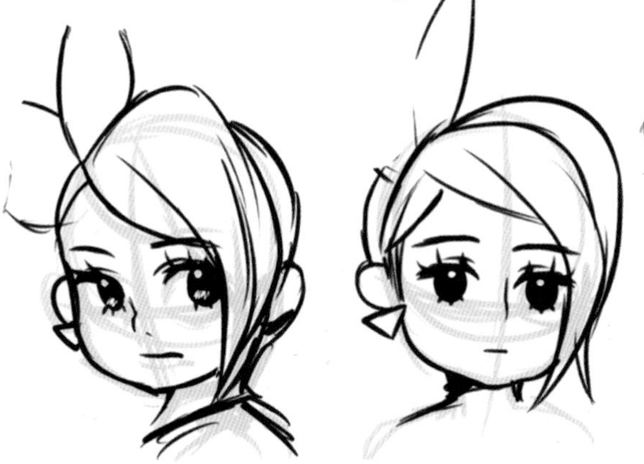

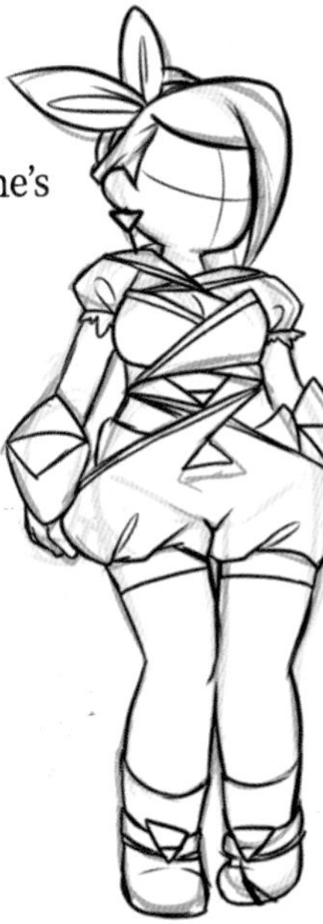

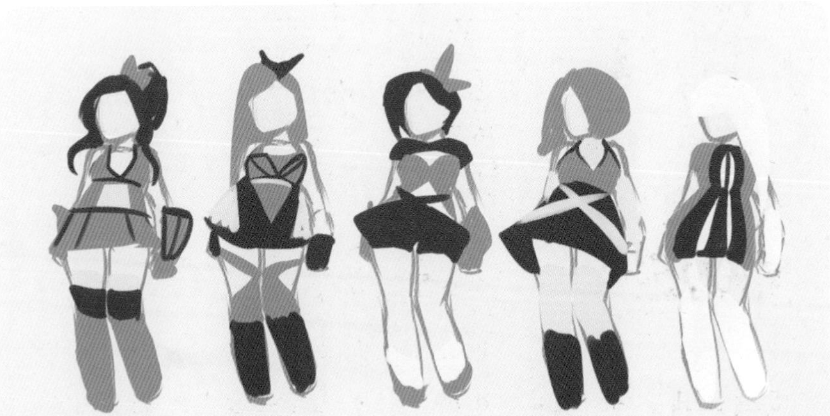

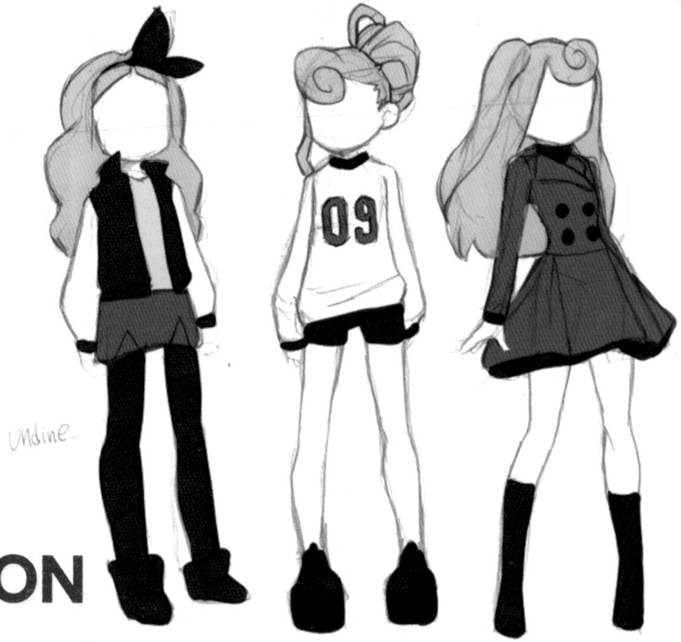
Undine

FASHION

I really love these little fashion studies Oscar did of the different girls! Versions of some of these show up in the first chapter. You can really see their different personalities in the way they choose to dress. Oscar definitely knows more about actual fashion than I do. Ha ha!

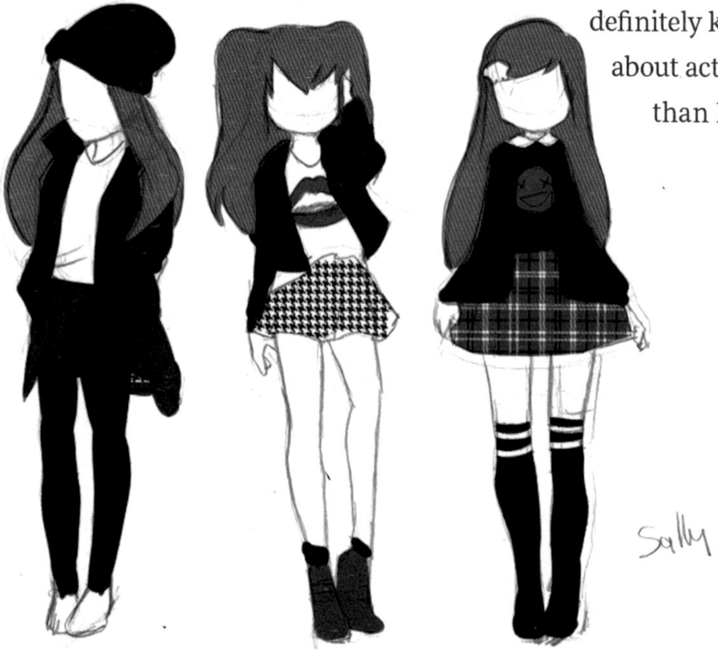
Sally

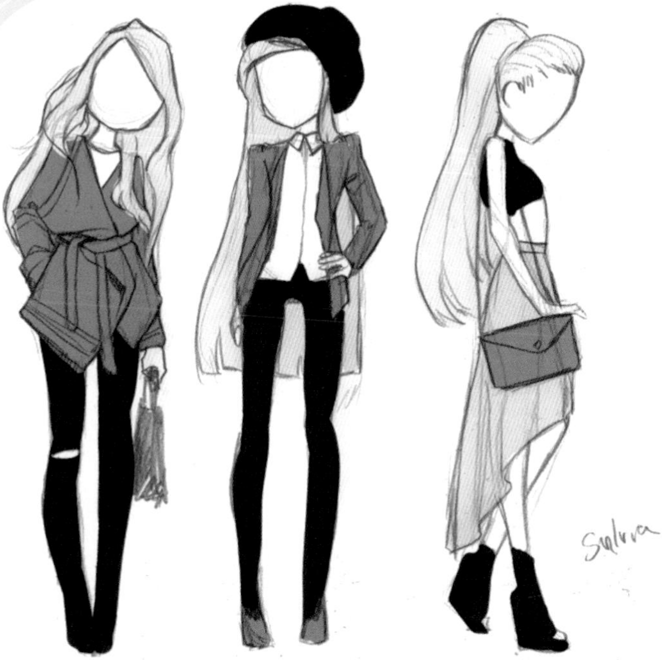

That said, the straight-haired Undine in Chapter 1 feels vaguely cursed now. I figure it's something she tries out every once in a while, before going, "Nah, forget it."

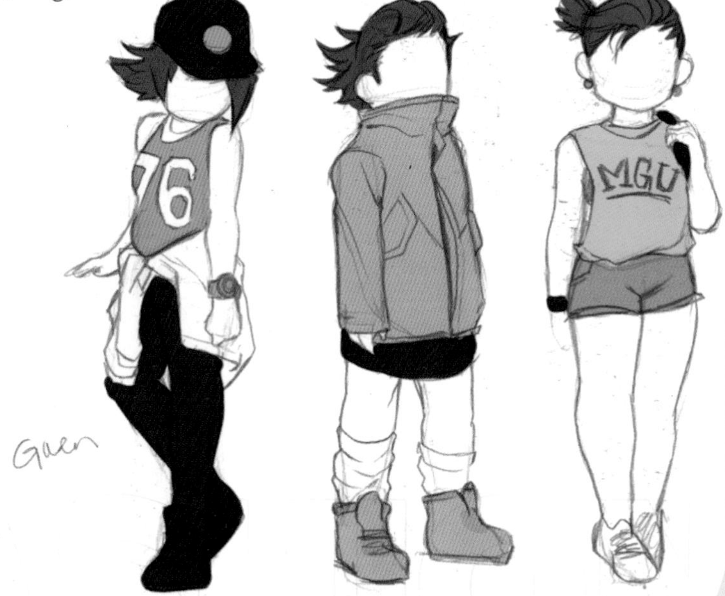
76
MGU

SLEEPLESS
DOMAIN

ABOUT
THE CREATOR

Mary Cagle is an artist from Texas, with a degree in Sequential Art from the Savannah College of Art and Design. She is a full time web comic creator. In 2009, she started with *Kiwi Blitz*, a teen sci-fi mecha series. In 2013, she traveled to Japan to teach English, and chronicled her time there in the comic *Let's Speak English*. During that time she also started *Sleepless Domain*, a comic inspired by her love of magical girl anime and manga! She can usually be found drawing late at night, surrounded by many cats. The cats are very important to her.

Author Site:
sleeplessdomain.com

Social:
twitter.com/cubewatermelon